SPIRITS UNEARTHED

ALSO BY ALICE DUNCAN

The Daisy Gumm Majesty Mystery Series

Strong Spirits

Fine Spirits

High Spirits

Hungry Spirits

Genteel Spirits

Ancient Spirits

Spirits Revived

Dark Spirits

Spirits Onstage

Unsettled Spirits

Bruised Spirits

Spirits United

Spirits Unearthed

Shaken Spirits

Scarlet Spirits

Exercised Spirits

Wedded Spirits

Domesticated Spirits

Library Spirits

Spirits Adopted

Rosy Spirits

The Mercy Allcutt Mystery Series

SPIRITS UNEARTHED

A DAISY GUMM MAJESTY MYSTERY
BOOK 13

ALICE DUNCAN

April, 2019
Paperback ISBN: 978-1-64457-071-5
Hardcover ISBN: 978-1-64457-072-2

ePublishing Works!
644 Shrewsbury Commons Ave
Ste 249
Shrewsbury PA 17361
United States of America

www.epublishingworks.com
Phone: 866-846-5123

Thanks to Stephanie Cowans for giving me the idea for this book. Thanks to my niece, Sara Krafft, because she actually is magic. And, as always, thanks to Lynne Welch, Sue Krekeler and Julia Anderson for being such great beta readers. They're always full of ideas, and I do so appreciate them, especially now that my brain's gone dry!

YOU'RE INVITED

Now you can experience the smells and flavors of Aunt Vi's kitchen, just like Daisy! We were fortunate enough to convince Aunt Vi to share one of her mouth-watering recipes. When you finish the story, page ahead for *Aunt Vi's Swedish Smothered Chicken* which is not to be missed. Enjoy!

ePublishing Works!

ONE

"This is stupid," said Sam Rotondo as he limped through Mountain View Cemetery in Altadena, California.

Monday, two weeks before Christmas in 1924, and the weather had turned frigid. That is to say, it was darned cold for Pasadena, California, where the weather seldom, if ever, gets truly frigid. It must have been in the low forties. That might account for the reason Sam Rotondo, my fiancé, was in such a foul mood. Or maybe the cold weather made his wounded leg hurt. I don't know. All I know is that he didn't want to do what I wanted him to do.

To give him the benefit of the doubt, I must say that walking to my late husband's grave was a struggle for him. He still had to rely heavily on his cane, given to him by Dr. Benjamin after Sam was shot in the thigh by an evil woman. As it had rained recently, the cane kept getting stuck in the moist soil and Sam kept having to yank it out.

Spike, my late husband's brilliant dachshund, frolicked around Sam and me. I'm still not sure if dogs were allowed in the cemetery, but nobody kicked us out, so what the heck.

"It's not stupid," I told Sam. "It'll make me feel better."

"It's stupid whether it makes you feel better or not," Sam grumped.

"Oh, stop it. You enjoy complaining, don't you?"

"No. I don't enjoy complaining. Ow!"

He had inadvertently stepped into a hole with his left leg, the one that had been shot, and I guess he wrenched it pretty badly.

"Watch where you're going, Sam," I said. Not awfully sympathetic of me, I know.

"Cripes. This is stupid."

"You've said that before."

Spike at least was enjoying himself. He ran this way and that way and generally tore around, as happy as a hound ever was. He had a nice big yard at home to snoop and sniff in, but it was nowhere near as large as the cemetery.

"That's because it is," snarled Sam.

"Pooh." I walked over to him and took his arm. "Really, Sam. I appreciate you for doing this. You're a sweetheart."

Sam said, "Huh." He said that a lot.

"I love you, Sam."

"Then why are you torturing me?"

"I don't mean to torture you. Lean on me, okay?"

"No need. I can use my cane."

"Thank you, sweetie."

"Huh."

Told you so.

But we made it to Billy's grave eventually. I stood beside it, looking down and wishing Billy was still alive. On the other hand, then I'd have two men in my life, and one was almost more than I could handle. Poor Billy had suffered terribly after the Great War. He'd been gassed and shot and had been in constant pain until he'd finally taken matters into his own hands and drunk an overdose of morphine syrup. I understood his reason, but I'd suffered mightily after his death. It's hard to lose a person you've known and loved all your life, even when you knew it was bound to happen eventually.

Sam had suffered, too. His late wife, Margaret, was buried not far from Billy. They had moved to Pasadena in hopes the warm, dry

Pasadena air would help relieve Margaret's tuberculosis. It hadn't. But he'd been a policeman in New York City, and he'd had to wait until a position with the Pasadena Police Department had opened up. He'd grabbed it with both hands as soon as he could, but he still felt guilty about not getting Margaret out of New York earlier than he'd been able to. But, as I'd told him many times, *nothing* can cure tuberculosis, and he'd done his very best for the wife he'd loved with all his heart, just as I'd loved my Billy.

For the record, I felt guilty about Billy, too. I'd sometimes been short-tempered with him when he was grumpy. But he'd been grumpy because he'd hated being crippled and having mustard-damaged lungs.

In other words, life is never fair. To anyone.

My aim that day was to tell both Billy and Margaret that Sam and I were engaged to be married, and we hoped we had their blessing.

So technically, Sam was correct. This trip *was* stupid.

Heck, I made my living—a darned good living—as a spiritualist-medium to the wealthy ladies of Pasadena who had more money than brain-power. If I actually *could* talk to dead people, I'd have asked for Billy's blessing regarding Sam and me a long time ago. I remained relatively undaunted, however, because it seemed somehow important to me to say the words to Billy, even if his soul had long since departed this earth. And I wanted Sam to say the words to Margaret, too. He probably wouldn't, so I'd have to say them for him, Sam not being one to ask for people's blessings on a regular basis. Well, I wasn't either, but this trip to the cemetery just felt right.

Still staring at Billy's beautifully carved headstone—it said "Sacred to the memory of William Anthony Majesty. Beloved husband of Daisy. July 12, 1897-June 10, 1922. Rest now as you could not in life. *The Good Die First*"—I said softly, "Billy, you got your wish. You asked Sam to take care of me after you were gone, and he's going to do just that—"

Sam said, "Huh," interrupting me.

"Anyway," I continued. "We're not just marrying because you

asked him to take care of me. I know it sounds impossible, but Sam and I have come to love each other."

The reason Billy would have found this fact unbelievable is that Sam and I had begun our relationship a few years prior, mercilessly antagonistic to each other. It had taken time and exposure to show us the other's lovable side. Time, exposure and, almost certainly, Spike.

I continued, "I hope Sam and I have your blessing for our union. We don't know when the ceremony will take place, because Sam got shot in the thigh by another dreadful woman named Petrie —not all the Petries are ghastly, but a lot of them are—and is still recovering, but we'll get married one of these days."

Spike rushed up to Sam and me, a man's shoe clutched in his teeth, his tail wagging deliriously.

"What the—?" said Sam, glancing down at Spike.

Distracted from my purpose, I too, peered at my dog. "Where in the world did you find that, Spike?"

Because he was a dog, Spike didn't answer. Rather, he dropped the shoe at our feet, smiling up at us. Don't tell me dogs can't smile, because they can. In actual fact, he looked quite pleased with himself.

"Where'd you get hold of a shoe, Spike?" Because I knew Sam's leg hurt, I was the one who bent and picked up the shoe. It was quite heavy, for a shoe.

I squealed when I saw the reason for its unusual weight. The stupid shoe held a foot! I dropped it and clutched Sam's arm.

"What the—?" said Sam once more, startled and staggering a bit.

"Sam! That shoe has a foot in it!"

"What?"

"It's got a foot in it!" Because I figured I should, I bent and picked up the shoe again, tentatively, by one of its laces. It smelled awful. "See?" I said, thrusting the shoe and foot at Sam.

He recoiled. "Where the hell did you find a foot in a shoe, Spike?"

Once more Spike didn't answer for the reason stated above. I noticed dried blood on the ankle part of the foot and grimaced. "Sam, could Spike have dug up a grave? Good Lord, the managers of the cemetery will kill us if he did."

"Don't be silly," said Sam, as gracious as ever. "He couldn't dig up a grave. Even if he could, he'd have found a coffin, not a foot in a shoe."

"Oh. I guess that makes sense."

"This isn't right," said Sam, master of the obvious.

"We'd better see if we can find the rest of the body, if there is one," I said tentatively. I didn't want to look for loose bodies in the cemetery.

"Oh, there is one," said Sam, sounding even grouchier than he'd sounded before. "You make a habit of stumbling over bodies. I should have figured you'd find one in a graveyard."

"I don't either!" I cried, miffed. "Anyway, the graveyard is full of bodies."

"Not fresh, falling-apart ones."

"It doesn't smell awfully fresh to me," I muttered. The shoe was truly disgusting. It stank and it was covered in dirt. I stared down at my dog, who still looked up at us, happy as a clam. And how anyone knows clams are happy is beyond me.

"You know what I mean," growled Sam.

"Yes, I do." I gazed at him. "So *do* we need to search for the rest of the body? Or should we telephone the Altadena Police Department?"

"There is no such thing as an Altadena Police Department. The community of Altadena has a Los Angeles County Marshal's Office, which I think is housed in Pasadena, to investigate crimes committed in Altadena. But I don't know their telephone number. I guess we can dial the operator, but we'd better find the rest of the body first."

"Do you think this was the result of a crime?" I asked, gazing at the icky foot.

"Well, now, I just don't know. Maybe somebody cut off his foot and tossed it into the cemetery. Just for a lark, you know?"

"There's no need to be sarcastic, Sam Rotondo."

5

"Huh."

"We can call the county marshal from our house, can't we?" I asked tentatively.

"Where the heck else would we call from?" asked Sam as if my question had been as stupid as our reason for visiting the cemetery that day.

He was wrong, and I told him so. "Listen to me, Sam Rotondo, *you* might want to tell the county marshal that Billy's dog was digging up bodies in the Mountain View Cemetery, but *I* sure don't!"

"Hmm. I guess you've got a point."

"Darned right I do."

With a look that told me he considered me, if not insane, then as close to it as made no difference, Sam said, "We're going to have to come up with some story as to how we found a fresh foot in the cemetery."

"Oh, dear."

"Right."

"Well, we can say we...stumbled across it." Darn! I wish I hadn't said *stumbled across*, since Sam had accused me more than once of stumbling over bodies.

"Guess we'll have to. Damn it, now I have to walk around in this soft grass some more, and my leg is killing me."

"Why don't you sit on..." I looked around. Aha. "Sit on that bench," I said, pointing. "Spike and I will search the place."

Appearing doubtful, Sam said, "I don't know. I'm not sure I trust you."

I threw my arms out. "What in the world can I do in a cemetery? All I'm looking for is a body, for heaven's sake! There has to be a body somewhere close by. Otherwise, Spike couldn't have found its foot." Ew. That sounded terrible.

Wrapping his scarf over his chin and nose—sewn by my own two hands out of a pretty flannel plaid material I'd found at Maxime's Fabrics—Sam sat with a grunt on the bench I'd mentioned. "All right. But don't take too long."

"I guess we'll have to take as long as necessary. The rest of the body might not be nearby, you know," I pointed out.

"Nuts. If you don't come back in five minutes, I'll holler for you. I don't trust you. Or Spike."

Spike wagged at Sam, as if Sam had just praised him to the skies.

"Darn you, Sam Rotondo! And Spike's on your side."

Sam said, "Huh. Smart dog."

"Fiddlesticks." But Spike and I turned around. Although I didn't much want to, I again picked up the grisly shoe. I showed it to Spike, and said, "Spike, find it."

Spike looked up at me oddly. Technically, "Find it" wasn't one of the commands he'd learned at the Pasanita Obedience Club for Dogs, to which I'd taken him a couple of years prior to this incident. However, Spike had come in first in his class, was smart as the proverbial whip, and I guess he deduced from my voice and posture —and, perhaps, the stinky shoe—that I wanted him to find the rest of the body from which the shod foot had come. Therefore, he turned and began trotting off. I trotted after him through the slushy grass.

Good thing I'd worn my comfy old walking shoes, because they were going to be soaked by the time I got home that day.

TWO

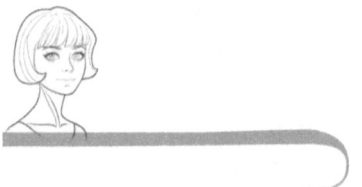

Fortunately—or unfortunately. To this day, I'm not entirely sure—Spike led me to a marshy puddle of mud not far from Billy's grave, but tucked away in a corner of the cemetery. It looked to me as though the latest rains had created the mud, and that the site had originally been pretty thoroughly smoothed over.

Because of the recent downpours, however, the loose soil had washed away somewhat, leaving parts of a man's leg exposed. I knew it was a man because of the soaking-wet tweed trousers covering the leg. The foot belonging to the leg was gone. Spike wagged like mad. I suppressed a gag of nausea.

"Good boy, Spike," said I. Then I spun on my heel and almost raced back to Sam. Spike, who seemed to want to stay at the mud puddle and snoop some more, finally came when I ordered him to. He was *such* a good dog! Nobody else ever obeyed my commands.

"Sam!" I shrieked.

Startled, Sam leapt from the bench to his feet, staggered a bit, and uttered a loud, "Damn!"

I winced and said, "I'm so sorry, Sam. I didn't mean to hurt your leg."

"Yeah, yeah. I know." He glowered down at me. Sam was a tall man, and when he loomed like that, I felt particularly small. "What the heck did you scream for?"

"I didn't scream," I said, probably inaccurately. "But we found the body. It looks as if someone had buried it in the ground, but the recent rains unearthed some of it." I glanced once more at the foot-filled shoe.

"Hmm. I'd better take a look." He grabbed his cane and limped after Spike and me as we walked back to the body. Spike positively raced to the site, probably hoping for more goodies to show us. I called him back and made him heel. He didn't want to, but he heeled. I absolutely adored that dog.

Sam planted his fists on his hips, his cane sticking out behind him, and gazed down upon the muddy body. I could tell he wasn't pleased. "Cripes. Can you tell who it is? If you know, I mean."

"No." I shook my head. "I...I guess we'll have to uncover more of it before anyone can tell who it is. Was. Unless it's a stranger to these parts." It occurred to me that I probably shouldn't use the pronoun "it" in reference to a most-likely-murdered human being, but I wasn't sure what else to call it. Him. Whoever.

Sam said, "Cripes," again. "How are we supposed to do that?"

"Um...I'm not sure. I expect Spike would love to dig some more, but that would only make him dirty and disturb more of the...corpse. I guess."

Still staring at the mud-caked remains, Sam said, "Well, can you find a fallen branch or something? Maybe I can dig around and we can see more of the body. It's possible a vagrant died and someone planted him here, although I don't know why anyone would do that."

"I don't, either, although I suppose it's possible." Sam's scenario didn't sound awfully credible to me, mainly because Altadena and Pasadena weren't full of vagrants, both being respectable and relatively high-class communities. "I'll look for a branch."

After glancing from the body to Spike, Sam said, "Better take Spike with you."

"Right."

So I called my dog and he came with me, even though he

wanted to dig up and probably gnaw on some more of the body. Poor Spike. I was always spoiling his fun.

The Mountain View Cemetery was well kept and had lovely grounds. The caretakers of the place didn't leave branches lying around for too long at any one time. However, after walking approximately seven and a half miles over and around various graves and headstones, Spike and I eventually found what looked to me as though it might be a fair to middling stick with which to scoop mud from a hole. Spike and I carted it back the seven and half miles (I'm exaggerating; it only *felt* like seven and a half miles) to Sam, who still stood guarding the remains. Poor Sam. His leg must have been killing him by that time.

He frowned at me. "Took you long enough."

"Go chase yourself, Sam Rotondo. *You* try finding loose branches in this cemetery. The guardians of this place keep it clean. It took us this long to find this one stupid branch."

I thrust it at him, which turned out to be a mistake, because he took a step backward and must have wrenched his bad leg again. "Damn it!"

"I'm sorry. But I wish you wouldn't swear," I said.

"I'll stop swearing when my damned leg stops hurting."

I merely sighed heavily.

Nevertheless, Sam, after eyeing the branch, turned it around so that its larger end pointed at the ground, and started scraping. Spike wanted to help, but I wouldn't let him. Poor Spike.

After he'd dug and scraped for plenty long enough to work up a sweat and, I'm sure, violate his leg even more severely, Sam stepped back, panting, and squinted down into the hole he'd dug. "Can you see it any better now? I can't stoop very well because of my leg. I can tell it's a man—at least I think it's a man—but I don't recognize the face because it's covered with mud. But I don't want to scrape around much more because...Well, the corpse is decomposing, and I don't want to disturb it or rub any of it off the bones."

"Ew." I didn't want even to look at the body's muddy face, but I knew where my duty lay. Therefore, sucking in a breath of clean air for courage, I walked over to the face Sam had partially revealed.

Horrid sight. "What's that thing on his chin?" Whatever it was, it stuck up through the mud in a little point.

"I have no idea," said Sam.

I gasped. "Good Lord!"

"What? Who is it? Do you recognize him?"

"No," said I, slapping a hand to my hammering heart. "But if that muddy, pointy thing is a goatee on the face, it might be Marianne Grenville's dreadful father. He's the only person I know in these enlightened times who wears a stupid goatee."

Sam glared at me. "Who the devil is Marianne Grenville, and who's her father?"

"Good Lord, Sam, don't you remember? It was two years ago. Marianne Wagner ran away from home and then married George Grenville. This may be…perhaps used to be…Doctor Everhard A. Wagner. And he was a ghastly man! I hope it's he, and if it is, I'm glad he's dead. I only hope Marianne or her mother didn't kill him. He deserved to be murdered, but they'd only get into trouble if they did him in."

"Jeez," said Sam. "What did the guy do?"

"For one thing, he used to beat up on his wife and daughter. He also…" Nerts. This was embarrassing. "He used to…touch Marianne in inappropriate places. Mrs. Wagner's the one who gave me the money to buy our Chevrolet. She thanked me for helping to rescue her daughter. Marianne's the presumed-to-be-a ghost I exorcized from Mrs. Bissel's basement. Remember?"

Still frowning, Sam said in a second or two, "I remember. You said it was a cat living down there. I knew you were fibbing."

"It wasn't a mere fib," I declared vehemently. Perhaps a trifle too vehemently, since I still felt kind of guilty about my part in rescuing that particular damsel in distress. "If I'd told you the truth, you'd have forced Marianne to go back home and be mistreated by her old man some more. I think, once everyone knew Marianne had been found and was safe, people began finding out things about Doctor Wagner. Unsavory things. I understand his medical practice kind of took a nosedive."

"Proud of yourself?"

"For ruining his business? Actually, yes, unless his wife is suffering from the loss of income. For helping Marianne escape from a terrible home, yes. I'm very proud of myself, thank you." I gave Sam as good a glare as he was giving me. "If the police ever tried to help people like Marianne and her mother, people like me wouldn't have to get involved, you know."

Sam stopped frowning and heaved a huge sigh. "Yeah, yeah. However, the police can't just butt into other people's lives."

"Yes. So I've been told before. Even when that awful Mr. Bannister nearly murdered his wife."

"We could have done something if he'd succeeded in murdering her."

"A whole lot of good *that* would have done the poor woman!"

"You think the police should run roughshod over the population? I think that's what happens in dictatorships and old tsarist Russia."

"Phooey. But I guess you're right." I hated admitting it.

"Anyhow, I'd better take another look at the body and try to determine how he died. I don't dare remove any more mud for fear his flesh will come off with it."

I said, "Ew," again.

"And it's going to hurt my leg, so if you don't want to listen to me swear, you'd better take Spike for a walk around the grounds."

"Can't I do it for you?"

"No." Succinct. That was my Sam. "Police business."

"I'm sorry, Sam."

"I'm sure."

"I *am*. I don't want your poor leg to hurt any more!"

"I know it. But move out of the way so I can take a closer look at the body. I'd like to give the marshal some kind of idea of how he died. If I can tell at this stage of the game."

I did. And he did, uttering several grunts of pain on his way down to his knees. He was silent for what seemed like a day or two, and I got itchier and itchier, wanting to know what had caused the death of the man whom I assumed to be Dr. Wagner.

And who would dump a body in a cemetery? This whole

scenario didn't make sense to me. I wanted to ask Sam questions, but he was already in a pretty bad mood, I knew he was in dreadful pain, and I didn't want to make things worse.

However, by the time he finally shoved himself to his feet, I was about to climb out of my skin in anticipation. "Well?" I asked.

"Well what?"

"Darn you, Sam Rotondo! What was the cause of death? Could you tell?"

"Give me a handkerchief," said he. Not very enlightening.

Nevertheless, I withdrew a hankie from my handbag and passed it to him. He wiped his hands, and I noticed red stuff mixed with the dirt as he wiped. I decided that hankie didn't need to be laundered. I could make zillions more, so I'd just throw that one away.

"So?" I asked after he'd taken approximately a hundred years to clean his hands as he stared down at what was left of the dead man. "Did you figure out what did him in?"

"Yeah." And he stopped speaking.

Wanting to pummel him about the head and shoulders, I demanded, "Well, what *was* it? How'd he die?"

"Somebody bashed in his skull. Looks like several blows with some kind of blunt instrument."

"Ew. If it's Doctor Wagner, I didn't like the man, but that sounds like a painful way to go."

"Yeah. It probably was. Anyhow, we have to get to a telephone." He looked troubled. "I don't like leaving the body unguarded."

"Why? Do you think someone will want to steal it? This isn't Victorian England, Sam. Medical students don't have to dig up graves or murder people in order to study anatomy anymore."

"That was in Scotland, and they weren't medical students. They were just a couple of drunks trying to make a buck."

I stared at my fiancé. "How the heck do you know that?"

"I like to read."

"So do I, but I've never heard about…those men."

"Burke and Hare. Anyway, that's not relevant. I don't like to leave the body unattended."

"I can stay here if you want to go down to Marengo and call the county marshal."

"Cripes, no! With my luck, you'll find six more bodies while you're waiting here."

"That's not fair, Sam."

"Huh. But let's get to the machine. I'll have to ask for Margaret's blessing another day. And I took the whole damned day off so we could come here."

"I know, Sam, and I'm sorry. This isn't fair."

"What is?"

He had a point. Nonetheless, I attached Spike's leash to his collar. Then Sam, Spike and I walked back through the muddy cemetery to Sam's big Hudson. There I toweled off Spike's dirty feet—I'd come prepared—and Sam drove us from the cemetery in Altadena to my home in Pasadena.

When we got to my family's tidy bungalow on South Marengo Avenue, I gave Sam the privilege of getting in touch with the Los Angeles County Marshal's Office. I wouldn't know what to say to them.

The only member of my family at home at the time was my father, Joe Gumm, who had a bum ticker and could no longer work at his job as chauffeur to rich people. Great guy, my father. He beamed at us when we walked through the front door, but his smile faded when he saw the expressions on our faces. Well, Spike was still jolly, but Sam and I probably looked as upset as we were.

"What's wrong?" asked Pa.

"Your daughter did it again," said Sam, sounding grim. He marched through the living room and dining room to the kitchen, where our telephone hung on the wall.

That 'phone got a lot of use, mainly because people were always calling me and asking me to read their palms, deal out tarot cards or consult my "spirit control," a guy named Rolly. Not my fault. I named him when I was ten years old, and I really don't think childhood blunders should be held against one forever. Heck, I'd named myself Desdemona back then, too, thinking it was a much classier name than Daisy, which is my real name. I'd have named both Rolly and me something else except that we both had a reputation by the time Spike found that wretched shoe in the cemetery.

As Sam limped into the kitchen, Pa looked at me quizzically. "What happened?" he asked.

"Spike found a shoe with a foot in it at the cemetery."

"He did *what?*"

Feeling a bit snarly, I said, "You heard me."

I love my father. He's one of the most wonderful people on the face of the earth. I was mightily peeved, however, when he shook his head and said, "Good Lord, Daisy, Sam's right about you. You stumble over bodies everywhere, don't you?"

"He is *not* right! Anyhow, this wasn't my fault. Spike found this one."

"Someone dumped a corpse at the cemetery? Really?" Pa appeared astounded, which only made sense.

With a sigh, I sat on one of the dining-room chairs and said, "Yes. Somebody evidently murdered whoever it was. I think, although I'm not sure, it's the body of Doctor E.A. Wagner."

"Who's Doctor Wagner?"

I heaved another sigh. "Remember when I exorcized the ghost from Mrs. Bissel's basement a couple of years back? Well, that ghost turned out to be Marianne Wagner, who isn't a ghost at all, and she'd run away from home because her father was a cruel monster."

"Yeah? I remember that episode. A little. So he's a monster, is he?"

Because I didn't want to go into lengthy explanations, I said only, "Yes."

Sitting beside me, Pa took my hand. "I'm sorry, sweetheart. It must have been unpleasant for you."

"It was. But it was Sam who had to inspect the body to figure out what caused his death." I shuddered. "It hurt his leg and must have been...really awful."

"I'd say so."

Sam's rumbling basso-profundo voice issued softly from the kitchen for several minutes. Then Pa and I heard the receiver click into the cradle, and Sam limped from the kitchen to flump into one of the dining-room chairs.

"So what now?" I asked him.

"Gotta meet the marshal at the cemetery."

"How long will it take the marshal to get there?"

With a shrug, Sam said, "Don't know. They aren't that far away. On Foothill and Lake." He heaved himself to his feet.

"That's close to Mrs. Bissel's house," I said, surprised, as the only official building I'd ever noticed in that area was a local branch of the fire department. Not that I'd been looking.

"Probably. Nine-forty East Foothill. Right there on the corner."

"Yes. Mrs. Bissel's place is on Foothill and Maiden Lane. The marshal's office must be almost across the street from her."

"Very close then," said he.

"Crumb. We should have called from her house."

"Probably better that we didn't. We don't want to advertise a crime all over town before we need to."

"I guess you're right."

However, before he could escape, I said, "Stay there for another little minute, Sam. I know your leg is aching"—I didn't react to the hideous frown he shot at me—"so I'll get you a couple of aspirin tablets before you go."

"Thanks."

Burning to ask my next question but not quite yet, I went to the bathroom, shook out three aspirin tablets from the bottle, and side-stepped into the kitchen to get a glass of water for him to take them with. I don't think that sentence is correct. Oh, who cares?

"Here you go, Sam. Maybe these will ease your pain a bit. You're going to have to stand around a lot, aren't you?"

"Yes." He took the aspirin and the water. "Thank you. Want to go with me?"

THREE

So surprised was I at this question, my mouth fell open and nothing came out of it for several seconds. Under normal circumstances, Sam will do *anything* to keep me away from his cases. Maybe he didn't care this time because it was the county marshal's problem? I didn't know.

Evidently I was silent too long. Sam's face crunched up into an expression of exasperation, and he said, "Well? You're always trying to pry into my cases. Do you want to come with me to the cemetery or not?"

"Yes!" I cried, perhaps too loudly. I saw Sam wince. "I'm just so surprised you asked me to!"

"You don't have to screech at me," he mumbled.

Pa laughed.

I leaped from my place at the table, startling Spike, which I regretted, and raced to Sam, to whom I gave a big, smacking kiss. Deciding it was safer not to ask why he wanted me along, I didn't.

"You don't have to be so thrilled. You're the one who's going to have to identify that rotting corpse, you know. Provided it turns out to be whoever that man you told me it was, is." His nose wrinkled. "Did that make sense?"

"I know what you meant," said I. "That's why you want me along? In case I can identify who it is? Was?"

"Yeah. And it's the county's case, so I won't have much to do with it. I hope."

I didn't voice my own hope that they'd want Sam right, smack in the middle of solving the crime. Once we were back in his Hudson again, however, I did ask a pertinent question. Or maybe it wasn't, but I wanted to know the answer anyway. "Who's going to notify the next of kin?"

"Don't know yet."

"You're always so helpful, Sam."

He shot me a grin. "I know. That's why you love me."

"Right." Actually, he was partially correct. He drove me nuts when he refused to discuss his cases, but he was always there when I needed him. "Thank you for letting me tag along with you."

"You're welcome."

We said no more as we tootled up Fair Oaks to the cemetery. The county marshals had shown up before us. Two uniformed men stood outside their official automobile, arms crossed, one of them carrying a large satchel, and both looking as though they'd rather be somewhere else. I didn't much blame them, but they'd signed on for this duty.

As Sam pulled into the dirt parking lot, the two uniforms started walking our way.

"Detective Rotondo?" one of them asked. I squinted, but couldn't see a badge or anything on his coat. Maybe he attached it to his shirt. Or maybe he kept it in his wallet. That's where Sam kept his.

"Yes," Sam said, getting out of the machine. He walked over to my side and opened my door. I, too, stepped out.

The second officer said, "Is that a civilian?"

"Yes," said Sam.

"She shouldn't be here."

"She's the one who found and may have identified the body."

"Oh. Well, then, I guess it's all right." He held out a hand to me. "I'm Marshal Evans."

Taking his hand, I said, "Daisy Majesty."

He dropped my hand like a hot rock, nodded and turned to Sam with the same hand held out. "Detective Rotondo. Can you lead the way to the corpse?"

With a sigh, Sam said, "Yes. It'll take me a while because I have to use this thing." He shook his cane as if he wished it were human and he could somehow damage it with the shake.

"Take your time," said Marshal Evans.

Sam turned to me. "Lead the way, Daisy. You can move faster than I can."

After receiving a nod of agreement from Marshal Evans, I led the way. Sam lagged a little way behind us. I got the impression he just didn't want to get involved in this particular case and wasn't going to put himself forward in any way whatsoever.

The ground was still squishy. Fortunately, I hadn't changed my damp shoes for another pair, so the mud and grass didn't hurt them any more than they were already hurt.

After about three or four minutes, the group of us arrived at the would-be grave of the corpse that might be that of Dr. Wagner. Sam put a large paw on my shoulder, I guess to give me courage. "Here it is." I pointed. "I think, although I'm not positive, that it's Doctor Everhard A. Wagner. If it is he, his wife is Diane Wagner, and his daughter is Marianne Grenville. She's married to George Grenville. His sons are named Gaylord Wagner and Vincent Wagner."

"Thank you, Mrs. Majesty." Marshal Evans grabbed a tarpaulin out of his satchel, spread it on the ground and knelt. I was impressed by his state of preparedness.

After carefully wiping away mud and grit with a cloth, Evans asked, "Do you recognize him?" He looked up at me. His face displayed displeasure. I'm sure mine did, too. Dr. Wagner wasn't a pretty sight.

"Yes. That's Doctor Wagner, all right." My nose wrinkled of its own accord.

"Did he live here? In Altadena?"

"He lived in Pasadena," I said.

"Do you know if the Pasadena police have received any missing-person reports on the fellow?"

"Don't have a clue," said Sam, shaking his head.

"Hmm. And who were his next of kin again?"

I repeated all the names. The other officer, who hadn't introduced himself, wrote them down.

Evans said, "You know their address?"

"No. It's in Pasadena, but I don't know the street or number."

"Hmm." He peered closely at the earth surrounding what was left of Dr. Wagner's head. "Looks as though he was killed elsewhere and dumped here."

Dumped? Ew. On the other hand, we were talking about Dr. Wagner, and he surely didn't deserve any respect.

"Huh," said Sam, his hand tightening on my shoulder. "Does that make it a county case or a city case?"

With a sigh and a grunt, Evans rose from his tarpaulin. "Henry, will you please fold up that thing? I'll call the coroner. He's in Pasadena, so I expect you're going to have to be involved in this one, Detective Rotondo."

"Great," said Sam, his hand nearly denting my shoulder by that time. He was clearly not happy to hear the news. "Merry Christmas."

"Right," said Evans. He grinned.

Henry, who never did get introduced to Sam and me, stood guard over the body while the rest of us walked back to the parking area. Sam opened the passenger door of his Hudson and I climbed in. Then Sam and Marshal Evans drew away from the machine and commenced chatting with each other. Typical. Sam wanted me out of the way before he'd discuss the case. Darned men.

When he eventually entered the driver's side of his Hudson, he growled, "This is terrific. Now I have to notify the next of kin."

"Do you have their addresses?"

"No. We're driving to the marshal's office, where all will be revealed."

"Why does Marshal Evans think Doctor Wagner was killed elsewhere and then driven to the cemetery?"

"Not enough blood in the soil."

Another ew.

"Want to come with me when I notify his wife and daughter? I'll tackle the sons by myself, but you know both ladies, so it might make them feel better if you're with me."

"Sam!" I cried. "You're letting me butt in! You've never done that before."

"I figured I might as well let you come with me, because I *know* you'll get involved anyway since you know some of the people involved. Plus, as you're so fond of telling me, people are more apt to speak frankly to you than to the police, especially when it comes to family problems."

I shot him a beaming smile. "I *knew* you'd see it my way one of these days."

"Oh," said he grumpishly, "I've always seen it your way. I just don't like it."

"Hmm."

He grinned. The fiend. He loved teasing me and getting me all upset for nothing.

Sam's Hudson followed the marshal's auto up to the marshal's office, which wasn't very far away from the cemetery, and we all got out and trundled inside the building. There, one of the marshal's minions first called the county coroner and then grabbed a telephone directory and looked up Dr. Wagner's address and that of George and Marianne Grenville. Sam jotted the addresses in his pocket notebook.

"Any listings for..." Sam glanced at me. "What are the sons' names?"

"Gaylord and Vincent," said I. "Last name Wagner."

The minion scoured the telephone book for Gaylord and/or Vincent Wagner, then shook his head. "Maybe they live with their mother."

"Maybe," said I.

"That it for now?" Sam asked.

"Guess so," said Marshal Evans. "I'm going to write up a report on this. Then I expect your chief and mine will get together and decide who's going to do what regarding the case. I'm sorry, Detective Rotondo, but if most of the people involved are Pasadena residents, especially if we determine the man was killed in the city, you'll probably have to take the case."

With a sigh, Sam said, "I'm used to it. May I use your 'phone to call the station? I want to know if anyone's filed a missing-person report on Doctor Wagner. Any idea how long he's been dead, or do you have to wait for the coroner to report?"

"Better wait for the coroner. The recent rains might have interfered with decomposition. I imagine he's been in the dirt for two or three days at least."

Yet another ew.

So Sam called the station, determined no missing-person report had been filed for Dr. Wagner, hung up the receiver and told Evans so.

"Does that seem odd to you?" asked Evans.

"Don't know. According to Daisy here, Doctor Wagner was a bad man who mistreated his wife and daughter. Maybe they didn't care if he went missing. I don't know anything about his sons."

I said, "From everything I've ever heard, they're as bad as he is. Was. You know what I mean. Well, I don't know if they beat up on women, but they're both snobs and supercilious and…Well, not very nice."

"Hmm," said Evans.

"His daughter ran away from home a couple of years ago, but that turned out all right. She's married to the Grenville fellow now," Sam said. "He owns that big bookstore downtown on Colorado."

"Ran away from home, did she? Not a ringing endorsement as to the state of affairs in the family."

"Right. Do I need to know anything else before I visit Mrs. Wagner?"

"Don't think so. I'll telephone you with any information I receive, and we'll send a report to you at the police department."

"Thanks," said Sam, not meaning it.

Marshal Evans smiled at him, and Sam and I walked back to his car.

"So, I have Mrs. Wagner's address in my notebook. I also have that of her daughter and son-in-law. Where do you want to go first?"

"Um…I don't know. What do you policemen usually do?"

"Tell the wife, then, if the kids live elsewhere, get in touch with them."

"Then let's go to Mrs. Wagner's house. Where is it?"

Sam reached into his front jacket pocket, pulled out his little notebook and handed it to me. "You tell me."

His handwriting was quite nice, for that of a man. Legible, anyway. Smallish. Neatish. I squinted down at the pad. "Um…It says here she lives on El Molino Avenue south of Colorado Street. Nine fifty-three."

"Must be a nice place. That's a fancy neighborhood."

"Yes, it is. The houses down there are huge and beautiful."

"We don't typically get calls to go to places like that."

"Except for Mrs. Pinkerton."

"Except for Mrs. Pinkerton," he agreed.

Mrs. Pinkerton was my very best, most lucrative client. That was because her daughter, Stacy, was a horrible person and was always getting into trouble. Since Mrs. Pinkerton actually believed the bilge I spewed as a spiritualist-medium, and since she always hoped the tarot cards or the Ouija board would change their minds and predict that Stacy would become a good person someday, she called upon my services a whole lot. Anyway, the police had been obliged to visit Mrs. Pinkerton's house on several occasions because of Stacy's appalling behavior. Well, and then there was the time the Ku Klux Klan tried to kill her gatekeeper, but that's another story altogether.

Wow. The Wagner home was impressive. Gigantic and creamy yellow, it looked cheerful even on a crisp December day.

"Shoot, Sam, how many rooms do you suppose that place has?"

He drew his Hudson to a stop outside the huge lawn to allow us to gape for a few minutes. "I don't know. Six or seven hundred?"

"May be," said I, still gaping.

The place had a black wrought-iron fence surrounding it, but the front gate stood open, so Sam turned right, tootled his car up the drive and parked it next to the stairs leading to a gigantic porch that wrapped around most of the house. The place appeared to have approximately a zillion windows, and I couldn't quite feature Dr. Wagner in that house. It looked too friendly a place in which an ogre like him might dwell. I'd have expected a dark and gloomy house—one that looked more apt to house a troll. Like, say, a cave or something along those lines—but this sure wasn't one of those.

Sam exited the Hudson on his side, walked around and opened my door.

"Thanks, Sam." I got out of the car.

"Any old time."

"You're still grumpy, aren't you?"

"Why wouldn't I be? I took a day off because you had a whim to see our late spouses' graves and ask a couple of coffins for a blessing on our union, and I ended up saddled with another murder on my hands. It's as if you attract them. Like honey attracts flies."

"I don't, either."

Actually, as I thought about the dead bodies that seemed determined to show up here and there in my vicinity—no matter where that vicinity was—Sam was right. What a melancholy reflection.

Sam said, "Huh," and we climbed the stairs to the porch.

We passed a charming table and a couple of chairs sitting on the porch, and I was surprised yet again. The whole place seemed warm and welcoming. Strange. I couldn't imagine the evil Dr. Wagner allowing his wife to decorate the place, but it sure didn't fit what I knew of him. Maybe he had the rack, thumb screws, and iron maiden locked in the basement.

The door was some kind of wood—I don't know one kind of wood from another unless it's birds-eye maple—and massive. Wide; what they used to call a "coffin door," because folks used to lay out dead bodies in their homes until the undertakers brought the coffin, moved the corpse into it and carried it away. The door had to be wide enough to accommodate the folks carrying coffins out. It was the first evidence of something that reminded me of Dr. Wagner. Nobody'd be using this door to haul out his coffin, however.

Sam rang the bell.

Nothing.

Sam rang the bell again.

Still nothing.

"Damn," said my beloved, ringing the bell once more and pounding on the door for good measure. "Ow. Hard wood."

He was still shaking his hand and looking crabby when the door finally opened to reveal a scared-looking maid in a black dress and a white apron. She squinted at us and didn't speak.

"We need to see Mrs. Wagner," said Sam to the girl.

"Um...She's not available to see visitors right now."

Withdrawing his wallet, Sam showed the girl his police credentials. "Police business. She will be available to see us."

The girl licked her lips, still looking scared, and said, "Um...I don't—"

"We need to see Mrs. Wagner," said Sam. "Now." He didn't raise his voice, but when he used that tone on people, they generally did what he told them to do. It was deadly, that tone.

The girl jumped about seven inches and backed up. "I...I..."

Deciding the poor thing needed a friend, I said softly and soothingly, "It's all right. We really do need to speak with Mrs. Wagner. It's important, or the police wouldn't be calling."

She gave up. "Follow me then," she said, sounding as if she expected to get a whipping for her action.

Lordy, the Wagner men even intimidated the staff who kept their charming home neat and tidy.

The frightened girl led us up a staircase to the second floor, turned left and walked down a wide hallway. When she reached a door at the end of the hall, she tapped lightly on the door then pushed it open. "She's on the balcony," said the girl, pointing to an open door on the other side of the room. She turned and fled.

Sam and I exchanged a glance. I'm not sure what Sam's glance denoted, but mine probably showed bewilderment.

Undaunted—or perhaps only slightly daunted on my part—we walked to the open door and stepped outside onto a gorgeous balcony with a wrought-iron railing protecting folks from falling into the lovely gardens exposed thereby. Mrs. Wagner sat huddled in a chair with a quilt wrapped around her and her feet resting on a hassock. She turned with a jerk, then winced.

Rushing over to her, I cried, "Oh, my Lord, Mrs. Wagner, I'm so sorry! What in heaven's name happened to you?"

FOUR

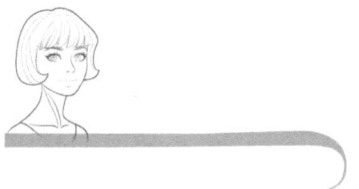

The woman was a mess. Her face featured a mass of bruises, which were evidently not of recent origin because they were turning green around the edges. I took her hands and gazed down upon her. She made a truly pathetic picture, hunched, wrapped and brutalized. She wasn't the first battered woman I'd seen, but I felt particularly sorry for her.

"Mrs. Majesty?" she quavered, as if it was difficult for her to speak. The bruises on her throat probably accounted for that.

"Yes, Mrs. Wagner. It's I. I'm so sorry..." My words trailed off. I was sorry her late husband had used her as a punching bag? I couldn't say that.

Fingering a swollen cheek, she said, "I'm glad you're here." Then she began crying as if her heart were broken. It probably was.

Still holding her hands, I knelt before her. "Did your husband do this to you?"

She nodded, still crying. I contemplated fumbling in my handbag for a hankie, but she held my hand tightly, so I didn't.

"I'm so sorry." Repetitive, Daisy Gumm Majesty. But I didn't know what else to say. *Why didn't you leave the bum years ago? Why didn't you go live with your daughter and her husband?* I'm sure they wouldn't have minded. *Why didn't you knife him while he was sleeping?* Heck, she could then have messed up the room and blamed his death on burglars or something.

Feeling totally helpless, I said softly, "Mrs. Wagner, Detective Rotondo here has some news for you. It…It might actually make you feel better, although I don't suppose I should say that."

Diane Wagner dipped a hand into a pocket of the robe she wore under her quilt and pulled out a hankie. After wiping her eyes, she said, "The only thing that would make me feel better is knowing Everhard will never come home again." She wiped her eyes once more. "Although, that would still leave the boys."

"Good Lord! Do they beat you, too?"

She shook her head and winced again. "No, but they're not awfully nice boys."

Boys? They were men, curse it! Not-very-nice men, even according to their mother.

"I'm sorry," said I yet again. Then, still kneeling, I scooted to one side of her, allowing Sam to loom over her. She shrank back some more.

Because I was irked with my beloved, who didn't quite know how to handle problems of this nature—crying women, I mean—I said gently, "Sam, why don't you pull up that chair over there. Then you can speak to Mrs. Wagner more easily."

"Good idea," said he, grabbing a chair and sitting in it. He still looked menacing, because that's just how Sam looked, but at least he no longer towered over her. He spoke softly when he addressed the woman again. "I have some new for you that will probably come as a shock, Mrs. Wagner. I'm sorry."

Good Lord, now *he* was sorrying her. Oh, well. Just went to prove I wasn't the only one who lacked imagination in the face of trying circumstances.

"Please tell me he's dead," whispered Mrs. Wagner.

I don't know if Sam was shocked but I, oddly, was not. If I'd had to live with a man who did that to me, I'd want him dead, too.

"That's what I'm here to tell you, all right," said Sam.

Mrs. Wagner's eyes opened as wide as they could, considering the swelling around them. "He is? Are you sure?" She buried her abused face in her hands and muttered, "Thank God." She resumed crying, this time with relief, unless I missed my guess.

Rising to my feet—my knees were sore by that time—I patted her on the shoulder. When she winced, I stopped patting. What an evil man Dr. Wagner had been!

"Detective Rotondo needs to ask you some questions, Mrs. Wagner—"

"Oh, please don't call me that! Call me Diane. Anything but Wagner."

"Very well, I understand," I said, using my most soothing tone. "Detective Rotondo will need to ask you some questions, Diane."

After giving her eyes another wipe, she said, "All right. What do you need to know?" She squinted, decided that didn't feel good, and opened her eyes wider once more. "What did he die of? He didn't have a heart, so it couldn't have been a heart attack."

Guess we knew how she felt about her old man, didn't we?

Placing one of his huge hands over one of hers in her lap, Sam said gently, "I'm afraid he was murdered, Mrs.—Diane."

She stiffened. "Murdered? How? Who did it?"

"He was struck on the head with a blunt instrument, and we don't yet know who did it."

"Good Lord. I probably should tell Gaylord and Vincent. Not that they'll be heartbroken. I'll call Marianne, though. Perhaps she and George will allow me to stay with them for a while. They've asked before, but I was afraid Everhard would find out where I was and take it out on them."

"Your late husband doesn't sound like a very nice man, Diane," said Sam, foregoing subtlety since it would have been wasted anyway.

"He was mean and hateful, and I'm glad he's dead. I'd like to thank whoever did it." She glanced from Sam to me. "That sounds terrible, doesn't it?"

"After having met him and Marianne and you, it doesn't sound terrible to me," said I, though her words had startled me a little bit —but not much. I'd had dealings with beaten-up women before. I'd

29

discovered the ones who wished their abusers dead had been receiving the brunt of their violence for long enough to understand abuse like that was in no way connected to feelings of love or esteem.

"Can you think of anyone else who might have wanted him out of the way?" Sam asked.

Diane heaved a sigh and commenced thinking. After several seconds of that, she said, "He had problems with so many people, it's difficult to pinpoint just one. Lately, he was in what sounded like a feud with another doctor in town, but I don't know the other man's name." She shot me a quick glance. "I fear his business suffered a decline after Marianne left home. And that's not your fault!" she hastened to add, looking at me squarely. "You assisted Marianne, and I'll always be grateful to you for that. She didn't deserve what that man did to her." She shook her head. "How can a man be all charm and niceness until you marry him, and only then show his true colors? Why does that happen?"

"I don't know," said I, peering at Sam and hoping he wouldn't turn into a monster after we were married.

Naw. Sam was always Sam. I'd only recently begun to appreciate him for that.

"He hated George Grenville for marrying Marianne. He and the boys never got along well, either, but he didn't dare beat up on them once they were big enough to fight back. He was at odds with so many people, it's difficult for me to recall them all." She sighed.

"Take your time," said Sam, still being gentle with the woman. "Do you think your sons might know the names of any of Doctor Wagner's particular enemies?"

"I'm not sure. They might. They've both been living at the Pasadena Golf and Tennis Club for some time now."

"I didn't know men could actually live there," said I, earning a frown from Sam.

"Oh, yes, many young men—wealthy young men"—Diane grimaced—"stay there. All their needs are taken care of, and all they need is money, which Vincent and Gaylord have."

I decided that answered my question, so I clamped my lips together.

"How long has Doctor Wagner been away from home?" asked Sam.

After heaving a soulful sigh, Diane said, "Four days. I was scared to death every minute of every day that he'd come back and light in to me again."

"Couldn't Marianne help you?" I asked, being unable to suppress the question, even in the face of Sam's frown.

"She could, but Doctor Wagner hated George Grenville, and he…behaved horribly to Marianne."

"Even after she and Mr. Grenville were married?" said Sam before I could get the same words out of my mouth. His glower told me to keep it that way.

"Yes. He went out of his way to annoy George and harass Marianne."

"How did he do that?" Sam beat me to the question again that time.

"Oh, he'd go to Grenville's Books and create a scene for no reason, calling George a cheat and a liar in front of customers. Things like that. I'm not sure how he harassed Marianne, but I do know she was afraid of even stepping outside her house for fear her father would get her."

"Get her? What do you mean by 'get her'"? asked Sam.

Shaking her head, Diane said, "Kidnap her, I guess. Poor Marianne didn't like to talk about it, and neither did George. They were both trying to spare my feelings." She chuffed out a small breath of hopelessness. "As if they could. I had to live with the demon."

"Out of curiosity," said Sam as if he weren't sure he should be asking, "did you ever consider leaving your husband? He doesn't sound like a person I'd want to be around for very long at any one time."

"Oh, yes," said Diane promptly. "I considered it all the time, but I was fairly certain he'd find me and bring me back again and beat me some more. He did this sort of thing a lot," said she, spreading open her blanket and revealing discolored arms that went all too well with the bruises on her face. With a small shrug she added, "Or he might have just killed me."

"Didn't your sons stick up for you?" I asked, perhaps too strongly. But, honestly! What kinds of sons could stand around and allow their father to brutalize their mother?

"They tried," said Diane.

"How is that?" Sam asked before I could.

"They'd tell him to stop hitting me. And he would. Stop hitting me, I mean. Until Gaylord and Vincent left the house, and then he'd tear into me even more brutally than before."

"I'm surprised none of your children reported your husband's abuse to the police department," said Sam.

Both Diane and I shot him meaningful glances. I guess he caught the meanings therefrom, because he sighed and said, "Yes. I know. The police are pretty helpless in cases of family violence."

"Oh, I'm sure they'd have cared if Everhard had succeeded in murdering me, although he'd probably have tried to cover it up some way or other. Pretend someone had entered the house and murdered me while he was away or something."

Precisely the scenario I'd considered her enacting on her husband. I'd grown up in a loving family and had married a wonderful man; it was depressing to know so many other families weren't as lucky as I. Providing luck had anything to do with it; I didn't know. Still don't, for that matter.

"So you can't think of the names of anyone who particularly disliked Doctor Wagner, Diane?"

"I'll think about it," she said. "I'll give Marianne a call." She didn't look as though she wanted to.

"Would you rather we inform your daughter, Diane? We'll be happy to do it. You probably need to rest and take in the news," Sam asked, his voice still gentle.

"Oh, would you?" she said, relief palpable in her voice. "I'll call them later, but I would *so* appreciate you breaking the news."

"We'll be happy to do that, Mrs. Wag—er, Diane," said Sam.

"Thank you. Will you be going to their house? I mean, will you visit them or telephone them?"

"It's better to break this sort of news in person," said Sam. I was pretty sure the "in person" scenario was preferred because the cops could assess the person's reaction to the news, but I didn't tell Diane that.

"Thank you. They live up on Catalina Avenue." She gave Sam the address, which he wrote in his little notebook. "It's an adorable, sweet place. Not huge and impressive like this monstrosity."

Monstrosity? I thought her home was gorgeous and charming.

"Very well. We'll visit the Grenvilles next," Sam told her.

She heaved a huge sigh. "Thank you. I really didn't want to deliver the message via the telephone wire, and I can't get around very well yet, thanks to my late husband."

I don't believe I'd ever heard a woman sound so bitter. I understood completely. Mrs. Wagner wasn't the first brutalized woman I'd met in my shortish life.

"We'll be glad to do that for you, ma'am," said Sam. "Would you like us to give your daughter a message to come see you or anything? We can tell Mr. Grenville to come here, too, if you'd like."

"Thank you. That would be kind of you. George's bookstore is closed on Mondays, so I expect they'll both be at home. They have such a nice little place." She sighed again. "I gave you the address, right? On Catalina? Near Washington?"

"Yes, thank you, we have it."

"And the boys are at the Pasadena Golf and Tennis Club. I think I already told you that." She passed a hand over her brow, as if wiping away cobwebs. "I'm sorry. My head has been swimming ever since Everhard did this to me."

"Have you seen a doctor?" I asked.

"No. Everhard *was* a doctor."

"Yes, but…Well, I think you should see another doctor. Someone who actually cares about his patients. I'll be happy to call Doctor Benjamin for you, if you'd like him to call on you, Diane. He's a wonderful, caring man."

More tears leaked from the poor woman's eyes. "Thank you, dear. Yes. That would be nice. I've always liked Doctor Benjamin. *So* unlike Everhard."

"That's for sure," I agreed.

"Very well, ma'am," said Sam, rising from his chair. "Well go break the news to your daughter and son-in-law now."

She gazed up at him. "Thank you. You just delivered the best news I've heard in two years. That sounds terrible, doesn't it?"

"No," said Sam, not one to mince words.

"Diane, if there's anything at all I can do to help you or Marianne, other than call Doctor Benjamin for you, please let me know. I'll be happy to do whatever I can, although I can't imagine what that might be," I said. Then I felt silly.

"You did both of us the greatest favor you could ever bestow when you rescued Marianne, Mrs. Majesty."

"Please just call me Daisy. Everyone does."

She gave me a faint, painful smile. "Daisy. Perhaps you can come over and visit with Marianne and me, if she stays here. I hope she'll invite me to stop at her place for a few days. I miss her so very much."

"You haven't seen her very often of late?" I asked.

"Not nearly enough. She was frightened of Everhard and didn't dare come near this house."

"That's so sad," I said, taking her limp hand. "I'm sorry. I hope things will improve from now on."

"You're very kind, dear. They can't help but improve now that Everhard is dead. He was an evil man." She shook her head.

We left her after another round of farewells. Sam and I walked out to his machine in silence.

FIVE

W e'd driven almost all the way up El Molino Avenue to Washington before either of us spoke, and then it was Sam. "Not a happy family."

"Not a happy family," I agreed. "I feel so sorry for women like that. I wish there was some way the authorities could help them."

"I do too, to tell the truth. But we aren't allowed to barge into people's homes without being asked, unless some crime has been committed."

"Beating up a fragile woman isn't a crime?"

"Of course it is." Snappy. Sam often got snappish when he was frustrated. "But we can't do anything about it unless someone complains. And then half the time the abuse only gets worse, just as Mrs. Wagner said. I wish we could just shoot men like Doctor Wagner and do the world a favor, but we can't."

"People shoot mad dogs."

"Yeah. But people aren't dogs."

"Maybe not, but they're certainly animals."

"True. Most people aren't as nice as most dogs."

"That's true, too. How sad."

Sam hung a right on Washington Street and drove to Catalina Avenue. He said, "What's their address again?"

"Turn right when you get to Catalina, and it should be right there. On the..." I contemplated the address in my head. Not a mathematical genius, I. "It should be on the right side of the street. Thirteen-oh-five."

"Got it."

The Grenville home was one house down from the corner of Catalina and Washington. A lovely location. Catalina was a shady street, and the Grenville house was not unlike my family's nice bungalow on South Marengo, only larger and fancier. Also, Catalina was lined with oaks and not pepper trees as was Marengo. "Hmm. This is it?"

"Yes," said Sam, turning off the ignition. "Pretty place."

"It sure is, although I guess Mrs. Wagner was right in that it's not as huge as their home on South El Molino."

"Nice, though."

"Yes, it is. Gee, when Harold told me George Grenville lived on Catalina, I thought he meant one of those sweet little bungalows a little south of here."

"Maybe to him, this *is* a sweet little bungalow."

After a split-second of contemplation, I said, "You're probably right." Harold's own home in San Marino was gigantic.

Sam exited his side of the Hudson and came around to open my door. I got out and gazed at George and Marianne's house. A gray Cadillac was parked in the drive, and the place wasn't fenced and gated. Still, it was relatively large and lovely, a typical Pasadena bungalow. I vaguely recalled George Grenville driving a dark Cadillac, so perhaps he and Marianne were home.

"Well," said Sam. "Nothing ventured, nothing gained." He took my arm and drew me to a stop. I'd begun marching up the drive to the front porch. "Only this time, let me do the talking, all right?"

"Of course, I will."

Sam rolled his eyes. Darn him!

"I will!" I insisted.

"Of course, you will" Sam repeated. Then he allowed me to walk again.

The Grenville's front porch was large and roofed, and it, too, had a table and a couple of chairs parked on it. I didn't know why folks left their outdoor furniture outside in the wintertime, but what the heck. They were rich and I wasn't, so they played by different rules from those my family followed.

I allowed Sam to ring the electrical doorbell and heard chimes inside the house. They sounded quite pretty. "Chimes," said I, smiling.

"Chimes," said Sam. "Lovely." He was being sarcastic, so I pinched his arm.

Before he could say "Ow," the door opened and George Grenville stood there, looking nervously at us from behind a screen door. Then he recognized me.

"Daisy!" he cried, clearly mystified by my presence on his front porch, but relieved. Perhaps he'd expected Marianne's bad-doctor father to show up. He turned. "Marianne, it's Daisy Majesty!" He looked back and took in the presence of Sam. Turning once more, he said, "And...And that policeman fellow. You know the one."

She should. Sam had driven her mean old father out of Grenville's books one day two years past when he'd been creating havoc therein.

"Detective Rotondo," Sam supplied.

"Detective Rotondo," George repeated, unlocking the screen door and allowing us entry to his home. "Come in, both of you. I hope this isn't bad news."

He really did look worried.

Marianne came at a trot from somewhere else and stopped beside her husband. She said, "Daisy! How good to see you. Unless..." She clapped her hands to her cheeks. "Oh, please don't tell me he's killed Mother! Oh, Daisy!"

"No, no," I said, breaking Sam's rule before I'd been inside the house for six seconds. I swear...

"Please, Mr. and Mrs. Grenville," said Sam. "May we come in

and sit down? I have some bad news to impart, although it isn't about your mother."

"Thank God," Marianne whispered, seeming to deflate.

"Come into the living room," said George, leading the way.

The place was furnished with nice stuff. Bookcases—unsurprisingly—lined a wall in the living room. George gestured to a sofa and a couple of chairs. "Take your pick," said he.

Sam and I shared the sofa. George and Marianne, still both seeming quite wary, sat on a couple of chairs opposite us. Suddenly Marianne jumped to her feet. "Oh, I'm so sorry! I should have offered you tea or coffee or—"

"There's no need for that, Mrs. Grenville. Please sit down again. I have some unfortunate news to tell you."

Marianne reached for George's hand, and he took hers in what looked like an almost-painful grip.

Re-seating herself, she asked, "What is it?" in a strangled whisper.

"I'm sorry to have to tell you that your father has been killed."

George gasped. Marianne swallowed hard.

"By killed, do you mean...?" Evidently George didn't want to say the word aloud.

"Someone murdered him, yes," said Sam.

"Thank *God*," whispered Marianne. "Thank *God*! Oh, but it wasn't Mother who did it, was it? Not that she shouldn't have, but—"

"No, no," said Sam, holding out a hand as if to keep her from bolting up and running around in circles. "We just came from visiting with your mother. She's fine. Well..."

"She's not fine, is she? He beat her up again, didn't he?" asked Marianne.

"I fear he did."

"I hate him *so much*!"

"Marianne," said George, sounding a cautious note. "Perhaps we should let the detective tell us what happened."

"Of course," she said. "Of course. I'm sorry."

"No need to be sorry, ma'am," said Sam in his official voice, softening it for Marianne's sake. "But your father was found murdered this morning, and I will need to ask both of you a few questions."

"Go ahead," said Marianne. "We have nothing to hide." She gave us a grim smile. "As you've probably already figured out, I loathed the man. He was a beast to Mother and me. I'm glad someone finally killed him. He had so many enemies, it might be difficult to whittle down the pile."

"Interesting. Do you have any names for me to write down?" Sam took out his notebook and poised his pencil over same, waiting for something to write.

"Besides us?" Marianne asked. Then she glanced at George and grimaced. "I'm sorry. I didn't mean that. We'd never have done anything to hurt Father, but he's been harassing George at the store and he keeps…Er, he kept coming over to our house and just sitting in his automobile across the street, staring at the house. I was afraid to leave home for fear he might do something to me."

"He truly was a monster, wasn't he?" I asked before I could remember to keep my mouth shut. Happened a lot with me.

"Yes. He was." She squeezed her husband's hand. "I'm surprised George put up with me because of him."

"It sounds almost as if he were stalking prey," muttered Sam, writing.

"Exactly," said George. "I went out there and shouted at him a few times and he'd go away, but he always came back. I think the man was mad."

"So do I," said Marianne.

"He'd been going to the bookstore and creating a ruckus?" asked Sam, still writing. "How often did he do that?"

With a shrug, George glanced at Marianne. She glanced back and gave him shrug for shrug. Finally George said, "Ever since we were married. I wanted to ask Marianne's mother to stay with us, but she always said she feared what he might do to us—and to her—if she did come to live here. She seemed to think he might go completely crazy and burn the house down or shoot us or something along those lines."

"He probably would have," whispered Marianne.

"What about your brothers?" asked Sam. "Did they get along with their father?"

"I have nothing to do with either Gaylord or Vincent. We... aren't on friendly terms."

"Why is that?"

After thinking for a few seconds, Marianne said, "Well, they aren't brutal, as was Father, but they're not nice. They treated me like dirt, and they treated George even worse than that."

"How did they treat you, Mr. Grenville?"

"Hmm. I don't know. It's difficult to explain, except that they've always been supercilious and uppity. Not at all like their sister or their mother." This time it was he who squeezed his wife's hand. She smiled tenderly at him. Nice couple, at least on the surface.

"Did they ever...I don't know. Behave inappropriately? Like, hitting people or anything? They didn't beat up on your mother or you, Mrs. Grenville?"

"No. Never. They just didn't seem to care one way or another if Father treated our mother badly." She shook her head. "I'm not sure how to describe it. I guess what I'm saying is they didn't care about anyone but themselves. Not even Mother, who is a wonderful, sweet woman and didn't deserve the punishment Father dealt her or the indifference Gaylord and Vincent exhibited toward her."

"I see," said Sam. "Your mother told us your brothers have been living at the Pasadena Golf and Tennis Club for a while. Do you know anything about that?"

"Not a thing," said Marianne. "Although it doesn't surprise me, as many of their friends also live there. Anyhow, any time Father got particularly nasty, the two of them would vanish. They very seldom tried to help Mother. Once or twice they did, but Father held the purse strings, so to speak, so I guess they didn't dare rebel too openly."

"I'm sorry," said Sam, and I could tell he meant it. "Do you think your brothers might have had anything to do with your father's death?"

Marianne started a bit. "Gaylord and Vincent? I...I don't know.

I doubt it. They didn't like to do anything for themselves. That's why they live at the club. They like being waited on." She shook her head. "I'm sorry. That's not fair to them. Many of their contemporaries live at the club. I guess they like it better than living at home or in an apartment by themselves. They get waited on, and their friends are always nearby." She made a face. "I don't care for many of my brothers' friends, but that's not their fault."

I almost asked her why she didn't like her brothers' friends, but a glance from Sam told me not to.

"Do either of your brothers hold a job? I mean, are they lawyers or doctors like their father or anything like that?"

"Those two?" George guffawed. "No. They only liked spending the old man's money. As Marianne told you, they didn't like to do things for themselves. They preferred being waited on hand and foot."

"From what I've heard, your father's practice has been declining for a couple of years, Mrs. Grenville. Do you know anything about that?"

"No," said Marianne. "But it wouldn't surprise me. After…Well, after I ran away and Daisy and George rescued me"—She gave her husband another glowing smile—"I think people began to see him for what he was."

"And that was?" asked Sam.

"A hateful and cruel man. Mother said his business had been off, and he was having big arguments with other doctors in town." She frowned. "And, of course, he treated her even worse than he used to. Which was my fault for running away." She had to wipe away a tear.

"It wasn't your fault," said the loyal George. "Your father was completely to blame for everything that happened to his business. He was a vicious brute of a man. Marianne's right, though. In recent weeks, I've been hearing rumors of him getting into spats with other medical men in the city."

"Any names you can think of, Mrs. Grenville?"

"Um…Not offhand, although I'll think about it. You might talk to Gaylord and Vincent. They were closer to the man than either

Marianne or me, even though they didn't like him either. Still, they might know something." He shook his head. "He spent so much time spying on Marianne and harassing me, I'm surprised he had any business at all. I don't know when he did his doctoring. As I said, he always seemed to be skulking around us. And beating his wife." He grimaced. "Terrible man. It's wrong of me to say so, but I'm glad he's gone."

"So am I," said Marianne.

"So am I," said I. Then I shut my mouth again. But really, can you blame any of us?

With a sigh, Sam said, "So am I." Then he said, "Thank you for your time. Please give me a call at the station if you can think of the names of any people who might have wished Doctor Wagner ill." Sam dug a business card out of his coat pocket and handed it to George.

"Pretty much everyone who ever met him wished him ill. Murder him...? I don't know who would do that. But I'll definitely think about it." George glanced at me. "You're friends with Harold Kincaid, aren't you? Well, I know you are, because you and he both helped Marianne when she ran away."

"Yes, we're good friends," I said.

"He might have more scuttlebutt than I have because he has a physician friend, Doctor Greenlaw. I've seen the two of them dining together at the Castleton. In fact, I do believe Doctor Greenlaw is staying at the club, too."

The Hotel Castleton was an elaborate and gorgeous hotel on South Lake Avenue in Pasadena. Harold had taken me to dine there, too, and it didn't surprise me that he and Fred Greenlaw dined there together from time to time. "Thank you, George. I'll definitely ask Harold if he can think of anyone who might have hated Doctor Wagner enough to do him in."

"Besides the members of his family," muttered Marianne, who seemed to have gained confidence now that she knew her old man was out of the picture forever.

With a smile, George said, "Yes. Besides his family."

Sam and I rose, and George and Marianne followed suit.

"Thank you for your time, Mr. and Mrs. Grenville. Please give me a call if you think of any one person who might have disliked the doctor more than anyone else. Actually, any and all names will help. We're not swimming in clues at the moment."

"Will do," said George.

"I'll think, too." Marianne looked at her husband and broke into a broad smile. "Oh, George, let's go to see Mother. I've been so frightened of my father that I haven't paid Mother the attention she deserves."

"Sounds like a good idea to me. We should have her stop with us for a while."

Marianne gave her husband a smacking kiss on the cheek, and George blushed. He didn't ordinarily display his affections in front of others.

I thought they were cute as bugs. Not that bugs are cute, but… Oh, never mind.

SIX

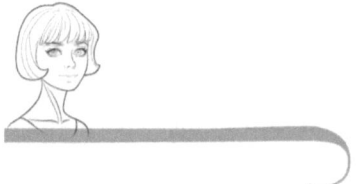

S am and I rode down the hill to my family's bungalow on South Marengo. He said, "I'm going to have to interview the two sons by myself, because I don't think they allow women into the Pasadena Golf and Tennis Club."

"I know they don't," I said, feeling bitter. The one time Sam actually wanted me to help him with a case, and I was prevented from doing so by a stupid rule. Men's clubs. I think there should be women's clubs that exclude men. Hmm. Maybe there are. Not that it mattered to me. I had a job to keep me occupied.

"I'll give you a report tonight," said Sam, grinning. He knew how galling I considered the Golf and Tennis Club's anti-female bias.

"Thanks, Sam. I'm not sure what Vi will be fixing for us, but I know it'll be spectacular."

"I know it, too."

My beloved aunt, Viola Gumm, was probably the best cook in the entire universe, and my family got to eat her meals every day. She was also Mrs. Pinkerton's cook, but she always made enough to bring to the family when she left work. Bless the woman. Neither my mother nor I could cook a lick. In fact, it's safer for everyone if neither of us even enters a kitchen. Lowering reflection, but true.

When Sam pulled up to the curb in front of our house, Pa was outside with Spike on a leash. That is to say, Spike was on the leash, and Pa was holding it. I said, "You don't need to open my door, Sam. I'll just help Pa walk Spike." I leaned over and kissed his cheek. "Don't forget to tell us everything tonight."

"I won't." Sam waved to my father, who waved back, and he began slowly rolling his Hudson down Marengo Avenue, aiming, I was sure, for the Pasadena Golf and Tennis Club. Darned men.

Spike greeted me warmly as usual, and Pa smiled down upon the both of us. That's because I was on my knees loving my dog. "Want to go with us on our walk?" asked Pa.

"You bet. I'm all dressed for it." That's because I hadn't changed since Sam and I went to the cemetery that morning. Which made me think of something. "By golly, I'm hungry! Sam and I didn't have any lunch yet."

Pulling out his pocket watch, Pa said, "Shoot, Daisy it's one o'clock. Want to eat before we walk?"

"No. I don't want to disappoint Spike. But I'll definitely be ready for a sandwich when we get home."

"Some of Vi's great meat loaf is waiting for you in the Frigidaire," said Pa, grinning. "I know how much you like that."

"So do you. Gee, I wish I'd asked Sam to come in for lunch." I felt guilty. Poor Sam had to work too many hours.

"I'm sure he'll find food somewhere."

"I'm sure, but it won't be as good as Vi's."

So we took a short walk around the block. My wet shoes kind of squished and were uncomfortable, but what the heck. When we got home again, I changed shoes and then made myself a sandwich with the remains of last night's meat loaf on some of Vi's magnificent bread. I really wanted to telephone Harold Kincaid, but I needed to eat first because my tummy was growling like an angry bear. Spike, as usual, sat at my feet, pretending he was starving to death. If you only looked at his eyes, you'd believe him. If you looked at the rest of him, you'd know better. I suppose the same could be said for a whole lot of us humans, too.

Anyhow, as I was chewing my last bite of delicious sandwich, the telephone rang. Nothing unusual there. Our 'phone was always ringing, and the person on the other end of the wire generally wanted to talk to me. I was forever getting calls from rich women wanting me to conduct séances or visit them with my bag of tricks (Ouija board, tarot cards and crystal ball). Because I was in the process of masticating, Pa answered the 'phone for me. I gave him a little wave of thanks.

"Yes, Mrs. Majesty is at home. I'll get her," said my darling father. He allowed me to swallow my last bite of lunch and take a sip of water before he whispered, holding his hand over the receiver, "Don't know who it is."

Interesting.

Taking the receiver from Pa, I said, "Good afternoon. This is Mrs. Majesty."

"Good afternoon, Daisy. This is Laura Frasier."

Mrs. Frasier! I hadn't heard from her for quite a while, but she was a good client. "How nice to hear from you, Mrs. Frasier. How are your darling dogs?"

Mrs. Frasier bred and showed miniature pinschers, as Mrs. Bissel bred and showed dachshunds. Mrs. Bissel's life's aim was to have one of her dachshunds entered into the American Kennel Club's Westminster Dog Show, the be-all and end-all of doggie glory. Mrs. Frasier was working her own personal fanny off trying to get the AKC to recognize miniature pinschers as a breed so that she, too, could show off her dogs at Westminster. I'm not altogether sure how the AKC could fail to recognize a miniature pinscher. Heck, since I'd known Mrs. Frasier, I'd been able to recognize the breed whenever I saw it; however, I do believe the AKC meant something different by the term "recognize" than did I. I really didn't much care, but I'd never tell Mrs. Frasier or Mrs. Bissel that.

"Oh, Daisy, I'm glad you're home! Have you heard the ghastly news? Well, I guess it isn't terribly ghastly for poor Diane Wagner, but still...Her husband was *murdered*!"

Yes, indeed. I'd heard that news, all right. I'd found the body. With a little help from my dog.

"Goodness," said I in my comforting spiritualist's voice. "What a dreadful thing to happen."

"You didn't know the man if you think that," said Mrs. Frasier, being quite blunt. "He treated Diane and his daughter terribly. And those boys of his...Well, all I can say is I'm glad they aren't in my family."

"Yes, I had heard he wasn't a nice man. I've also met the Wagner boys and can't say I liked them much," I said soothingly. "Still, murder is a hard pill to swallow."

"It certainly is. And what I'm hoping to do is bring the matter to a quick close by having you conduct a séance and determine who did the deed! Then I don't know whether we should tell the police or just send the murderer a thank-you card."

Merciful heavens. "My goodness, Mrs. Frasier, you really didn't care for the man, did you?"

"He was a brute, and he treated his wife and daughter like dirt, only worse."

"Yes, I've heard that."

"You can believe it. Because *I* know it's true! Diane Chapman Wagner and I have been friends since our school days, and she's been at the mercy of that fiend for far too long."

"For her sake, I'm glad he's no longer able to torment her," I said, trying to be tactful.

"It's not that easy. Now the police are dogging her. I fear they think she killed him!"

Her words surprised me. "But how could they? His body was found buried at Mountain View Cemetery!" Whoops! And how, Mrs. Frasier might ask, could I know that? Oh, well. Not the first time I'd regretted my tendency to blurt things out. Trying to cover my error, I added, "At least, that's what I've heard."

My goodness, but news traveled fast! I think the telephone has a good deal to do with that.

"Well, you'd know all about it, since you visited poor Diane to deliver the news."

Oh, yes. I'd forgotten that part. "Well, yes. Detective Rotondo asked me to accompany him when he spoke to Mrs. Wagner. And also to her daughter, Mrs. Grenville."

"Lord, yes. Oh, Daisy, I do hope George didn't kill the man. Not that he didn't deserve it, but still..."

"Why would he kill his father-in-law?" I asked, although I already knew.

"That awful man persisted in bullying the both of them! He made trouble in the bookstore, and, according to Diane, he terrified poor Marianne so much that she was scared to leave her own home for fear her father would kidnap her and...Well, I don't know what he might have done, but given that he was exposed as a...a...well, an evil man after Marianne ran away, it wouldn't have surprised me if he'd murdered *her*. I wouldn't blame George or Marianne if either of them killed the man, although I suppose that sounds awful."

"No, it doesn't," I said, still attempting tact. "I agree with you, actually."

"Well, then, can you conduct a séance here as soon as possible? I'm sure Rolly will be able to guide us in the right direction."

That was more than I was sure of. Nevertheless, I played my part. "Indeed, I can, Mrs. Frasier. Let me just check my calendar."

For the record, I didn't really have a calendar on which to keep track of my business. It was a good business and I earned considerably more money than most females who had to hold paid employment at the time; therefore, I could pick my own work hours. For the most part. Sometimes, especially in the case of Mrs. Pinkerton, I'd be called and asked for Rolly to give emergency advice. Because Rolly was me, the advice mainly consisted of common-sense suggestions. Since Mrs. Pinkerton had no common sense of her own, she seldom took Rolly's advice. Which, of course, created more business for me.

I'm sorry. I didn't mean to sound so cynical.

"It looks as if this coming Wednesday is free, Mrs. Frasier. Is that too soon, or will it be all right with you?"

"That will be perfect! Thank you so much, dear. How's your little dachshund doing?"

"Spike is fine, thank you. We all love him so much." I gazed down dotingly upon my pooch. "Right now he's telling me he's starving to death, but I don't believe him."

She laughed. "That's a dachshund for you. Their eyes fib for them. You really ought to get a min-pin, dear."

"I think one dog is about all we can handle at the moment, Mrs. Frasier, but thank you."

"I don't think a person can ever have too many dogs," said the immensely wealthy Mrs. Frasier. If you had enough money, I don't suppose you *could* have too many dogs, because you could hire people to take care of them for you. For example, Mrs. Bissel, the dachshund lady, had a man in her employ who did nothing but take care of her kennels.

Leaving the dog issue alone for the nonce, I said, "What time would like to hold your séance?"

After a moment's contemplation, Mrs. Frasier said, "I think eight o'clock would be a good time. I'm not going to give a party beforehand, so it will be easy to plan for Wednesday. Just a few people will be there, including Diane and Marianne, if she's willing to come. I doubt either one of them will be busy that night, since Doctor Wagner's body was only found today. Has Marianne ever attended one of your séances?"

"No. Mrs. Wagner went to at least one séance I conducted, right about the time Marianne disappeared, but I've never seen Marianne at one."

"I hope she'll come to this one. And I'll have to ask Madeline, too, because she's so overwrought about that hellish daughter of hers. And Griselda. She's another one who's tried to help Diane over the years, but none of us could assist her very much."

Griselda was Mrs. Bissel. Madeline was Mrs. Pinkerton, and she'd been overwrought about Stacy for years and years, although Stacy's recent trouble was worse than ever. Definitely a problem child, Stacy Kincaid.

"And Harold Kincaid! I'd love to have Harold come to the séance. He's so amusing and kind."

"He is indeed," said I of one of my very best friends.

"Wonderful. Thank you so much, Daisy, and I look forward to seeing you on Wednesday."

"I'm looking forward to it, too, Mrs. Frasier."

You might have noticed that, while my clients all called me by my first name, I was always formally polite and called them Mrs. Whatever. Just one more aspect of my odd job.

Mrs. Frasier and I each hung up our receivers, and I was about to clean off the kitchen table when the stupid telephone rang again. Sighing, I turned and lifted the receiver. "Gumm-Majesty residence. Mrs. Majesty speaking."

"Oh, Daisy!" cried a voice I recognized all too well. I suppressed a sigh.

"Good afternoon, Mrs. Pinkerton."

"Actually, it *is* a good afternoon!"

"It is?" I blinked at the receiver, only then recalling I hadn't shooed off any of our party-line neighbors. Ah, well.

"Yes. I mean, I'm still in a state about Stacy, but did you hear about that terrible man, Doctor Wagner? Somebody *killed* him! I'm so happy for Diane! Well, as long as she didn't do it."

A trifle surprised, I said, "Yes, I did hear that. In fact, Mrs. Frasier just telephoned to set up a séance for the day after tomorrow. She's hoping Rolly can discover the identity of the murderer."

"Marvelous! Well, as I said, as long as it wasn't Diane or Marianne. Or George, of course," said Mrs. Pinkerton, who sounded almost happy for the first time since her daughter's arrest for abetting a murderer and committing other vile crimes. "I don't suppose it was. I don't believe any of them has it in them to kill anyone, even anyone as detestable as Doctor Wagner."

"I don't think so, either," said I, wondering if Mrs. P would get to the point of her call any time soon.

"Well, dear, I was going to ask you to do a séance at my house for Diane, but if Laura has already set one up, I'll just attend hers."

Without being invited? I didn't ask. "That sounds like a good idea, Mrs. Pinkerton." Although I was afraid to ask, I thought it only proper to do so; therefore, I said, "How are you doing these days? I haven't seen you for…Well, since Saturday." And today was

Monday. But I honestly did hear from her most days, so this was almost a drought.

"Thanks to Harold and you and Rolly, I'm feeling better, Daisy. Thank you. I'm still terribly upset about Stacy, but Harold has finally convinced me there's nothing more I can do for her at the moment."

Bless Harold's heart! I didn't think *anyone* could penetrate Mrs. Pinkerton's elephant-like ability to remain miserable, no matter what. Not that I think elephants are miserable. I meant about their hugeness and thick skin. Oh, never mind. "I'm so glad to hear it," I said honestly.

"Yes. Harold said I've done everything I can do up until now. I hired that lawyer, and I make sure she has spending money at the jail and sent Father Frederick to speak with her. And I do believe that Buckingham fellow from the Salvation Army has been to speak with her, too."

"I'm sure he has," said I, thinking warmly of Johnny and Flossie Buckingham, another two of my best friends. Johnny had saved Flossie from a life of sin and degradation—heck, they were now joyfully married and parents of a delightful little son—and he'd done his best to save Stacy, too, but some problems were too difficult even for Johnny. "Captain Buckingham is a special and caring man."

"Yes, he is," said Mrs. P with sigh. She hated that it had been a Salvation Army person and not an Episcopalian who had kept Stacy on the straight-and-narrow path for as long as she'd been able to stand it, which was not long enough. "Still, I do wish Stacy had... Ah, well. It's past time to worry about it now, I guess."

"I'm sure you've done everything in your power to help Stacy, Mrs. Pinkerton. It's also past time Stacy began taking responsibility for her own actions." This was a bold speech for me to deliver to Stacy's mother, even though it was the truth.

"That's precisely what Harold's been telling me. Over and over. Yes." Another sigh. "I know you're right. And so is Harold."

I remained silent for once.

"But I'm so glad Laura is having you conduct a séance for poor

Diane. I'm sure I'll see you on Wednesday. Oh, but Daisy, do you think you could possibly visit me tomorrow? Just for a little while? Just so Rolly can assure me I'm doing the right thing by Stacy? Please?"

See what I mean? Rolly, being me, told her the same thing every single time he spoke to her. But she lived in hope that he would change his tune. As Rolly and I were one, she didn't have a prayer of that ever happening. Anyway, even if Rolly told her Stacy was an angel come to earth, the Pasadena Police Department still held her in a cell for abetting a cold-blooded murderer. The PPD didn't put as much stock in Rolly as did Mrs. P.

"Of course I can come to see you tomorrow, Mrs. Pinkerton. Will eleven o'clock be a good time for you?" That way I could visit the library beforehand, return my family's stack of already-read books, and see if Miss Petrie, my favorite librarian, had tucked away any other gems for us.

"Eleven would be perfect, dear. Thank you so much."

"You're very welcome, Mrs. Pinkerton." Bravely daring, I added, "Although I doubt Rolly will have any information for you other than that he's already imparted." Seventeen billion times.

Very well, so I exaggerate every now and then.

"I know it, dear. But you and Rolly are such a comfort to me in these dismal times."

"That's good to know, Mrs. Pinkerton."

"You're a sweet girl, Daisy. I wish my Stacy were more like you."

Pshaw. "Thank you, Mrs. Pinkerton."

"It's only the truth, dear."

I was glad to hear it, I think.

"Rolly and I will be over to see you tomorrow, Mrs. Pinkerton. Try to bear up and take Harold's excellent advice to heart."

"I will, dear. Thank you."

We disconnected, and my gaze paid a brief visit to the ceiling. After having catered to wealthy women for more than half my life, I'd come to understand that money, in fact, couldn't buy happiness. It could, however, buy the next best thing to it, and that was pretty much everything else in the world.

Because I was already at the telephone, I dialed Harold's number. Roy Castillo, his houseboy, a nice lad whom Harold had saved from slavery a few years back, answered the telephone. Yes. Slavery. I swear, sometimes I despair of the world.

"Good afternoon, Roy. This is Daisy Majesty."

"Good afternoon, Mrs. Majesty. Mr. Harold isn't at home now. I expect that's whom you called for."

Roy's grammar was better than most of the native-born American citizens I knew. He'd originated in Tortuga, which is an island somewhere. Geography is another of my not-so-well-developed characteristics.

"Yes, it was. Thanks, Roy. Will you please ask Harold to telephone me when he gets the time? It's not urgent, but I'd sure like to talk to him."

"Happy to do that, Mrs. Majesty."

"Thanks, Roy."

We each hung up, and I couldn't think of anything else of a productive nature to do. Therefore, I dust-mopped the floors, dusted the furniture, and settled in our comfy living room to read for a bit until Vi came home. Spike joined me, although I don't think he was interested in the book.

SEVEN

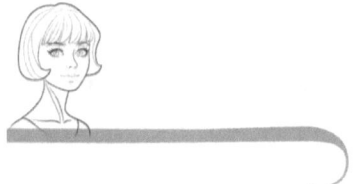

Sam showed up at our house a little early that evening. We Gumms and the remaining Majesty dine at six p.m. Not a fashionable hour, but good for those of us who actually had to work for a living and arise early in the morning. At five-thirty, Spike raced to the front door even before Sam twisted our doorbell.

"Sit, Spike," said I to my dog. He sat, bless him. He was *such* a well-trained hound. I opened the door and smiled at my beloved. "Evening, Sam. How was the rest of your day?"

"Glamorous and exciting," he said, sounding exhausted and cranky. Everything was as usual, in other words.

"I'm sorry." I looked down at Spike whose shiny black tail was sweeping the floor excitedly. Thanks to my recent housekeeping, there was no dust for him to stir up. "Okay, Spike," I told him, giving him the word to cease being a good dog and resume being man's best friend. Woman's too, by gad.

Grunting, Sam leaned over to pet Spike, who had commenced leaping on his right leg. Sam had strategically put his right leg forward, sparing his wounded limb from Spike's friendly mauling.

"Yes, buddy, it's good to see you, too," said Sam.

"Let me take your hat and coat. Do you need more aspirin?"

Handing me the items I'd requested, Sam said, "Yes, I could use a couple more aspirin tablets. Thank you."

"You're more than welcome. I'm so sorry your day didn't go as we'd planned it to." Heck, we'd been aiming to take lunch somewhere after we received our late spouses' blessing for our eventual marriage, and then spend some time at his darling bungalow in a court of same on South Los Robles Avenue. What we'd planned to do there is nobody else's business. Poor Sam hadn't even been privileged to eat a meat-loaf sandwich. "I hope you managed to get lunch somewhere."

With a sigh, Sam limped to the dining room and sat. He said, "No time. I'm famished."

"Oh, I'm so sorry! I should have made you a sandwich to eat on the way to that stupid club."

"Thanks for the thought. It's all right," said Sam, sighing. He smiled up at me, though, and that made me feel less guilty

"Did I hear someone tell Daisy he's famished?" asked Vi, grinning as she poked her head out of the kitchen and looking at Sam.

"You did, Vi. It's been a rough day."

"I heard about it from Mrs. Pinkerton," said Vi. "Actually, Harold told me about it. You and Daisy don't seem to have much luck avoiding dead bodies, do you?"

"No," said Sam. "We don't."

"Which isn't my fault," I said, defending myself before I'd been attacked. I guess I was a little sensitive about the dead-body issue.

Vi only laughed. Sam sighed again and said, "May I have a couple of aspirin tablets? Then I'll tell you about the rest of my day. After I left you here, I mean." He sniffed the air. "Something sure smells good."

"Thanks, Sam. And the house always smells good when Vi's cooking." I went to the bathroom, shook two tablets out onto my palm, detoured through the kitchen to fetch a glass of water, and delivered tablets and water to my fiancé, who had commenced rubbing his face with his hands. He really did look exhausted, poor thing.

I allowed him to swallow his aspirin tablets before I began grilling him. And I didn't grill hard. The man was already worn out.

"Did you find the Wagner brothers at the Pasadena Golf and Tennis Club?" I asked after waiting a few seconds to make sure Sam had settled into his chair and the aspirins had begun making their way to wherever aspirin tablets did their magic.

"Yes. Mrs. Wagner was right. A lot of rich young men live there." Sam made a grimace of distaste. "The Wagner brothers appeared broken up about their father's death, and both of them even shed a tear or two."

I felt my eyebrows shoot up. "They did? Really?"

With a shrug, Sam said, "They seemed to. They acted more emotionally wrenched than either the late doctor's wife or daughter."

"Did you believe them to be sincere in their feelings?"

"How should I know? I'm not a mind-reader. That's more along your lines than mine."

"No need to get snippy."

"I don't mean to be snippy," Sam said with another sigh. "I'm just tired."

"I'm sorry, Sam."

"So tell me about your day. I'm sure you didn't spend it idly. I expect you were on the telephone talking to everyone in town about the doctor's murder."

"Not everyone. In fact, I didn't telephone anybody except Harold, and he wasn't home. People telephoned me."

"Huh."

"Mrs. Frasier asked me to conduct a séance on Wednesday night to ascertain the doctor's murderer."

"I'm sure that will be helpful."

"Don't be snotty. Then Mrs. Pinkerton called. She was over-joyed about Doctor Wagner's death. I guess I was a little surprised, but not a whole lot. Evidently nobody liked Doctor Wagner."

"Evidently. The two sons said he'd been having a real feud with another doctor in town. Hasn't come to pistols at dawn yet, but the

two men apparently had words all the time. Bitter words, and sometimes in public."

"Oh? Can you tell me which doctor?"

With a shrug, Sam said, "Why not? You're already involved in
the case. Have you ever heard of a Doctor. Ferdinand? Doctor
William Ferdinand?"

"Um..." I thought hard for a couple of seconds. Darned near
sprained my brain. "No. I've never heard of him."

"Well, he's the one purportedly feuding with Doctor Wagner."

"Did Gaylord or Vincent tell you why?"

"Claimed they didn't know. I'll have to talk to Doctor Ferdinand,
of course. I was hoping maybe you could tell me something about
him and why the two doctors were at each other's throats."

"Neither of the sons could tell you?"

"Don't know if they *could* tell me. They *didn't* tell me, and that's
what matters. I'll have to find out why they were fighting via another
route. Nothing's ever simple."

"No. It doesn't seem to be. I'm sorry, Sam."

"Not your fault."

Boy, there was a first!

"By the way," Sam said after a moment or two of silence on
both our parts, "Mr. Pinkerton's two sons also live at the Pasadena
Golf and Tennis Club."

"I didn't know that. But if I had a choice, I don't think I'd want
to live in the same house as Mrs. Pinkerton, either."

"Tut, tut," said Sam, grinning.

Deciding to leave the Pasadena Golf and Tennis Club and all its
inhabitants alone for a while, I asked Sam, "Would you like me to
ask Doc Benjamin if he knows anything about the two other doctors
and why they might be feuding?"

"Couldn't hurt, I suppose."

I pressed a hand to Sam's forehead, surprising him into a little
start. He said, "Ow!" I guess because his bad leg had twanged.

"Just checking to see if you're feverish. You *never* ask me to snoop
into your cases. Sorry if I startled you."

"I figure this one was a lost cause from the beginning. You're involved whether I want you to be or not."

"I know. Poor Sam." Delighted, I said, "Why don't you rest in the living room with Pa while I set the table. I think Ma's resting up from working at the Hotel Marengo all day."

"Thanks. Think I'll do that." He sniffed the air again. "What's cooking, Vi? Whatever it is, it smells great."

"Swedish-style smothered chicken and, according to reports from the Pinkerton home, it *is* great. I'll let everyone here decide for themselves."

"Huh. I've heard of Swedish meatballs, but not Swedish smothered chicken."

"I've never even heard of Swedish meatballs," I told my beloved. "When Vi makes meatballs, she generally serves them with that delicious Italian sauce you told her about."

"Ah. We Italians. We might not be good for much, but the food is great." Sam tried to smile as he rose to his feet, but I guess his leg pain vanquished his smile, because he ended up grunting and frowning.

"I'll be so glad when your leg heals completely, Sam," I said with huge sympathy. Sam didn't deserve to be crippled because of some evil people's evil actions. But, according to our darling doctor, Doc Benjamin, he wouldn't be crippled forever and the leg would eventually stop hurting so much. The waiting time was hard on him, though, and he probably used his leg too much. I'm not sure how much was too much, but his leg kept hurting. I know it hurt Sam more than it did me, but I still felt for him a good deal.

After Sam had joined my father in the living room, I heard the two men begin talking about the upcoming Rose Bowl game. The competing football teams were coming to Pasadena from Notre Dame, known for some reason mysterious to me as the Fighting Irish—I mean, wasn't Notre Dame Cathedral in France? Ah, well. Anyway, Notre Dame aimed to play Stanford University's football team. My father and Sam knew a good deal more about sports than did yours truly, who didn't much care, even though baseball was supposed to be the USA's national pastime and men seemed to love football. All I knew were that the coaches of the two teams involved in the upcoming bowl game had interesting names: Knute Rockne and Pop Warner.

"That really does smell good, Vi. What's the difference between Swedish smothered chicken and anybody else's smothered chicken?"

As I began setting the table, Vi said, "I have no idea. I got the recipe from Evelyn McCracken. She has all sorts of foreign recipes, and she's happy to share them."

"Isn't she the one who told you about that Mexican sausage?"

"Chorizo. Yes." I could hear the smile in Aunt Vi's voice. She truly loved to cook, a love that baffled me. I guess everyone has an idiosyncrasy or two.

"Does Mrs. McCracken still cook for Mrs. Bannister?"

"Yes, she does."

"How's Mrs. Bannister doing these days?" I only asked because I, along with Harold Kincaid, Flossie Buckingham and a few other noble souls—not that I'm calling myself noble, mind you—had probably saved Mrs. Bannister's life a few months prior. She was yet another victim of a brutish, cruel man.

"She's much better, according to Evelyn. She still credits you, Harold and Flossie for saving her life."

"Aw, that's sweet."

"It's the truth," said my aunt, always one of my staunchest supporters, even when I got myself involved in unusual problems.

"Actually, you're probably right, although Flossie and Harold played a bigger role in her rescue than I did."

"That's not what Evelyn said."

"Oh." I was pleased, although I tried not to gloat. In truth, those several weeks during which Harold, Flossie and I hid Mrs. Bannister from her evil husband, had been extremely nerve-wracking. They'd culminated in the shooting of Sam Rotondo, too, so I guess there wasn't really much to gloat about. Sometimes I hate the truth.

"What kinds of serving dishes will you need for this Swedish treat, Vi?" I asked my marvelous aunt.

"A serving bowl for the buttered noodles."

My mouth began to water. Anything buttered is all right by me.

"And another, larger serving bowl for the smothered chicken. Then we'll need the bread basket, and you'd better set out bread-and-butter plates, too, because the sauce will cover most of everyone's plates."

"Yum. I can hardly wait."

"Then you'll need two more serving dishes, one for the buttered carrots and another for the green beans."

"Oh my goodness, Vi, I don't think I can wait until dinnertime!"

"You're going to have to, Daisy Majesty," Vi said with mock sternness.

Ma entered the kitchen, yawning. "Oh, my, it smells good in here," said she.

"Smothered chicken, Swedish style," I informed my mother as if I knew what I was talking about.

"What's the difference between Swedish chicken and any other kind of chicken?"

"That I don't know," I told her. "But Vi can explain."

"No, I can't," said Vi. "That's just the name of the recipe, and I don't know what it has to do with Sweden."

"Oh," said Ma, and she finished helping me set the table.

At six o'clock precisely—she was like a finely tuned watch—Vi called me in to the kitchen to begin carrying out viands to the table. "And tell your father and Sam to come to the table," she added.

So I did both of those things, and we all took our places around the dining table. We had a nice dining room. It led directly from the kitchen, and boasted a built-in china hutch and side board. I'd stacked the plates at Vi's place at the head of the table as she'd told me to do, and placed various bowls and dishes elsewhere on the table. I did use the bread-and-butter plates, and we all put them to good use. After Pa said the usual grace over the meal, we dug in, Vi filling each plate with chicken and sauce, and each of the rest of us passing around the noodles, vegetables and dinner rolls.

The meal was spectacular. But then, all of Vi's meals were spectacular.

"Boy, this chicken is delicious," said Sam in a variation of what he always said when he got to eat one of Vi's meals. "I didn't even know Swedes used chicken."

"I suspect every culture dines on chicken or some other types of birds," I said after swallowing a bite of chicken and noodles. "Vi makes regular old meatballs, too, sometimes." I frowned. "Or maybe she doesn't. Usually the only time we get meatballs is when we have Italian sauce with them. She said Swedes make meatballs, too."

"I didn't know the Swedes made meatballs either. I thought we Italians were the meatball kings. Most of the Swedish stuff I ate when I was a kid in New York consisted of pastries and other kinds of sweets."

"I think all countries have their own variety of meatballs or meatloaf. Not to mention chickens, ducks and geese," said Vi. "After all, we humans have to eat more or less the same things."

"I guess that's true," said I, adding my bit to the conversation. Not that I knew beans about cooking, but I had been to the Middle East and read a lot of *National Geographic* magazines. "Except for people in Africa, who probably eat kudus and wildebeests and other ungulates like that, we basically have the same major meats available to us, and then we use what we can get from local sources."

"What's an ungulate?" Ma wanted to know.

"Horses and antelopes and animals like that. I think," I said, trying to remember the last article about Africa I'd read in *National Geographic*. "I expect people who lived in the Wild West ate buffaloes and antelopes. They used a lot of lambs when we were in Egypt and Turkey. I love lamb."

"So do I," said Ma, who was kind of a picky eater.

"They use different kinds of beans there, too. Not like our baked beans, I mean. They just grow different vegetables in the soil they have to work with, I suppose."

"Makes sense to me," said Pa, grinning. He knew all about cooking and me. Well, by that time in our lives, everyone did.

"We Italians eat a lot of beans, too," Sam said. "Beans are cheaper than meat, and they're filling."

"What kinds of beans do Italians eat?" I asked, curious.

Sam shrugged. "Darned if I know. My mother fixed noodles and beans a lot. Called them *pasta e fagioli*. Only we pronounce it *past'fazhool*. That's Italian for noodles and beans. We Italians make approximately six million different types of pasta." Sam sometimes exaggerated, too. At least, I think that was an exaggeration. Maybe it wasn't. What I didn't know about food and cooking could and did fill shelves and shelves of books in the library.

"Hmm. I don't think I've ever had pasta and beans together," said I musingly.

"They're good," said Sam.

"You'll have to tell me what your mother puts in with her beans and pasta, Sam," said Vi.

"I'll find out. All I know for sure is garlic and tomatoes." Sam savored another bite of chicken with his buttered noodles. "Depending on where your family comes from—Sicily, Tuscany, Rome, or wherever—you'll find different shapes of noodles. Some of them are tiny and look like rice. The rice-shaped ones are called orzo."

"My goodness, I didn't know that," said I. Not that I needed to because, as mentioned several times already, cooking and I didn't get along. "Didn't we eat some kind of noodle called couscous when we were in Turkey, Sam?"

"Don't remember," said he, taking another bite of his noodles and chicken. After he swallowed, he said, "I suspect all cultures have noodles of one kind or another."

"By the way," said Pa, dropping the beans-and-pasta theme, "Herb Hull gave me a couple of bushels of apples today. Do you want to help me dig out the cider press from the basement, Daisy?"

"Sure. I love fresh apple juice." Pressing apples for juice and cider was one job even I couldn't mess up. So far, anyway.

"Save some of those apples for pies, you two," said Vi.

"You betcha!" said I, thinking about Vi's marvelous apple pies. Of course, everything she made was marvelous.

"How do you make juice and apple cider?" asked Sam, looking puzzled.

"You never made apple juice in New York City?" I asked, surprised.

"Naw. We Italians only make wine."

We all laughed, even though he was probably telling the truth.

"We have an old wooden apple press we brought here from Massachusetts," Pa said. "We keep it covered in the basement until apple season. Then we haul it out, press the apples and make juice. Vi will turn some of the juice into cider." He peered at my aunt. "What's the difference anyway, Vi?"

"Cider has cinnamon and sugar. Sometimes I'll add allspice. The juice is just the juice. I'll preserve the cider in jars, but we have to drink the juice while it's still fresh. Apples can be stored fairly well as long as they're kept in a cool, dark place, so we tend to make juice and cider out of most of them, and then I'll used the rest of them for pies, tarts, applesauce, or whatever. I'll dry some of them, and when they're out of season and we can't live without apple pie for another minute, I'll make a dried-apple pie."

"Interesting," said Sam, sounding as though he meant it.

"You can help us press the apples if you want to," I offered.

"Thanks," said he, eyeing me as though he thought I were up to something.

"But I don't want you carrying the press up the basement stairs," Pa told him. "It wouldn't be good for your leg."

"Is the thing heavy?" Sam asked.

"Not awfully, but you still shouldn't help carry it," I told him. "As Pa said, it's an old wooden one. I guess Pa's grandparents used it on their farm. Is that right, Pa?"

"Yup. We had an apple orchard. Tons of apples. Used to sell 'em to the grocers in town, give them to our friends, and make gallons of juice and cider."

"I'll be darned," said Sam. "I guess I missed a lot, living in the city all my life."

"Maybe so," said I, "but you had a whole lot more interesting experiences in New York City than we've had in Pasadena. Heck, the food alone in New York is so varied, I'll bet you never ran out of new things to eat."

"Not in my family. We were Italian all the way. Although I did get to eat some falafels and other Arabic food when I was with my friend Armen."

"Oh, yes, I remember you told us about Armen. You got to eat a lot of Middle-Eastern food with him, didn't you?"

"Well, I wouldn't say a lot, precisely, but his family cooked the way they were brought up. Mine cooked the way they were brought up. I don't think either the Italians or the Armenians used cider presses. Come to think of it, I'll bet both Italians and Armenians had olive presses, though. They had to get olive oil somehow."

"I've never even thought about olive oil," said Vi meditatively. "But I expect you're right, Sam."

"Maybe they'll do an article about how to make olive oil in the *National Geographic* someday," I said.

Everyone laughed, but I was serious. Oh, well.

"Have you heard from your nephew recently?" I asked Sam. Frank Pagano, the son of one of Sam's many sisters, ran away from home a month or so ago and landed in his uncle's bungalow. Sam hadn't appreciated Frank's visit one little bit. Neither had we, mainly because Frank pilfered stuff.

"No, thank God," said Sam. He sounded as if he meant it.

And the telephone rang.

EIGHT

I t was Harold. "Harold! Did you hear the news?" I asked excitedly.

"About somebody finally bumping off that Wagner bimbo? Yup. Past time, if you ask me."

"Me, too, but I don't want it to be…Wait a minute, Harold." I cleared my throat. "Will our party-line neighbors please hang up your receivers? This call is private and it's for me."

Three clicks. My gaze paid a visit to the ceiling. "Mrs. Barrow? Will you please hang up your telephone? This call is for me."

Another, louder, click. If Mrs. Barrow hadn't helped solve a murder case once, I'd have been inclined to holler at her. It's not nice to listen in on other people's private conversations. Mind you, I'm sure the calls to my house were more interesting than any calls she ever got, but still…

"Party line," said Harold. "You really ought to spring for a private wire, you know."

"That's expensive Harold. Not all of us are rich, you know."

"I know. I know."

"But Harold, has Doctor Greenlaw ever said anything to you about Doctor Wagner? According to the reports I've been hearing,

Doctor Wagner has been having a terrible fight with another doctor in town." I put my hand over the receiver and hollered into the dining room. "What's that doctor's name, Sam?"

Sam limped into the kitchen. He didn't look at all peeved, as he usually did when I poked into his cases. Guess that's because I could give him more information than most of his other sources. He said, "Ferdinand. Doctor William Ferdinand."

I uncovered the receiver and said to Harold, "Doctor William Ferdinand."

"Don't know him. I've never heard Fred talk about him. Why? What was Wagner's beef with Ferdinand?"

"I don't know. That's why I'm asking you."

"Sorry. Can't help you there. I'll ask Fred. Heck, you could ask Fred yourself, for that matter."

"I think I'd rather you ask him, thanks. I really don't know him very well."

"You're just afraid he's mad at you because of that Bannister affair."

I heaved a sigh. "Yes. That's probably it. I don't want to disturb him again."

With a laugh, Harold said, "He's not mad at you, but I'll ask him if he's heard why Doctors Wagner and Ferdinand were beefing with each other."

"Thanks, Harold. You haven't heard anything else about Doctor Wagner, have you?"

"Other than that everybody hated him and they're all glad he's dead? No."

"But do you know why everybody hated him? I mean, I know why *I* hated him. And I know why Diane and Marianne hated him, but why did everybody else hate him?"

"Because he was a creepy pill and gave everyone the jitters? He was a really unpleasant person. I think that idiotic goatee made him even more ghastly. That's all I know about him. Nobody's seen much of him recently, according to people I know. So maybe he hit the skids or something."

"I know his business went downhill after Marianne's escape."

"Escape. Good word for it."

"I think so, too. Thanks, Harold. Talk to you later. Oh, wait. Is Doctor Greenlaw staying at the Pasadena Golf and Tennis Club?"

"Yeah. Until his house is built. Why?"

"Just wondered. The Wagner brothers are staying there, too."

"Lucky Fred," said Harold sarcastically.

"Right. Thanks, Harold. See you soon."

"I guess we'll see each other Wednesday evening at Mrs. Frasier's place. I understand your spirit control plans on figuring out who murdered the bad doctor."

"Right," I said again, this time with a sigh. "Wish Rolly and me luck."

Harold laughed again and hung up his receiver. I did likewise and turned to Sam. "He doesn't know why the two doctors were at each other's throats."

"Figured as much," said Sam, sounding almost as weary as he looked. "I'm going to take off now, Daisy. I aim to talk to Doctor Ferdinand tomorrow. If you could see Doctor Benjamin, maybe we can compare notes later in the day."

"Sounds good to me." Something occurred to me. "Say, Sam, your juju didn't get hot when you were speaking with anyone in particular today, did it?"

During the last murder case Sam worked on, the Voodoo juju given to him by Mrs. Jackson, a real, honest-to-goodness Voodoo mambo from New Orleans, got so hot it nearly burned his skin any time he was close to the murderer. Sam didn't like to believe the thing had actually communicated with him, but I couldn't think of any other reason his juju might have acted up only when he was in the presence of the killer. The one Mrs. Jackson had given me never did anything at all. It just hung on its woven cord around my neck and…Well, that's all it did. I thought Sam's was considerably more interesting than mine, although I'd never tell Mrs. Jackson that.

Sam slapped a hand over his chest and frowned. "For God's sake, Daisy, you're not going to start in on that Voodoo nonsense again, are you?"

"If you'll recall, Detective Rotondo," I said coolly, "that juju told you who the murderer was. Quite distinctly. It got so hot, you had to take it off at one point. You *do* recall that, don't you?"

"Yeah, yeah. I recall that. Pure coincidence."

"Sure it was. Tell me another one, why don't you?"

"Nuts. Jujus and Voodoo are just superstitious nonsense."

"If you still believe that after what happened last month, you're a hard case, Detective Sam Rotondo."

He grinned and chuckled. "Yeah. I've heard that before."

I laughed, too, and Spike and I walked Sam out to his machine. We smooched a couple of times, but then he had to go home to rest, and I had to wash the dishes. Therefore, Spike and I watched as his big old Hudson rolled away, and then we walked slowly back to the house.

After I'd washed the dishes and put them all away, I contemplated reading for a while, but I was kind of pooped, too, after the excitement of the day, so Spike and I went to bed. We slept like the dead for many hours, but we were both bright-eyed and bushy-tailed on Tuesday morning. After visiting the bathroom, I practically bounced into the kitchen, ready to begin my day of spiritualist-mediuming and snoopery.

"You're looking perky this morning," said Pa, eyeing me from the kitchen table as I tied the ties on my bathrobe.

"I'm feeling perky. Are Ma and Vi still here?"

"They are. It's only seven, sweetie." He smiled broadly at me. "Your aunt left some breakfast for you in the warming oven."

"Bless Vi's heart." I trotted over to the warming oven, found a plate filled with waffles and sausages and silently blessed Aunt Vi again.

Vi and Ma strode into the kitchen, pulling on their hats and coats. The weather remained chilly. Well, heck, it was December, even if we did live in paradise. More or less.

"Good morning, dear," said Ma, coming over to kiss me on the cheek.

"Morning, Ma. Would you like me to drive you and Vi to work this morning?"

"No, thanks. It's nice out, if a bit brisk. The walk will be pleasant."

"I don't need a ride, either, thanks," said Vi. "I think Harold will bring me home. I'm planning something special for tonight's dinner." She smiled wickedly. She's the only person I've ever met who could find pleasure in surprising her family with food. If I ever tried to feed us, every day would be a surprise, but not a good one.

"You're a peach, Vi," said I, lavishly buttering my waffle and then reaching for the maple syrup, which was sent to us each Christmas by a relative in Massachusetts.

"I know it. Will you be visiting Mrs. P today?"

"Yes. At eleven."

"Come to the kitchen after you're through with her, and maybe I'll feed you some lunch."

"I love you, Vi! You, too, Ma. But Vi feeds us."

My mother, who didn't have much of a sense of humor, actually laughed.

After cleaning up the breakfast dishes, I went for a walk with Pa and Spike. Spike was so well trained that he would heel off the leash, but I attached his leash to his collar anyway, just in case we encountered a stray cat or something. Spike was the best-behaved dog I knew, but I didn't want to take any chances.

When we got back home, I opened my over-stuffed closet to find a suitable costume for the day. I aimed to visit Dr. Benjamin, the library and Mrs. Pinkerton, so I had to look businesslike. Plus, the weather required warm clothes. Therefore, I chose a newish butterscotch-brown flannel suit I'd made not long before from material I'd bought on sale at Maxime's Fabrics. With it, I wore a white shirtwaist, a dark green man's tie, neutral-colored stockings, my brown shoes with a low Louis heel, and a brown cloche hat with a dark green ribbon around it.

After I'd put everything on, I looked into the cheval-glass mirror and asked my dog, "What do you think, Spike? Do I look like a professional spiritualist-medium? And will my old black coat look all right with the brown and green?"

Spike wagged his tail, and I took that for approval. So I got out the brown handbag that went well with my shoes, stuck everything I'd need in it, and exited the bedroom. Pa sat at the kitchen table reading the morning *Star News*.

"Anything in there about Doctor Wagner's death?" I asked him as I pulled on my brown gloves.

"Only a paragraph on page two. Let me see...Ah, here it is. 'The body of Dr. Everhard A. Wagner was found Monday morning. The cause of his death is unknown at this time. Dr. Wagner was a well-known medical practitioner in the Pasadena-Altadena area for at least fifteen years. He is survived by his widow, Diane Marie Chapman Wagner; his daughter, Marianne Louise Wagner Grenville; and his two sons, Gaylord Sidney Wagner and Vincent Chapman Wagner.'" Pa looked up at me from his paper. "You look nice. But there isn't much here that you don't already know. I guess the paper didn't want to get into the murder issue."

"Probably not," said I, heading for the table beside the front door where my family puts already-read books. I picked them up and headed for the side door. Our Chevrolet perched at the foot of the side porch steps, ready for me to get in and drive. Spike wanted to go with me, but I convinced him that Pa needed his company more than I did. "He was definitely murdered, so I don't know if the folks at the newspaper are just fudging or don't quite know how to write an article about a rich doctor being bumped off. It sure wasn't an accidental death."

"For certain?"

"For certain. Heck, if he'd died by accident, why was his head bashed in, and why was he buried in a shallow grave at the Mountain View Cemetery? Not in a coffin."

Pa grinned. "You have such a way with words, Daisy."

"Nerts." I kissed my father on top of his head, bent down to give Spike a farewell pat, and headed to the machine. I piled the books on the passenger seat and climbed into the driver's seat. It was *so* nice to have a car that didn't need to be cranked. I don't think I'll ever cease being grateful for that.

My first stop was Dr. Benjamin's office on Beverly Way in Altadena, which was a good deal north of our bungalow on South

Marengo Avenue. I wanted to visit his office before I did anything else, because Doc Benjamin had office hours in the morning and made house calls on his patients in the afternoon. As long as he hadn't been called out to deal with an emergency, he could usually be found in his office during the morning.

Evidently I was the first person to visit him that day, because no one else sat in the outer office when I got there. Mrs. Benjamin, his wife and office help, smiled at me.

"Good morning, Mrs. Benjamin," said I, smiling back.

"Good morning, Daisy. You're looking healthy as a horse. I hope you're not feeling ill."

"Nope. I'm hoping to ask your husband a few pertinent—or maybe impertinent—questions about something else."

"Ah," said she, winking. "A mystery?"

"Kind of," I said, wondering if it would do any good to ask her what she knew about Dr. Wagner. "Is the doctor free?"

"No. He charges for his time." Mrs. Benjamin giggled. She was such a sweet woman, and I liked them both so well that I giggled, too.

"I'll be happy to pay him for his time," I told her.

"Don't be silly, dear. He's just sitting in his office smoking. You know him."

"I do indeed." Dr. Benjamin was seldom without a cigarette halo around his head. He smoked almost constantly. I didn't think all those cigarettes were good for him, but I didn't know any more about medicine than I did about cooking, so I never mentioned my fears to him.

"Go on back. He'll be pleased to see you. How's your delightful detective doing?"

Sam? Delightful? Yes. He was—when he wasn't in his stoic and grim detectival mode—and it was nice to know other people thought so, too. "He's fine, thank you. We both got an unpleasant surprise when we visited the cemetery yesterday."

"Oh, good Lord, don't tell me it was *you* who found that awful man's body!" said Mrs. Benjamin. She knew about my penchant for stumbling over dead bodies, too.

"I'm afraid it was," I said. "I wanted to ask Doc about the man." Then, figuring why not, I asked, "Do you know what he was doing these days? I understand his professional life hasn't been... robust for the last couple of years."

Mrs. Benjamin sniffed. "I should hope not. I didn't know him well, but I've heard stories." Her voice dropped to a sepulchral tone on the last couple of words.

"What kinds of stories?" I asked eagerly.

"Hmm. You'd best ask the doctor, dear. I'm really not supposed to spread gossip. If it *is* gossip."

The way her lips pinched together led me to believe that, if the tales she'd heard were mere gossip, she'd be surprised to learn it.

Fascinating. I opened the door to the hallway leading to Dr. Benjamin's office and practically tap danced down the hall to his door. I found him standing at the window, looking out onto the gray December day. His office offered a view of Lake Avenue, which was one of the main north-south streets in Altadena and Pasadena. Several businesses shared space on Lake, including the Altadena Public Library, a grocery store, a bakery and several other shops. Some private residences also occupied lots on Lake Avenue, but it seemed to me that businesses were gradually taking over the avenue. I guess that sort of thing constituted progress in our modern age.

NINE

When I opened the doctor's office door, he turned and smiled as though he were glad to see me. I returned his smile. Even though he'd cracked his window open a teensy bit at the top, his office reeked of cigarette smoke. He waved some of it around, probably in an effort to reduce the smudgy atmosphere. Didn't work.

"Good morning, Daisy. You don't look as though you need my medical services."

"Thank you, Doctor Benjamin. I don't, really. I came to ask you some questions about Doctor Everhard Wagner."

His smile turned upside down. "The man was murdered," he said in a flat tone.

"I know. Sam and I found the body yesterday morning when we visited Mountain View Cemetery."

His smile returned, he plopped into his chair and gestured for me to take a seat opposite his desk. "You certainly have a knack for finding murdered people, don't you, my dear?"

Instantly, I said, "I don't do it on purpose!" My reputation for falling over dead bodies was getting on my nerves. I couldn't help it, for Pete's sake! If folks left dead bodies strewn all over the place in my vicinity, it wasn't due to any flaw in my character.

He laughed. "I know it isn't your fault, sweetheart. I just like to tease you."

"You and everybody else I know," I said upon a deep and heartfelt sigh. "But since Sam and I were together when we found the body, Sam asked me to ask you if you knew what Doctor Wagner had been up to recently. According to lots of people, his medical practice had been seriously damaged after his daughter ran away and he was exposed as a wife-beating brute."

With a grimace of distaste, Dr. Benjamin said, "That's one way of putting it."

"Do you know why he and Doctor—Oh, pooh, I can't remember his first name. But a doctor whose last name is Ferdinand was mentioned as a particular enemy of his. Do you know why that was?"

Doc Benjamin sat and pondered my question for several seconds. Then he said, "I don't like spreading rumors, Daisy."

"Are they mere rumors? Or was Doctor Wagner up to something sinister? And if he was, is that the reason Doctor Ferdinand was so angry at him?"

"Hmmm. Are you sure Detective Rotondo wants you probing into the Wagner case? You're not fibbing to me, are you, Daisy?"

"No!" Indignant at the thought I might be dissembling, I went on, "If you don't believe me, call Sam at the police department!"

"Don't get mad at me, sweetie. Just checking. Last I heard, he was peeved with you for involving yourself in one of his cases. I do believe that was one of the reasons for his nasty leg wound." He grinned as if he didn't mean it, but I suspected he did.

"He wouldn't have got shot if he hadn't followed me secretly," I muttered, feeling guilty.

"I'm sure that's so, but his secretly following you might have saved your life, you know."

I huffed out another sigh. "I know."

"And you sure he won't mind you asking me about the two doctors?"

"Absolutely. This case is different. Sam and I found the body together, went to the Los Angeles County Marshal's Office together, and he really, honestly and truly, asked me to ask you about Doctor Wagner. And Doctor Ferdinand, if you know."

"All right. I believe you."

I humphed again, which only made him laugh once more.

"Well?" I said, still indignant. "Will you tell me what the evil Doctor Wagner was up to, or do you not know?"

"Oh, I know, all right."

"Well?"

"It's not pleasant, Daisy."

"Nothing about Doctor Wagner was pleasant. Including his death."

Doc Benjamin leaned over his desk and peered closely at me. "How'd he die?"

"Got his head bashed in."

"That doesn't sound very nice."

I shrugged. "Neither was he."

With another laugh, Dr. Benjamin said, "All right. My under-standing is that not long after Wagner's business declined when he was exposed as whatever it was you called him, he got into the illegal abortion business."

"Abortions? Oh, my!"

"Yes. Unpleasant, I know. And I also know that William—that's Doctor Ferdinand's first name—was upset because Wagner did a sloppy job on quite a few of his patients. Also, William is a Roman Catholic, and his church is vehemently opposed to abortion. I believe, however, that it was the sloppiness of Wagner's work that mattered more to William. He…Well, he had to deal with the after-math a couple of times." He grimaced. "As did I."

"You mean Doctor Wagner messed up women's abortions?" I'm pretty sure I had a disgusted look on my face, because I felt disgusted. Totally, absolutely, positively disgusted. I mean, I don't approve of abortion, but if a woman is desperate enough to rid herself of a baby, there had to be a *really* good reason for her to do so. The decision alone would be a painful one to make, and if she then went to a doctor whom she presumed to be honorable only to have the procedure botched, well…I didn't even know what to think about that, except that Dr. Wagner fell even further in my esteem, and he'd been below dirt level for years.

"That's precisely what I mean," said Dr. Benjamin, not inclined to laugh anymore. "He ruined two young women's chances for ever bearing children, thanks to the sloppiness of his work. Those are the only two I know of. There may well be more."

"That's terrible," I said, meaning it. In fact, I kind of felt like crying but didn't for once.

"Terrible is one word for it. To treat an already-desperate young woman like a piece of meat is…Well, despicable is the word that comes to my mind."

"Despicable works. Those poor girls. I mean, I don't suppose they should have…well, got themselves in trouble, but still…."

"Still. Yes, I know. And it's not always the woman's fault, you know, Daisy. You do know that there are men in the world who take vile advantage of women if they can. You're not naïve. I know for a fact you've dealt with some…problems that certain women have endured."

I heaved yet another deep sigh. "Yes, I have. I've never considered a woman being…well, assaulted and getting with child. That must be horrible."

"Yes. It must be."

I got the impression Doc Benjamin had seen more than his share of young women who'd been violated in one way or another, and he didn't like it. Didn't blame him one little bit.

"I don't suppose you have the names of any poor girls who were…butchered by Doctor Wagner, do you?"

After a short spell of silence, the good doctor said, "If I do know the names of any young women who were in trouble and who went to Doctor Wagner, I couldn't divulge them, Daisy. That would be a gross violation of a patient's privacy. I'm sorry, but that's a doctor's golden rule. After, of course, 'First, do no harm'".

"Of course. I didn't mean for you to violate anyone's privacy.

And is that 'do no harm' thing really part of a doctor's…whatever you call it?"

"*Primum non nocere.* Those words, 'first, do no harm' aren't actually part of the Hippocratic Oath, but the oath means that. There's also a part about absolutely respecting a patient's privacy. And that's another part of the oath I won't violate, even under torture." He grinned.

"You're kidding me!"

"Well, actually, I was about the torture part. But I take the privacy part of the oath seriously and I won't violate it, even for you."

"I understand," said I, humbled. "Doctors carry a heavy burden. I didn't know those things were part of the Hippocratic Oath."

"I know you didn't." His tone had softened. "And it wouldn't surprise me if some of the young women I've seen would love to talk to you, just for the consolation an understanding soul can provide. And I know you have an understanding soul."

"Thank you. So do you." I sniffled. "You were so good to Billy and me during those awful years when he suffered so much."

"Poor Billy," said the doctor.

"Poor Billy," I agreed.

"And poor you."

"I guess so."

"I know so. You went through hell, Daisy, and you've borne up admirably. That's why I almost wish I could divulge the names of a couple of my patients to you. But I can't, and that's that. But you know, some truly good young women get 'into trouble,' as the time-honored saying has it. Oh, they might have used poor judgment or done something indiscreet, but none of them deserved what that butcher Wagner did to them."

"I've got to visit the library today. I think I'll read the Hippocratic Oath. You guys are held to strict standards. Well, most of you are."

"We choose to practice strict standards. That's why a villain like Doctor Wagner is anathema to us."

"You really do think he was a villain, don't you?"

"He butchered several young women whom I had to treat after he was through with them. So, yes, I believe he was a villain."

"He seemed to hate woman," I mused.

Another moment of silence while Dr. Benjamin looked thoughtful, and then, "I do believe you're correct about that. I'd never thought of his attitude and actions in that way before, but I think you're right."

"But that doesn't bring us any nearer to who killed him."

This time the doctor's silence made me look up from my folded hands, which I'd had atop my handbag in my lap. His face revealed a troubled mind.

"What's the matter, Doctor Benjamin?"

He shook his head. "As I said, I can't violate my patients' confidences. I wish I could tell you more, but I can't."

Well, dagnabbit, now I was *really* curious. Peering closely at the doctor, I saw his lips were pinched and his brows furrowed, as if he were in some distress. What did this mean? Clearly he knew some of Dr. Wagner's victims. Could he know of a young woman who had been violated by Dr. Wagner and then...

My mind boggled. Good Lord! Dr. Wagner couldn't have violated his own *daughter*, could he? Marianne? My mind boggled some more.

But merciful heavens! What an idea. Could that vile man have raped his own daughter, impregnated her, and then ruined her chances of ever having children? If that were the case, the man truly *had* been a monster! I opened my mouth, knew instantly that Dr. Benjamin wouldn't answer any of my prying questions, and shut it again. Darn it! And I was absolutely *certain* Marianne wouldn't confess to anything so...gross and disgusting. And so horribly sad. Even though, if what I were thinking had happened, it wasn't her fault any more than stumbling over dead bodies was mine.

The doctor and I sat in silence for a few more moments, and then I said, "Well, I thank you for your time, Doctor Benjamin. I know Sam will appreciate learning what you told me."

"You're welcome."

And then, because I couldn't hold in my rage another single second, I said, "I'm *glad* that awful man is dead! What a fiend he was!"

"Can't argue with you there, Daisy. You're fortunate in your family."

"I sure am. And in my family's choice of doctors. Thanks again, Doc."

"You're more than welcome, Daisy. Please give my regards to your family for me."

"I will. We need to have you and Mrs. Benjamin over for one of Vi's special dinners again soon."

"Your aunt has invited us for Christmas Eve dinner, so we'll see you soon. There's nowhere else either of us like to dine as much as at your place. Your aunt has an angel's touch in the kitchen."

I rose and smiled at him. "She sure does. Just like you have an angel's touch with your medical arts."

He laughed, we shook hands, and I left his office. After saying good-bye to Mrs. Benjamin, I tootled off to the Pasadena Public Library, thinking unpleasant thoughts about Dr. Wagner the entire way.

I also thought about Marianne Grenville. If Dr. Wagner had done what I suspected he might have done to her and then ruined her chances of having a family, it might give both her and George a motive for doing away with the ghastly man. Oh, dear. I wasn't sure if I should tell Sam my private thoughts. After all, I wasn't bound by any oath, Hippocratic or otherwise.

On the other hand, if I was wrong about Marianne and her old man, blabbing might lead to disastrous consequences, although I couldn't offhand think of what those consequences might be.

George and Marianne arrested for murder? I couldn't make myself believe that killing Dr. Wagner was an evil act. His entire life was evil. Putting him down was, to my mind, in the nature of putting down a rabid dog.

Oh, dear, dear, dear, dear. I didn't know what to do, but I hoped I'd come to some sort of resolution before I saw Sam again. Bother. Life could be so troublesome and unsettling.

TEN

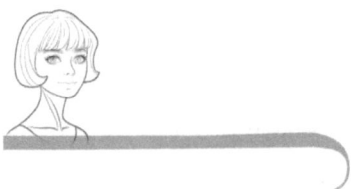

As luck would have it, my favorite librarian, Regina Minerva Petrie—one of these days to become Regina Minerva Browning—sat behind her desk in the reference section of the library. I was happy to see her because, if anything could keep my mind from dwelling in the sewer of Dr. Wagner's life and death, books could.

Miss Petrie appeared quite attractive that day. Thanks to my influence—and I'm not bragging. It's the simple truth—she'd learned how to fix her hair more artfully, use a tiny bit of makeup to great advantage, and now wore attire that was both professional and good-looking. None of her old, boring brown or gray ensembles these days. She appeared darned near perky as I approached her desk after dropping off my family's already-read books at the returns table.

"So nice to see you, Daisy! I've saved some books for your family."

"You're a peach, Regina. I do so appreciate you. You've been of more help to my family and me than anyone else in the world, except maybe Doctor Benjamin."

Can you tell I was still in a state? Well, I was.

Regina blinked at me several times. "Are you all right, Daisy? You look a little worried. I hope nothing's wrong in your world."

Nothing wrong in my world? Heck, no! I made a valiant attempt to put my emotions back into the mental bag in which I generally held them.

"Just a little bit of unpleasantness going on around me," I said, smiling and hoping the expression looked genuine.

"I'm sorry." Her distress was definitely genuine, and I felt like a rat.

"No, no. I mean everything's fine. It's just...Well, you probably read about that doctor who was found deceased at Mountain View Cemetery. Sam and I found him. It wasn't any fun."

Slapping a hand to her cheek, Regina said, "Oh, my Lord, Daisy. I'm so sorry!"

Happens all the time. I didn't say that out loud. "It was...unsettling."

"I can imagine."

"But how's Robert these days?"

As I'd anticipated, mentioning her beloved Robert Browning—not the poet, but a scientist who worked at the Underhill Chemical Company and sometimes colluded (that doesn't sound very nice, but I don't mean it that way) with scientists and professors at the California Institute of Technology—made everything else in Regina's world disappear. She beamed at me.

"He's just fine, thank you. I'm so grateful to you for introducing us, Daisy. I've never been happier."

"That makes me happy." I meant it, too.

She sighed with joy. "Oh, but look what I saved out for you and your family!" She reached for a shelf under her desk, pulled out three books and quietly placed them on her desk. "*The Bandit of the Black Hills*, by Frederick Faust—that's a pseudonym used by Max Brand, if you know who he is—was one I thought your father would like."

"The cover alone makes it something Pa would want to read," said I, picking up the book and gazing at the villainous-looking fellow on the front of the book. "What else do you have? Do I sound greedy?"

She laughed. "Not at all. I understand completely. If it weren't for books, I'd have gone mad years ago."

"Me, too." No lie there. "What's that one?" I asked, pointing at the next book in the stack.

"I think you'll really like this one. It's *Craig Kennedy Listens In*, by Mr. Arthur B. Reeve. Craig Kennedy is a scientific detective. Very entertaining story."

"Oh, I've loved Mr. Reeve's other Craig Kennedy books. Thank you!"

"You're most welcome. Last, but not least, I've saved *A Passage to India*, by Mr. E.M. Forster. It's not the happiest book in the world, but I did sort of get lost in Mr. Forster's depiction of India and the various Indian and British characters. I hope you'll enjoy it as much as I did."

"Thank you! I've always wanted to read more about India. I think Rudyard Kipling did that to me."

Regina laughed. "I think Rudyard Kipling did that to a lot of us."

"Oh," said I, as if just recalling a duty, although it had been on my mind ever since I'd sat in Dr. Benjamin's office earlier that morning, "do you have a copy of the Hippocratic Oath somewhere?"

"The Hippocratic Oath? Are you going into medicine, Daisy?"

I managed a chuckle. "No, but I was talking to Doctor Benjamin this morning, and he mentioned it. I guess all doctors are supposed to take the oath and honor it. I got the feeling the doctor Sam and I discovered the body of yesterday didn't honor it. If that sentence made any sense."

"Yes, it made sense." She hesitated for a moment or two, and then said, "I've heard awful things about him. And I understand you helped his daughter escape from his clutches a couple of years ago. I thought that was very brave of you."

"Good Lord, does *everyone* know I had a hand in helping Marianne? I thought the Wagner family wanted to keep it a secret." I frowned. "I know *I* sure wanted my name kept out of the matter."

"Things leak out," said Regina philosophically.

"I guess so," said I, wishing things could be kept in better order. Shut in a locked drawer to which only I had the key, for example. I tried to shake off my feeling of disquiet. To distract her from the Dr. Wagner scenario, I asked, "Have you and Robert set a date yet?"

Distraction worked. With a dreamy smile, Regina said, "We were aiming for June, but we're not precisely glued to the month. Almost everyone gets married in June, and I personally think an autumn wedding would be nice. Of course, we'd have to wait a few more months, but that's all right." She breathed in a deep breath and let it out slowly. "He's such a wonderful man, Daisy. And we'd never have got together without you."

Oh, boy. Matchmaker-in-chief; that was me all right. "You probably would have found each other even without me. You seem to have been made for each other, really."

"I don't know. Neither one of us is precisely a social butterfly."

I smiled. "True, but sometimes love finds a way." After hearing what I'd just said, I nearly gagged. I'm not usually so stupidly sentimental.

"That's true. After all, if it weren't for your first husband's horrible illness, you'd never have met the detective, and now the two of you are engaged."

She still looked dreamy, and I didn't want to ruin her mood, but still…Maybe Regina should know the truth.

"Actually, it was Mrs. Pinkerton's good-for-nothing daughter, Stacy Kincaid, who first brought Sam and me together. If Stacy weren't a total poop, I'd never have met him."

"She's that awful girl who was in cahoots with my wicked cousin, wasn't she?" She shuddered almost dramatically. Drama and Regina Petrie don't often go together; at least not that I'd seen before.

"She's the one, all right. Wretched brat, and her mother's had to put up with her dreadful behavior for years now. Don't know why she didn't kick the kid out a long time ago."

"Oh, but Daisy, you wouldn't throw out a child of your own, would you?"

Thinking back over the year and taking into consideration all the evil people with whom I'd had to deal, I wasn't sure about that. However, I didn't think Regina needed to know it. "Probably not," said I without much conviction. If I ever bred an animal as vile as Stacy Kincaid or Percival Petrie (Regina's criminal cousin), I'd wish for foresight so that I could have the child drowned at birth if necessary.

That sounds awful, doesn't it? Well, I guess I don't really mean it.

Or maybe I do.

Anyhow, nobody has the foresight to see what a baby will grow up to be or how it will act as an adult. I don't care what lies fortune-tellers spout, nobody can predict the future. Please don't tell any of my clients I said so. Not that I was or ever had been a fortune-teller.

Oh, pooh. Never mind. Whatever happened in the possible-child-of-mine's future, I guess I'd just deal with it when it got to me. As my aunt, father, mother and assorted other kinfolk are fond of saying, "No sense borrowing trouble." Actually, Vi's more apt to say, "Sufficient unto the day is the evil thereof," but I don't like that saying as well, since evil and I don't get along too well.

"Thank you so much for the books, Regina. I know I'm going to enjoy them. Even the *Passage to India* one. Now that I don't feel so affected by that awful war, I'm able to read things that aren't jolly without going into a deep melancholy. Although I'm never going to be able to read *An Amazing Interlude* again." Mind you, that was a good book, but Mary Roberts Rinehart wrote it during the war, and it featured a young woman from the United States who wanted to help the war effort. By the end of the book, you still didn't know if she and/or her handsome and brave French soldier would even survive, much less thrive.

"I understand. That book got to me, too, and I didn't have your personal…What would you call them? Connections? To that war."

"I guess that's as good a word as any," said I, thinking wistfully of my late husband as he'd been before the war. "But can you direct me to a copy of the Hippocratic Oath? Just because I'm interested in reading what doctors sign on for. If you know what I mean."

"I understand completely." Regina rose from her desk chair and led me to the reference section of the library. Somewhere in the 500 stacks, she pulled out a book. "This should have it printed out. This is a reference book, so you can't check it out, but you can read it, and if you want to write it down, I can lend you a pencil and some paper."

"Thank you! I don't need to copy it down. I just want to read it. I'll take it to a table and look at it, and then I'll be sure to put it back in its right place."

With another sweet smile, she said, "You're one of the few people whom I trust to do exactly that."

We exchanged knowing looks—although I'm not sure what we knew—and I lugged the heavy tome to a table, pulled out an even heavier chair, sat, gently plopped the book on the table, opened the book and looked. It was in *Greek*, for pity's sake! Fiddlesticks.

But wait. There was an English translation after the Greek. Shoot, the beginning of the original text refers to Greek gods by name: "I swear by Apollo the Healer, by Asclepius, by Hygieia, by Panacea, and by all the gods and goddesses, making them my witnesses, that I will carry out, according to my ability and judgment, this oath and this indenture."

Interesting, and I guess I'd just learned where our English words hygiene and panacea came from. Dr. Benjamin was correct in that the words "First, do no harm" don't appear in the text. Modern-day translations undoubtedly left out the Greek-god references. It was a worthwhile oath, I decided after reading the whole thing. Too bad some doctors—like Dr. Wagner, for example—failed to abide by its dictates.

I carried the sixty-pound volume—there I go, exaggerating again—back to the 500 stacks, put it into its proper place, picked up my family's latest load of books, waved good-bye to Regina, and took the books to the check-out counter. Then I left the library and drove to Mrs. Pinkerton's palace, which was north and west of the Pasadena Public Library, on Orange Grove Boulevard—"Millionaire's Row," according to some local wits. Those wits were right. Both Mrs. Pinkerton and Mrs. Frasier lived in mansions on Orange Grove, which was a gorgeous street lined with huge estates. Mind you, our own neighborhood was nice, but South Marengo Avenue couldn't hold a candle to Orange Grove if you compared Marengo's inhabitants to those who lived on Orange Grove. Therefore, I didn't bother. Comparing the streets or their inhabitants, I mean.

After I parked my family's almost-new Chevrolet in front of the gigantic front porch of the Pinkerton place, I trod up the marble steps, patted one of the marble lions on its head, picked up the brass door knocker hanging from a brass lion's mouth, and whacked the knocker against the brass knocking plate. Almost instantly, Featherstone, the Pinkertons' butler, opened the door.

"Good morning, Featherstone!" I always greeted him exuberantly, mainly because I'd never once, in all the years I'd been working for Mrs. Pinkerton, seen him smile or deviate an iota from his butler act. He even had an English accent, by golly! Sometimes I tried to tease him, but not so much recently. He had his pose as a butler to maintain, just as I had mine as a spiritualist-medium to do likewise.

"Mrs. Majesty," said he. "Please come this way."

So I went that way, following him, although I could find my way to Mrs. P's front drawing room blindfolded and walking backwards by that time. But I didn't want to cause Featherstone any distress, so I never veered off course. I doubt he would have reacted if I had veered, but he might have suffered internal unease, and it would have been mean of me.

Entering the drawing room, I saw Mrs. Pinkerton seated on a beautiful sofa across the room. She'd been reading the latest issue of *Vanity Fair Magazine*. My family didn't subscribe to *Vanity Fair*, which published some short fiction pieces, lots of articles about celebrities, fashions, and who was doing what with whom. Sort of a gossip magazine for rich people, I reckon. When she glanced up and saw me, she smiled hugely.

Boy, was *that* a change from her usual mood when I came to call. Generally speaking, especially during the past several months, she'd been hysterical, weeping, in a nervous twit, or exhibiting a combination of all of those things. Not today. I sent up a silent prayer of thanks to the Creator. I had enough on my mind already. I didn't need a panic-stricken Mrs. Pinkerton with whom to deal.

"Good morning, Daisy dear. How are you today?"

"I'm fine, thank you, Mrs. Pinkerton. And you?" I asked as I carried my pack of spiritualist paraphernalia over to the sofa and pulled up one of Mrs. P's gorgeous medallion-backed chairs across the table from her. Taking a breath and a chance, I added, "You don't seem as upset today as you've been recently."

"Have a seat, dear. No. Harold has convinced me of the error of my ways. I have always loved and continue to love my daughter, but she's going to have to deal with her problems without me bailing her out this time."

Right. Unless one counted hiring the most expensive legal counsel available in Pasadena and making sure she wanted for nothing. Well, except freedom, but she didn't deserve freedom.

But good heavens! I could hardly believe my ears. I hope this new attitude on Mrs. P's part wouldn't spell the end of my spiritualist-medium business.

Naw. She could never hold on to a good mood for long. She'd be panicking again soon; I was sure of it.

"I'm so glad to hear it," I said, and I meant the words sincerely, and not just for Mrs. P's sake, but for mine as well. She was much easier to deal with when she wasn't in a frightful tizzy. "You've done everything you can do for Stacy, Mrs. Pinkerton. She stepped in the mud all on her own this time, and she should have to deal with the consequences of her actions."

Letting out a largish sigh, Mrs. Pinkerton laid the magazine on the coffee table set before the sofa. "I know. Sometimes it's hard for me to keep my spirits up, but Harold is forever prodding me to buck up. And I know he's right."

"Harold is a good son," I said. "And he's wise, too."

"Yes. He is," agreed Harold's mother. "Much wiser than I."

He sure was. Naturally, I didn't say so. Rather, I said, "Would you like to consult the Ouija board, or have me deal out a tarot hand for you today, Mrs. Pinkerton?"

"Yes, please. I'd like to speak to Rolly through the Ouija board first."

"Certainly. Don't forget that Rolly can't answer questions about anyone but the person asking." I'd told her the same thing several thousand times, but it bore repeating. Mrs. P didn't learn easily.

"I remember, dear." She gave me a sweet smile.

So I pulled out my Ouija board, which I kept in a lovely bag embroidered by my very own hands. The board was an older model board, but I'd polished it up and kept it well-groomed. Neither my Ouija board nor I would ever present a less-than-perfect veneer to my paying clients. I set the board on the coffee table with the letters and numbers facing Mrs. Pinkerton. I'd learned to read upside-down years earlier. I set the wooden planchette in the middle of the board, and Mrs. P and I lightly placed our fingertips on it. You're not supposed to put any weight on the planchette, because—so legend has it; I personally don't believe in any of it—you might in that way prevent the planchette from moving easily over the board. Hogwash, all of it. Still, it's how I made my living so I adhered to the rules.

Once our fingertips rested lightly on the planchette, Mrs. P said, "Very well. This question isn't strictly about myself, but I would like to know, since I'll be among the guests, if Rolly will be able to help you determine the murderer of that beastly Doctor Wagner."

I was about to administer another teensy lecture about only asking questions pertaining to herself, but evidently Rolly had a different idea that day. Since Rolly is me, this surprised me a good deal. At first I wasn't sure what was happening and glanced sharply at Mrs. P to see if she was attempting to manipulate the planchette. But she had her gaze fixed firmly on our fingers, so I squinted again at the stupid planchette and felt it move on its own. I swear, it did.

Now here's the thing. I never moved the planchette using physical force. Never. However, since my mind was the functioning party to any Ouija-board transactions I perpetrated, the planchette always did what I wanted it to. It probably comes down to me unwittingly directing the planchette, even if it doesn't feel as though I'm physically moving the thing. It's a stupid triangular-shaped piece of wood, for cripe's sake. It couldn't *possibly* move without some input from the human in charge.

Except that day. The confounded, mindless piece of polished wood zipped around the board without my involvement. Not *any* involvement. Neither physically nor mentally did I direct the planchette where to go. It went anyway. All on its own.

Don't feel bad if you don't believe me. I wouldn't believe me either, if someone said that to me. But it happened anyway, whether I believed it or not.

In answer to Mrs. P's question, the planchette skimmed lightly but firmly to the "Yes" on the upper left-hand side of the board.

Shoot. What did this mean?

"Oh, I'm so glad!" Mrs. P exclaimed. "Will you be able to tell us who the murderer is, Rolly?"

Darned if the blasted planchette—being used by *me*, curse it, not the fictional Rolly—didn't shudder a bit and stay on the "Yes".

I didn't approve of this. However, evidently Rolly, or the planchette, or the spirits in the room, or whatever was there didn't care if I approved or not. When Mrs. P said, "Can you tell us the name or the killer?"

"Yes," said Rolly. Or me. Or the gods. Or perhaps I'd gone completely 'round the bend and insanity now ruled my fingers. As that was a distressing thought, I attempted to banish it.

Didn't work. As if impelled by forces beyond my control, I asked whatever entity was governing things at the moment, "At the upcoming séance at Mrs. Frasier's house, will you tell us the name of Doctor Wagner's killer?"

I swear to God, I didn't do a single, solitary thing to that pesky planchette. I only sat there like an idiot and watched the wooden object upon which our fingers lay slide sleekly to the "No" in the upper right-hand corner of the board.

"Oh, but if you know who it is, why won't you tell us?" asked Mrs. Pinkerton in a pleading voice.

When the wretched planchette spelled out "Not my job," I

suspected Sam Rotondo had somehow monkeyed with the dratted board, although I had no idea how he could have. But darned if Rolly didn't sound just like him. Well, the planchette sounded like Sam, at any rate. All right, it didn't *sound* like him, because it was speechless, but...

Honestly, I don't know *what* I mean. Stunned didn't come even close to what I felt during that Ouija-board session. By the time I left Mrs. Pinkerton, she was gleeful.

I wasn't.

ELEVEN

About thirty minutes after our Ouija-board session started, it ended, and I was intensely glad of it. I still felt shaky as I walked from the drawing room to the kitchen to avail myself of Aunt Vi's promised lunch. My feelings stumbled around inside me like reeling drunkards, and I felt a trifle sickish in my tummy, but I decided what had happened with the Ouija board and Rolly was a mere fluke, prompted by the unpleasant stresses of the last day or so. Not to mention talking to Dr. Benjamin that morning and my deplorable supposition concerning Marianne Grenville and her late, unlamented father.

I only hoped I was right and my life would come to its senses soon, if not instantly. I prayed for instantly.

"Good heavens, Daisy, what happened to you?" said Vi as soon as I'd set foot in her kitchen lair.

"Do I look that bad?" Guess my prayer had gone unanswered. Again. I sighed and sat on one of the chairs placed at the kitchen table against the wall.

"You only look a trifle pale, dear. Are you feeling all right?"

"Um…Yes. I'm fine. I just had a little Ouija-board session with Mrs. Pinkerton."

"Oh, dear. Was she in a state?"

"Oddly enough, she wasn't. It's just…Well, I don't know. Something weird happened."

"Oh, is that all?"

I stared at my aunt. "What do you mean, 'Is that all'? It scared me to death!"

Her eyes narrowed and she gazed upon me with some concern. "I'm sorry. What scared you?"

I shook my head. "It sounds stupid."

"That's all right, dear. If it will help you feel better, please tell me about it."

"Well…" Shoot, I felt like an idiot. "Well, the Ouija board kind of got away from me when Mrs. P and I were using it."

"It got away from you? It ran out the door? I'm not sure what that means, Daisy." Vi, bless her, sat in a chair near mine and took one of my hands, which she squeezed reassuringly. "I don't understand, dear."

"I don't, either. It spelled out things I hadn't intended for it to spell out." Beginning to feel a little more peeved than spooked, I blurted out, "And it sounded just like Sam!"

Peering hard at me and obviously puzzled, Vi said, "Goodness. I thought your Ouija-board antics were all make-believe."

"So did I."

"What did it say? Or does it speak?"

"It doesn't speak. It spells things out. Since I made Rolly up when I was only ten, it's not supposed to be able to spell well, but nobody remembers that part. Anyway, it spells correctly these days."

"If it's you, I expect it does," said Vi, still squinting. "But whatever happened, dear? You really do look a trifle frazzled."

"Frazzled. That's a good word for it." I took in a deep breath and released it. "When Mrs. Pinkerton asked the Ouija board—well, she thought she was asking Rolly, but you know what I—"

"Yes," said Vi, probably not meaning to interrupt, but knowing what I was going to say because I'd said it so often. "I know what you mean."

"Well, when she asked the Ouija board—which she thought was

being ruled by Rolly—if it or he—Oh, bother. When she asked it if it knew who'd killed Doctor Wagner, darned if that idiotic planchette didn't just zip right up to the 'Yes' at the top of the board!"

"Oh." Vi let my hand go with a little reassuring pat. "That doesn't sound too terrible, sweetie."

"Maybe not to you. But I hadn't intended it to say it knew who the murderer is. Was. Well, you know what I mean."

"Yes, I think I do. But I'm still not sure what has you so upset, Daisy. Tell me about it while I fix your lunch."

"Thanks, Vi. Let me see if I can make this make sense. If that makes sense." I heaved a sigh. "Oh, dear."

"You just sit there and relax, sweetie, and think about what happened. Then you can tell me so that I can understand."

I almost heard the unspoken "I hope" she didn't utter. And how could she understand what had happened when I didn't?

Fiddlesticks. I thought hard for a moment or two, watching Vi as she moved around the kitchen. Looked as if I were going to be eating a sandwich for lunch that day. That was all right by me.

"Very well," I said at last, hoping I'd mentally sorted out what had happened and what my feelings were. "The thing is that, even though I know I'm the one doing the thinking during a Ouija-board session, I never consciously direct the planchette to do anything. It just does what I want it to do, because I'm the brains behind it." If brains were involved. I was beginning to think my own personal brain had acquired leaks. "Maybe brains isn't a good word."

"It's a fine word, dear," said Vi with a short laugh.

Well, she *could* laugh. She hadn't just been involved in an uncanny Ouija-board session. But never mind that.

I went on. "But today, I had aimed to tell Mrs. Pinkerton that Rolly—that is, the Ouija board—didn't have a clue who murdered Doctor Wagner. *I* sure don't know who did it. But the stupid planchette went to the 'Yes' and just sat there."

Vi turned to peer at me from the stove, where she stirred something in a small saucepan. "That sounds odd," said she.

"It *was* odd! Ridiculously odd! I don't have a single, solitary notion who the killer is, but the stupid planchette said it *did* know. What's more, when Mrs. P asked if it knew the killer by name, it stayed on the 'Yes'. But *I* don't know the murderer's name, so if I don't know, how could the Ouija board know?"

"I don't know," said Vi.

My elbows rested on the table, and I sank my head into my hands. "I don't, either. And then, when Mrs. P asked if it would reveal the name of the killer at Mrs. Frasier's séance tomorrow night, it said it wouldn't."

"Oh?" Vi had commenced ladling out what looked like soup into a pretty flowered bowl. Mrs. Pinkerton had lovely china. Several patterns' worth, according to Vi and my friend Edie Applewood, who worked as Mrs. P's lady's maid. "Why is that? Did it tell you?"

I lifted my head in time to see Vi use a spatula to lift a toasted sandwich from the stove-top grill and on to a flowered plate that matched the flowered bowl. Then she cut the grilled sandwich into two neat triangles. Whatever my lunch was going to be that day, I probably wouldn't be able to it justice.

Or maybe I could. Just because my brain was in a muddle didn't mean I couldn't still enjoy food, right?

Putting the bowl, plate, some silverware—real silver silverware, in Mrs. P's house—onto a tray and adding a napkin, Vi brought it to me and set it out on the table as if she were a waitress.

"Thanks, Vi," said I, looking at what appeared to be a toasted sandwich with cheese, ham and tomatoes on it. The soup was definitely cream of tomato. Vi made the best cream of tomato soup in the entire world. That shouldn't surprise anyone, since she makes the best everything in the entire world. "This looks spectacular."

"I used pumpernickel bread, because I know you like it."

"You're so good to me, Vi."

"But go on with your story. Maybe the séance will solve the murder and Sam will be happy with you."

"For once," I said for her, since she'd never say such a thing.

"Nonsense. Sam loves you to death, Daisy. You know that."

Another sigh. "I know it. And I love him. But that doesn't solve the problem of who killed Doctor Wagner."

"But I don't understand. According to you, the Ouija board said it—or Rolly or…well, I don't know—But you said it said it knew who the killer was and even the killer's name."

"Yes, *it* claims to know. *I* don't have a single, solitary clue."

"Well, then, but the Ouija board—or whatever—said it *does* know. If it knows the killer's name, why won't it say who it is?" She wrinkled her nose. "Not that I believe in that sort of thing, you understand."

"I understand," I said after heaving a sigh.

"Then why won't it say the killer's name?"

"Beats me, but when Mrs. P asked if it would reveal the name at the séance, it said it wouldn't. And then, when she asked why it wouldn't, the stupid thing spelled out 'Not my job'. I swear, Aunt Vi, it sounded just like Sam!"

"Really? Why wouldn't Sam tell you the name of the murderer if he knew?"

"Sam *would* tell if he knew. But Sam *doesn't* know."

A moment of silence passed while I bit off the end of my absolutely scrumptious sandwich. While Vi had cut the sandwich in half, she didn't bother removing the crusts, which was all right with me since that seems a terribly wasteful habit. That's probably why rich people did it. To prove they're richer than the rest of us mere mortals and could afford to waste food and money.

I'm sorry. I'm not really crabby most of the time. I hope.

"Um…I don't understand, dear," said Vi.

"Neither do I."

"But…but aren't you and Rolly the same thing? I mean, you made up Rolly, didn't you? So how could he know something you don't know?"

I took a sip of soup. Amazing. It tasted as if Vi had sautéed some onions and maybe some mushrooms and added them to the plain old tomato soup. Not that Vi's tomato soup is ever plain or old.

"That's the thing!" I said, splashing my spoon into my soup by accident. I guess frustration does that to a person. "I'm sorry, Vi," said I, blotting up the spill with my napkin. "I don't *know*. I never would have said Rolly knows who the murderer is because *I* don't know who the murderer is!" I set my spoon beside my bowl and gazed sorrowfully down upon my delicious lunch. "I'm so confused, Vi. This has never happened before."

Never mind the time I was at a séance and the ghost of Eddie Hastings suddenly popped out of my mouth. Or the time I was playing a fortune-teller at one of Mrs. Pinkerton's parties to benefit the Pasadena Humane Society and my stupid crystal ball showed me a bunch of trees, thereby leading to the rescue of a kidnapped butler. Those things were disconcerting enough, but I'd never, ever, not once, lost control of the Ouija board's inhuman, inanimate, unconscious, lifeless, carved wooden planchette.

Until that day.

"I'm sorry, dear," said Vi. She was concerned; I could tell. She also had no more idea what to do about my problem than did I. I also got the impression she didn't think the problem was a big deal. Guess it wasn't to her, but her job didn't include spiritualist-medium-ing.

Nerts.

After heaving another heartfelt sigh, I said, "I just don't know what to do. Maybe I won't have to do anything. Maybe Rolly or the Ouija board or the planchette or something will relent and deign to surrender the killer's name at tomorrow night's séance." I didn't believe it.

Neither, evidently, did Vi. She rose from her chair, her face a pattern-card of disbelief. "Well, dear, I don't know if that will be any better."

"What do you mean?" I gazed at my aunt in surprise.

"If that crazy thing spells out a name, who's to say it's right or wrong? I mean, you can't just go around accusing people of murder without proof, can you?"

"But I wouldn't be the one accusing anyone," I said feebly.

"Perhaps not, but who will believe that, dear? You're supposed to be in charge of all those spiritualist…whatever you call thems. Arcana? I'm not sure if that's the right word."

"I think it is," I said, drooping slightly.

"Well, then, aren't you the one who's supposed to be in control of those things?"

"Yes."

"But in this case you aren't?"

"Right."

Vi stood there for a moment or two, peering down at me with concern. We were in agreement there. I was concerned, too.

However, that didn't stop me from finishing and enjoying my delicious lunch.

TWELVE

W hen Sam came over that afternoon for a discussion about our various doctor visits and any new insights we'd gathered from our inquiries, I still wasn't sure what to tell him.

Oh, I had no trouble telling him what Dr. Benjamin had revealed about the dreadful Dr. Wagner's abortion racket. It was all the other stuff, including my thoughts regarding what might have happened to Marianne, thanks to her father, that gave me pause. I mean, that was only a guess on my part and a particularly ugly one. Only it felt right. I wished it didn't.

And I *really* didn't want to delve into what had happened between the Ouija board and Mrs. Pinkerton that morning. He'd only laugh. I wasn't sure I could handle being laughed at, as I was still off kilter and feeling out of control. In my own realm, for the good Lord's sake! I mean, I'd invented my spiritualist-medium self out of whole cloth when I was ten! All of a sudden to lose control of what I'd come to think of as my own personal domain made me nervous. Quite nervous. Scared, actually.

Oh, dear.

"Yeah, I heard about the abortion business Doctor Wagner was conducting from Doctor Ferdinand. The man nearly turned purple with rage when he told me about it." Sam grinned.

"I imagine he disapproved," I said, my own disapproval clear to hear. I didn't think anything about this case was laughable. "So do I. I don't think it's anything to grin about."

Sam said, "Sorry. It's not funny, but Doctor Ferdinand reminded me of my mother and father. Roman Catholic to the core. Nobody, but *nobody*, is allowed to abort a baby, even if everyone involved knows the poor thing will starve to death once it's born because there are either already too many mouths to feed or it's damaged somehow. I didn't mean to make light of the situation with Wagner. That man was a bastard."

I blinked at Sam's words, not quite knowing what to say.

"Sorry about the bad language," said he, clearly misinterpreting my silence.

"Oh, no!" I said, startled. I don't think Sam had ever apologized for using bad language before. "It's not that. It's that I thought you were a Roman Catholic, too. Do you believe in abortion?"

"'Believe' in it? Yeah, I 'believe' in abortion, because it happens. Sometimes a woman will abort a baby naturally. In other cases, evil men like Dr. Wagner might help them along. Do I approve of abortion?" He held out his hand flat and wobbled it a bit in what I gather is the universal gesture for "I'm not sure."

"Really?" Don't ask me why, but his equivocal answer surprised me. Sam wasn't known for being wishy-washy about anything.

"Really." He grinned again. "Surprised?"

"Kind of. I mean, you're a Catholic, and—"

Sam interrupted me. "I haven't been a practicing Roman Catholic for years now. I thought you knew that."

"Well, I guess I did. I remember when your nephew was here—"

Another interruption. "I don't *want* to remember when he was here."

With a small laugh of my own, I said, "I don't blame you. But I remember Frank being appalled that you'd go to a church other than the Catholic Church. I think he disapproved."

"That in itself is a good-enough reason not to attend Catholic services. Anything my idiot nephew disapproves of can't be all bad."

"He was a problem, all right." I sat still, pondering what to say next. At the moment, Sam and I were seated next to each other on one of the benches in our inglenook. A fire burned merrily in the fireplace. Spike had sort of melted himself over both of our laps, which was easy for him to do since he had such a long body. When he lay like that, he also got patted by two pairs of hands instead of one. Spike was a smart dog. Quite unlike Frank Pagano, Sam's nephew, if you wanted to think about the two males in that way.

But I'm straying from the point again. Sorry.

"You have something more to tell me, don't you?" said Sam, peering at me closely. "What is it? Spit it out."

Blast! How did he know I was concerned about something? He had begun to know me too well for my own good, Sam had.

I waffled. "It's nothing, really."

"I don't believe you."

"Well! That's not very nice, Sam Rotondo." I attempted to sound offended but couldn't quite carry it off.

"Nuts. Just tell me what's bothering you."

"You'll laugh."

"Good. I could use a good laugh."

"Or maybe you'll get mad."

Beginning to frown, Sam said, "All right, now I *definitely* need to know what's bothering you."

"You won't believe me."

Rolling his eyes—not an unusual gesture—Sam barked, "Just tell me, dammit!"

"All right, all right. When Mrs. Pinkerton and I were using the Ouija board this morning— Stop rolling your eyes at me!"

He stopped. "Go on." His voice was flat as the proverbial pancake.

"When we were using the Ouija board, it said it knew who Doctor Wagner's murderer is. Was. Even the killer's name."

Sam stopped frowning and began looking puzzled, which made sense to me. "Yeah?"

"Yeah."

"Well, who was it? According to your Ouija board."

"I don't know."

Exasperation from Sam. "For God's sake, Daisy! What do you mean it knows and it doesn't know? That doesn't make even more sense than it usually doesn't make."

"It's not my fault. The planchette got away from me."

"What the devil does that mean?"

"Just what I said, blast it! I didn't push it or anything. It just moved on its own."

"And it said it knew who the murderer was?"

"Yes."

"Well, then, who was it?" he demanded.

"It wouldn't say."

Shaking his head hard, Sam sat back against the embroidered cushions I'd made for the inglenook bench, looking pretty darned frustrated.

"I knew you'd be mad at me," I said, feeling meek and frustrated. Even *I* could hardly believe what I was telling him.

"I'm not mad at you," said Sam.

"You look mad."

"I'm not, but Daisy, if you know who the murderer is, *tell* me!"

"But I *don't* know. It was the…Crumb. This sounds so impossible. But it was the Ouija board that said it knew. I didn't have anything to do with it."

Looking closely at his face, which was turning kind of eggplant-colored, I sighed and said, "I knew you wouldn't believe me. It sounds incredible."

"Yes," he managed to say through clamped teeth, "it does."

After heaving a huge sigh, I said, "But it happened. Just the way I told you. The Ouija board said it knew who the killer was but wouldn't reveal the person's name."

A few silent moments ensued, during which Sam's face lost some of its purplish color. I was glad of that. Purple really isn't his color. Eventually he said, "Did your board tell you why it wouldn't reveal the murderer's name?"

"Yes. It said revealing the name wasn't its job."

"*What?*"

"You heard me. It…Well, it reminded me of you, actually."

"Good God."

I decided to change the subject before Sam keeled over from frustration. His color still wasn't great.

"But I learned something else about Doctor Wagner. That is to say, I *think* I learned something. I'm not sure. It may be a wild guess on my part, but the thought came to me when I was talking to Doctor Benjamin."

Sam sucked in a big breath. "Go on," he said, his voice tight.

"Evidently several other doctors in town had to…mop up after Doctor Wagner's lousy work. With abortions, I mean."

"Yes, Doctor Ferdinand told me that, too. That was another thing that infuriated him about Wagner." He shook his head. "Truth to tell, I'm glad Wagner's dead. Someone probably should have killed him years ago."

"Yes, but…" Darn. If I told him my supposition about Marianne, Sam would take my theory as a reason to look more closely at Marianne and George as suspects in the vile doctor's murder. On the other hand, I felt obliged to tell him my suspicion, hoping he'd scoff. If he scoffed, I wouldn't worry so much.

"Go on," he said again, his voice sounding not quite as dangerous as it had earlier.

"All right. I may be totally wrong about this, but I got a funny feeling as I was talking to Doctor Benjamin that Doctor Wagner might have…Lord, this sounds awful."

"Just say it," said a frustrated Sam.

"I got a feeling that perhaps—and I don't know this to be true—that perhaps the evil doctor impregnated his own daughter and then botched her abortion."

"He *what*? Doctor Benjamin told you that?"

"No, he didn't tell me that. He couldn't, because that would have been a violation of his Hippocratic Oath."

"His what?"

"Oh, you know. It's the oath all doctors take in order to be doctors. They have to keep their patients' information confidential."

"Oh, yeah. I've heard of it, now that you mention it."

"Anyway, he told me other women had been given abortions by Doctor Wagner, and he did such a lousy job, they can no longer bear children. If he did that to his own daughter—and I know he… well, touched her inappropriately—then it might give Marianne or George a motive for killing him. Doctor Wagner, I mean. And they'd have been right to do it, so I hope it's not true, because the law and I don't see eye-to-eye on the matter of Doctor Wagner's death."

Sam scrubbed his face with his hands. When he emerged, he said, "But that's only a guess on your part."

"Yes…Kind of. Although…Doctor Benjamin looked extremely troubled as we were talking. He couldn't tell me the names of any of Dr Wagner's victims because of whatever they call it. Doctor-patient privacy or something like that. Because of that oath they have to take."

"So you don't know for sure that Mrs. Grenville got pregnant by her old man and was then butchered by him."

"No, I don't know for sure. I just…sort of gathered as much from Doctor Benjamin's demeanor and the things he said. If you know what I mean."

"Good Lord," said Sam, again scrubbing his face with his hands. "I guess I can talk to the Doc Benjamin. Maybe he'll let on to a copper if that's what happened in the Wagner family, but he probably won't. That's part of his job, maintaining his patients' confidentiality."

"Yes. That's what he told me."

"And I don't know how well the Grenvilles would react to direct questions from a policeman about such a…ticklish suspicion." Sam tilted his head and peered at me, speculation writ large on his features.

"Shoot. You want me to talk to Marianne, don't you?"

With a sweet—for him—smile, Sam said, "You love to butt into my cases, remember?"

"Hmm. I'm not particularly eager to butt into this one in that way."

"You're the one who brought up the problem. If it is a problem."

"I know. Nerts, Sam. How in the world can I approach Marianne about such a horrible...I don't even know what you'd call it. Assumption? Supposition? Hypothesis? On my part? She'd probably kick me out of her house and never speak to me again."

"You're the one who's always telling me people are more apt to talk to you than to a copper. And you're right. Especially when it comes to stuff like this."

"Well, yes, but...Some things are difficult to talk about, no matter who you're talking to."

"Yes, indeed," said Sam, grinning like the fiend he was. He knew I'd capitulate and question Marianne, drat him.

Vi called for me to set the table for dinner, so I had to disturb Spike, who grumbled a bit. But Sam carried him from the inglenook to the sofa, and he calmed down again. Spike, I mean, not Sam. I wasn't sure what Sam's state of mind was at that moment. My own was considerably rattled. Confused. Worried. Peeved. A trifle queasy. All of those things. Combined, they made my innards uncomfortable.

My mood lifted some when I walked from the living room into the dining room and smelled whatever Vi had fixed for our dinner that night. "Oh, boy, Vi. That smells heavenly!"

"It is, if I do say so myself," said my aunt in a smuggish voice. She had every right to be smug. After all, it wasn't everyone who could be the best cook in the world.

So I set the table, Ma called Pa and Sam in to dinner, we all sat down, and Pa said grace. Vi had promised us something special for dinner that night, and she sure delivered. A large rib roast of beef with roasted potatoes, gravy, Yorkshire pudding, green beans with almonds, her feather-light dinner rolls, and a green salad graced the table. Vi cut the roast and handed out plates decorated with large slices of tender roast beef, and we passed everything else.

"This is one of the most delicious meals I've ever eaten, Vi," said Sam, altering his usual during-dinner praise for my aunt.

"It is wonderful," said Ma.

"I agree," said Pa.

I couldn't talk because my mouth was full, but I nodded with vigor. Poor Spike sat at my feet and gazed mournfully up at me.

After I swallowed, I asked, "Is something special going on with the Pinkertons, or did you just decide to honor everyone with a gigantic rib roast and Yorkshire pudding?"

"I thought Mrs. P deserved a special meal because of everything that hateful daughter has put her through recently. Hoping to keep her spirits up, you know." She grimaced. "Sorry, Daisy. Didn't mean to bring up spirits at the dinner table."

"That's all right," said I. "I'm over it."

"Over what?" asked Ma, peering at me curiously.

I *really* didn't want to get in to another discussion about my runaway planchette, so I only smiled and said, "Nothing, Ma. Just had an interesting session with Mrs. Pinkerton and the Ouija board today."

"Oh. That sounds better than usual," said Ma. "Generally you find sessions with that woman tiring."

"True enough," I said.

Apparently Sam swallowed wrong, because he began coughing. I whacked him on the back.

Really hard.

THIRTEEN

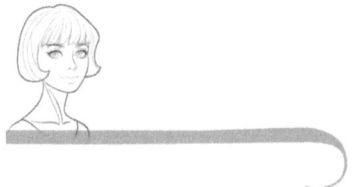

The following day, Wednesday, I decided to pay a call on Marianne Grenville before my courage gave out.

Well...Truth to tell, my nerves hadn't yet risen above ground level regarding this particular duty I'd assumed. I didn't look forward to it, nor did I think Marianne would ever speak to me again if I dared broach the topic of my suspicion. Or maybe it was less a suspicion than a preposterous conclusion based on rickety evidence. Banana peels. I didn't know what it was. Come to think of it, I didn't know where Marianne was, either. She might be at her mother's place. Or her mother might be at her place. I decided to try the Grenville home first.

Unfortunately, Marianne was there, smiling up a storm, with her mother standing right behind her, likewise smiling. Diane Wagner's bruises were still evident, but they were mostly yellowish-green by that time.

"Daisy! How good to see you. Please come in," said Marianne, standing aside and waving me into the entryway.

"It truly is good to see you, Daisy," said Diane. "I don't think I've ever been happier than I've been these past couple of days. I suppose that sounds awful of me, doesn't it?"

"No. Not at all," said I. "The truth sometimes hurts, but other times it's a huge relief to tell it out loud." Shoot, I'd already begun preparing the groundwork for my monstrous questions.

"I just made a pot of tea," said Marianne. "Mother and I were going to have tea in the living room along with some shortbread cookies Mother made last night. Please join us."

"Thank you. That sounds delightful," I said, wishing it were true. Mind you, I love shortbread and I'm fond of tea, but I still wasn't sure how to approach the subject I'd come to Marianne's house to discuss.

"I'm selling the house," said Diane Wagner. "It's going to take weeks to sort through everything and decide what I want to keep and what I don't, but I'll be pleased to see the last of it."

"The house on El Molino?" asked I.

"Yes. I can't wait to be rid of it."

"You know, when Detective Rotondo and I visited you on Monday, we both thought the house was lovely and cheerful. In fact, I was surprised, since I…Well, I knew what kind of man Doctor Wagner was."

"I told Mother the same thing," said Marianne, carrying a tray into the living room. The tray was silver, and the teapot and cups were beautiful.

"What a lovely china pattern!" said I, glad to be diverted from my purpose.

"Thank you," said Marianne, setting the tray carefully on a coffee table in the living room. Mrs. Wagner and I sat on two chairs near the table. "It's Coalport, and the pattern is called 'Indian Tree'. It belonged to my Grandmother Chapman."

"On my side of the family," added Diane. "Doctor Wagner's side of the family brought nothing of value to our marriage."

With a soft laugh, Marianne said, "That's not true, Mother. You know father was the only bad seed in that family. Grandmother Wagner was a lovely woman."

Diane Wagner huffed, but then gave up her bad mood with a little chuckle of her own. "You're right, of course. My late husband's parents didn't know what a monster they'd bred because no one ever told them." Frowning once more, she said, "Although I doubt they'd have believed me if I'd told them."

"Probably not," agreed Marianne. "No one wants to believe their children are bad."

"True," said Diane. "I don't want to believe it, but I fear Gaylord and Vincent might take after their father in too many ways."

My ears perked up. Marianne poured tea and gave Diane and me a cup each. Diane reached for a piece of shortbread. I didn't, but only because I wanted to say, "Do you really think your sons are...not-very-good people, Mrs. Wagner?"

Diane chewed her cookie, took a sip of tea and gazed thoughtfully at me. "I...don't really know. I don't believe either one of them is as awful as their late father. However, I also don't believe either of them is...well, kind-hearted and generous, if you know what I mean."

I didn't, but I decided not to question her further about her sons. One ghastly question per day was my limit. I took a piece of shortbread, too, and nibbled an end. It was good, but nowhere near as good as Aunt Vi's Scotch shortbread, which she didn't make often enough to suit me. Mind you, if I didn't know I'd burn the house down, I'd have attempted to make it myself. Vi had told me often enough that Scotch shortbread is one of the easiest recipes a person can bake. That's unless you're talking about me as the cook. I could pretty much be guaranteed to mess up anything I attempted to create in the kitchen.

"I don't know," said Marianne musingly. "I don't believe Gaylord and Vincent are *bad* men. At least not bad like Father. They just...don't like to do anything for themselves. They prefer to be waited on. They told me often enough that they feared Father would lose all his money before they could inherit it." She shook her head as if in mystification.

Since no one in my family had ever inherited anything from any other member of my family—except for red hair and blue eyes, I mean—I could understand the Wagner sons' worry in theory, but it seemed pretty selfish to me. Heck, I'd been working since I was ten years old. I don't think either of the Wagner sons had ever worked a day in their lives.

Yet both Diane and Marianne knew their male kin better than I did. I hadn't been impressed by either of the Wagner sons the few times I'd met them, but neither of them had impressed me as actively evil, as had their father.

"I suppose that's because they grew up being waited on," said Diane with a sigh. She sipped more tea. "I wanted to be firmer with them, but their father ruled the roost." She shuddered slightly.

Reverting to the subject of the Wagners' El Molino house, I said, "But your home on El Molino really does look cheerful and inviting, Mrs. Wagner."

"Diane, please. Please don't call me Mrs. Wagner. It didn't take more than two or three weeks for me to understand I'd made a dreadful mistake in marrying that man, and I don't want his name. In fact, I'm going to get my name changed back to my maiden name, Chapman, as soon as possible. As for the house, yes. Doctor Wagner did allow me free rein when it came to the decorating and furnishing of that house, although, of course, he had to approve of the ideas before anything was done. He wanted to project a welcoming image, even though the image lied. That house carries with it horrible memories, and I can't wait to be shut of it forever."

With a sigh, Marianne said, "Yes. I have no good memories of life in that house either. It's a shame, because you're right, Daisy. It really does look cheerful and inviting. Talk about putting up a false front." She took a vicious bite of shortbread. "Still. It seems a shame to sell it after you've put so much work into it."

Mrs. Wagner only uttered a soft "huh" sound.

"I'm sorry," I told both women. "I know bad things happen in families. My own family life has been happy, and both of my parents are wonderful people."

"Yes, they are," said Diane. "And so are you." She gave me a warm smile.

Very well, I could feel heat sneak into my cheeks. One of the perils of having red hair is that it often comes with the problem of frequent blushes. "Oh, I don't know about that," I said, trying to pretend I wasn't turning hot.

"That's not true," said Marianne. "You saved my life. And I'm not exaggerating."

"Yes," said Diane Wagner. "You honestly did save Marianne's life." She clamped her mouth shut, and it looked to me as if it cost her some effort to open it in order to sip more tea.

Oh, dear. This appeared to be about the right time to probe. Still unsure how to go about it, I said, "Um...about that..." Hmm. What about that? Fah.

"What about that?" asked Marianne, speaking aloud my unspoken words. "It's the truth."

I plunged into the water. It might turn icy, or it might boil over, but I had to find out the answer to my evil-minded question. "Very well, I spoke with Doctor Benjamin yesterday, and Detective Rotondo spoke with Doctor William Ferdinand. Both doctors said Doctor Wagner had begun performing illegal abortions to make up for the loss of his legitimate business as patients turned to other doctors."

The two women's heads straightened, and they looked at each other for a tense moment. Then Diane let out a long sigh. "Yes. He had."

"And it wasn't a new procedure for him, either," said Marianne, her voice brittle. "I...I...I...Well, I don't want to talk about it." She bowed her head and lifted a napkin to her eyes, which I guess had begun to drip.

"I don't blame you for not wanting to talk about it, Marianne. But I do know one of the reasons you ran away from home was because your father...did...unspeakable things to you."

"He did that, all right," muttered Diane. "I..." Her voice trailed off.

"What Mother is trying to tell you is that when she attempted to intervene, he beat her almost to death. And then he still did unspeakable things to me."

"Um...Did any of those unspeakable things result in a..." Oh, good Lord. How to phrase the question so it didn't sound as repulsive and revolting as it was?

Marianne solved my problem for me. "Are you trying to ask if that monster impregnated me? Yes, he did. And then he aborted the unborn child. And...And I'll never be able to have children with George!"

After shakily setting her teacup on the tray, she broke down and sobbed as if her heart were broken. Diane left her chair to join her daughter on the sofa and threw her arms around her.

"I'm so sorry," I whispered, feeling lower than the roots of the four-o'clock plants that bloomed beside the back deck in our yard at home. I don't know if you've ever grown four-o'clocks, but in the spring and summertime, they bloom every afternoon around four o'clock—hence, their name—but their roots are almost impossible to dig up. They look like huge sweet potatoes, and they cling to the soil as if to life itself. Which, come to think of it, I guess is precisely what they *are* doing. Difficult plants, if fragrant. But they spread like crazy if you don't watch 'em and thin them out occasionally. That's how come I knew about their troublesome roots.

Got off-subject again. I'm sorry, but the subject is so horrifying, can you blame me?

Anyway, back to that unhappy living room.

"I *hated* him!" declared Marianne through her tears.

"So did I," her mother declared right afterward.

"So did I," I said, still whispering. "I can't even imagine what your life was like. Either of your lives."

"I wish I *had* killed him!" said Marianne, her words wobbly. "If anyone deserved to die, he did."

"I wish I'd had the nerve to kill him, too," said Diane. "But I was a coward. A *damned* coward." I got the impression she hadn't cursed very often, if at all, in her life until that day. "To do that to his own daughter! He deserved to suffer. I hope whoever killed him made him suffer before they put him out of his misery."

"*His* misery?" said Marianne, trying for a bitter laugh and almost achieving it. "*Our* misery is more like it."

"So true," said Diane, sobbing along with her daughter now.

I felt like a rat, and I wasn't sure what to do. Get up and leave? No. That would be cowardly. Which I was, but…Oh, dear.

"I'm so sorry," I repeated. Weak, Daisy Gumm Majesty; extremely weak.

Then, because I'd started the problem, I took my life in my hands and joined the two women on the sofa. Putting a hand on one each of their heaving shoulders, I said, "I sincerely apologize for unearthing ugly memories. I understand from Detective Rotondo that the police now know Doctor Wagner was performing illegal abortions. And many women, according to Doctors Benjamin and Ferdinand, were as cruelly hurt as you were, Marianne. I'm glad Doctor Wagner is dead, too. I'm only sorry it took this long for someone to do him in."

To my astonishment, both women turned and threw their arms around me. It was a rather uncomfortable situation for yours truly, being nearly smothered by emotion-wracked females, but I deserved worse than that.

"No, no!" cried Marianne. "I'm *glad* you know! People *need* to know what a horrible person he was. Mother suffered with him far longer than I did."

"I should have left him," muttered Diane into my shoulder. "I was *such* a coward."

"Nonsense," I said. "You know he'd have found and killed you if you'd attempted to get away from him." Thinking of a situation in which I'd found myself—Sam would say I'd hurled myself into it, but he's wrong—a couple of months prior, I said, "There are too many men like him, and there aren't enough laws to control them. Anyway, half the time the police don't even *care*! It's a terrible problem."

Thinking of my darling fiancé, who actually *did* care about stuff like that, although he claimed he couldn't do anything about it, I amended my previous statement slightly. "At least, most policemen turn a blind eye upon what happens behind a family's doors. Not all of them, but the ones who *do* care have their hands tied when trying to take care of problems like Doctor Wagner."

"I know," sniffled Marianne.

"That's true," added Diane, sniffling in her own right.

"Detective Rotondo would like to line all the men who hurt women up against a wall and shoot them."

If Sam ever found out I'd said such a thing, he'd probably stand *me* up against a wall, although I doubt he'd shoot me. I could already hear his most deadly tone in my head though. Sam didn't have to raise his voice to inspire terror in a person's heart. Trust me about this. That tone had even quelled his rotten nephew's more grievous tendencies. Most of the time.

"I know." Marianne pulled away from me, crumpled her napkin in her fist and swiped at her face as if she wanted to rub off her features. I cringed in sympathy with her soft-as-silk skin. "You were the first person besides Mother who ever knew the least little thing about that man, and you saved me."

With a couple of sniffles of her own, Diane pulled away from me, too, and said, "Yes, and I'll be forever grateful to you for it."

"I...don't deserve your thanks. Really. I just couldn't send Marianne back to such a situation."

"Other people wouldn't have bothered to help me," said Marianne, still sniffling. "Except for you, that kind Mr. Kincaid and George were the only people who cared about why I ran away from home and assisted me. I don't know what would have happened to me if you hadn't. Or Mother. That man literally held her captive. As his personal slave."

"Yes, he did. But oh, what he did to you was so much worse."

I agreed with both women, but I had to know one more thing. I didn't want to ask my next question either, but I did.

"Um...Have you told George about what your father did to you and what the result was?" I asked Marianne, hoping she'd say no, although that wouldn't speak highly of her character. Still, it was an embarrassing and humiliating admission to make to the person who wanted you by his side for his life. Then again, he probably deserved to know. Still, if George had wanted children...

Oh, boy, I wished I were out of that house!

But Marianne surprised me. Stiffening her spine, she said firmly, "Yes. I had to tell him the truth, because I loved him. He loved me, but he deserved a wife who was…a whole woman. If he wanted children, he'd have had to look elsewhere." She turned her face away from both her mother and me, and I understood. What an unspeakable thing to have to tell a man with whom one wanted to start a family. But Marianne had spoken the unspeakable, and I thought highly of her for doing so.

"That must have been hard to do," I said. It was more of a whisper, actually.

"It was. But it wouldn't have been fair to George if I hadn't told him."

"And God bless him, he said he only loved Marianne more for confessing the hideous truth to him!" said Diane, beginning to drip tears again.

I handed her a clean hankie. I'd brought extras with me because I'd anticipated tears—providing I gathered enough courage to ask my snoopy questions. By that time I was glad I had, but I still felt mighty uncomfortable.

"Yes," said Marianne, sniffling herself. "George was absolutely wonderful."

"He's a good man," said I, knowing the statement, while true, was weaker than a newborn kitten. "A very good man."

"The best," agreed Marianne.

I didn't know about that—I preferred my gruff and grumpy Sam to the staid and well-read George Grenville—but I allowed Marianne her prejudice. George Grenville must stand in her life as a golden idol. And he was, to her. I admired him.

I admired them all: Diane, Marianne and George. Mind you, Marianne and George had nearly driven me 'round the bend at the time during which I attempted to rescue her, but they'd improved upon further acquaintanceship. In fact, George had actually stood up to Marianne's wicked father right there in his book store while Billy and I were present. I'd squashed the awful man's hat flat, but that was nothing compared to what he deserved. At the time I didn't fully understand precisely what he deserved. I understood it all now, however, and I, too, hoped he'd suffered before he'd died.

That's not very nice of me, but it's the truth.

Dr. Wagner had been a poisonous man, and he'd poisoned his whole family. Not to mention the lives of countless other people. I'm not sure why no one had ever sued him for malpractice. I suspect it had something to do with the shame of having one's family's dirty linen aired in public. Such a lawsuit would be obscene and scandalous, and everyone tried to avoid scandal. I would never reproach anyone for that, but silence in some cases meant evil people like Dr. Wagner got away with far too many devilish deeds.

Heck, Fatty Arbuckle's career had been ruined, and he hadn't done anything wrong except preside over a drunken party in San Francisco. He'd been acquitted of murdering that poor girl whose name I can't remember by three separate juries, but his career in the pictures was over.

Which just went to show once again, if more proof were needed, that life was completely unfair.

Dr. Wagner had got what he deserved, but he'd received his deserts far too many years after his iniquitous career had begun. Heck, he was a lot older than Fatty Arbuckle, and he'd done far worse things than the comic actor, but he'd lived into his fifties—I'm guessing there—and that was at least thirty years more than he'd deserved.

Eventually I managed to pry myself away from the Wagner women—well, I mean Diane Chapman and her daughter, Marianne Grenville. I applauded them for wanting to drop the "Wagner" part of their names like hot coals as soon as they possibly could.

And now I knew for sure that both George and Marianne had excellent motives for murdering Marianne's father.

Bother. I hate when things like that happen.

FOURTEEN

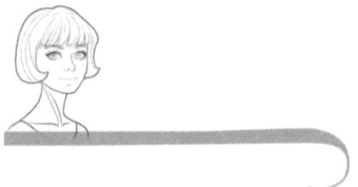

However, there wasn't much I could do about the truth, and I knew I had to tell Sam what Marianne and Diane had revealed to me.

I didn't want to. Sam would surely be convinced George did in the evil doctor because of what the doc had done to George's beloved wife. I still didn't think so. I simply couldn't make myself believe either George or Marianne would do such a thing as beat Dr. Wagner over the head several times with a blunt object. They weren't violent types. Besides, the evil doctor must have splattered his killer with a ton of blood, and I had a feeling Marianne—and maybe even George—would shrink and faint from the sight of so much blood.

Or maybe one or the other of them *had* murdered the beast. Or maybe they'd even been in cahoots with each other. I'd been wrong about people before. Far too often for my own personal comfort.

Sam sat in his office at the Pasadena Police Department, frowning down at a mess of papers on his desk when I walked through the door, making the heads of all the officers sharing the room lift their heads, gaze my way, and grin. They always did that, and it always embarrassed me. Nevertheless, I knew it to be my duty to tell Sam what I'd learned. I'd decided to visit him right after I left the Grenville place before I ran out of courage and decided to keep the women's secrets…well, secret. So I sat in the chair beside his desk and, in spite of his frown, told him what I'd just learned. I did so in a whisper so no one else would hear me.

Sam sighed heavily before he said, "That gives the three of them the best motive for the man's murder I've heard so far," he muttered. I got the impression he didn't like admitting it any more than I did.

"I still don't think any of the three of them did it."

Lifting his head, he gazed into my baby blues with his black-olive eyes. "And why is that? Because you like them? People other people like do bad things all the time. You must have figured that out by this time, what with you stumbling over corpses all the time."

"Stop blaming me for finding bodies, darn you, Sam Rotondo."

"I'm not blaming you for the crimes themselves. You're just sort of…I don't know. You're like a magnet for dead bodies or some-thing. The Typhoid Mary of crime."

"I am not." But we'd been over that same ground countless times—which might possibly mean he was right. "Anyhow, you're going to have to find some kind of proof that anybody did it, and I'll bet you can't, at least for Marianne, Diane and George. I mean, say George and Marianne were in it together. Which one wielded the blunt instrument? George? He's probably not strong enough to whack a person that hard, and neither is Marianne."

"If Mr. Grenville hit the man enough times, he probably could have caved in his skull."

My nose wrinkled of its own accord. "Wouldn't Doctor Wagner have objected?"

"Who knows? Maybe Grenville drugged him."

"Nerts. Supposing George *did* manage to overcome the evil doctor and batter him to death, then what happened? Did he and Marianne dump Wagner's body in the back of George's Cadillac and drive it to Mountain View?"

"Somebody did," said Sam doggedly. In fact, he often reminded me of Spike, who never gave up on a scent.

"Well, don't stop looking for suspects just because George and Marianne and Marianne's mother have a motive. According to Doctors Benjamin and Ferdinand, they were far from the only people in Pasadena with good, if not better, motives to do in Doctor Wagner."

"True. But I don't know any of the other people's names."

"That's no excuse for quitting."

"I'm not quitting," Sam said. "But I don't have a lot to work with here."

"Hmm. I suppose not." Something occurred to me. It had probably occurred to Sam a couple of days prior to that moment, but I figured I'd ask anyway. "Did you find Doctor Wagner's records somewhere? I mean, did he keep records of his patients and procedures?"

"Probably. Our men are still searching the house. We only found the body a day and a half ago, you know, and the judge signed the search warrant yesterday."

"It seems like longer ago than that."

Sam shook his head. "I know, but it wasn't."

I looked up to take a peek at the clock hanging on the wall near Sam's desk, but it seemed to have stopped at five o'clock on one day or another. "What time is it anyway? Do you know?"

Sam bent his left arm at the elbow, shook his coat and shirt sleeve down, and squinted at the wristwatch he wore. "Need my reading glasses, curse it. But it looks like eleven forty-five."

"Is that too early for lunch?"

After peering from his watch to me and staring for a second or two, Sam said, his tone of voice suspicious, "Why?"

"I'm inviting you to lunch, you big oaf! If your leg can stand it, we can walk to the Crown City Chop Suey Parlor up the street. My treat."

Sam thought over my invitation for approximately two and a half seconds, shrugged, and said, "Sure. Why not? I'll even let you pay."

"Thank you."

"You're welcome." He rose to his feet, pressing hard on his desk to take as much weight as possible off his left leg. Raising his voice slightly, he said to the room at large, "Going to lunch. Back in a bit."

The rest of the men in the room, most of whom I knew by sight if not by name, all grinned at the two of us.

"Take your time," called one of them.

"Have a good time," another one said.

"Will do," said Sam with a grin of his own. He snagged his hat from the coat tree right next to the office door, slapped it on his head, and we left the station, Sam's cane tapping as he walked.

"How's your leg today?" I asked, peering with concern at the implement he wielded. I was beginning to worry about Sam's slow recovery.

"It's better. Still hurts. Helps if I stay off it."

Feeling guilty, I said, "I should have parked the Chevrolet in front of the station so you wouldn't have had to walk up the block."

"Nuts. A little exercise is good for it. Doc Benjamin said so."

"I hope so. I should get more exercise than I do, too. Walking Spike around a few blocks with Pa in the morning doesn't pump up the old muscles much."

"Yeah, but you do laundry and clean house and so forth. That gives you plenty of exercise."

"Maybe."

But I didn't want to talk about exercise. I wanted to talk about Dr. Wagner's murder. Since I wasn't totally insane—yet—I waited until we were seated in a snug corner of the Chinese restaurant up the street from the police department and had placed our orders before I brought up the subject. I loved Chinese food. Still do, for that matter.

"All right, Sam, what's happened so far? Have you talked any further with the two sons? Do their alibis hold up?"

His eyebrows dipping like a fuzzy V over his eyes, Sam said, "I'm the copper here, not you. I'm the one who's supposed to ask the questions, not you."

"That's unfair, Sam! We're in this one together. Even *you* said so. You even asked me to talk to people."

"All right, all right. We're still checking everyone's alibis, including the sons'. I don't know anything at this point." As if he begrudged saying so, he added, "I appreciate the information you gave me at the station."

"You're welcome. I didn't want to tell you because I knew you'd jump to the conclusion that George or Marianne or Diane—or all three of them—did the dirty deed. Dirty only insofar as the scene of the crime was muddy. Whoever did in that horrible man deserves a medal or a lot of money. Or both."

"Vindictive little thing, aren't you?"

"If vindictive means I think he got what he deserved, then yes, I am. He was a foul, degenerate, despicable creature. I'd rather deal with a rattlesnake than a person like that. He doesn't deserve to be called a man."

Not that I held a grudge or anything.

With a grin, Sam said, "Not that you hold a grudge or anything."

I laughed. "If anyone deserved to have a grudge held against him, it was that detestable doctor."

"I agree."

Our food arrived, and we both dug in. I especially loved the spare ribs.

When the first pangs of our hunger had been dulled, I said, "I'm holding that séance tonight at Mrs. Frasier's house. If I learn anything from the gathering, I'll tell you as soon as I can."

"Wonderful. I can hardly wait to hear what your precious spirit control tells you tonight."

"Don't be mean, Sam. It's not my fault the Ouija board did something without me directing it."

"Huh."

I gnawed a bit of meat from my sparerib, annoyed at my beloved. "It's not," I insisted after I swallowed.

"Right."

I gave up. However, lunch was good, and I actually paid the bill, even though Sam tried to wrest it away from me. But I liked to keep my word, and I'd invited him, darn it!

Dinner at the Gumm-Majesty house that night was good, if not quite as spectacular as it had been the night before. Vi had made a lovely beef-and-noodle soup using left-over rib roast and vegetables. She made some delicious cornbread to eat with it. I adored Vi's cornbread slathered with butter and drizzled with honey.

"Wonderful, Vi," said Sam, discreetly slurping soup. He didn't make any slurping noises; sorry if I gave that impression. He was a tidy diner.

"Especially on such a cold night," said Ma.

"Thank you," said Vi. "Just leftovers."

"Not *just* leftovers," said I. "You made a wonderful whole new meal from the leftovers. That takes talent. Definitely more talent than I possess."

"We all know about you and the war between you and the kitchen," said Pa, chuckling.

He was right, darn it.

At any rate, dinner was delicious. Since I had to work that evening, Sam helped me with the dishes, and then he took off for home. So Spike and I inspected my closet for séance-worthy attire. There was a whole lot of it jammed into the closet, thanks to my adoration of sewing and need for suitable business costumes. At least that's my excuse for my somewhat extravagant wardrobe, and so far nobody's quibbled with me about it. Heck, I earned the money I spent on fabric and notions, and there was plenty left over for household expenses. I also made clothes for everyone else in the household.

Does it sound as though I'm trying to justify my too-many clothes? Guess I am, although inside, I *know* there's no need to apologize for it. Really. Honestly.

Oh, never mind.

Eventually Spike and I decided on a fairly new gown I'd made of dark green satin. It had long sleeves and very little decoration. The skirt was asymmetrical, falling to ankle-length from an embroidered patch on the right hip. The rest of the skirt varied from that one fall of fabric to a discreet six inches above my ankles. Tasteful. I always attempted to be tasteful in both my attire and my demeanor.

The dress's material was shiny and quite lovely—and marvelously inexpensive thanks to Maxime's year-end sale of fall and winter fabrics and colors. I'd bought it in late December of 1923, so the fabric was about a year old, but the gown itself was a new creation. It went stunningly well with the emerald engagement ring Sam had given me and which his father, who owned a jewelry store in New York City, had designed. I had to hide my juju in my handbag, but I kept the bag with me. Not that I believed in the overall good-luck-giving capabilities of Voodoo jujus, but it couldn't hurt to carry it with me, could it?

After I'd fixed my makeup—pale powder with a mere touch of mascara on my eyelashes and a wee bit of pencil on my eyebrows—I looked pretty darned good if I do say so myself. I'd brushed my hair into a sleeker bob than usual, using a dab of Columbia Grease-less Hair Cream; and decided to be daring and use the skinny green hair band I'd created out of leftover green satin studded with golden sequins I'd bought at Nelson's Five and Dime. It looked quite elegant when I kind of wove it into my dark red bob, and I was impressed. Heck, the total cost of creating the hair band had been about three cents. I tell you, I might not be good for much, but I was a heck of a good seamstress and spiritualist-medium.

Once I'd donned my séance costume, put on my black pumps and grabbed my handbag—into which I'd put my juju—I shook out the black, crushed-velvet cape, the fabric for which I'd snagged at a junk sale at church. I think it used to be someone's ball gown in the 1890s or thereabouts—and threw it over my shoulders. Then I walked to the living room and made a grand entrance, which would have been grander if Vi hadn't already gone up to bed.

"So, how do I look?" I asked my mother and father, twirling in front of them.

"Beautiful, sweetheart," said Pa, bless him.

"My goodness, Daisy, you really do look wonderful. I don't think I've ever seen you wear your hair quite like that," said Ma.

"No, you haven't. I tried to press out its waves with a little hair tonic. And I've never used a hair band before. Do you like it? I feel kind of like Anna May Wong, only with red hair and not so much money."

"Who's Anna May Wong?" asked Ma.

"You don't know who Anna May Wong is?" I asked my mother, awed.

"Heck, even *I* know who Anna May Wong is," said Pa.

"She must be famous," said Ma.

"Very," said I. "She's a movie star. She's Chinese, so her hair is black. And her hair is straight, and I can't make mine go completely straight. Heck, Ma, she starred in *The Thief of Baghdad*, with Douglas Fairbanks! We saw that movie at the Crown."

"Hmm. Now that you mention it, I guess I do vaguely recall that picture. Oh, now I know what you mean about looking like her. She has a bob!"

I love my mother. "Precisely," I said.

"Wasn't she the very first woman to cut her hair like that?"

"No, I think that was Irene Castle."

"I think I've heard of her."

Laughing, I said, "I'm sure you have. She and her late husband, Vernon, were famous ballroom dancers."

"Oh," said Ma, clearly at sea. My mother didn't follow fashions in either pictures or dancing. Good thing I did it for her, or she'd still be wearing those long, lumpy dresses women wore in her youth.

"I'm sure you look better than either Irene Castle or Anna May Wong," said my staunch and loyal father. "Even if you don't make as much money as they do."

"Thanks, Pa. I do try to look as good as possible for my clients. And heck, my job is kind of like an actress's. In a way."

"You do it very well, according to all reports," said Pa. "Too bad Sam isn't here to see you."

I agreed with him, although I only said, "Pooh. He wouldn't even notice."

But he would have. And he'd have approved. I was sorry I hadn't asked him to come to the evening's séance. Oh, well. A girl can't think of everything, can she?

FIFTEEN

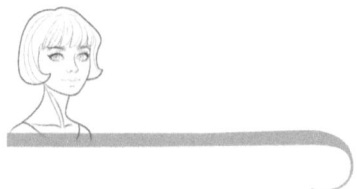

I arrived at Mrs. Frasier's Orange Grove estate at about seven-thirty that night. The séance was scheduled to begin at eight, and I wanted to be sure I had the séance room arranged the way I wanted it to be.

At the most, I allow eight people to attend my séances. More people than that can become unruly. Or, if not actually unruly, at least not as quiet as they should be. Mind you, I've never yet presided over a completely silent séance, no matter that I always tell the attendees to sit still and be quiet. Somebody always shuffles, sneezes, moans, groans, or scrapes his or her chair across the floor. In the case of Mrs. Frasier's home, the room in which the séance would be held had a gorgeous Oriental rug under the table, so chair-scrapes were unlikely. The rest of the noises would probably occur, however.

Mrs. Frasier's butler, a fellow named Cruikshank, admitted me to the house and showed me to the drawing room. Most of the rich people for whom I worked had drawing rooms instead of the plain old living rooms with which the rest of us mere mortals had to deal. There I go, being snide again. So sorry.

One of the first people I spotted in the drawing room was Diane

Chapman. Very well, she wasn't Diane Chapman yet, but she hated the Wagner name so much, I was letting her use it before the court said it was all right. Nice of me, huh?

I headed for her chair but was intercepted by Mrs. Pinkerton before I reached my goal. Only then did it occur to me that I hadn't heard from Mrs. P since Monday! Good heavens, was the world coming to an end?

"Daisy!" she shrieked. She was a big shrieker, Mrs. P. "It's so good to see you. I've missed you these past couple of days. I do so hope you can help Diane and Marianne this evening."

"So do I," I said, my voice registering its soft, spiritualistic tone, hoping it might make an impression and Mrs. P would speak more quietly. Didn't work. I'd expected that.

Clapping a hand to her bountiful bosom, Mrs. Pinkerton bellowed—very well, so I just exaggerated again—"I just *know* you'll be able to solve this thing." Finally lowering her voice—thank heaven—she added, "Not that I want it to be solved. The man was so horrid, whoever did him in deserves a reward."

That seemed to be the general sentiment regarding the late, unlamented Dr. Everhard A. Wagner. It had been voiced by Mrs. Pinkerton more than once to my certain knowledge, and by pretty much everyone else I'd spoken to about his demise.

Luckily for me, Harold Kincaid appeared at his mother's side before she could drag me into a corner and monopolize me for the rest of the evening. "Daisy, my dear," said he. "Let me take you to see Diane and Marianne before the séance." Turning to his mother, he said, "You can chat with Daisy after the séance, Mother. Diane and Marianne need her now."

"Oh, of course! You're *such* a thoughtful son, Harold," tittered Mrs. Pinkerton.

With a smile, Harold hauled me away from his mother. Under his breath, he muttered, "Damned right, I'm thoughtful. Hell, *someone* in the family has to be."

"Stop saying funny stuff, Harold. I want to look like a spiritualist, and giggling doesn't match the image."

"That wasn't meant to be funny," said Harold. "It was the truth."

"I know. I'm sorry."

Harold didn't acknowledge my sympathy because we'd reached Diane's chair by then, and she'd been joined by Marianne. I smiled graciously at both women, who smiled graciously back at me. Diane's bruises still showed, but she'd managed to subdue them with powder. Marianne smiled shyly at Harold and me.

"How are the two of you this evening?" I said gently. "Well, I hope. I also hope this evening's séance will prove of benefit to you."

"I hope so, too," said Diane, taking my gloved hand in her right hand and covering it with her left. "You were of *such* comfort to me two years ago. I'll never forget how much hope you instilled in me at Griselda's séance."

Oh, boy. Two years prior, I'd had Rolly tell the poor woman that Marianne wasn't present on the so-called Other Side, which meant she was still alive. That particular séance had been held in Mrs. Bissel's house, the basement of which had been Marianne's hiding place until I found her there. I was glad to know Rolly's words had given Diane comfort, but I'd felt like a vile fraud ever since that night, as I knew full well Marianne had been, at the precise time I'd held the séance, hiding in the little cottage behind Grenville's Books.

Nevertheless, I said, still softly and soothingly, "I'm so glad."

"You saved my life back then," said Marianne, smiling at me. "And I'm grateful to you for helping Mother, too. And you didn't tell on me. I felt so bad for deceiving Mother." She gave a little sniffle and dabbed at her eyes with her hankie, which looked to me as if it had been used a time or two already.

"Harold and George did every bit as much as I did," I told them, lying nobly. Neither Harold nor George had wanted to get involved back then, but they'd been persuaded, bless them both. And then George had nearly driven me crazy by practically showing Marianne off in public. I'd had to speak severely to both George and Marianne, and they hadn't appreciated it until they realized why I'd been so adamant about keeping Marianne hidden. Golly, doing good deeds can give a person ulcers sometimes, can't it?

"Nonsense. You were the one who saved me," said Marianne.

"Well, I'm glad to have helped." Glancing around the room and discovering all of the séance attendees had arrived, I said, "But I must prepare the room for the séance now. I'm happy the two of you could come this evening."

"I have no one in my life who can dictate what I can and can't do anymore," said Diane, her smile nearly triumphant. "I had to go against my late husband's wishes to attend that one séance at Griselda's house."

"I'm sorry you had to go through that, Mother."

"It was worth every blow, just to know you were still alive, darling."

Every blow? Good Lord, did she mean her detestable husband had beaten her up for attending my séance? The man was rising to the status of Jack the Ripper in my mind. I wouldn't have felt guilty if I'd murdered him myself. On the other hand, I did feel guilty about Diane having braved his wrath in order to attend one of my phony séances. Hmm. Maybe I'd quit the spiritualist business after Sam and I got married.

Or maybe I wouldn't.

"But now the big bad wolf in both of our lives is gone," said Marianne, laughing softly. Her laugh sounded slightly strained to me. Poor thing.

After bidding the two women *adieu*, I walked over to Mrs. Frasier, a tall, lean woman, who was at that moment entertaining Mrs. Bissel by showing her some of the tricks she'd taught her miniature pinscher, Percy. Percy had once disemboweled my handbag and stolen a hankie therefrom, but I liked him anyway. At the moment, Percy was standing on his hind legs and waving his paws at Mrs. Bissel, who beamed down upon him.

"He's adorable, Laura. Just adorable. Although, as you know, I'm partial to dachshunds." Mrs. Bissel noticed me and said, "Oh, but it's Daisy! She has one of my dachshunds. What's more, she took it to the Pasanita Obedience Club's obedience class, and he did wonderfully!"

"How do you do, Mrs. Bissel? Mrs. Frasier. I see Percy is doing well." I leaned down to pet the frenetic little beast. He was a cutie, if a trifle too bouncy for me.

"Percy is doing superbly, Daisy. Thank you. Oh, and do you know what I just learned?"

I hadn't a clue, so I shook my head, still smiling.

"The AKC has just recognized miniature pinschers as a distinct breed! They'll be able to enter the Westminster Kennel Club Dog Show in February!"

"How wonderful for you," I said, thinking it must be nice to be rich and not have to think about anything but taking dogs to various dog shows.

"It is wonderful," agreed Mrs. Bissel. "Of course, *dachshunds* were recognized by the AKC in 1885." She sounded a trifle smug.

"That may be true, but min pins have been around for just as long as dachshunds. It's only that they weren't brought to the USA until later than dachshunds." Mrs. Frasier sniffed. "And *I* think they're the perfect breed."

"They're both delightful breeds," I said, trying to avert a war of words between the two dog breeders. If I were being honest, I'd have to say I preferred dachshunds to miniature pinschers, but honesty and my job didn't always go together, so I didn't. "However, I need to be sure the séance room is set up properly, Mrs. Frasier. May I do that now, please? I'll need a few minutes to collect myself after that."

"Oh, yes, dear. Of course," said Mrs. Frasier. "I understand you need to compose your mind to receive messages from your spirit control."

"Indeed," said Mrs. Bissel. "That's very important."

Right. It sure was.

Oh, dear, there I go again with the sarcasm. I'm sorry. I loved my clients; I really did. Just because I thought they were…well, kind of silly for believing the stuff I told them didn't mean they weren't nice folks.

"Here, dear. Let me show you the room." Mrs. Frasier gestured to Percy to come with us, and he heeled as if he'd been trained *almost* as well as Spike. "You probably remember it from the last séance you conducted here, but Percy and I will just take you there. Then you can let me know if there's anything you need."

"Thank you." I shook Mrs. Bissel's hand and leaned in to whisper, "I like dachshunds better than min pins, too, but please don't tell Mrs. Frasier."

Mrs. Bissel burst out laughing. Of all my clients, she was the most down-to-earth. Even if she was richer than Croesus, whoever he was. One of those old Greek guys, I think.

At any rate, Percy, Mrs. Frasier and I walked down the hallway to the room designated for the séance. I told her how happy I was for her that miniature pinschers were at last getting their just recognition from the American Kennel Club.

"Thank you, dear. We min-pin people have worked so hard for this honor. It's rewarding to have our work acknowledged."

"I'm sure it is. If all min pins are like your Percy, they're charming."

Pleased, Mrs. Frasier said, "Well, of course, Percy is special, but the breed in and of itself is wonderful."

The breed, if Percy was an example, was a teensy bit exuberant for me. I preferred Spike's more relaxed view of life and the world. Naturally, I didn't tell Mrs. Frasier that.

Opening the door to the séance room—I think it was a den or something during its every-day life—Mrs. Frasier said, "Here you go. I set the table up with the one cranberry-glass candle holder the way you like. If you need anything else, just ring for Cruikshank. He'll be at your bidding this evening."

Poor Cruikshank. Not that I aimed to overwork him. All he'd have to do was turn off the lights at the beginning of the séance and then turn them on again at the end of it.

"Thank you very much. I'll sit and meditate for a few minutes now."

Mrs. Frasier peered at what looked to me to be a solid-gold wristwatch on her slender wrist. "It's ten minutes until eight, so will that give you enough time?"

"That will be perfect. Thank you."

"Thank *you*. We're all so hoping the spirits will be able to direct us to the person who killed that terrible man. If we even want to know. We're all so happy he's gone, it might be better if we never find out."

"Yes. I've heard that same sentiment from several people since his body was found," said I, thinking that, no matter what happened during or after the séance, I would have to make a full report to Sam Rotondo. At that point, I wasn't sure I wanted to, especially if I did accidentally learn the name of the killer.

Unless, of course, the killer turned out to be someone I disliked. Then I'd have no trouble at all blabbing to Sam.

Bother. I'd have to tell Sam whatever I learned. Providing I learned anything, and since I was a fake, the likelihood of that was slim.

I felt better after I'd come to that conclusion.

Anyhow, I spent the next ten minutes sitting in the chair at the head of the table, which was oval—oval and round tables are my favorites at which to conduct séances because people seemed to fit better around them than at square tables—and was, I hoped, looking mysterious and spiritual when the séance attendees filed in.

They took their cue from my own demeanor, and what little chit-chat had been going on prior to their reaching the door stopped as soon as they entered. My head was bowed when they arrived, but I lifted it as soon as I'd counted enough footsteps so as to believe everyone who was supposed to be there was. There, I mean.

I gave the assembled guests one of my patented mysterious, spiritualistic smiles and said in my gentlest and most mystical spiritualist's voice, "There's no arranged seating. Please sit anywhere you like around the table." I added the "around the table" clause in case some wit said he or she wanted to sit on the table or in the corner or on top of the china cabinet something. I tried to avoid silly stuff like that. Heck, the whole notion of a séance was silly; it didn't need help.

So, as quietly as a small herd of people can be, they pulled out chairs, sat, and drew their chairs to the table. They all looked at me kind of like sheep, except for Harold, who knew I was a fake and honored my ability to keep my performance at its peak level at all time. Well, most of the time.

I don't mean to boast, but I really was good at my job.

Softly and sweetly, I said, "Please take hands."

Everyone took his or her neighbor's hand. There really ought to be a gender-neutral singular pronoun in the English language—aside from the word "it," which refers to non-human things. I hope someone will invent one someday.

Then I nodded to Cruikshank to switch off the electrical lights. He did so, and we sat at the table, everyone gazing raptly at the red glow coming from the cranberry-glass candle holder in the middle of the table.

Again I bowed my head and sat still for a few minutes. This was in order to convince my spirit control, Rolly, to come to me. As soon as he supposedly did, I moaned softly and sagged ever so slightly in my chair.

So. The evening got off to its regular, time-honored, standard spiritualist-medium-séance start.

After that, things got weird.

SIXTEEN

The weirdness didn't happen all of a sudden. I was firmly into my act, and all the attendees were behaving just as they ought when Rolly greeted me. As ever, he called me his "love," since we were supposed to be soul mates through eternity.

Then I said to Rolly, "Rolly, a new soul has crossed to the Other Side recently. A gentleman named Doctor Everhard Allan Wagner passed only a few days ago."

"'Aye, my love, so he did. But he was no gentleman. He was a very bad man.'" I hadn't intended for Rolly to say that. It just slipped out.

Murmurs of approval from around the table let me know Rolly hadn't said anything wrong. Good. I always feared I might slip up.

"Rolly," said I, "Doctor Wagner was cruelly done to death, and we are gathered here to discover who did the deed."

In his best Scottish accent, Rolly said in a voice about an octave deeper than my usual speaking voice, "'Why would you want to do that, love?'"

I swear to heaven, I hadn't meant to say that either. A couple of soft chuckles from séance attendees didn't quell the jolt of shock that zipped through me.

Internally scolding myself—I honestly didn't know where that comment from Rolly had come from—I said, "The police are looking for his murderer. Whoever killed Doctor Wagner needs to be brought to justice."

"'And what is justice?'" said Rolly. Against my will. That darned voice of his just seemed to have taken hold of my vocal chords.

In order to give myself a bit of space in which to recover my poise, I let out a soft murmuring moan. Scrambling to get my wits together, I said, "Murder is a foul deed, Rolly. Whoever killed the man was wrong to have done so."

"'If you say so, my love. I think he should have been done in twenty or thirty years ago.'"

Curses! This had only happened to me once before, when the voice of a murdered fellow had come out of my mouth. I'd had no control over myself then, and I seemed to have no control over Rolly now. Blast and heck!

"Rolly," I said severely, "murder is a vile act and a criminal one. Do you know who killed Doctor Wagner?"

"'Oh, aye. I know.'"

Assorted gasps from the audience. I doubt anyone heard my own personal gasp, which slipped out past my guard. But doggone it, Rolly *never* got out of my control! Well, except for the case of Eddie Hastings, the above-mentioned murdered fellow. If the voice of Dr. Wagner suddenly spouted from my mouth, I aimed to faint and end the séance right then and there. Well…I'd pretend to faint.

"You know who killed Dr. Wagner?" I tried not to sound as upset as I felt.

"'Oh, aye.'"

"Will you please tell us?"

After a small spate of silence, Rolly again spoke without my prompting. "'Ah, my love, I fear I canna do that.'"

"Why ever not?" I asked, even more severely.

"''Tisn't my job, my dear. Your police fellow needs to do that.'"

Almost jumping out of my skin at the catastrophe that seemed to be happening right there in the séance room, I asked, feeling pathetic and scared to death, "Can you at least give us a hint?" If that wasn't one of the stupidest questions I'd ever asked during a séance, I don't know what was. For Pete's sake, I was pleading with a fictitious spirit control I'd made up out of whole cloth when I was ten years old! And he kept saying things I didn't want to say and were against my volition.

"'Oh, aye. I can give you a hint.'"

Darn Rolly to heck and back! Why was he doing this to me? I'd *created* him, for pity's sake! I could jolly well un-create him, if this kept up.

"Well then," said I, yet more severely, "will you please do so?"

"'Oh, aye, if you wish it.'"

Damn him. Sorry for swearing. "Yes, Rolly, we wish it." I fear my voice was a trace harsh by that time.

"'My darling girl, the best hint I can give you is to look to the family.'"

Four or five people gasped.

Diane Chapman said, "Oh, dear God!"

Marianne Grenville fainted.

So, not knowing what else to do, I fainted too. My own personal faint was only partially fake. My wits were scrambled like morning eggs, and I felt as if my entire life had plummeted out of control. Therefore, I moaned piteously, slumped in my chair, my eyes fluttered shut, and I was so befuddled, I didn't even give Cruikshank the signal to turn on the lights.

I do believe Harold Kincaid took control of events at that point, because when I groggily attempted to straighten myself in my chair, I saw him attending to Marianne. Diane hovered at his side, clasping her hands to her bosom as if in prayer, and watching her daughter as if she feared Marianne might have had a heart seizure or something of that nature.

As for me, I wanted to fold my arms on the table, bury my head in them, and burst out crying. I'd never felt so awful in my life, except for when Billy died.

Several minutes later, I sat beside Harold Kincaid at the séance table, and the two of us were alone in the room. Harold had told Cruikshank to get the rest of the séance attendees out of there and call a doctor to see to Marianne. Cruikshank and another of Mrs. Frasier's minions had carried Marianne out of the room, and I didn't know what they'd done with her until later.

Shaking all over, I said, "I-I-I don't know what h-happened, Harold."

"Good God, Daisy, 'look to the family'? What was that about?"

"I-I don't *know*! I swear, Harold, I don't know why Rolly said that!" I began crying, feeling like an imbecile and wishing I were dead.

Frowning at me, Harold said, "Are you serious?"

"*Yes*! Yes, I'm serious! It was like...like that awful time when Eddie Hastings spoke through me. I hated it then, and I hate it now. Only this was *Rolly*! Oh, Harold, Rolly doesn't even exist!"

Later, I was glad Harold had thought to shut the door to the séance room because if he hadn't, other people might have heard my confession, and then my career would have been kaput, my credibility would be shattered, my entire family humiliated, and we'd have had to move to Massachusetts or maybe Outer Mongolia. We'd probably have been run out of Pasadena, tarred and feathered, on a rail. Not sure what people meant when they said someone was run out of town on a rail, but if Harold hadn't been wise enough to shut that door, I fear I'd have learned.

"Perhaps you need a rest, sweetie. After all, you found a body and have been dealing with my mother and the late doctor's family quite often recently. I think the myriad strains are getting to you." He patted my back and handed me a clean handkerchief. My own hankie was more than soggy by then.

"Th-thank you."

"You're welcome."

He sat silent for a while as I attempted to get my tears to dry up. At last I hiccupped and made one last swipe under my eyes, hoping my lightly applied mascara hadn't run down my cheeks.

Finally Harold said, "That's interesting, though, about 'looking to the family.' If what you're telling me is true—"

"It *is*!" I cried, feeling as though my last friend on earth had deserted me.

He patted me on the back again. "Don't be upset. I believe you. It's just...difficult to comprehend that it really happened."

"You're telling *me*. I almost died when I heard what was coming out of my mouth."

"Very strange," said he.

"Very," I agreed.

"But do you really think a member of Wagner's family might have done him in?"

"How the heck should *I* know?" I nearly burst into tears again. "It was Rolly who said that. I had no control over him. Oh, Lord, Harold, that's never happened before."

"Well...There was the Eddie Hastings séance."

"Yes, but that wasn't Rolly speaking. It was Eddie Hastings speaking through me. Rolly is my own personal invention, and he's never been beyond my control before tonight."

"Hmm. I don't blame you for being upset."

"Thank you a whole lot."

"Hey, Rolly isn't my fault."

"I know. I know. I'm sorry, Harold, but I feel *so* awful about what he—I—oh, whoever said it—said."

"I know, sweetie. Wish I knew what to do to help."

"You're doing it by remaining my friend, even in the face of this...catastrophe."

"I don't know if the séance qualifies as a catastrophe—"

"It does!"

"Then I'm sorry. And I remain your friend through thick and thin. Don't forget that I shot a man for you once."

"How could I ever forget that?" We'd been in Turkey, and Harold had only shot the man because we were attempting to rescue Sam Rotondo from some bad guys. Harold had been a true hero then, and he was a true friend now.

I told him so.

"Hmm. If you say so. I'd rather comfort you than shoot anyone else."

"I appreciate you for wanting to do both."

"Of course. What are friends for? Not that I wanted to shoot that guy, but..."

"I know. You did it because you had to."

Harold shuddered as he remembered that day near the shore of the Bosphorus Strait.

"I wish I could be of some use to you, Harold, but it always seems to be you who's rescuing me for one reason or another."

"Yes. I've noticed that."

"Oh, Harold, I'm so sorry!" I started weeping again. Pitiful. I was truly and disgustingly pitiful.

"Oh, for crying out loud, Daisy Majesty, drain the damned swamp and quit blubbering!" Harold actually shook me.

In doing so, he jostled the tears right out of me. I sniffled, wiped my eyes with his handkerchief again and said, "Thanks, Harold. I needed that."

"So did I. I've never known you to be so weepy, Daisy. If you keep it up, you'll remind me of Mother, and that will never do."

I almost smiled, but couldn't quite drum up a smile even for Harold that evening.

"Thanks again, Harold."

"You're welcome."

Because I knew I had to rise and face the music—or at least the séance attendees—soon, I asked, "Do I have makeup smears running down my cheeks?"

Peering at me critically, Harold said, "Not really, but I'd better do a touch-up job."

"You can do that? I don't have anything with me."

"Have any face powder?"

"Um...Yes. It's in my handbag, which is...I don't know where it is. Oh, Lord, Harold! My life is over!"

"Stop being so melodramatic, Daisy! Just stop it right this minute."

"All right," I said meekly. I didn't want to antagonize the person who might well be my last friend on earth.

"Good. Is this your handbag?" He picked up a small black bag from the table near where I'd been sitting.

"Yes." *Sniffle.* "I know I fool people for a living, Harold, but I honestly didn't intend Rolly to say any of those things." Another sniffle smote the air wetly.

"Yes, yes. You've told me that seven hundred times already. Stop overacting and sit still while I see what I can do to fix you," he commanded.

So, rather like Spike, only much meeker than my confident and obedient hound, I sat still while Harold wiped my cheeks with another hankie and daubed powder over my face. He frowned critically at me. "We're going to have to do something about those eyes."

"My eyes?" My right hand flew to one of them. "What's wrong with my eyes?"

"Swollen and red," said he. "But never fear. I have a solution. Just sit there for a few minutes. I'll be right back."

"Don't leave me!"

He rolled his eyes. I swear, he and Sam reminded me *so* much of each other sometimes. "Just sit there and be still. And stop whining, for God's sake."

Whining? Was I whining?

Shoot, I guess I was. I told myself to get a grip on my emotions. I was the best spiritualist-medium in Pasadena; all of my clients said so. Complete strangers had called me at home and told me they'd heard as much from some of those very same clients. Falling apart was definitely *not* part of my act.

As I waited in Mrs. Frasier's former séance room, I straightened my shoulders and told myself to buck up. I reminded myself that strange things happened occasionally. *Remember those waving pine trees in your crystal ball?* I asked myself. I nodded. Indeed, I did remember those stupid pine trees in my stupid crystal ball. I also remembered the terrifying time the late Eddie Hastings' voice had emanated from my own mouth. I guess, all things considered, this time wasn't as horrid as that time had been.

The door opened, and I realized I hadn't calmed down an iota when I jumped approximately twelve feet out of my chair, clapped a hand to my chest, and barely stopped myself before I screamed.

"Harold," I said, letting out a long, agonized sigh. "I'm *so* glad it's you."

"Who else would I be?" asked he, trotting to my chair and plunking himself down on the one next to it. Only then did I notice he carried a small bundle in his hands. "All right. Close your eyes and look at me."

"How can I look at you with my eyes closed?"

"Stop being so damned literal, Daisy Gumm Majesty! Turn your head so it's pointed toward me, shut your mouth and your eyes, and be still."

I obeyed without another word.

To this day, I'm not entirely sure what Harold did to me, but it involved ice, powder, and a soft rag. He worked on my face for I don't know how many minutes, but it seemed like hours. At last he sat back and said, "There."

"There what?"

"You may open your eyes now. You'll do fine, as long as you don't have hysterics when we join the rest of the group."

Only then did I recall we had another injured party or two in that group. I sucked in a gallon or so of air. "Oh, Lord, I forgot all about Marianne! How is she doing?"

"She's fine."

"Are you sure? Did an ambulance come for her?"

"No. She woke up and refused a doctor or an ambulance. She's still in the drawing room, and her mother and mine are hovering over her like buzzards."

"That's not a pleasant image, Harold Kincaid."

"How about fluttering like hummingbirds."

"Much better."

"Good. Now smile."

"I beg your pardon?"

"Smile, dammit! We have to go out there and beard the dragons.

I've told everyone the séance sapped your strength and it's taking a while for you to recover. So far I think they believe me."

"As well they should, because it did, and I did."

"I know, sweetie. Just don't project yourself as feeling robust. Pretend you're still all atremble at what your spirit control said."

"I don't have to act to do that. I *am* all atremble. I swear to God, Harold—"

"Yes, yes, I know. You didn't have any control of your control." He rolled his eyes again.

"It's the truth," I said, still pitiful.

"It's all right, dear. I believe you. And I'm a total skeptic. You'll have much better luck with the rest of the gang. So brace yourself. We're going to face the ravening horde. By the way, I don't know if I've told you yet, but that gown is stunning. Love the uneven hemline."

My gown? I looked down at same. Oh, yes. I remembered now what I'd donned for this wretched séance. I was glad Harold approved, although I didn't much care at that point. "Thank you."

"You're welcome. All right now. Here we go."

"Oh, Lord," I whimpered.

"Buck up, dammit!"

His harsh tone so startled me, darned if I didn't buck up. Good old Harold.

SEVENTEEN

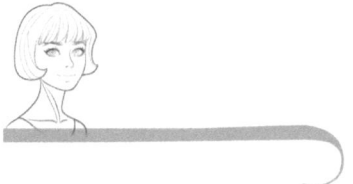

More than a little wobbly on my pins, I allowed Harold to take my arm, guide me from the séance room and down the hall to the drawing room. When I entered, all eyes shot straight at me. Oh, dear. I'm sorry about that sentence. The notion of shooting eyes is totally disgusting. What I meant was that everyone turned their heads and stared at Harold and me.

"Daisy! Are you all right?" Mrs. Frasier rushed up to me, an expression of concern on her face.

A little surprised—I'd kind of expected to be stoned, if only figuratively—I said softly and a bit shakily, "Yes, thank you. I'm so sorry about…what happened. Is Marianne all right?"

"She's awake and alert now," said Mrs. Frasier. "Lucy"—Lucy was one of Mrs. Frasier's housemaids—"brought in a tea tray, and I made sure Marianne drank a cup of hot, sweet tea with plenty of milk. And you should have one, too."

"Oh, but, I don't deserve—"

Harold pinched my arm, and I winced. He said, "That would be perfect, Mrs. Frasier. Thank you very much. Mrs. Majesty is definitely shaken. The séance was quite an ordeal for her."

"I know," said Mrs. Frasier in a thrilling whisper. "It must have been. Come here, dear. You, too, Harold."

She led us across the room. I almost didn't dare peer around for fear I'd see killing looks directed at me, but Harold pinched me again, so I peeked at my victims. For heaven's sake, they all watched me as if they feared I'd drop dead of something. Fright or spiritual collapse, I guess. They were almost right.

Mrs. Pinkerton, as Harold had already told me, still loomed over Marianne. Marianne sat on a sofa next to her mother, and as soon as Mrs. P saw me, she leapt up and made a rush at me. Harold, bless him, intercepted her by inserting his body between his mother's and mine, so there was no big collision.

"Oh, Daisy! How terrible for you! Are you all right, dear?" Mrs. P asked, tugging me away from Harold and nearly crushing me to her large bosom. "Poor Marianne fainted, too."

Too? Did everyone think I'd really fainted? I hoped so. I sneaked a peek at Harold from the one eye not smushed into Mrs. P's massive frontage.

"It took Mrs. Majesty quite a time to come out of her trance," said Harold, loudly enough for everyone in the room to hear. "This séance was harder on her than most of them are."

And *that* was the absolute truth. Nobody else needed to know why.

"Oh, Daisy!"

This cry had come from Diane, who left her daughter and hurried over to the group of us. Thank the good Lord, Mrs. P finally let me go. I staggered a trifle after she released me. I truly *was* adversely affected by that dratted séance.

As Diane elbowed Mrs. Pinkerton aside—quite a feat for the skinny Diane—she said, "Daisy, are you all right? You look terrible!" How kind. I didn't say so. She went on, "And Marianne is so afraid Rolly meant *George* was the murderer!"

"What?" My voice remained weak, and not because I wanted it to be. "I'm so sorry. I'm sure he didn't mean Mr. Grenville did the deed, Diane."

"But what *did* he mean? 'Look to the family'? What did that mean?"

"Mrs. Wagner, I think we'd better get Daisy settled somewhere before we ask her questions," said Harold, who, as I may have mentioned several times already, was my very best friend in the whole wide world. "She's a good deal unnerved by what happened."

"Oh," said Diane. "Oh, of course. I'm sorry, Daisy. Marianne and I are just so…worried. We're unnerved, too."

"I can certainly understand that," said I in a voice barely registering above a whisper. "The séance was…an ordeal for many of us."

Mrs. Frasier, tsking, led me to the other end of the sofa from Marianne. "Here, dear, let me pour you some tea."

"Thank you." Knowing where my duty lay, I turned to Marianne. "I'm so sorry, Marianne. I had no idea what Rolly was going to say. And I don't know what he meant by what he did say."

She smiled wanly at me. "It's all right. I know you can't predict what the spirits will tell you."

Not always, but usually. I didn't say that. "That's true, but I hate it when they say things I don't understand. Or things that don't address the question asked, as Rolly did this evening." That was diplomatic, wasn't it?

Probably not. Bother.

"I understand, Daisy," said Diane, taking over for her daughter, still standing over me and wringing her hands. "Marianne and I are only rather confused about Rolly's message."

Completely understandable. So was I.

"Here you go, dear," said Mrs. Frasier, handing me a cup of tea that looked as if it had been well stocked with milk and sugar.

Harold intercepted the cup and saucer. "Here," he said, placing the saucer on the coffee table in front of the sofa and handing the cup to me, not letting go of it until he saw I had a firm grip on the handle. "I don't want you dropping anything."

"Thank you, Harold. Thank you, Mrs. Frasier." I sipped the tea.

It was good, and I discovered, after drinking the cup dry, it really did help to perk me up slightly. Therefore, as soon as I'd returned the cup to the saucer and taken a deep breath, I turned again to Diane, who once more sat next to Marianne on the sofa. The two women held hands and both appeared nervous.

I said, repeating myself, "I apologize, Marianne and Diane. I had absolutely no idea what Rolly was going to say, and I also have no idea what he meant by what he did say." I sucked in some air and let it out slowly. "Does...I mean, did Doctor Wagner have any other family besides you two and the two younger Wagner men? Brothers? Sisters? Aunts? Cousins? Anyone at all?"

As if this idea were a new and welcome one, Diane and Marianne exchanged a glance.

After a moment or two, Diane said, "Um...He has a brother, but they hadn't spoken in years. His brother's name is Arnold Wesley Wagner, and as far as I know, he lives in Mississippi. Or maybe it's some other southern state. They weren't close. No one was close to Doctor Wagner." Some bitterness crept into her last sentence.

Suddenly Marianne, pressed a hand to her cheek, gasped and said, "Oh, my!"

I perked up minimally.

"Whatever is it, dear?" asked Diane.

"I just thought of something!" said Marianne.

Not overwhelmingly helpful, but at least they didn't seem inclined to beat me to a pulp or throw me off the Colorado Street Bridge.

"Yes?" I said, hoping for some clarification.

Mother and daughter stared at each other for approximately ten seconds. It felt like ten years.

Then Diane's expression blossomed with sudden understanding and she nodded. Marianne did likewise.

"It wouldn't surprise me," said Diane.

Huh?

"My word!" exclaimed Mrs. Pinkerton who, as ever, had managed to insert herself into the conversation. Then again, the entire séance crowd had come over to us and stood in a huddle around the sofa containing Diane, Marianne, Harold and me. "What an interesting notion!"

What notion was that? Totally confused, I.

"Yes," said Diane in a soft voice. "It is. Very interesting." After exchanging another look with her daughter, she said, her voice a bit harder than it had been, "It wouldn't surprise me to learn he had other children by other women."

This time it was I who gasped. I think a few other people did, too. Harold didn't. Man of the world, Harold.

Diane went on. "I'll have to get in touch with our attorney. He probably knows much more about my late husband's private life than I was ever privileged to know."

Not a ringing endorsement of her marriage, but we already knew her marriage had been a pit of misery.

"You know," said Marianne thoughtfully. "Gaylord or Vincent might know." She shrugged. "Or both of them. They wouldn't want to tell us if they did know about any…What would you call them? Mistresses? My late father might have had."

Mrs. Pinkerton's right hand flew to her mouth and she gulped audibly.

Diane said, "Yes. They might know. And you're right. They wouldn't tell us."

Her voice registering incredulity, Mrs. Frasier said, "Mistresses? Do you really think he might have had…mistresses?"

"It wouldn't surprise me," said Marianne, her voice dark; almost sinister. "In fact, it wouldn't surprise me to find out he had a whole 'nother family or two. Or even three. He was a bad man."

With a sigh, Diane said, "Yes. He was. A very bad man."

Mrs. Frasier said faintly. "My goodness."

The herd of people standing in the room nodded solemnly, as if a puppet master were in charge of their strings. Clearly Dr. Wagner's evil ways were a poorly kept secret in the upper echelons of Pasadena society.

"I'll ask Fletcher Kingsley," said Diane. "He's the family's attorney. He'll probably know, if anyone does, if Doctor Wagner had any other children. Or about…other people who were close to him.

Although how any woman could—But never mind. We all know what Doctor Wagner was."

Eight to twelve heads nodded, the faces attached to same looking grim, angry or solemn or a combination of the three.

About forty-five minutes later, during which interminable time I'd sat in the drawing room, speaking softly and apologetically to the victims of my séance and being reassured time and again, I managed to make my escape. I still felt terrible about what Rolly had said. Fortunately for me, no one present seemed to hold me accountable for Rolly's lousy behavior. They were far more forgiving of Rolly than I was. Stupid spirit control. It was the first time in my entire career I'd even considered trading Rolly in for another model.

Good Lord! If I did that, would Rolly haunt me?

I felt as though I were losing my mind. The feeling wasn't pleasant.

Harold walked me out to the Chevrolet. His bright red Stutz Bearcat was parked nearby. My family's Chevrolet looked like a fat old uncle compared to Harold's low-slung, snazzy car.

"So," said Harold, "that was kind of a fiasco, wasn't it?"

"Yes," I said, still feeling guilty and drooping, "it was. And I still don't know how it happened."

"You should have a woman-to-man talk with Rolly. He's getting too big for his britches."

"That probably should be funny."

"Yes. It probably should be. I'm sorry it's not."

I heaved a huge sigh. "So am I. I hope everyone's in bed when I get home, because I don't want to talk about this séance. Ever. But I'll have to eventually. And I'll also have to confess to Sam what went on here tonight."

"The good detective doesn't really believe in your spiritualist nonsense, does he?"

"Heavens, no! But I still feel obliged to tell him. I mean…Well, I mean, what if Rolly was speaking the truth?"

I couldn't see Harold's face clearly because the night was dark; however, the outdoor lights were on—this was a mansion, don't forget—and I was able to make out his dubious expression. "And you still claim Rolly spoke without any help from you, right?"

I stopped walking, deeply hurt by the note of disbelief in Harold's voice. "Yes," I said, wanting to cry again. "Yes, yes, *yes*! I had nothing to do with what he said! Do you honestly think I'd have said something like that on *purpose*? 'Look to the family?' Do you really, Harold? I thought you knew me better than that!"

"Don't get upset again, sweetie. Yes, I know you better than that. I just wonder if…Well, if the stress of recent events is getting you down. You don't believe in the spiritualist garbage you spout any more than I do, do you?"

"No," I said, whimpering slightly. "Except every now and then, something weird happens. Like that time Eddie Hastings came out of my mouth. And tonight." I started walking again, but not with any sort of lift to my walk. I was droopy and drooping. "Oh, Harold, this was almost worse than the Eddie Hastings séance! I thought I had complete control of Rolly! I always have had before. I made him *up*, for heaven's sake! If he starts doing stuff like he did tonight, I'm…I don't know what I'll do. Quit the business, I guess. But then what will my family do? I guess I can be an elevator operator at Nash's, but I won't make a tenth as much money as I do now."

"You don't have to worry about that yet, sweetie. Just continue as you've been doing, and I think things will work out."

"Why do you think that? What if this happens again?"

With a shrug, Harold said, "Just visit my mother more often. She'll love it, and you won't have to worry about Rolly because she'll believe anything that comes out of your mouth. Anyway, you can read the tarot cards instead. Or the crystal ball. Or the Ouija board."

"Rolly's supposed to be in charge of the Ouija board, too, you know. He did something without my prompting the other day with the board. *When* I was with your mother. I think he's beginning to take over my…What do you call it? My psyche. Or something."

"Nuts to that. Just slap him down."

"How do I do that?"

Another shrug. "I don't know. Throw that wooden triangle thing across the room and yell at Rolly?"

I think he was kidding, but I said, "I might just do that."

"Sleep well, Daisy. Don't take everything so seriously. I'm sure it will work out all right."

"If you say so."

"I say so."

I sure hoped he was right. As I drove home that night, I had serious doubts.

EIGHTEEN

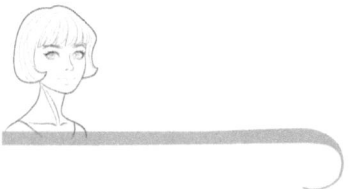

Thursday morning, I awoke with a heart heavy only partially because Spike had decided to sleep across my chest sometime during the night. I gently shoved him off and sat up in bed.

"Spike, whatever will I do?"

Spike didn't answer, which I'd expected. That morning I liked Spike infinitely more than I liked Rolly. Spike wagged his tail, which prompted me to hug and cuddle him until I remembered I needed to use the bathroom, which meant he probably did, too. So I let him out the back door leading from my bedroom to the back deck. Spike raced outside and down the steps and spent a good deal of time watering various plants. Mind you, I didn't see him do his watering. I raced to the human bathroom, leaving the bedroom door open so Spike could come in without disturbing anyone by barking to be let inside again.

Once I'd used the facilities, splashed cold water on my face, and peered into the mirror—I looked not unlike hell warmed up, darn it —I shuffled back to my bedroom. Spike had gone into the kitchen from which fragrant smells emanated. I wasn't hungry. That was most unusual.

Oh, dear. I hoped this didn't signal the beginning of another decline. After Billy died, I'd spun so far out of control and lost so much weight, folks told me I looked skeletal and nearly transparent. At this point, December of 1924, I still hadn't regained all the weight I'd lost.

I told myself that was a good thing. I hadn't been fat before Billy's death, but I'd been about as far from the bean-skinny ideal of femininity then in vogue as an ocean liner was from a rowboat.

Because I felt so shaky and puny, I decided to get dressed before I faced my family. In truth, I rather hoped Ma and Aunt Vi had already left for work, although when I glanced at the clock on my bedside table, I saw it was only a little past six-thirty a.m. And I'd come home after midnight. Good. If any of my family members asked why I looked so ghastly, I could blame my lack of looks on lack of sleep. Wouldn't be a complete lie.

It didn't take me much time to decide what to wear. I had no commitments except for making a telephone call to Sam, and I didn't have to dress well for that. I also didn't want to make the call, but needs must sometimes. Whatever that means.

After combing my hair—thank the good Lord and Irene Castle for the modern-day bob—I slipped on a newish blue housedress, some white cotton stockings, and my old brown walking shoes. I figured Pa and I would take Spike for a walk that morning as we usually did, and I could slip on a sweater and my coat and be plenty warm enough.

As soon as I walked into the kitchen, the 'phone on the far wall began ringing. At—I looked at the kitchen clock near the telephone—seven a.m.! Who in the world would be calling at this ungodly hour? Well, it wouldn't have been ungodly if you were a farmer or night-shift worker or something like that, but we Gumms and Majesty weren't. And neither were any of our neighbors.

The only person I could think of who might perpetrate such an inconsiderate act would be Mrs. Pinkerton in a tizzy. However, according to my friend and her lady's maid, Edie Applewood, Mrs. Pinkerton seldom got up before nine a.m. Must be nice to be rich.

Feeling annoyed as well as tired and grumpy, I stomped to the telephone, barely registering my father seated at the kitchen table with Spike at his feet.

Nearly ripping the receiver off the cradle and slamming it against my ear, I said—softly and soothingly, darn it—"Gumm-Majesty residence. Mrs. Majesty—"

"Yeah. I know all that," came Sam's voice, which sounded nearly as grumpy as I felt. "What I need to know is what happened at your séance last night."

"And you're telephoning at seven o'clock in the morning to ask me about it? The telephone rings in all our party-line neighbors' homes, too, you know. You probably woke them all up."

"Nuts. Working people have to get up early."

"Not *this* early unless they're farmers and have to rise at the crack of dawn to feed the chickens and slop the hogs!"

"Do farmers do that?"

"How should *I* know? I'm not a farmer! It's too early for you to telephone anyone who doesn't live on a farm!"

I heard an offended, "Hmph," from one of the people who shared our telephone wire. *So there, Sam Rotondo*, I thought.

Very well; I didn't feel awfully mature that morning.

After sucking in approximately twelve cubic feet of bacon-scented air—which made me feel better, actually—I said, still softly and sweetly, "Will our party-line neighbors please hang up your receivers? This call is for me. I'm terribly sorry it's so early. It was unconscionable to wake you all up so early on this"—I glanced out the kitchen window and almost groaned—"foggy December morning."

Three clicks smote my ear. I waited. "Mrs. Barrow?" I said, even still softly and amiably, curse it.

"It's real selfish of you to have people telephoning you so early in the morning, Mrs. Majesty." Mrs. Barrow's repugnant New York twang stormed through the telephone wires. "Inconsiderate, is what it is."

"Yes, it is, and I'm sorry," said I, hoping Sam's own personal telephone ear was turning red with embarrassment. It probably wasn't, Sam being Sam.

Mrs. Barrow's click at last smote my ear, and I said, "How dare you, Sam Rotondo? Don't you have any manners at all? You know we have a party line! What couldn't wait until a more decent hour?"

"Cripes," muttered Sam. "I didn't realize how early it is."

I humphed.

"Sorry," he added.

"I'm sure. Now what was it you wanted?" I didn't really need to be reminded.

"What happened at the séance last night? I heard rumblings about it."

"You heard *what*?"

"Cripes. Don't screech at me. I heard from one of the uniforms whose sister works for Mrs. Frasier that something odd happened. What was it?"

Before coffee? Before toast? Before bacon? Darn Sam Rotondo to perdition!

"Nothing happened!"

"Horsefeathers. It did, too. Now what was it?"

"For pity's sake, Sam. Rolly told everyone at the séance to look to the family when I asked him who committed the murder."

Silence greeted my announcement—which had been nothing but the truth, even if it didn't carry with it the emotional overtones and undertones Rolly's suggestion had elicited from last night's victims.

"That's it?" he said at last.

"That's it," I said, mad as an old wet hen, as my aunt was wont to say. I didn't have much to do with barnyard animals on a daily basis, but I could imagine how having a bucket of cold water thrown at a peaceful hen might affect its mood.

"That can't be it. Peterson said his sister was all agog."

"Agog, was she?" I tried to sound as sarcastic as possible.

"Yes. Agog. So what you told me can't be the sum total of what happened last night."

Nuts to the irritating man! "Listen, Sam. I didn't get much sleep, I just got up, and I'm tired and cranky. Let me eat breakfast, and I'll 'phone you back."

"Invite him for breakfast," my father said from his seat at the kitchen table.

I jumped, having forgotten all about him even being there. I turned, frowned, and said, "He doesn't deserve to be fed."

Pa laughed and said, "Sure, he does."

"Fiddlesticks." Nevertheless, I said into the receiver, "Pa wants you to come and have breakfast with us."

"He does?"

"Yes."

"Do you?"

"No."

"Be there in five."

He hung up.

"And a plague upon your house, you rat," I muttered as I hung up the receiver and turned. Planting my fists on my hips, I told my wonderful father, "Sam is an inconsiderate wretch. He doesn't *deserve* any of Vi's good cooking."

"Nonsense. He does, too. You're just cross this morning because you got in so late," said my aunt, entering the kitchen from the hall from the bathroom. When I turned to glance at her, I saw her smiling. Huh.

"Oh, my, is Sam coming over?" asked Ma, entering the kitchen from the dining room. She smiled, too. "That's so nice."

Spike jumped up from the kitchen floor and raced to the front door, barking madly. It was his oh-goody-a-friend-has-come-to-call bark, so I knew it was Sam. Five minutes, my left hind leg. He must have called from the pay telephone booth on the corner. Darn him! And here I was in my ugly blue housedress and clunky shoes.

Oh, well. Couldn't be helped. I followed Spike to the door and flung it open, scowling as viciously as I could.

"You," I said, glaring at Sam.

He had the grace to look slightly—only slightly, mind you—abashed. "Me," he said, leaning on his cane and attempting to produce an endearing smile. He was too big to be endearing, even in a Santa-Claus suit.

"Come in," I snarled.

I stepped aside, and Sam walked into the house. Because I hadn't told him not to, Spike commenced leaping upon Sam, his little doggie claws making furrows in his overcoat. I looked down at my dog, satisfied and hoping one of his claws would make a big hole in Sam's trousers. His overcoat was too thick to be damaged by a dachshund's short claws. Darn it.

"Cripes. I'm sorry I called so early," Sam said, hanging his overcoat and hat on the coat tree next to the front door. He knelt to pet Spike and looked up at me. "Is that the only reason you're so short-tempered this morning?"

Short-tempered, was I?

By golly, I was. I attempted to cheer up without much luck. "No," I said. "I didn't get any sleep, and Marianne Grenville fainted when Rolly told the assembled séance attendees to look to the family if they wanted to know who killed Doctor Wagner. Personally, I don't *care* who killed him! I think whoever it was deserves a million dollars and a fast car. Maybe two million dollars."

"Daisy!" came my mother's appalled voice from behind me.

Well, wouldn't you just know she'd be there to hear my ugly words? I borrowed one of Sam's favorite activities and rolled my eyes heavenward. What a stupid morning *this* was turning out to be.

"Sorry, Ma," I said, turning and attempting to smile at her. "I'm just tired." A glance at Sam. "And grumpy at having been telephoned too darned early in the morning."

"I'm *sorry*," said Sam again, pleading this time, and rising to his feet with a grunt and the aid of his cane.

"Pay no attention to Daisy, Sam," said Ma. "Sometimes those séances take a good deal out of her and really do sap her strength."

Bless my mother's heart! I had no idea she believed that!

I think I must have goggled in astonishment at her because she then said, "Well, they do, don't they?"

"Yes," I said, sniffling a trifle. "They do. Thanks, Ma."

"But that's no reason to be rude to a guest."

A *guest*? "Sam isn't a guest! He might as well live here, he's around so much!"

"Daisy," said my mother, tutting at me. "Poor Sam can't help being a lonely bachelor. After all, he didn't have a family to help him when his dear wife passed on."

God save me. Now Sam was a lonely, bereaved bachelor. And I was a shrew, I supposed. I didn't ask.

"Come to the kitchen," I told Sam, ignoring my mother's comment, and walking kitchenwards.

"Thank you, Peggy," said Sam. "It is lonely here, all alone in Southern California with my family in New York and all."

Bunkum. I didn't say so.

"You're welcome here any time," said Ma.

"Good morning, Sam!" said Aunt Vi, smiling up a storm as she tied a scarf under her chin, ready for the walk up to Colorado to catch a bus to Mrs. Pinkerton's place.

"Would you ladies like a ride to work?" asked Sam, sounding gracious.

I hoped they'd say "yes" so I could try to get over my bad mood.

"No, thank you," said Ma. "I only work up the street a bit, and the bus stop is right there on Colorado for Vi to catch."

Fiddle-faddle.

"Sure?" asked Sam, still sounding gracious, curse him and all his spawn.

Wait a minute. Some of Sam's spawn might come from me. Disregard that last curse, please.

"Come on in, Sam!" came my father's voice from the kitchen. "Bacon and cinnamon rolls, thanks to our wonderful Vi."

"Cinnamon rolls, eh?" I sniffed the air as I tromped through the dining room to the kitchen. By gum, there *was* a scent of cinnamon perfuming the air along with the heavenly aroma of bacon. Maybe the whole day wouldn't be as awful as the morning.

"Yes," said Pa. "They're delicious."

"In that case, Sam doesn't deserve any," I said.

"Daisy!" My mother called from the front door.

Sam laughed.

Botheration!

NINETEEN

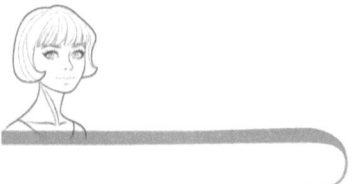

S am walked as softly as he could, considering his cane and the size of his policemanly shoes, through the dining room and paused at the kitchen door. "Listen, Daisy, I really am sorry I called so early. I won't stay if you don't want me to."

Scowling at him, I thought about telling him to leave but I didn't quite dare, what with my father sitting right there at the table and Spike cavorting at Sam's feet. And besides that, I loved the man. Even though his early-morning telephone call had been untimely. On the other hand, I'd woken in a bad mood, so I couldn't really blame Sam for my grouchiness.

"Oh, come in," I said, attempting to match Sam in the graciousness department. "And sit down. I'll get you a plate."

"You sure?"

Unable to restrain my grumpiness, I glared at him. "Don't press your luck, Sam Rotondo. I'm only being nice to you because Pa's here."

"Daisy," said my father, reminding me of my mother.

Then and there I decided I was going to rent a room at a boarding house.

But wait. If I moved to a boarding house, I might have peace and quiet and not be under constant scrutiny from my mother and father, but I also wouldn't be able to eat Vi's wonderful meals. My gaze fell to my precious hound. I couldn't have Spike with me if I lived in a boarding house, either. Nuts.

Although...It probably wouldn't take *too* long to save enough that I could afford to buy myself a little cottage somewhere. Spike and I could live there and be happy without people scolding us all the time.

Hmm. There was still the lack-of-Vi problem to consider.

Piddle. Guess I'd just have to stay here. I drew in another acre of delicious-smelling food aromas, and tried to perk up a trifle.

"If you're sure..." Sam hesitated, his hand on the back of one of the kitchen chairs.

I relented. "Oh, sit down, you big galoot. To tell the truth, the main reason I'm in such a foul mood is that wretched séance. It...It didn't go as I'd planned."

"Goodness," said my father. "Glad I didn't go out gallivanting earlier this morning. I can't wait to hear all about it."

"Me, either," said Sam, trying to sound as if he weren't relieved. And hungry. Couldn't blame him for that. The aromas of cinnamon and bacon and coffee were enough to make even me in my bad mood glad to be alive. Almost.

"Great. I love an audience," said I, heaping slices of cooked bacon on a plate and using a spatula to scoop up one of Vi's fabulous cinnamon rolls. For the life of me, I don't know how she did all the things she did in the kitchen. The only thing I'd ever succeeded doing in the kitchen was burning up a pot in which I'd been trying to boil water.

Sam didn't say a word until I set his plate on the kitchen table in front of him. I got a knife, fork and spoon from the silverware drawer—we didn't have real silver silverware, but that's what people call it—got a napkin from the napkin drawer, and set them carefully beside his plate.

"Coffee?" I asked in a pleasant voice.

"Yes, please."

"Orange juice? Or just peel an orange, if you want one." We

always had oranges, thanks to our two orange trees. One of them bore fruit in the spring and summer, and the other one bore fruit during the autumn and winter.

"Thank you," said Sam.

I stood back and gazed at him. He stared back at me.

"Well?" I said, my patience snapping slightly. "Dig in, darn it!"

"I'm waiting for you," said my beloved in a placating sort of voice.

"Oh," I said, feeling silly. "Thank you."

So I filled my own plate, got silverware and a napkin and sat across from him at the table. Pa sat at between us, smiling fondly at each of us in turn.

"Put some butter on your roll," I suggested. "Vi's cinnamon rolls are great even without butter, but butter makes them heavenly, especially since Vi left the rolls and the bacon in the warming oven, and the rolls are still hot."

"Thanks," said Sam. He carefully sliced some butter from the butter dish on the table using the butter knife provided for the purpose, and deposited it on his plate. In other words, he was being polite and mannerly this morning. Trying to appease me, I had no doubt.

I, too, took some butter. Then I broke off a piece of cinnamon roll and carefully buttered it with my table knife. *Lead by example*, I told myself. Not that Sam needed lessons in manners from me. His mother had taught him well.

"Oh, pooh. I forgot the coffee," said I, looking around and not seeing my coffee cup on the table. That's because I hadn't set it there.

"You two stay here, and I'll get coffee for the both of you," said Pa, bless him.

"Thanks, Pa."

"Thanks, Joe."

By the time I'd eaten half a cinnamon roll, two slices of bacon, and sipped about half a cup of coffee, I decided I might survive the morning. Perhaps even the entire day. In fact, I felt nearly human again.

Therefore, I set my knife carefully on my plate, delicately wiped my lips with my napkin, and launched into an elucidation of the prior night's séance. Sam must have recognized my mood to be unstable, because he didn't interrupt once during my narration. Pa said, "Wow," once or twice, but that was it as far as commentary from my audience went as I spoke.

When I resumed breaking bits of cinnamon roll, buttering them, and popping them into my mouth, Sam ruminated. Sort of like a cow.

I'm sorry. Guess my mood hadn't improved a whole lot at that point.

I was swallowing the last of my coffee and contemplating another half or quarter of a cinnamon roll when Sam finally spoke.

"Look to the family, eh?"

"Yes. Look to the family."

"And you didn't…what? You didn't mean to say that?"

"I didn't. I don't know what possessed Rolly. Or what possessed me. Some demon from hell, maybe."

"Daisy," said Pa. "That's really not funny."

Bother! "It wasn't funny last night, either, Pa," I said, my voice grating unpleasantly. "I don't know how it happened. I didn't mean for Rolly to say any of the things he said last night."

"Hmm," said Sam noncommittally.

"Interesting," said Pa.

"Huh." I decided I'd probably better not eat any more food. My mood was so unsettled, another bite or two of cinnamon roll might adversely affect my digestion.

I did, however, remember my manners—a little late. "Would you like another cinnamon roll, Sam? Or a half of one? Or more bacon?"

"Thank you. I'd love another half of a roll and another piece or two of bacon, please." I guess he recalled who did the cooking at our house and who was no longer in the house. "If the bacon's already prepared. Don't want to be a bother."

It was a trifle late to worry about bothering people, I thought spitefully. However, I held my tongue, took Sam's plate and waltzed over to the stove. "No bother at all," I said. I think my voice actually sounded sincere. Maybe with a little more practice, I could be human again. "Want anything else, Pa?"

"No, thanks," said my father.

"Thank you," said Sam as I set his plate before him.

"You're welcome."

As for me, I decided eating an orange might be a good idea. Might give me some much-needed nutritional sustenance and perhaps, with a jolt of vitamin C rushing through me, I'd feel better. Couldn't feel a whole lot worse. So I snatched a Valencia orange from the bowl in the middle of the table. Valencias being what they were, I rose and got a fruit knife from the knife holder and commenced slicing the orange on the plate that formerly held my cinnamon roll and bacon.

"So in spite of what you wanted him to say, Rolly told everyone they needed to look to the family in order to find the murderer, did he?" asked Sam between bites.

"Yes."

"Out of curiosity, what *had* you planned to say," asked Pa.

"Beats me," said I. "I never know what's going to pop out of my mouth, but it's never anything concrete like 'look to the family'. I'd probably have said something vague, like, 'The police are getting closer and closer to the villain,' or something along those lines."

"Ah," said Pa.

"So nice to know Rolly appreciates the police," said Sam.

"Yes," said I, summoning up my grievance against him once more. "That makes one of us."

Sam grinned at me. He would. Every time he smiled like that, he made it difficult for me to stay angry with him. Telephoning at the crack of dawn, my aunt Fanny. I tried not to smile back at him, but I couldn't help myself.

After swallowing a bite of cinnamon roll, Sam said, "I don't suppose he gave you a hint about any particular family member we should look at, did he?"

"No. He did not. He was being particularly cantankerous last night, if you ask me." I'd cut my orange into sixths, and I chewed

orange from a piece of peel. Valencia oranges are sweet and delicious even if they do have seeds, and the juice felt good sliding down
my throat. I glanced up suddenly. "And don't you dare tell me *I'm*
cantankerous, Sam Rotondo."

"Wouldn't dream of it," said Sam with another angelic smile.
For the record, angelic smiles and Sam Rotondo doesn't really go
together very well. He's too big and block-like to carry off an
angelic image.

I sniffed. "Good thing." I peered down at my orange, then back
up at Sam. "I'm sorry I got so mad at you this morning, Sam. You
did telephone entirely too early, but I didn't mean to snap at you."

"That's quite all right," said Sam. "I'm—" He stopped speaking.

"You're used to it?" I asked, sugar coating my words.

"I'd never say that," said he.

"Huh," I said, borrowing a word from his vocabulary.

"Anyway, nobody else had a clue who might be the family Rolly
wanted people to look to?" asked Sam after swallowing more bacon.

"Nope. Although Marianne—or maybe it was Diane. I can't
remember—said she'd better talk to their family's attorney on the
chance the attorney might know if the philandering Doctor
Wagner had fathered any children with a woman other than
Diane."

"Daisy!"

I glanced from my orange slice to my father, who appeared
honestly shocked. Nice man, my father. Innocent, though.

"It wasn't I who thought of that, Pa. It was Doctor Wagner's
own daughter—or his widow—and if you knew what that doctor
put his daughter through, you wouldn't be so surprised by the question. Comment. Whatever it was."

Pa's nose wrinkled. "Good Lord."

"Something like that," I said, and bit into another orange slice.

"Did she mention the attorney's name?" asked Sam.

I wracked my brain. Not too hard, for fear it would rebel or
shatter or do something else awful. "Kingsley. Or Fletcher."

"Fletcher Kingsley?"

"Yes. I think that's the name. Do you know him?" I asked Sam.

"I know of him. A lot of Pasadena's wealthier citizens use him for family affairs."

"In this case, I guess it would be an affair outside the family," I muttered.

Pa opened his mouth, but shut it again without uttering anything.

"Guess so," said Sam.

Pa began gathering up the breakfast dishes.

"I'll do that, Pa. You needn't bother."

"That's okay. You're not feeling well this morning, and I feel great. Might as well make myself useful."

And darned if he didn't wash up all the breakfast dishes. I dried them and put them away, determining that I'd been a hateful hag that morning, and no one except Sam—and maybe Dr. Wagner— deserved my wrath. Guilt washed through me.

"Sorry I was so touchy earlier, Pa," I said in a weak voice.

"Don't give it another thought," said my darling father. "You had a rough night"—He glanced at Sam, still sitting at the table sipping coffee—"and an early morning."

"You can say that again. Thanks, Pa."

"I'll never call early again," said Sam. "Promise."

Both Pa and I laughed, so I guess all was forgiven, although I'm not sure who needed forgiveness or from whom.

After the dishes were done, I said, "Want to go for a walk with Pa and Spike and me, Sam?"

Spike, who could understand English, even if he couldn't speak it, instantly began jumping up and down and running to his leash on a hook in the service porch and back into the kitchen, wagging his tail like an electrical fan. Smart dog, Spike.

"Sure," said he, bravely daring. "I'd like to talk about the case."

"I wish I had some sort of recording device. I'd love to have recorded that comment and keep it for all eternity."

"That's what your memory's for," said Sam with a lame smile.

"Right. Let me get my sweater and coat."

By the time I'd donned both sweater and coat and wrapped a scarf around my head to keep my ears warm, Pa had clipped

Spike's leash onto his collar, and both Pa and Sam had put on their own coats and hats.

We'd walked south about a block when I broke the silence that had settled among us. Well, except for Spike's excited snufflings and our own footfalls on the dried peppercorns dotting the sidewalk. During the spring and summer, the pepper trees lining Marengo Avenue made a gorgeous canopy over the street. During the winter-time, they dropped their berries. Folks, including us, swept their sidewalks religiously, but there were always stray peppercorns to step on.

Whoops. Got distracted again.

At any rate, I was the first person to speak during our walk. And I said the one thing I shouldn't have, thus making the day perfect so far. "So, what do you think Rolly meant by his 'look to the family' remark, Sam?"

A moment of silence preceded Sam's answer to my question, which meant I wasn't going to like what he aimed to say. I knew my Sam.

At last he said, "You're not going to like it."

Told you so.

"But I think Rolly was pointing his finger at George Grenville."

Figured as much. "Technically speaking, George isn't a member of the family. He only married into it."

"That makes him a family member," Pa said.

"I think so, too," said Sam.

"But you don't really think George killed that awful man, do you? Really?"

"That awful man, according to many reports, had been tormenting George Grenville and his wife, and he did other terrible things to her. Mr. Grenville clearly loves his wife, and I wouldn't blame him if he killed the doctor, but the law and I don't see eye-to-eye on some matters."

"True." I sighed. "It makes me furious to think that, *if* George did the deed—and I seriously don't think he did—he'd get into trouble for it."

"I'll have to talk to him again. You know that, right?"

"Because Rolly told you to? I thought you didn't believe in Rolly."

"I don't, but I believe in you."

"Awww. I think that's the sweetest thing you've ever said to me, Sam Rotondo."

My father chuckled.

Neither Sam nor I did.

TWENTY

Not long after we all got home from our walk, Sam departed for the Pasadena Police Department, located behind Pasadena's City Hall on the corner of Fair Oaks Avenue and Walnut Street. Pa sat in the living room to read one of the books I'd recently checked out of the library. Spike followed me around as if we were attached, and I went into my bedroom and sat on the small rocking chair in the corner to contemplate the state of the world—or at least of Pasadena, California.

Spike put his paws on my knees, and I bent to lift him on to my lap. The rocker was one chair in the house he couldn't leap on to because of its nature. Mind you, I could have stopped it from rocking so he could achieve his high jump, but he'd tried it a couple of times when I hadn't expected it, and the rocker had done its rockerly duty and rocked, precipitating Spike onto the floor in a shiny black lump. Poor baby. So I lifted him up and he snuggled on my lap. He was kind of long to spread himself out, but he could roll himself into a ball, not unlike the morning's cinnamon rolls, in fact, thus achieving comfort. I propped my feet on the cunning little stand I'd found in a junk shop and spiffed up with new paint and a chintz cover to match the one I'd made for the chair and commenced thinking.

My thoughts weren't bright, and I don't think my mood had anything to do with the weather which, while no longer foggy, was dank and chill.

"I know George didn't murder that hateful man, Spike."

Spike sighed in agreement.

"But I'll bet you anything Sam's going to arrest him."

This time Spike's sigh was one of disapproval.

"Marianne will be crushed, and she's already been through too much in her relatively short life. Diane will be frantic."

Spike let out a doggie chuff of sympathy.

"But if George *didn't* do it, who did?"

Evidently Spike had no opinion on that subject, because he didn't utter a sound.

"Sam ought to talk to those awful sons of the Wagners, Spike. Or maybe Doctor Wagner botched an abortion on someone whose nearest and dearest decided to get even."

More silence from Spike.

When the telephone in the kitchen rang, I nearly dumped Spike on the floor, the bell startled me so much.

Spike disapproved and said so.

Giving him a loving pet, I said, "I'm sorry, sweetheart. Got lost in my thoughts. Didn't mean to disturb you."

Being the kindhearted, forgiving soul he was, Spike didn't object when I lifted him onto the ground again. In fact, he wagged at me. I wish people were more like Spike. Heck, I wish *I* were more like Spike. Spike never held a grudge or disliked people on sight, neither of which attributes I owned.

When I walked out of my bedroom and into the kitchen, I saw Pa headed in the same direction.

"It's probably for you, Daisy," said Pa. "Want me to tell Mrs. Pinkerton you're away from home?"

"You'd actually lie for me?"

Pa shrugged and said, "Not on a regular basis, but the past few days have been pretty hard on you."

"Thanks, Pa, but I'll get it. You're the best father a girl could have, you know."

He gave me a broad, appreciative smile.

I love my family.

As ever when I answered the telephone, I said, "Gumm-Majesty residence. Mrs. Majesty speaking."

"Oh, Daisy," said Mrs. Pinkerton.

"Good morning, Mrs. Pinkerton." As her voice had held no hint of her present mood, I didn't know if I'd just lied or not, but I crossed the fingers of my left hand just in case.

"Oh, Daisy," repeated Mrs. P, "I wonder if you wouldn't mind bringing Rolly and the Ouija board over today. I'd love to ask Rolly some questions regarding the Wagner murder case."

The Wagner murder case? She sounded like a bad detective novel. "Don't forget that Rolly can't answer questions about anyone but you, Mrs. Pinkerton," I said, pretending to be as sweet and kind as Spike.

"I know that, dear, but Rolly has been so helpful recently, I just thought I might give him a chance to tattle a little more." She giggled.

I didn't. As far as I was concerned, Rolly could take a long walk off a short pier—well, except that he didn't exist. Fudge. Did I trust Rolly, however insubstantial I knew him to be, not to do something outrageous again?

No, I did not.

On the other hand, Rolly was how I made my family's living—and I'm not discounting the contributions from Ma or Aunt Vi. However, neither Ma nor Vi earned what a man would have earned for doing the same jobs they did. That is to say they *earned* it; they just didn't *get* it.

On the *other* other hand, if Rolly continued to be uncontrollable, I might just contract a fatal case of the screaming jimjams.

Humbug. Only one way to find out.

"I'll be happy to bring the Ouija board to you, Mrs. Pinkerton." I glanced at the kitchen clock. Shoot, it was still early. Only eight forty-five. "Will ten-thirty be all right with you?"

"That will be wonderful. Thank you dear."

"Certainly. Rolly and I will see you then."

We both rang off, and I turned, frowning, to see my father eyeing me from the door to the dining room.

"On call again today, are you?" he asked.

"Yup. Mrs. P just can't get enough of Rolly and me."

"I thought you were at odds with Rolly."

"I am, but I need him."

Pa laughed, and Spike and I returned to my bedroom.

This time, however, I didn't sit and meditate. Rather, I chose a warm outfit to wear on this bleak midwinter day. Oh, very well, that's a bit melodramatic. However, I laid said outfit on my bed, and retired to the bathroom, shutting the bedroom door behind me. I'd learned shortly after Mrs. Bissel gave Spike to Billy and me that there wasn't much Spike liked better than snuggling up on the clothes I laid out on my bed. Naturally, he had to dig a nest for himself in them, thereby wrinkling them almost beyond redemption.

In the bathroom I bathed, washed my short hair, rubbed Pond's Vanishing Cream on my face—it hadn't yet made my freckles disappear, but I lived in hope—and smeared cream-of-almond lotion over the rest of my body. If nothing else, I'd smell good. Using a dab of Rexall Hair Tonic, I brushed my hair into submission, which wasn't difficult to do since I'd had it bobbed. I have to admit that my hair was easy to work with, too, which made one element of my life manageable.

Now there only remained Rolly. Maybe Mrs. Pinkerton. Well, and Sam. Aw, fiddlesticks; the Wagner murder, too.

Because I had a few minutes to spare before I left for Mrs. P's estate, I decided to join Pa in the living room and read for a few minutes. Fortunately for me and the state of my blue-and-gray flannel suit with its wrap-around skirt and box coat, Spike was firmly settled on Pa's lap. Not that a few black or tan doggie hairs would have done much damage, but still...

I picked up *A Passage to India* and read the first two or three pages. Chandrapore didn't strike me as a place I'd particularly like to visit because it sounded as if it were smelly and dirty. The Marabar Caves sounded interesting, however.

Before I was able to read enough to determine if Chandrapore was as ugly as it first sounded, I had to put the book aside and fetch my hat, coat and gloves (all black). I also picked up my bag of spiritualist paraphernalia and then said good-bye to my father and my dog.

"Off to Mrs. Pinkerton's?"

"Yes. Wish me luck."

"Luck," said Pa.

Spike wagged. I gave them both a pat on the head and walked out to the Chevrolet, parked as usual at the foot of the side-porch stairs. My heart performed crazy flipping maneuvers as I drove to the Pinkerton palace. It was the first time since I'd invented him that I'd been afraid of Rolly. Had I summoned a demon from the pit when I was ten, little knowing what I was to launch into the world? Or had my last two experiences with Rolly been extreme aberrations? I prayed for the latter, but my heart continued to thump unpleasantly.

But Rolly behaved! He told Mrs. P he could only answer questions about her, and that he couldn't tell her who'd killed Dr. Wagner. Not only that, but when she asked why he couldn't, he didn't spell out that same snotty "Not my job" phrase, but just said he wasn't able to.

"But you said you knew who did it last night, Rolly," said Mrs. P, sounding a little pouty.

And darned if Rolly didn't spell out, "I'm sorry."

"So you didn't mean to say you knew who it was?" she persisted.

The planchette, supposedly guided by Rolly, swept up to the left side of the board and landed firmly on the "Yes."

Hallelujah!

And so it continued. For at least thirty minutes Mrs. Pinkerton tried to get Rolly to knuckle under and tell her stuff I didn't know, but he refused to be swayed. Or perhaps I was merely mindful on that day of my ultimate control over the make-believe Rolly. I'd probably become too complacent over the years.

At any rate, I was so relieved by the time I left Mrs. Pinkerton's presence, I nearly skipped all the way down the hall to the kitchen. My day, which had begun in misery, looked as if it were going to be smooth sailing from then on. Because I didn't quite trust the day or Rolly—or me, for that matter—I knocked before I pushed open the swing door to the kitchen. Didn't want to startle Vi as I'd done on prior occasions when I hadn't announced my coming before barging into her domain.

Vi was there, chopping cooked chicken into a small dice, using her knife so deftly, she created a positive blur of motion as she wielded it. She'd tried to teach me how to do that once. The lesson didn't stick. She glanced up from her cutting board and smiled at me.

"Feeling better, dear?" she asked.

"Yes, thank you. Sorry I was so grouchy this morning, but... Well, it's over now."

"Do you have time to wait for lunch? I'm fixing chicken-salad sandwiches with spinach-cream soup."

"Spinach-cream soup? Have you ever made that for us? I don't recall it."

"I'm not sure. It's just like any other cream soup, only with spinach."

"Oh."

With a laugh, Vi said, "See for yourself. There's a pot on the warming plate filled with the stuff. You'll probably get it for dinner, too, so I hope you like it." She tilted hear head toward the stove and sure enough, a pot sat on the part of the huge range used for keeping food warm.

So I moseyed over to it, grabbing a spoon from the kitchen drawer on my way, lifted the lid and dipped my spoon into the milky-green mixture contained therein. It didn't look particularly appetizing, but I trusted my aunt. I was right to do so.

"Oh, my, Vi, this is delicious! I'm glad we're getting it for dinner."

"So glad you like it, dear."

"I love it. You've made other kinds of creamy soups for us before, haven't you?"

"Of course, I have, but not usually until this time of year, when it's cold."

"Makes sense."

I wanted to continue dipping my spoon into the soup and eating more but restrained myself. "Rolly didn't upset Mrs. Pinkerton today."

"I thought it was you Rolly upset yesterday and the day before."

"Hmm...Yes, it was. But today he behaved himself."

"Or you remembered who's boss."

Or he did. "Yes, that's probably it."

"I'm glad you feel better. You're not still mad at Sam, are you?"

"No," said I. "I didn't mean to be so grumpy with him, even if he did call too early."

"Poor Sam."

Huh.

Vi's chicken-salad sandwich and creamy spinach soup were both delicious, and I left for home stuffed to the gills and happy to be alive.

The feeling didn't last long.

TWENTY-ONE

W hen I drove up our driveway on Marengo Avenue, I noticed a large gray Cadillac parked in front of our house next to the sidewalk. It looked like the Grenvilles' auto, and I wondered why they were visiting.

Turned out they weren't. When entered the house via the side-porch door, I heard sobbing noises coming from the living room. Oh, dear. I wanted to run and hide, but knew that to do so would be cowardly, so I walked through the dining room to the living room, my heart sinking slightly with each step.

There I saw Marianne seated on our sofa, Spike at her feet, and Pa with an arm around her shoulders, attempting to comfort her. When I walked in, he looked up and an expression of pure relief sneaked across his face. That was a bad sign; I knew it.

Nevertheless, my courage didn't fail me. Actually it did, but I entered the living room anyway and walked to the sofa. Not a long journey, unfortunately.

"Whatever is the matter, Marianne?" I asked in my comforting spiritualist's voice as I approached her and Pa.

She jumped about six feet—she'd be great if the sitting high jump were an Olympic event—thereby dislodging my father's arm.

Then she leaped to her feet and rushed at me like Spike going after a ball. Bracing myself, I briefly hoped she didn't aim to batter me to death. I was, if not taller, at least heavier than she, so I'd probably have prevailed. But I didn't want to fight, curse it.

However, she stopped right in front of me, wiping her eyes with her bare hands. Then she screamed, "Detective Rotondo arrested George! Oh, Daisy, he didn't do it!"

In this particular case, I knew the "he" she spoke of was George and not Sam, and that Sam had arrested George, although George hadn't killed Dr. Wagner. The English language is quite odd sometimes, especially when it comes to pronouns.

And then she sort of crumpled up. I managed to grab hold of her before she hit the floor, but I think I dislocated something in my shoulder while doing so, because it ached for a week after my deft catch. Pa rushed over and helped me guide the weeping woman back to the sofa. This time I sat next to her, believing it to be my duty. After all, I was responsible for Rolly and his idiotic pronouncements.

"I'll go make a pot of tea," Pa said softly, and he hightailed out of the living room as if pursued by a pack of screaming devils. Wise man, my father.

I wished I could join him, but I knew where my duty lay. Therefore, I said, "Did the detective actually arrest George, or did he only take him to the station for more questioning, Marianne?"

She tried to answer my question, I think, but she was blubbering so hard I couldn't understand her. I sighed, a trifle irked, even though I did feel sorry for the dear thing.

"Marianne," I said softly. "Please try to get yourself under control. You really need to tell me what I need to know."

Bless Pa's heart, he came into the living room bearing with him a couple of clean dish towels. He was clearly happy to be relieved of an onerous duty, but he wanted to help me take over for him.

"Here, Marianne," I said since she hadn't stopped weeping. "Use this towel and dry your tears. I need to know what's going on."

Furiously wiping her face with the towel, she gasped out, "I-I-I j-j-just t-t-told you!"

"You told me Detective Rotondo has arrested George, and I want to know if he really *did* arrest George, or if he merely took George to the police station to ask him more questions."

Sniffling and wiping more tears, Marianne gazed at me out of drowned blue eye. "Is-is there a difference? The detective took George away in a police car. From the book store! In front of all his customers!"

Egad. If Sam really did haul George out of Grenville's Books while customers meandered around, I might just have to speak to my beloved by hand. Not only did I believe George to be innocent of the crime in question, but taking him away in front of a bunch of his customers would be bad for his business even if it were proved beyond the fraction of a doubt that he was innocent of the crime for which he was being questioned. My early-morning annoyance with Sam Rotondo resurfaced and began bubbling like a witch's cauldron over a hot fire.

"I'm really sorry about this, Marianne. I'm sure George didn't kill your father, and I'm also sure the police will find the true culprit."

Unsure of any such thing—about the police finding the real perpetrator, I mean—I put an arm around Marianne's shoulder and tried to hug her and make her feel better. Didn't work.

"Daisy! What am I going to *do*? George didn't kill my awful father! That stupid spirit control or whatever you call him told everyone to look at the family! That's not fair to us! Neither George nor I had a single, solitary thing to do with killing my father, and neither did Mother!"

"I know, Marianne. I honestly didn't know what Rolly was going to tell everyone during that darned séance. Anyhow, I'm certain neither George nor your mother would have done—*could* have done —such a thing."

Wiping away more tears with a dish towel, she scowled at me. "If *you* don't know why he said it, who does?"

Feeling helpless and guiltier than a dozen murderers, I said, "I-I don't know. I'm sorry."

She slapped the coffee table in front of the sofa with her damp towel. "Well, you being sorry certainly helps a lot, doesn't it?"

"Here's some tea for everyone."

My father's chipper voice made both Marianne and me start. Marianne gasped, must have swallowed wrong, and commenced coughing and turning red. Lord, Lord, could the day get any worse?

The answer, of course, was yes. It could and did.

I finally persuaded Marianne to take sips of warm, sweet tea in between coughing bouts, and eventually she calmed down. Pa stood in front of the two of us, looking bewildered and as if he didn't know what to do.

Since I knew no more than he what should be done, I only sat with Marianne until she downed the last of her tea. Sniffling, she eventually stopped coughing, although tears still flowed, but I think these tears were caused by her coughing fit. At last, she stood.

Because I didn't want to stare up at her looking like the dolt I was, I rose too. Pa, I noticed, seemed to be on the alert, in case Marianne decided to slap me silly. At that point, I wouldn't have blamed her if she did.

"Marianne," I said in a last effort to calm her shattered composure. "I'm so sorry George was taken away by the police the way he was. That was...unfortunate."

"*Unfortunate*! Is *that* what you call it? The police practically proclaimed George's guilt before all the customers in the bookstore! That's not unfortunate. It's beastly."

She was right. I told her so. "Yes, it was a beastly thing to do, especially since they probably only wanted to ask him more questions."

But it was also possible they'd found something linking George to the murder. Policemen didn't generally rip people—especially people of a certain social standing, which George was—away from their places of work for no good reason. I didn't—still don't, in fact—believe wanting to ask more questions counted. Had someone found evidence pointing to George?

I sure hoped not. I didn't want George arrested for the crime even if he did it. Which adds one more boulder to the scales weighted against my overall character. Still and all, George was a good guy; Dr. Wagner had been evil and vicious and had deserved to die. I swore then and there—to myself; I didn't speak aloud—that I was going to grill Sam Rotondo like one of Aunt Vi's T-bone steaks—not that we Gumms and Majestys got T-bone steaks a lot—the next time I saw him.

Which, of course, was that night when he came to dinner. Thursday nights were choir-practice nights for me, and I didn't have very much time to chat before I had to leave for the church. Therefore, as soon as I heard Sam's Hudson's engine turn off, and even before Spike could begin his happy barking frenzy, I tore out the front door to assail Sam before he could enter the house. If I'd tried to grill him in front of my mother and aunt, they'd have scolded me. I raced to the Hudson even before Sam could extricate himself from its front seat. He glanced up at me, surprised.

I grabbed the sleeve to his overcoat and tried to yank him from the automobile. Sam being a large, obelisk-like fellow, I didn't succeed. I could, however, still use my voice, and I did.

"Sam Rotondo, Marianne Grenville came over here this afternoon, hysterical, telling us you'd arrested George Grenville inside his bookstore in front of his customers for the murder of Doctor Wagner. Is that true? Did you really do that?"

Squinting at me as he struggled out of his car—his left thigh still hurt him a good deal—he said, "We did no such thing."

I'd been bent over him, ready to spew more venom, but his words brought me upright in a trice. Whatever a trice is.

"You didn't?"

"No, we didn't. *I* didn't. A couple of uniforms visited the bookstore and asked to speak with him some more down at the station so we could get a comprehensive statement from him."

"You haven't already done that?"

"We have his original statement. We wanted to ask him some more questions."

"Why?"

"Because we're conducting a murder investigation, for God's sake!"

"Don't get snippy with *me*, Sam Rotondo! Why'd you have to haul him out of the bookstore in front of his customers?"

"First of all, I didn't do anything at all to him. I wasn't there. Second, Grenville said he'd be happy to come with Doan and Underwood to the station."

"If that's so, why was Marianne so upset? Honestly, Sam, she was a wreck."

"I don't know. She's an emotional woman. How'd she even find out?"

Good question. "I don't know."

"Well then, stop yelling at my men and me for doing our jobs."

"Nerts to that. She's been upset ever since her father's death was reported. What's so all-fired important that you had to haul George to the station during the day? Couldn't you have waited until the store closed? It's only open until six p.m., for crud's sake."

"Dammit, I don't want to stand out here in the cold arguing with you about the Wagner case."

"That's too darned bad, because I'm going to talk to you about it whether you want to talk to me or not. We have to do it here, because we can't talk in front of my parents and Vi, confound it! Did something new come to light that points the finger at George? And don't you *dare* try to cut me out of the investigation now. We're in this one together and have been from the first, don't forget."

"How could I forget?" said Sam, sounding grouchy.

Too bad. I was grouchy, too, and I'd also had to deal with Marianne. "Tell me what's going on, Sam, or I won't let you eat Vi's dinner tonight."

"Criminy. At least let me sit on the porch, will you? My leg's killing me."

"All right, but if you don't tell me everything, *I'll* kill you and save your leg the trouble."

He didn't even crack a grin. Grunting, he sat on the top porch step and stabbed his cane into the hydrangea bed beside him. "We found a bloody baseball bat in the Grenvilles' potting shed."

"You found a *what*? In *where*?"

"You heard me."

"But…don't you have to have a warrant or something in order to search other people's property?"

"Yes."

"How'd you get a warrant? Neither George nor Marianne looked guilty enough for a judge to sign a warrant. At least, not to me, they didn't. What happened?"

"We got a call at the station telling us to look more closely at Mr. Grenville."

"From whom?"

With a shrug, Sam said, "It was what we call an anonymous tip."

I huffed. "And it came from the murderer, I'd bet."

"Possibly. I don't know." Another shrug from Sam.

"An anonymous tip was reason enough for a warrant? I don't believe it."

"Sorry to burst your bubble, but we got a warrant. And that's principally because of the anonymous tip."

"That's crazy!"

"Not entirely. Don't forget that my men have families, and members of their family work for rich folks all over Pasadena and Altadena. My men know more about the Grenvilles than you'd think."

"Hmm. What else led to the judge signing a warrant?"

Before answering me—he probably knew I'd hate whatever he aimed to say—Sam took in a deep breath and let it out in a whoosh. "Judge Carpenter is a member of the Pasadena Golf and Tennis Club. One of the guys who works at the club told him about the bloody bat."

"How did *he* know about it?"

"His brother works as gardener for the Grenvilles. He found the bat in the potting shed."

"Someone must have planted it there. The real killer, I mean."

"I hope you're right. All I know as of this minute is that my men found a bloody bat in the Grenvilles' potting shed, and they went to Grenville's Books to talk with Grenville about it."

"That sounds like a mighty fishy story to me, Sam. I can't

picture George Grenville playing baseball. When he was at school, he never played sports. He's always been more likely to visit a museum or go to the library for fun than play a ball game."

"That may well be true. Anyway, it wasn't any fault of mine that the damned bloody bat was found on Grenville's property. Am I allowed into the house for dinner now?"

"Well…I guess so."

"Thanks heaps."

"You're welcome. But Sam, I know George didn't kill that man, and I think you're putting an awful lot of weight on a so-called anonymous tip. I also think Judge Carpenter should have had more real evidence before he signed the stupid search warrant. Well, I guess there's the gardener, too."

"Precisely," said Sam as he grabbed his cane from the hydrangea bed and whacked it against a porch step to get the mud off.

Shoot. The gardener thing sounded bad, although I still didn't believe George Grenville would own or use a baseball bat on purpose. Heck, even in school, he was a member of the chess club and never participated in sports. "Still, I think you're jumping the gun."

"I'm not jumping anything, and there's no gun involved in this one. It's a baseball bat."

"Funny, Sam Rotondo. The police are over-reacting to something George Grenville never touched in his life."

"Maybe we are. I had nothing to do with it, though."

"Why not? I thought you were in charge of the case."

"I am, but I wasn't at the station when the call came through. I had to keep an appointment with Doctor Benjamin this afternoon. Doan thought the tip and the baseball bat together were strong enough evidence for us to snoop some more in the Grenvilles' business, and Judge Carpenter agreed."

"Hmph. I always sort of liked Doan, but today he sounds like an idiot."

"We have to do our jobs, Daisy."

"And why didn't you tell me you had an appointment with Doc Benjamin? I'm interested in your health, you know, Sam Rotondo."

"I forgot," said Sam. I didn't believe him.

"Hogwash. You're just worried your leg will never get better, and you wanted to spare me."

"How is not telling you about a doctor's appointment sparing you?"

Good question, darn it. "Well…I just think that when a man and woman are engaged to be married, they should share everything."

"Right. That's why you always share information with me."

"I *do* share!" Recalling the recent Bannister investigation and a couple of other little episodes in my past, I added, "For the most part. Sometimes I can't share because it's other people's business."

"Of course." He struggled to his feet. I noticed his face appeared more ragged and rugged than usual. He'd clearly had a rough day.

My sympathy stirred, I said, "Did Doc Benjamin give you bad news?"

"Not really. Just the same old thing. It'll take time. And the wound will heal completely, but it may pain me forever, depending on the weather or the type of activity I'm doing."

"I'm sorry, Sam."

"Yeah. So am I."

We entered the house together, and Spike finally got to display his affection for Sam.

I felt crummy. Mainly because of Marianne and George, but also because of Sam. That ghastly woman who'd shot him in the thigh could have easily shot him through the heart. In fact, if I hadn't stuck a kitchen towel over the wound and held it there, he'd have bled to death. I shuddered.

"Here," said Sam, putting his coat over my shoulder in the mistaken belief that I was cold.

"Thanks." I didn't clue him in.

TWENTY-TWO

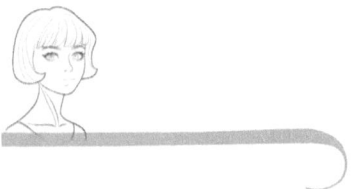

That night's dinner which, for me, was a repeat of that day's lunch, was delicious. The only difference was that Vi served a roasted chicken after we ate the creamy spinach soup.

My mood was a little grim as I washed the dinner dishes and put them away. I was terribly worried about George and Marianne Grenville. But I didn't have a single, solitary idea how to go about proving George's innocence.

The discovery of that bloody bat was disturbing. For all that George Grenville was apt to read all day and all night and never play a game of ball, he might have kept a baseball bat someone had given him as a gift or something.

Piffle.

Nevertheless, when the time came, I bundled up in my hat, coat and gloves, and walked out to say farewell to my family and Sam. Sometimes Sam went to choir practice with me and just sat in one of the front pews in the sanctuary and listened. I wished he'd join the choir because he had a magnificent bass voice, but I'd have to pester him about that later. After all, he grew up in the Roman Catholic Church, so we Methodists were quite a step for him, although he didn't seem to mind joining us at our church services.

His nephew had been horrified that Sam would actually step foot into a church that wasn't Catholic. I think Frank's attitude endeared us Methodists to Sam, actually. Frank wasn't a nice guy, and he'd been a sore burden for Sam to bear.

Anyhow, Sam said he had paperwork to do that evening, so I drove alone to the church, which was just up the street on the corner of Marengo and Colorado. My mood wasn't chipper.

As soon as I set foot in the choir room, Lucy Zollinger cornered me.

"Oh, Daisy! Did you hear about that awful Doctor Wagner? Somebody *murdered* him!"

"Yes, I know."

"Oh." Lucy sounded disappointed.

"That's only because Detective Rotondo and I found the body," I said to make her feel better. I mean, if you have a choice bit of gossip, it's a let-down when the person you're gossiping to already knows about the piece of gossip. Did that make any sense? Oh, never mind.

"Good Lord, you did? I swear, Daisy," said Lucy, squinting at me oddly, "you trip over dead bodies every time you turn around, don't you?"

"No!" Blast and heck! Was I really getting a reputation for finding corpses? "Sam and I just happened to be in the cemetery that morning and Spike—you know, my dog—brought us a shoe with a foot stuck in it."

Lucy stepped back and gazed at me with horror. Guess I should have softened the truth slightly. Fiddlesticks. I seemed to be having no luck at all communicating with people that day.

"Well, I didn't mean it precisely that way. I mean, yes, Sam and I went to the cemetery, but that was because I wanted to...to..." Phooey. What I'd wanted to do sounded idiotic now. "Because we wanted to visit the graves of our respective spouses—I told you Sam's a widower, didn't I?"

"Yes, I vaguely remember that. The poor man."

The poor man? How about poor me? I'd lost my beloved spouse, too. But I didn't feel like stirring up trouble.

Therefore, when I resumed speaking, I only said, "We took Spike along, and *he* found the body. I didn't."

"Still..." Lucy didn't appear mollified.

"Anyhow, it's not my fault. Shoot, Lucy, you and I were in church *together* when that horrible Mr. Underhill was murdered. So you might as well say that *you* keep finding dead bodies."

"Not as often as you do," she declared stoutly.

Piffle. "Let's talk about something else, all right?"

"Yes, all right. Murder is too grim a topic for church. Oh, but Daisy, I'm so excited about Christmas! It will be Albert's and my first Christmas together!" Lucy had wed Mr. Albert Zollinger several months prior and they seemed to adore each other, which I thought was sweet.

"That's nice, Lucy. I'm so glad you and Mr. Zollinger found each other."

That was true, if only partially. After the Great War, there were no longer enough young men alive to wed all the young women wanting husbands. When Lucy and her Albert began seeing each other, I'd felt sort of bad that Lucy had to settle for a man so much older than she. Nevertheless, I'd never seen Lucy happier than during the past year, so I was probably only being hateful for thinking she'd settled for someone less than she deserved. On the other hand, Lucy herself was no beauty queen. Tall, lean and kind of rabbity, she might not have been able to attract a young man even if the late war hadn't killed off most of them.

Good Lord, what an obnoxious, judgmental person I can be without half trying, huh? I apologize—especially to Lucy and her Albert. Sometimes I wonder why God allowed me to sully His sanctuary. Melancholy thought. I mentally slapped myself hard and shoved all evil-minded judgments aside, where they occupied only a tiny amount of brain space. I hoped they'd stay there.

"How are you going to handle the families? Spend Christmas Eve with one and Christmas day with the other?"

Lucy's smile turned upside down. "Poor Albert has no family left, so we'll be celebrating both days at my parents' house. If I can learn how to cook well enough, I hope we can host a Christmas Eve party next year. That would be such fun! But I don't think you've seen our new house, have you?"

"You have a new house? That's wonderful, Lucy!"

"We just bought it. Albert is so good with finances, you know. We'll be moved in by Easter."

"Where is it? I'll have to write down the address, and you can show me through it one of these days."

"Absolutely! You're one of the very first people I want to see it. After my parents, of course."

"Of course. What's the address?"

"Fifteen-eleven North Holliston Avenue. Oh, Daisy, I just love the house. It's one of those sort-of Spanish-style homes, and it has four bedrooms."

"Wow. Do you aim to fill all those bedrooms with children?"

Lucy blushed scarlet. "I hope we will have children one day, but not quite yet."

"I'm sorry, Lucy. I didn't mean to pry into your business."

"That's all right. Both Albert and I would rather settle in and get comfy in the house together before we try for children."

"Makes perfect sense to me." Which, for one of the few times that day, was the truth.

Lucy went on, "We've been living in Albert's apartment at the Castle Green, you know."

"I know. I love the Castle Green. It's a lovely place. I performed a séance there once."

Shaking her head, Lucy giggled and said, "You and your séances."

I heaved a little sigh and said, "It's a living."

"I know." She placed a hand on my shoulder and gazed at me sorrowfully. "You've been through so much, Daisy. I honestly don't know how you've managed to do all the things you do."

I was beginning to wonder the same thing, only I don't think Lucy and I shared opinions. Lucy probably meant how I'd lost my husband and had to work for a living. I wondered how I'd managed to turn into a miserable, lying old hag. Well, not old. The hag part certainly seemed to fit that evening, though.

"The Castle Green is beautiful, but I'm glad we'll have our own house now!"

"That's a nice address, Lucy, on Holliston. It's a pretty street."

" Yes, it is. But, well..." Lucy laughed. "I hate to say this, but Albert and I generally dine at the Castle Green, so I don't have to cook. But I'll be happy to have a home all to ourselves. I'm praying it won't take me long to learn to cook a lot better than I can now."

"Oh, yes. I know the feeling well," said I, recalling my many dismal failures in the kitchen of our bungalow.

"I've picked up several cookbooks at Grenville's Books," Lucy said happily.

"How nice. I love Grenville's Books, too." I only hoped it would remain open and a viable business after the Wagner case had been solved.

"It's my favorite bookstore," said Lucy.

Before I could add my praise to Lucy's regarding George Grenville's bookstore, a loud voice from the sanctuary said, "Ladies and gentlemen."

The voice belonged to Mr. Floy Hostetter, our choir director. He'd been itchy lately, what with getting the choir all tuned up for Advent and Christmas and so forth. This coming Sunday, the first Sunday before Christmas, we were doing a mix of Advent and Christmas hymns. I love Christmas carols. So many composers have contributed wonderful music to the season.

On the coming Sunday, Mr. Hostetter had chosen as our anthem "Savior of the Nations, Come," which is, according to him, a hymn sung primarily in Lutheran Churches. That's probably because Martin Luther translated it from the Latin. Then a fellow named Reynolds translated it into English. At any rate, the song had a very...I don't know what you'd call it...Medieval tone to it? Not that I know beans about Medieval music, but this particular Advent hymn sounded really old to me.

I'm probably wrong.

Anyhow, the choir had been struggling a bit with it, so I'd known before I'd arrived that Mr. Hostetter would want us to go over it several times. Having been summoned, Lucy and I, and all the other stragglers in the choir room hied ourselves out to the chancel.

"Everyone, please take your seats," said Mr. Hostetter, frowning.

Without whispering or even making moving noises, we took our seats. All of us choir members appreciated Mr. Hostetter, but he could get a teensy bit crabby at times. He particularly didn't approve of chatter during choir practice. The fact that his frown was most often directed to Lucy and me, who sat in the front row together, led me to believe he didn't aim on taking any guff from us that evening. And for good reason. Occasionally—very occasionally, mind you—Lucy and I would whisper to each other during choir practice.

"Take out 'Savior of the Nations, Come,'" directed Mr. Hostetter.

We dutiful choir members did as bidden. Mr. Hostetter nodded to Mrs. Fleming, our organist, she began the introduction to the hymn, and we all joined in where we were supposed to join in. Boy, this was the first time *that* had happened! The last few times we'd rehearsed the hymn, it had been definitely ragged, which I thought served Mr. Hostetter right for selecting a Lutheran hymn. Not that I have anything against Lutherans, you understand; it's just that the hymn felt weird on our Methodist tonsils.

Fortunately, on Christmas Eve we'd sing "Come, Thou Long Expected Jesus," which fit on my tongue much better than "Savior." That's probably because the words to "Long Expected" were written by Charles Wesley, one of Methodism's founders. Of course, on Christmas Eve, we'd sing "Silent Night," too. This is probably blasphemous, but I don't care for "Silent Night." I think it's boring.

I'm sorry, God.

Anyway, after we'd sung our way through "Savior to the Nations," Mr. Hostetter told us to get out "O Come, All Ye Faith-ful," which most of us could sing by heart at that point.

After we plowed our way through that one, Mr. Hostetter pinned Lucy and me to our chairs with a stiffish frown. We hadn't been chatting! Honest.

"Mrs. Majesty and Mrs. Zollinger, I would like the two of you to sing a duet during the third verse of 'What Child is This' on Christmas Eve. Do you each know your part?"

Lucy and I nodded in unison. We were asked to sing duets a lot, Lucy being a soprano and me being an alto, and both having good voices. We looked at each other, and I whispered, "Come over Saturday, and we can practice." That's because we Gumms and this Majesty had a piano at home.

Afraid to whisper back, Lucy only nodded. We both turned our attention back to Mr. Hostetter, who said, "All right, let's sing 'What Child' now. Remember, only Mrs. Majesty and Mrs. Zollinger will be singing the third verse."

You probably already know this, but "What Child" is sung to the tune of "Greensleeves," and was supposedly written by King Henry VIII. Knowing King Henry's history, I'm surprised music created by him had been allowed to enter the doors of any church, but I'm glad it did, because it's pretty. Even if Henry himself was a pig.

Dang. There goes my judgmental self, leaping o'er obstacles to get to a quick conclusion. Truly, all I knew about Henry VIII was stuff I'd read about him. As a Methodist, I probably should thank him; otherwise, my family and I would certainly have been Roman Catholics instead of Methodists. Still, he seemed like man of dubious character.

I should talk. Phooey.

Anyhow, Mr. Hostetter tapped his little baton thing on his metal music stand and nodded at Mrs. Fleming, who began the introduction of the song. We did a pretty good job on that hymn, too, except that Mr. Finster, a bass, began singing the third verse. He caught himself almost instantly, so Mr. Hostetter didn't yell at him.

"Very well," said Mr. H when we'd knocked down "What Child." "I know your won't do that on Christmas Eve, Mr. Finster."

"Of course not," said Mr. Finster. "I apologize."

"That's all right," said Mr. H. I guess he felt benevolent that evening.

And so it went. We went through all of the hymns we'd be singing on the coming Sunday, Christmas Eve, and Christmas Day, and I was all hymned out when practice ended. As Lucy and I put our hymnals and folders away, she said, "I'm going to gargle with hot salt water when I get home. This was the most intense choir practice I think we've ever had."

"I think you're right," said I. "And that's a good idea about gargling."

Lucy's Albert met her right outside the choir's door, and I was pleased to see their enthusiastic greeting one for the other. What's more, they walked to their automobile with Albert's arm over Lucy's shoulder. I thought that was sweet. See? I'm not totally bad.

"Mrs. Majesty?"

I'd been so busy thinking about how lovely a couple Lucy and Albert made—even if he was a million years older than she—that I started and whirled around when I heard my name.

Slapping a hand over my heart, I said, "Mrs. Dermott!" Violet Dermott was another alto. Much older than I, she had pretty white hair and always looked as if she'd just been discharged from a beauty parlor, with perfect, very lightly applied makeup and stylish clothing.

"I'm sorry I startled you, Mrs. Majesty."

"That's all right," I said, laughing. "I was so deep in my thoughts, I didn't hear you behind me."

She laughed a little, too, and then sobered. "I-I'm not sure I should be telling anyone this, but…Well, I know you're engaged to that nice detective fellow."

That nice detective fellow? Huh. Mind you, *I* adored Sam, but he could come across as quite stiff and formal if you didn't know him. That's because he had to project a stern and policemanly demeanor.

"Yes," I said. "Yes, I am. Um…did you want me to give him a message or anything?"

Mrs. Dermott stood before me—we were approximately the same height at five-feet, four-inches or thereabouts, so neither of us had to stand on tiptoes or stoop—and appeared nervous. Interesting.

"Well…Oh, I don't know. I just thought perhaps someone might be interested in something my son said to Mr. Dermott and me last night at dinner."

"What did your son say?" I asked her, wishing she'd speed up her narration. I was tired after a long, extremely frustrating day, and all I wanted to do right then was go home and read a bit more of *A Passage to India* with my hound on my lap before retiring to bed.

"It's…Well, it's probably nothing, really, but he said something that surprised me. It might have to do with the death of that awful Doctor Wagner."

In a flash, all thoughts of Spike and India flew out of my head, and I was all ears.

TWENTY-THREE

"My goodness, Mrs. Dermott, please tell me what your son said. As you know, Detective Rotondo is investigating the Wagner case, and he'll be overjoyed to get any information at all." Incorrect word selection, Daisy Gumm Majesty. I hedged and said, "I mean…I don't suppose overjoyed is the proper word for it, but… Well, I'm sure you know what I mean."

"Yes, of course." Mrs. Dermott smiled sympathetically. Perhaps she'd had a rough day, too.

"Thank you for your understanding."

"It must be difficult to investigate such horrible crimes."

"Yes, it is." I experienced a mad urge to grab the woman by her shoulders and shake information out of her. Couldn't she see I was exhausted?

"Well, our son, Claude, works at the Pasadena Golf and Tennis Club. He's the assistant manager there."

"How nice for him."

"Yes, it's quite a responsible position, and he does a good job."

"I'm sure. But you said he heard something?"

"Oh. Oh, yes, he did."

Yeesh. I wasn't physically able to stand there palavering with the woman all night, darn it. I'd fall over in a heap if she didn't spit it out soon. "Yes?" I said sweetly.

"He overheard several of the young men who reside there last night. Evidently, they were laughing together in the locker room. They'd been playing handball, you see."

"I see." I didn't care, but I saw.

"The club isn't merely for golf and tennis. Young men actually live there."

"Yes, indeed." I forced my face to remain serene.

"Well, Claude was in one row of lockers, and these fellows—he didn't know how many there were, or who they were, but he thought there were at least three of them—were in another row. I guess there are several rows of lockers in the club." She paused again, and I suppressed the urge to strangle her.

"Yes?" I said once more, wishing she'd get to the point.

"Well, Claude said they were laughing about something someone in the club did."

"Yes? What did this other gentleman do?" My voice was still sweet as candy, curse the woman.

"According to what Claude heard, someone hid something in Mr. George Grenville's home somewhere."

I waited, but she didn't continue.

"Um…Did your son say what it was they'd hidden?" Bet I knew.

"No. He didn't, but he felt uncomfortable about having overheard their conversation. He doesn't ordinarily eavesdrop, you understand."

"Of course not." I'd bet on that one, too, but against Claude's fond mother. And again, I'd probably win.

"But he was a trifle concerned about their nonchalance, given the circumstances of Doctor Wagner's death. Not that the man didn't deserve to die, but I heard from a friend who was in Grenville's Books yesterday that the police had come into the bookstore and carted George Grenville off to the police station. Claude is worried whatever that person—whoever he was—hid on Mr. Grenville's property might have something to do with Doctor Wagner's murder." Her face screwed up into a caricature of its usual oldish, stylish face. "Do you think it's important? I mean, does it even make sense?"

It made a whole lot of sense to me. "Yes," I told Mrs. Dermott. "It does make sense, and I'm sure Detective Rotondo will be more than happy to learn what your son overheard." A thought occurred to me, and I said, "Please tell your son not to be alarmed if Detective Rotondo or another member of the Pasadena Police Department visits him at the club. They'll only want to question him about what he heard from those men."

"Oh, no! He can't do that! I mean, nobody from the police can go to the club to question Claude! Oh, dear. Now I'm sorry I said anything."

The poor woman appeared stricken with fear. "My goodness, Mrs. Dermott, why ever not?"

"Because if one of those men who were talking ever learn Claude overheard their conversation and told the police about it, he might be in *danger*! One man has been murdered already, and whoever was talking in the club yesterday might have done it! Some of the young men who live there are...Well, they aren't wholesome young men. Claude has told us more than once that many of those boys don't do anything but drink and waste their parents' money. A disgrace, is what I call it." Mrs. Dermott frowned heartily.

Can't say as I blamed her. There was a lot of irresponsibility in young people going around in those days. Bright young things seemed to care for nothing and no one, and only wanted to go to parties and drink their lives away. I think the war had a lot to do with their attitudes, but I also think Mr. F. Scott Fitzgerald, in glorifying their frivolity, had contributed to the seeming epidemic of lousy behavior in so many of the youth of the day. Stacy Kincaid, to my mind, was a prime example of how not to live one's life. She had all the money in the world, didn't have to work, played all day every day, and had actually ended up participating in horrible crimes!

But I think I got distracted again.

"I didn't know," I said, not speaking the precise truth. I didn't know too many men who lived at the Pasadena Golf and Tennis Club. However, of those I did know, I thought the Wagner boys were warts on the skin of society. On the other hand, I knew Dr. Fred Greenlaw to be a peach of a guy.

"Oh, yes. Claude said most of them are nothing but wastrels and louts! And Claude has no idea where and how those silly boys get their liquor, but he's told us more than once that drunken parties take place there."

"Good heavens," said I.

"So the police simply *can't* question Claude at work. You do understand that, don't you?"

"Y-y-yes," I said slowly, thinking furiously. "But the police will certainly need to question your son about what he heard. Perhaps he could drop in at the police station sometime tomorrow? Or call and set up an appointment with Detective Rotondo? Or…I know!"

"You do?"

"Yes. Please have your son telephone me, and I'll set up a time and place for him and Detective Rotondo to speak. That way none of the men who talked about hiding something at the Grenvilles' place will ever have to know your son had anything to do with the matter. I mean, they won't know he overheard them talking and then told anyone. I mean, if you use me as a go-between, those worthless boys will never know your son heard anything at all. I mean…Oh, dear. I'm not sure what I mean."

"Ah. I think I do. You want Claude to telephone you, and then you'll get together with the detective and tell him Claude needs to tell him what he heard? And perhaps Claude and the detective will set up an appointment somewhere other than the Pasadena Golf and Tennis Club to meet and discuss the matter?"

I don't know about anyone else, but I was getting terribly confused. Nevertheless, I said, "Yes. Exactly. Our number is in the telephone book. We're listed under Gumm, and we live on Marengo. Just south of the church a couple of blocks."

"Yes, I remember you live close by. So do we, but not quite so close." She opened her handbag and took out a little notebook and pencil. Gee, she was about as organized as I was. I approved. "Just tell me your number, I'll write it down, and then I'll have Claude telephone you."

"Thank you. I'll call Detective Rotondo as soon as I get home, and perhaps I can give your son a definite time and place for the two of them to meet. Your son will need to talk to Detective Rotondo in person, because otherwise my word on the matter would be…I can't remember what it's called. Hearsay, I think."

"Heresy? Oh, surely not!"

"No. Not heresy. I think that's a religious term. Hearsay is a legal term, and hearsay isn't accepted in court." As a matter of fact, I almost got into fisticuffs with an attorney during a trial when he told the judge what I'd said was hearsay, and I maintained it wasn't. But I didn't want Mrs. Dermott to know that.

"I don't understand legal jargon."

"Nor do I. But I think this strategy will work."

"Thank you, Mrs. Majesty. I feel better for having spoken with you. I still don't want Claude to be involved in this matter, though. Some person murdered that awful doctor, and if it's one of the men Claude heard talking at the club, he might be in danger, too."

"True. I think we can prevent anyone from knowing Claude heard a thing."

"I hope so. Not that I'm sorry Doctor Wagner is dead. He used to abuse Diane terribly."

"Yes, I know."

"But I'm sorry. That wasn't a very Christian thing to say, was it?"

"I don't think God will be unhappy with you for telling the truth."

"Thank you, Mrs. Majesty. We all felt so sorry for Diane."

"As did I."

"Thank you, dear. I'll have Claude give you a ring."

We said our good-byes, and I finished walking to the Chevrolet, contemplating the state of things and of human beings.

I hadn't understood until recently that pretty much everyone in Pasadena seemed to know about the evil Dr. Wagner and his victims. Too bad nobody ever tried to do anything about him before his life ended in murder. Then again, he probably didn't deserve any better than murder. Then again *again*, his wife and daughter had deserved infinitely better than what he'd done to them.

Bother.

Anyway, if anything Claude Dermott had overheard at the Pasadena Golf and Tennis Club helped the investigation into Dr. Wagner's murder, Sam would be pleased. I hoped. As I drove home, I wondered whom Claude had overheard at the club. I hoped it wasn't Dr. Fred Greenlaw, because I liked him. Perhaps the Wagner boys had done their father to death. That would solve the crime, but Diane and Marianne might be upset.

But what the heck. The worst that could happen to Diane or Marianne had already happened; at least I thought so.

I was about to collapse from fatigue by the time I finally got home from choir practice that night. It was almost nine o'clock, later than usual, and too late to telephone anyone, but I still thought I'd better call Sam before Spike and I hit the sack.

Pa and Spike were the only beings still awake in our bungalow when I entered through the side entrance. Spike greeted me with hysterical wagging and leaping—but he didn't bark out a welcome. That's because I'd thought to put my finger to my lips in preparation. He knew the signal for silence. Boy, I do believe I had the best-trained dog in the whole world. I knelt and hugged and petted him.

"What a good boy, Spike!" I told him. It was nothing but the truth. Spike knew it and wagged harder.

"You looked worn out, sweetheart," said Pa.

Gazing up at him from my kneeling position, I said, "Is it that obvious?" Crumb. I really must look haggard if Pa had noticed.

He chuckled softly. "You just seem a little tired, is all. You're as lovely as ever, of course."

Getting to my feet with an audible grunt, I said, "Of course."

"Choir practice went well?"

"Oh, yes. We managed to sing 'Savior of the Nations, Come' without one person messing it up, and Lucy and I are singing a duet during verse three of 'What Child Is This?' at the Christmas Eve service."

"I love to hear the two of you sing together," said Pa, which made me smile.

"Thanks, Pa. Lucy's coming over Saturday so we can practice."

"Fill the house with music. That's what I like to hear."

"But now I have to telephone Sam."

Pa frowned. "At this time? Isn't it kind of late?"

"Yes, but it's important."

"If you say so."

"I think Sam will think so," I said a little stiffly. "And that's what's important."

"Right." Pa smiled to let me know he wasn't upset with me.

Therefore, although I didn't much want to, I walked to the kitchen, looked at the clock on the wall—it was then nine-o-three—and dialed Sam's telephone number. I didn't bother shooing party-line neighbors off the wire, since I didn't aim to impart anything of particular intrigue. Well, not anything that would intrigue nosy neighbors, anyhow.

Sam picked up his receiver on the second ring. He sounded trepidatious, if that's a word. I expect he equated late telephone calls with bad news, being a policeman and all.

"Sorry to call so late, but a member of the choir has some information for you that I believe might be important."

"Oh? What?"

"Not on the 'phone. I'll either telephone you at the station or visit you and give you the info. Just wanted to warn you some information is coming."

Silence.

Hmm. Perhaps this telephone call hadn't been precisely important after all.

"Are you there?" I asked in a small voice.

"Yeah. I'm here. So somebody said something to you, but you can't tell me what it was."

"Not over the telephone!" I realized I'd raised my voice and lowered it again. "Shoot, Sam, I just wanted to give you fair warning some vital information might be coming your way. Will you be in the office tomorrow?"

"Yeah. Desk duty tomorrow. Doctor Benjamin's orders."

"Why?" I asked instantly. "What's wrong? What happened?" My worry level soared astronomically.

"Nothing's wrong," he said in a weary voice. "I already told you anyway. Doc just said I've been overdoing it with the exercise lately. All that walking in cemeteries isn't good for me, apparently."

"Pooh. You didn't walk all *that* much."

"It hurt."

"I know." Feeling guilty, I added, "I'm sorry."

"Good."

I got the impression his mood had improved. The rat. "Good night, Sam," I said.

"Good night."

"Love you."

"Yeah. You, too."

Men. I swear....

TWENTY-FOUR

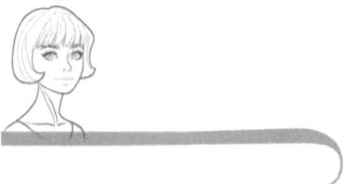

Aunt Vi was just about to leave the house for Mrs. Pinkerton's mansion when I walked into the kitchen on Friday morning. It was approximately seven a.m. I'd considered what Mrs. Dermott had told me as I'd dressed that morning, and I thought I'd come up with a keen way for Claude Dermott and Sam to speak together about the Wagner case without arousing the suspicions of anyone at all.

Smiling, Vi said, "Good morning, Daisy. I hear you got in late last night. Long choir practice?"

"It was a little longer than usual. Mr. Hostetter is having us sing a really odd Lutheran hymn on Sunday. It's pretty, but it's...well, kind of odd."

"Interesting."

"Say, Vi, I have a really...I don't know what you'd call it. Impertinent? I guess that's as good a word as any. I need to ask you a terribly, awfully, really and truly impertinent question."

Vi had been tying a scarf over her head in order to go out into the cold morning. She stopped and stared at me, her hands at the sides of her head, each one holding the end of the scarf and making her head appear kind of like a large bat. "An impertinent question? Good heavens, Daisy, what do you need to ask?"

"You shouldn't be asking impertinent questions, Daisy Gumm Majesty," said Ma, frowning as she walked into the kitchen. Her scarf was already securely tied over her head. "That's impolite, and I taught you better than that."

Piffle. "I know, Ma, but this is in aid of the Wagner investigation. Mrs. Dermott told me last night that her son heard something that might be important to the investigation, but she doesn't want the people he heard talking to know it was Mrs. Dermott's son who gave the information to Sam." I was getting confused again. Nuts.

"Go ahead, Daisy," said Vi. "Just ask. I'm sure I won't be offended."

"You might be," I told her, probably looking as penitent as I felt. "I wondered if you'd mind having three guests for dinner tonight. That's besides Sam. So it would be five of us and three of the Dermotts, if they're able to make it. I hope the whole family can come, because it will appear less obvious that the younger Mr. Dermott wants Sam's attention if they all attend."

"Three extra people? Without any notice? Daisy, that's—"

"I wouldn't mind at all!" exclaimed Vi, interrupting Ma's objection, bless her heart. "I get off early on Fridays, I'm planning to fix a leg of lamb with popovers, and that's no trouble at all. I'll just have Mr. Larkin deliver a larger leg of lamb than I'd planned for earlier."

Oh, boy, I absolutely loved leg of lamb.

"I'll pay for it," I said, hoping to quell my mother's irritation.

"Nonsense. Mrs. Pinkerton will pay for it," said Vi, laughing. "She pays for most of our meals, you know."

"I guess I did know that," I said because it was true, but I hadn't really thought much about it before.

"She doesn't mind?" asked Ma, blinking at Vi.

"Not at all. She appreciates Daisy so much, she's actually *ordered* me to charge our butcher's bill to her. Mr. Larkin approves, too." As Mr. Larkin was the butcher at Jorgenson's Market, where all the rich people's servants shopped, I expect he did approve.

Ma turned and looked at me, her expression changing from one of annoyance to one of admiration. "My goodness. I had no idea."

"Well, I guess she thinks she owes us or something," I said, feeling a bit funny about someone else buying our family's meat. That sounds strange, doesn't it? Oh, well. Rich people have always baffled me, and they continue to do so.

"It's thanks to Daisy that we eat so well at our house," said Vi.

"Now that's just not true," I told my aunt, reality smacking me upside the head. "Even if Mrs. Pinkerton bought our meat for all eternity, without you to cook it for us, we'd have died of ptomaine years ago."

"That's the truth," said Ma, ever candid.

"Nonsense. Neither of you enjoys cooking. You have other talents."

"I guess," said I.

"Yes, I suppose so," said Ma.

Spike, who was looking up at all of us with hope writ large in his eyes, wagged his tail. We were in the *kitchen*, for Pete's sake. The kitchen was where *food* resided. I guess he couldn't figure out why we were standing there jawing when we were supposed to be eating and dropping things for him to eat.

"Anyhow, we'd best get going, Peggy," said Vi to Ma.

"Want me to drive you to work?" I asked, believing I owed Vi a helping hand even if that hand only steered the Chevrolet.

"No, thanks. I enjoy the walk," said Vi.

"As do I," said Ma.

So they left to go to work, and Spike and I stared at each other for several seconds, my mind running around in circles, kind of like a hamster on a wheel. Spike's mind was on food, so I eventually gave myself a little shake and got busy. I fed him first, of course, and then went to the stove to see if Vi had left anything edible for Pa and me to eat.

Speaking of Pa...

"Where's Pa, Spike?"

Spike didn't answer, but Pa was clearly not at home. He was

probably out walking or chatting with one or two of his approximately ten million and three friends.

Bless Vi's heart, she had left breakfast for us. Sausages and scrambled eggs waited for me in the warming oven. So I brought my plate to the table, poured myself a cup of coffee, and enjoyed my almost-solitary meal. Spike got two little pieces of sausage. After eating, I peeled and ate an orange, all the while hoping the telephone would ring. Boy, *that* almost never happened. But I wanted to hear from Claude Dermott, confound it.

However, the first telephone call I received on Friday morning wasn't from Claude Dermott.

At nine o'clock, after nearly jumping out of my skin when the 'phone rang, I'd just lifted the receiver and said, "Gumm-Majesty residence. Mrs. Majesty speaking," when Mrs. Pinkerton screeched at me. I sighed and held the receiver away from my ear.

"*Daisy!*"

"Good morning, Mrs. Pinkerton. I hope nothing has happened to put you in a state." Was that going too far, me suggesting she was in a state?

Naw.

"Oh, Daisy, I just heard from Stacy!"

"Did she telephone you from the jail?" Lordy, her old man had escaped from San Quentin once; I hoped Stacy hadn't inherited the escapist gene from him.

"*Yes!*"

Thank God.

"Oh, Daisy, she's *so* unhappy!"

As well she should be, thought I. Naturally, those words didn't issue from my mouth. Rather, I said, "Oh?"

"Yes! They're treating her very badly, Daisy!"

As well they should, I thought. I didn't say those words, either. "How are they doing that?"

"They don't let her use the telephone as much as she wants."

Tut-tut. How tragic. Hmmm. What should you say, Daisy Gumm Majesty? Should you be brave and daring?

Why not?

"Mrs. Pinkerton, I know Stacy is frustrated because her freedom has been severely constrained, but you do understand that she was in part responsible for a couple of murders and assisted in a human-trafficking operation, don't you? One involving children? Who were imported into the United States for…immoral purposes? If anyone needs her freedom curtailed, I believe it's someone who's done those things. Do you really believe Stacy should be given her freedom before she learns how to use it properly?"

Harsh words. I hoped Mrs. P wouldn't fire me.

She gulped. I heard her. "I never thought of it precisely like that," she admitted.

"Perhaps you should. It might give you a different perspective about the reality of your daughter's transgressions. She really put her foot in it this time, Mrs. Pinkerton. You must know that. Hasn't Harold told you how culpable Stacy was in the Bannister affair?"

"Yes. Yes, he has. Several times. I…I didn't want to believe him. But then the lawyer told me the same thing."

"And I'm the third person to do so. Well, the fourth, if you count Rolly."

Another gulp. "Yes. Yes, you are. Well…Actually, you're the fifth. Algie told me so, too."

That surprised me. Algie, Mrs. Pinkerton's roly-poly, cherubic husband, didn't appear on the surface to have so much common sense. Just goes to show you can't tell a book by its cover, I reckon.

"My goodness," I said, mainly because I couldn't think of anything more intelligent to say.

"Oh, my. To think I should have reared such a child. It makes me terribly ashamed, Daisy."

"Stacy is an adult, Mrs. Pinkerton. She chose her own way. She was on the right path at the Salvation Army, but then she allowed her baser nature to override her new training. Captain Buckingham will do his best to redeem her. And don't ever forget that you reared a wonderful man in Harold."

Was that a little thick and gooey? Aw, so what? The poor woman needed some kind of consolation, and I was pretty sure she wouldn't get it from Harold, who was sick and tired of his mother's connip-tion fits. I *knew* she wouldn't get any comfort from Stacy.

"You're right. I know you're right, Daisy. You're so wise for your years."

Tell Sam that, I thought. Then I thought about offering her my services, but I didn't want to. So I didn't.

"Um…Do you think you can come over today, dear? I'd love to talk to Rolly and the Ouija board. And the tarot cards. If you don't mind?"

Gee, she usually considered me to be at her beck and call. Strange.

"I should be happy to visit you today, Mrs. Pinkerton. I do have to wait for an important telephone call, however. As soon as I receive the call I'm expecting, I can give you a firm time."

"Oh, thank you, dear. You're so obliging. Harold keeps telling me I take hideous advantage of you."

Bless Harold's heart!

"I hope you don't think I do, Daisy. I don't mean to, you know."

"I know, Mrs. Pinkerton. You don't take advantage of me." Not hideous advantage, anyway. Besides, she paid me a whole lot of money, and that took the edge off unpleasantness. In other words, I hadn't just uttered a huge lie. Just a little weensy one.

As soon as I'd hung the receiver on its cradle, I resumed being edgy and nervous. Darn it! Claude Dermott *had* to tell Sam what he'd heard. Didn't he realize that?

I told Pa so when he got home. He'd only been outside picking oranges, and he brought in a basket full of them.

"Oh?" said Pa, looking curious.

"I'll tell you on our walk," I said, nearly biting my nails with anxiety. Not that I'd ever do that. Desdemona Majesty, famed spiri-tualist-medium to wealthy women in Pasadena, would never bite her nails. Daisy Gumm Majesty would, though, curse it. When the 'phone rang, I uttered a soft scream, leaped out of my kitchen chair and dashed to the instrument hanging on the kitchen wall.

Remembering my profession in time, I spoke in my low,

measured spiritualist's voice. "Gumm-Majesty residence. Mrs. Majesty speaking."

"Um, is this Mrs. Majesty?" a male voice said, sounding nervous.

Hadn't I just said as much? Rather than bellowing at the caller, I said, still softly and soothingly, "Yes. Is this Mr. Dermott?"

"Yes. Yes, it is. My mother told me to call you in order to—"

"Yes," I said, cutting him off. How rude, huh? "Please say no more over the telephone, Mr. Dermott. Would it be possible for you and your parents to come to our house this evening for dinner? We dine at six o'clock. The person you need to speak to will be here, too."

My heart hammered to beat the band as silence reigned for what seemed like eons. At last, Claude Dermott spoke. "Uh...You want us to come to dinner? All of us?"

"Yes," I said, wishing the guy were a little quicker on the uptake. Couldn't he understand I was attempting to disguise the fact that *he* was the one who had the important information to impart? "If your entire family joins us, that would be best." I prayed for him to figure it out before I had a heart attack.

"Oh!" he said, I hoped with sudden understanding. "Oh, yes. Yes, I see. Um, I'll telephone Mother and get back with you. Is that all right?"

"Yes, only please do so quickly. I need to tell a few other people about this meeting. You understand?"

"Um, yes. Yes, I understand. Thank you, Mrs. Majesty. I'll call you back as soon as I can."

"Thank you."

We each returned our receivers to their respective cradles. At least I did so with mine, and I presume Claude did so with his.

"What's up?" asked Pa, eyeing me curiously.

I heaved an enormous sigh and sank back into my kitchen chair. There I explained what Mrs. Dermott had told me the night before and said I hoped we'd have three extra guests for dinner that night, so Claude Dermott could tell Sam his story without possible murderers knowing it was he who spilled the beans. Providing they really were beans and not just…well, nothing.

Pa's eyes widened as I told the story. "Three extra guests? Is that all right with your aunt?"

"Yes. I asked her. Believe it or not, she seemed pleased. I'll never understand her love of cooking."

With a chuckle, Pa said, "We all have our gifts, I reckon."

"That's what Vi said." I wasn't sure I believed it. My own gifts, such as they were, seemed paltry compared with the ability to feed people. I mean, Vi's gift was a life-saving one; Ma's was a useful one. Mine was…silly.

But before I could commence beating up on myself, the telephone rang again. I jumped up to answer it, and was so relieved to hear Claude Dermott's voice, my knees nearly buckled. Guess stress and strain really were getting to me.

"Mrs. Majesty?" he asked for the second time that day right after I'd told him who I was. Again I wanted to holler at him but restrained myself.

"Yes?"

"My folks and I will be pleased to dine at your home tonight. You said six o'clock?"

"Yes. Thank you. We don't dine at a fashionable hour, I guess, but it works for us."

He laughed. "We don't, either, because my father and I have to get up early to get to work. Your invitation is very kind. I've heard all about your aunt's cooking skills."

"You have?" Merciful heavens, Vi was famous!

"Indeed, I have. I think everyone in the city has heard about your aunt and her way with a meal."

I was so pleased, I could hardly stand it. I had to tell Vi what Claude had said when I was through with Mrs. Pinkerton. "Thank you! If you've heard good things, they're absolutely true. She's the best cook in Pasadena."

"So I've heard. My mother was so excited when I told her of your invitation, I thought she might faint, and I know she's telephoning all her friends."

"My goodness."

"Well, maybe she didn't almost faint, but she was sure pleased. And she's definitely telephoning all her friends."

"I'll be sure to tell Aunt Vi," I said.

"Please do. We're all looking forward to dining at your house this evening."

"Wonderful. And will you please bring a list of the people who live..." Rats. I struggled to say something that wouldn't titillate our party-line neighbors. "A list of the fellows who live there?" That was indefinite, wasn't it?

"Oh. You mean...Ah. Very well. You want a list of current residents."

"Yes. Thank you."

"I'll be happy to do that."

"Thank you! And Det—" Whoops! "And my fiancé will be pleased to meet you."

"I'll be happy to meet him, too."

We'd see about that, I reckoned. We said our good-byes and ended the call.

"Oh, my!" said I as soon as the receiver hit the cradle. "I'm *so* relieved!"

"Guests for dinner?" Pa asked, grinning at me.

"Guests for dinner," said I, and I picked up the telephone receiver again.

"What's up? You don't usually make telephone calls on purpose."

"Have to call Mrs. P. She wants to talk to Rolly. And I'll call Sam, too."

Chuckling, Pa walked out of the kitchen, headed, I was sure, to the living room, where he'd probably pick up *Craig Kennedy Listens In*, by Arthur B. Reeve. He'd just started it the night before. I still hadn't conquered *A Passage to India*, but that's only because I hadn't had much time to read. I was enjoying the book. Very exotic setting, if you were me.

Anyhow, I called Mrs. Pinkerton, told her I'd be at her home at eleven o'clock—it was then ten o'clock—then called Sam.

"Yeah?" came his gruff greeting when the officer at the front desk had transferred my call to his office.

"You're always so gracious, Sam," said I, feeling positively light-hearted for some reason. I mean, just because Claude Dermott had telephoned didn't really mean anything.

"Yeah. People tell me that all the time," said my beloved.

I laughed. Don't ask me why. "Well, you may become gracious. The Dermotts are coming to dine with us tonight."

"And that's the reason I should be gracious?"

"Yes! Because——" Whoops. Almost forgot again that we had a party line. I'd really have to look into getting a private line. Private lines couldn't be all *that* expensive. Could they? I didn't know. "Yes, because you'll get to have leg of lamb and popovers tonight! With guests."

"We're going to dine on the guests?"

Trust Sam.

"Yes, Sam, darling. We're going to have leg of lamb for the main course and eat the guests for dessert."

"Sounds great. The usual time?"

"The usual time."

"Excellent."

He hung up. I swear....

TWENTY-FIVE

Mrs. Pinkerton enjoyed our time together.

I'm lying. She was a total wreck. Mind you, this condition wasn't unusual for her, but she'd been almost cheery after the séance I'd held at Mrs. Frasier's home. I hadn't expected her mood to last, and that Friday morning I was proved correct. I wasn't happy about it, but I'd anticipated it.

After Rolly and the tarot cards had told her the very same things they'd told her countless times already since her evil daughter's arrest and incarceration, she bade me a teary farewell. I tried to be as soothing and consoling as I could be, and then I scrammed out of her drawing room and nearly ran to the kitchen.

My wonderful aunt had prepared lunch for me!

"Oh, Vi, I didn't expect you to fix lunch! Why, you didn't even know I was coming."

"Yes, I did. Harold told me."

It was only then I noticed Harold, who stood near the back door, grinning like an imp. He was so adorable in a cuddly, Teddy-bear kind of way. "Harold!" I rushed over and gave him a big hug, although to this day, I'm not sure why I did that. Guess I was just relieved and happy and…I don't know. He was my best friend, you know?"

"Daisy, whatever is the matter with you?" he asked, laughing and returning my hug.

"I don't know. I guess I'm just relieved. We might have a break in the Wagner case." I don't know why I said "we," either.

"Oh? What happened?" Harold said.

"My goodness!" Vi said.

"What kind of break?" asked Harold, peeling my hands from his shoulders. "Did someone confess or something?"

"No, but the Dermotts' son, Claude, overheard an incriminating conversation at the Pasadena Golf and Tennis Club. Several men were laughing about having hidden something at the Grenvilles' house."

"My goodness," said Vi again.

"Who were the talkers?" asked Harold.

"Claude didn't know," I told him.

"Hmm. That doesn't sound awfully helpful to me." Harold frowned.

"Maybe not, but then again, maybe the murderer was among those laughing."

With a shrug, Harold said, "Maybe."

Tilting my head a bit and staring at him, I said, "You know, it's possible somebody who's been living at that club really *is* the murderer."

"Maybe," Harold said again.

Vi said, "What did that young man overhear again, Daisy? Someone laughing about…what?"

"Whoever he heard, they were laughing about having hidden something in George Grenville's place. Somewhere. I don't know where, but it might have been the potting shed. That's where the police found the bloody baseball bat."

"Yuck!" said Harold.

"My goodness," said Vi.

"Hearsay," said Harold succinctly. "Even if you knew who was talking."

"It's hearsay now, but we may be able to figure out a way to get them to confess."

"You don't even know who they were," Harold reminded me.

"I know. But maybe the young Mr. Dermott's testimony might lead to the killer. Or something."

Harold grinned. "Or something."

"Oh, forget about that awful murder and sit down and eat your lunch, Daisy. I made enough for Harold, too."

"You're the queen of the kitchen, Mrs. Gumm," said Harold.

"Yes. You are," I agreed.

"Go along with the both of you," said Vi, gesturing for Harold and me to sit at the kitchen table.

So we did. And Vi served us delicious chopped ham sandwiches along with little carrot and celery sticks. She also added several olives to both of our plates. I loved olives. So, evidently, did Harold, because he gobbled them down as if he were starving. Harold and Spike had that characteristic in common. They were both a teensy bit chubby, but both could convince you with their eyes that you were mistaken; they weren't at all chubby, and you were mistaken in thinking they were.

I didn't believe either one of them.

We discussed the conversation Claude Dermott overheard as we ate our delicious lunches.

"You probably know more than I about who's living at the Pasadena Golf and Tennis Club, Harold. Claude Dermott is going to bring me a list of current residents, but I might as well get my own list started. Can you give me a list of names? Besides Fred Greenlaw, I mean. I suspect the murderer is young." I leaned down, picked up my handbag, and dug out my cunning little notebook and pencil.

"Why do you suspect that?"

Harold's question startled me, and I pondered it. "Um...I don't know."

Vi said, "I don't see why the murder had to be committed by a young man. Or even a man."

"Whoever committed the murder had the strength to carry the body to the cemetery and bury it," I said.

"Ah. Yes, I see," said Vi. "So it was probably either someone young, or there was more than one person involved."

"Right," said I. "So if Harold can think of any people who live at the club, my list and the list the younger Mr. Dermott brings tonight might give Sam a place to start looking. I guess the people don't have to be young."

Harold nodded as he chewed. "Most of the men living there *are* young, however. Perhaps not in the first blush of youth, but not elderly."

"I guess there's a reason they call it the Golf and Tennis Club," I said. "Not too many elderly folks play either game."

With a chuckle, Harold said, "You're wrong there, but let's not get started on that. I'll try to think of people I know who live at the club."

"Thanks, Harold," said I, wondering why an old person would even *want* to play tennis or golf. Heck, I wasn't old, and I didn't want to participate in either sport. On the other hand, I didn't particularly want to participate in any sport. My family wasn't filled to the brim with sporting-mad folks. That's probably because the members of *my* family, unlike those in many Pasadena, families, had to *earn* the money they lived on and hadn't inherited it. I didn't say that aloud, since it sounded mean-spirited and petty.

"First of all, both of my brothers-in-law have been staying there for quite a while."

"Mr. Pinkerton's sons? His polo-playing sons?" I was kind of surprised, although not very much. I wouldn't want to live with Mrs. Pinkerton if I were either of them.

"Yes. Clark and Carl, and they do play polo. But they're both nice fellows, and they're both engaged to be married to nice women. Then they aim to move to a house. One house for each couple, that is. In fact, I do believe they've both made offers on homes."

"Must be nice," I said. But I wrote their names down on my list. "Anyone else?"

Munching on a bite of sandwich, Harold shut his eyes and tilted his head toward the ceiling, as if that might help him think. "Let me see," said he. "Who else? Fred Greenlaw—the younger one—has been living there until the house he's having built is finished, but you already knew that. The Wagner sons have both lived there for quite some time. Theodore Ferdinand—"

"*Ferdinand*, did you say? I'm sorry, Harold. I didn't mean to interrupt you, but did you say Ferdinand?"

Harold opened his eyes and blinked at me. "That's all right. And yes, I said Ferdinand. Teddy Ferdinand. His old man's a doctor. What's so all-fired important about Teddy?"

"I don't know, but a Doctor Ferdinand—I can't remember his first name—had been in a vicious feud with Doctor Wagner, or so Sam found out recently."

"Huh. Not sure that means anything. Teddy is a nice-enough fellow. Didn't follow his father into the medical profession."

"What does he do for a living?"

"Not much, if what I've heard is true. Teddy can be something of a hot-headed fellow at times, though, and I know he adores his father, whom"—Harold grimaced—"he calls Pop. I didn't know about his old man and Wagner feuding. Interesting. I can see Teddy taking up the cudgels in defense of his father, although don't quote me on that."

"I won't," I said, ruminating about the sins of fathers and how those sins might affect their sons. "If the young Ferdinand was also angry with Doctor Wagner—and he might have had good cause, given the nature of Doctor Wagner's transgressions, even if he wasn't peeved about his father's grievance with him—he might have had a motive for doing in the evil doctor."

"Maybe," said Harold. "But let me think some more before you condemn anyone. I'm certain there are more fellows I know who live at the club." He recommended thinking. "Jacob Levine has lived there for a few months. He's a banker. Phil Martin. He's a lawyer, and —Say, I think Phil was courting Marianne Wagner for a while there."

"Really? I didn't know anyone had courted her except George."

Harold gazed at me with pity. "Daisy Gumm Majesty. For the

longest time, everyone in Pasadena thought Doctor Wagner was a very wealthy man. And he was, for a while. The daughters of very rich men get courted, even if those daughters are shy and withdrawn, as Marianne was, if I recall her correctly from parties."

"Yes," I said musingly. "She was. That's about all I remembered about her when Sam first told us she was missing." Poor Marianne. Small wonder she'd been shy.

"Phil is still looking for a moneyed young woman to marry. He doesn't like to work. Kind of like the Wagner boys and Teddy Ferdinand. He's got some kind of income, but I don't know where it comes from."

"I didn't know there so many lazy, idle young men living in Pasadena," I said with a sniff.

"Tons of them," said Harold, grinning.

"Shameful," said Aunt Vi, who'd been listening in. That was all right with me.

"I think it's shameful, too, Vi," said Harold. "I'd rather work for a living than depend on a spouse's inheritance. That's what my father did, and he was enough of an example for me."

Vi tutted.

"Can you think of anyone else who lives at the club?" I asked Harold.

After pondering for several seconds, during which he polished off the rest of his sandwich, Harold said, "Not offhand, but that doesn't mean there aren't more fellows staying there."

"Why do so many young men want to live there?" asked Vi.

"Good question, Vi. Yeah, Harold, why do they? You'd think they'd either remain with their parents until they married or get an apartment or live in a boarding house if they wanted their independence."

"If you have an apartment or a house, you have to take care of it yourself, sweetie. And all the boarding houses I've seen don't cater to the likes of the wealthy young men who belong to the Pasadena Golf and Tennis Club. Everyone I know who lives at the club, except for Fred, enjoys being catered to, but they don't want to get carped at by their parents. You know, 'Go out there and get a job, you indolent lout,' and stuff like that."

"Oh, my. That kind of makes me feel sad, Harold."

With a shrug, Harold said, "If it's any comfort, most of the men my age whom I know aren't like that."

"And a good thing, too," said Vi.

Harold laughed. "Anyway, I'll keep thinking about who might live there, and I'll call you if I can think of anyone else. I'll ask Del. He'll probably have a name or two for you."

For the record, Del was Harold's... I don't know what you'd call him. Lover? Well, whatever he was, Harold and Del lived together.

"Thanks, Harold."

"Even if Sam also agrees that somebody planted the baseball bat, how do you aim to prove it?" asked Harold after Vi had removed our sandwich plates and presented us each with a pretty cut-glass bowl filled with tapioca pudding. She'd even whipped some cream to put on top.

"This is astonishingly good, Vi," I told her. Then I said to Harold, "I'm not sure how to prove anything, but we'll think of a way."

"Yes, this is magnificent pudding, Vi. I've never tasted better."

"Thank you both. I put a little almond extract in it to give it a little...Punch, I guess."

"It's punchy, all right. It's spectacular," I told my wonderful aunt.

"It is indeed," said Harold.

"Anyhow, getting back to the murder, if the conversation Claude Dermott overheard leads to anything, I'm sure we'll figure out a way to trap the murderer."

"Confident wench, aren't you?"

"I trust Sam." I said in staunch support of my fiancée. Grumpy he occasionally might be, but Sam was a darned good detective. And he was only grumpy because of his poor wounded leg.

After a moment during which, I presume, Harold thought, he tilted his head to one side and said, "I might have an idea for you. Don't know if it will help, but it can't hurt."

"What is it?" I asked, all ears. Well, and mouth and stomach. That entire lunch was perfection.

"Fred Greenlaw lives at the Pasadena Golf and Tennis Club."

"Yes, I know. You've told me that several times. So what?"

"So there's going to be a Christmas get-together at the club tomorrow night. Why not have a gypsy fortune-teller there? I'm sure Fred can arrange it all. You don't require much time to prepare, do you?"

Did I? After approximately three and a half seconds of consideration, I shrugged. "No. All I need is my costume, which is hanging in my closet, and my crystal ball and tarot cards. I think I'll leave the Ouija board at home." Something occurred to me. "Will there be other females there, or will I be the only one? I'd feel really…I don't know. Conspicuous and embarrassed, I guess, if I were the only woman present."

"Naw, there will be lots of women there. It's the club's annual Christmas bash, and all the members bring their wives, female friends and, in Fred's case, his sister."

"Oh, I like Hazel Greenlaw!"

"Everyone likes Hazel, and she'll be glad to see you again, too."

"Sounds good. What time should I show up, or will you pick me up? I'd love it if you would, because I won't feel so much like an interloper if I attend with you."

"Sure."

"Thanks, Harold. Do you think Sam should come, too?" If Sam knew I was attending a Christmas party where a possible murderer might lurk, he'd be furious unless he were there with me.

"Of course. If the party yields results, he'll need to be there to arrest the bad guys."

"Oh. Of course. Silly me."

"Silly you," Harold agreed, the beast. "Anyhow, he doesn't look like a copper when he's all dressed up. When the two of you came to my mother's house for that dinner party a couple of months ago, you'd never have known he wasn't an Italian count, he looked so grand in his dinner jacket."

"That's sweet of you, Harold. I'll tell Sam you said so."

"Probably not a good idea," said Harold, grinning at me. "But definitely make the detective come. By force, if necessary. Remember that if we actually *do* discover something, we'll need him."

"True."

With a slight frown, Harold added, "In truth, I wish we could have a couple of other policemen there. Just in case, you know?"

"Do you really think someone might get out of hand?"

"Somebody murdered Doctor Wagner. And, while he needed killing, you and I don't."

"True. Thanks, Harold. Maybe Sam can get a couple of other officers to hang around outside during the party."

"Wouldn't hurt," said Harold.

"Thanks, Harold. I appreciate you suggesting this."

"Not a problem. I hadn't planned to go to the club's party, since I'm not precisely a sports fan, but Del has to attend mass at Our Lady of Perpetual Misery tomorrow night, so I might as well go to the party while he does that."

"Harold Kincaid, you're a caution!" Vi exclaimed. "Whatever is Our Lady of whatever you said it was?"

"He means St. Andrews, Vi. Harold and religion don't mix well."

"Oh, my," said my aunt, faint disapproval in her voice.

"I don't mind religion," Harold said, probably to appease Vi. "I just don't much care for the Roman Catholic Church."

It was the right thing to say to Vi, who considered Roman Catholics not much better than idolaters. And don't mention Baptists around her, either. She thinks they're all barefooted, illiterate backwoodsmen who wrestle bears every day and eat with their fingers. I don't know why.

I felt better about things when I left Mrs. Pinkerton's house. My tummy was full of good food, Harold had solved the problem of how to get the members of the Pasadena Golf and Tennis Club and me in the same room together, and we were having leg of lamb for dinner. Life didn't get much better than that.

TWENTY-SIX

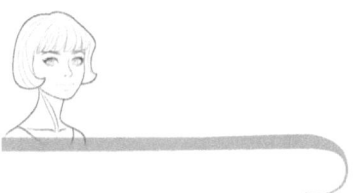

V i left the Pinkerton mansion with me that day since, as she'd said, she got off early on Fridays. As I drove us home, we discussed the Wagner case. By the time we got to our bungalow, we hadn't come to any earth-shaking conclusions about the matter.

As Vi prepared dinner for a party of eight, rather than the usual five she generally had to feed, I cleaned up the house. It didn't require a whole lot of cleaning since we were neat people, but I dusted the furniture, ran the dust mop over the polished wooden floors, and carpet-swept the various rugs in the various rooms. The place positively sparkled when the doorbell rang at around five-thirty that evening.

I knew Sam was at the door before I even reached it, because Spike had told me it was he. Spike has a special way of greeting his favorite friends.

"Evening, Sam," said I, lifting myself on my tiptoes to give him a little kiss.

"Evening," said he, kissing me back. He handed me a pretty bouquet of flowers. "Here. For you."

"Thank you, Sam! These are lovely."

"You're welcome. Everything set for tonight?" He sniffed the air.

"It sure smells like it is." He knelt with a pained grunt and gave Spike a thorough petting.

I smiled in approval, glad Sam loved my dog. "Leg of lamb. With popovers."

As he hung his hat and coat on the coat tree, Sam said, "Sounds delicious. I'd never even heard of a popover until I met your family."

"Old English recipe, according to Vi. You can make it in a big dish and call it Yorkshire pudding, too. Not that I know from personal experience, you understand. Sometimes she serves it as Yorkshire pudding, and sometimes she prepares the same batter and pours it in to a popover pan."

"What's a popover pan?"

"You know how much I know about cooking, Sam Rotondo."

"True, but you might have witnessed the preparation of these particular popovers. You also know what a popover pan is, so I'm sure you can explain to me what one is."

"You're right. Vi's pan is a heavy cast-iron thing that looks like a muffin tin, only black. She says you have to heat it in the oven with some kind of grease before you pour the popover batter into it."

"Sounds complicated."

"Everything related to cooking is complicated for me." I gazed up at my beloved. "I'm sorry, Sam. You're getting a lousy cook as a wife."

"That's all right. You have other talents." He grinned down at me.

I'm pretty sure I blushed. "Well, I hope you enjoy your popovers."

"I'm sure I will. I didn't think the British had any tasty culinary customs. When I was in England chasing you and Harold, they fed me stuff like cheese-and-pickle sandwiches and sausage rolls." He gave a judicious head-tilt. "The sausage rolls were good, but the rest of the stuff I ate there was pretty bland."

"Not like the Italians, eh?"

He grinned again. I was pleased to see his mood had improved since we'd spoken on the telephone earlier in the day. "Can't beat Italians when it comes to food."

"You might well be right," I said as I led him into the dining room. There I rummaged through the china cabinet until I found a nice vase. "These will be a beautiful centerpiece," I told him, retreating into the kitchen to fill the vase with water.

"Glad you like them."

"Oh, how lovely!" Vi exclaimed when she saw Sam's flowers. "What a nice thing to do."

"What?" said Sam, standing in the kitchen door and rubbing his hands, which, I knew because I'd felt them, were cold from the outdoors. "I thought it was traditional for a man to bring flowers to his best girl."

"That's so sweet," Vi gushed.

As for me, I squinted at Sam, wondering if he was up to something. He must have read my mind, because he smiled and said, "What? Isn't it a tradition?"

"Whatever it is, the flowers are pretty, and I appreciate them, Sam Rotondo."

"You're more than welcome, Daisy Majesty."

Okay. I guess that took care of that. I placed the vase of flowers in the center of the table. I'd had to add an extra leaf—to the table, not the flowers—in order to accommodate that evening's extra diners. The flowers did look nice there.

About fifteen minutes after Sam's arrival, the Dermotts twisted our old-fashioned doorbell. Sam, Spike and I went to the door to greet them. Mr. Dermott, too, held a bouquet of flowers, which he thrust at me.

"Thank you for inviting us this evening," said he.

"Thank you for the flowers!" I exclaimed, not having anticipated them, although I guess it was also a tradition to bring hostess gifts to people who invited you to dinner. Not that I was the hostess, but... Well, maybe I was, come to think of it. Just because I couldn't boil an egg, didn't mean I hadn't spearheaded this evening's get-together.

"You're more than welcome," said Mrs. Dermott as she, her

husband and her son walked into our house. I noticed her glancing around, as if checking to see if our home was as nice as she thought it should be.

Personally, I thought our home was perfect, but I wasn't Mrs. Dermott.

I'd met the Dermotts, except for Claude, at church get-togethers. Claude never came to church with his parents, but I knew him from years back when we'd both been little. We'd attended Sunday school together. He looked a lot like his mother, only taller.

Mr. Dermott was also tall, although not quite as tall as Sam. I made introductions all around, not leaving out Spike, who adored having people visit. To a person, the Dermotts claimed to adore Spike. Good thing, too.

Sam and Mr. Dermott helped Mrs. Dermott off with her coat and hat as I went to get another vase, into which I ran water and then stuck the Dermotts' flowers. Then I took that vase into the living room and put them on a doily on top of the piano. They looked good there. By that time the Dermotts and Sam had ambled into the living room. There Sam asked Claude to repeat what he'd heard at the club.

Claude did so, and Sam asked, "And you have no idea who was talking when you heard them?"

"No. I'm sorry. I didn't feel comfortable looking to see who they were. Well, whoever it was might have murdered someone. I didn't want to be next on the list."

"Understandable," said Sam.

"Oh, and here's the list I made of the club members. It's supposed to be confidential information, but…Well, I thought this was a valid exception." He peered closely at Sam. "You're not going to tell anyone I gave you that list, are you?"

"No," said Sam, looking at the paper in his hand before folding it and putting it into his jacket pocket. "This will remain our secret."

"Thank you." The words came from Claude along with a sigh of relief.

As for me, I thought Claude was kind of a sissy. Then again, he probably didn't get in trouble for snoopery as I sometimes did.

When Vi called us in for dinner, Claude had approved Harold's notion of Sam and me (and Harold) attending the following night's Christmas party. Sam didn't seem particularly thrilled, but I figured that was par for the course. And I just used a golfing expression! Boy, you just never know when you'll need a sporting term, do you? And such an appropriate one, too.

Dinner was spectacular, as usual. In actual fact, it was *more* spectacular than usual. The lamb was succulent, the popovers delicious, and Vi served us baked Roman beauty apples for dessert. When Mrs. Dermott asked her for the baked-apple recipe, Vi said she just cored the apples, put a dab of butter in the holes, and sprinkled them with cinnamon and sugar. The recipe sounded simple, but I knew if I ever tried it, I'd ruin it somehow. It's actually quite depressing to know one is a total failure at something so necessary to life as cooking.

Vi served the apples with thick, delicious cream. Perhaps I couldn't actually spoil cream, although it would probably be better for my family if I didn't attempt to do anything with cream except eat it.

After dinner, Ma and I stacked the dishes in the kitchen with the understanding I'd wash them after the Dermotts left. We all gathered in the living room and chatted some more, mainly about Dr. Wagner's murder.

"I didn't know him well," said Mr. Dermott at one point. "I only knew who he was, and I'd heard rumors that he mistreated his wife. We aren't rich enough to travel in the doctor's circles."

"Nonsense, Henry. You provide a very good living for us."

"Yeah, Pop, who wants to be rich, if you have to be like the Wagners?" said Claude, the dutiful son.

"I wouldn't mind being rich," I said.

Everyone turned to look at me. I shrugged. "Well, I wouldn't."

"Too bad you're aiming to marry a policeman then, isn't it?" said Sam. He smiled as he said it, so I don't think he was annoyed with me, although sometimes it's hard to tell with Sam.

At long last—far too long, in my opinion—the Dermotts took their leave. They thanked us over and over for inviting them to dinner. All three of them told Vi they'd never eaten a better meal. I'm sure that was true, but I was tired and wanted them gone quite a while before they left. But at least we'd solidified party plans for the following evening. Shoot. Tomorrow Lucy was going to come over to practice "What Child is This?" I wouldn't be at all surprised if I got an emergency telephone call from Mrs. Pinkerton, and then I had to be a fortune-teller at an evening party. Saturday sounded as though it was going to be an exhausting day.

It was almost midnight when I put the last plate away, and I was bushed. Whatever *bushed* means. Just another one of those idiosyncratic English sayings, I guess. Sam had left when the Dermotts did. Ma asked if I'd like her to help with the dishes, but I declined her kind offer. After all, she had to work on Saturdays. Mind you, the Hotel Marengo only demanded a half-day of their employees on Saturdays, but still, I didn't have to get up early as she did.

Naturally, I did anyway. My room led directly off the kitchen and no matter how quiet my family tried to be in order to allow me to sleep, Spike and I always knew when the kitchen was occupied. I think this had more to do with the scent of food than noise on anyone else's part. Spike and I were both food-hounds.

After breakfast and after Pa and I took Spike for a longer-than-usual walk around the neighborhood, I telephoned Lucy Zollinger. She answered the telephone sounding happy, which made me happy. Lucy had always been an even-tempered sort of person, but since her marriage, she seemed almost giddy with joy most of the time. I approved, as if anyone cares about that.

"Hey, Lucy, it's Daisy. When would you like to come over to practice?"

"Actually, why don't you come here? We can dine in the restaurant here at the Castle Green. Albert said he'd be delighted to escort the both of us. Then we can use the piano in the Valley Hunt Club's parlor."

"Won't the members of the Valley Hunt Club mind if we use their parlor?"

With a delighted titter, Lucy said, "Oh, my, no! Nobody uses it except when they hold meetings and events here. The Hotel Green is the Valley Hunt Club's headquarters, you know."

"Yes, I did know. Well…Thanks, Lucy. That sounds like fun. I…" I hesitated. What I had almost said was that I expected an hysterical Mrs. Pinkerton to telephone me and beg me to bring Rolly and the tarot cards to her house for a reading or three. Then I decided that was ridiculous. Who was Mrs. Pinkerton to dictate how I spent my Saturdays? Well, besides being my most persistent and lucrative client. Hmmm.

Oh, heck. I could fit Mrs. Pinkerton in somewhere. The notion of taking luncheon at a fine restaurant at someone else's expense appealed to me more than attending to Mrs. P's whims.

"You what?" Lucy prompted.

"Not a thing," I answered. "I'd love that, Lucy. When should I arrive, and will we practice before or after we dine?"

"I want to show you our apartment first. Then I thought we'd take luncheon, and then practice. I don't suppose we really need much practice. We sing that hymn every year, after all."

"Yes, we do. I'm looking forward to seeing your apartment, Lucy. I love that hotel."

"I do, too. It's going to be a shock when we move to our own home, and I have to cook for poor Albert." She giggled, and I had a feeling poor Albert wouldn't mind. I also had a feeling Lucy was a *much* better cook than was I. Then again, most people were.

"Why don't you come here about twelve-thirty? Albert and I usually dine at one or thereabouts. Is that all right with you?"

"Perfect," I told her. "Thanks, Lucy. I'm looking forward to it."

"I am, too, Daisy. You're so talented."

I was? I didn't know that. But I didn't argue. "Thanks, Lucy. See you then."

We each hung our receivers on their cradles. I was about to turn around and head to the living room to resume reading *A Passage to India* when the telephone rang again. After glaring at it malevolently for no more than a couple of seconds, I answered it in my expert spiritualist-medium voice.

Mrs. Pinkerton. Although I'd anticipated this, I wasn't happy about it.

"Oh, Daisy! I know it's Saturday, and I *know* how busy you are, but could you *please* visit me today? *Please?*"

She sounded pathetic, which was normal. She'd had a brief respite from her woes, but it hadn't lasted long enough to suit me. Before answering her, I glanced at the clock on the kitchen wall. Ten-o-five. Doing some quick calculations in my head—which hurt. I wasn't a mathematical genius—I finally said. "Yes, Mrs. Pinkerton. You sound as if you are having a hard time, and that grieves me." Boy, could I lay it on, or couldn't I? "I'll be happy to visit you at eleven this morning. I have a luncheon engagement and will be busy all afternoon, so that's the only time I can come." Technically, that was a fib, but I hoped to get in a short nap between lunch and dinner so I wouldn't be totally worn out when I played detective—I mean fortuneteller—at the Pasadena Golf and Tennis Club's Christmas party that evening.

"Yes!" Mrs. P shrieked, hurting my ears. Darn the woman! I'd just offered to sell her a part of my day; why'd she have to shriek at me about it? But then, Mrs. P seldom needed reasons for her shrieks. "Thank you so much, dear! I'm so very glad you can come. Please bring the Ouija board and tarot cards."

"I shall."

"Thank you," she said again. Then she commenced sobbing, my glance paid a visit to the ceiling, and I heard Pa chuckle in the background. I turned my head and stuck out my tongue at him. Childish, I know, but he didn't mind. In fact, he chuckled harder.

After that was over, Spike and I retreated into our bedroom and I flung wide the closet doors. Things were getting squishy in there, and I decided it was past time for me to cull my wardrobe. I could donate the clothing I no longer wore to the Salvation Army. Flossie and Johnny were always thrilled to get donations to give to the deserving—and sometimes the undeserving—poor.

The weather remained chilly to us spoiled Pasadenans, so I decided to wear a fairly new gown I'd made using the rendition of a

Jean Lanvin creation I'd copied from a *Vogue* magazine at the library. The dress was a dark, chocolaty brown, which suited the weather, and had cream-colored inserts in the slashed bishop sleeves. The sleeves were a little poufy at my wrists, but I didn't think they'd get in the way of my knife and fork. Or the piano keys. The dress was ankle-length, and it was supposed to have a high collar, but I don't feel comfortable in high, tight collars, so I just rounded the neck band and left the collar off entirely. The waist was dropped, as was fashionable, and I could wear my brown cloche hat, brown shoes with a short Louis heel, and carry my brown handbag.

My gorgeous emerald engagement ring looked quite spiffy with the color of the gown. Cream-and-brown embroidery—in a pattern reminiscent of *fleur-de-lis*, at least to me—around the neckline and at the lowered waist made any other adornment unnecessary. Which was a good thing, since I didn't happen to have a string of matched pearls or an emerald necklace to go with my elegant chocolate-colored gown. Not that Sam wouldn't give me something like that if he had the money. Probably. His father could undoubtedly get a deal on the emeralds or pearls and create the necklace himself. But such a flamboyant piece of jewelry wouldn't fit my image as a sober-sided spiritualist-medium, so it was just as well.

I grabbed my Methodist hymnal from the piano stand before leaving home, figuring I'd need it once I got to Lucy's place.

Naturally, my first stop of the morning after I dressed myself was at Mrs. Pinkerton's house. There everything went as I'd antici-pated. In other words, Mrs. P was in a State (with a capital S), cried and moaned, and Rolly and the tarot cards told her the same things they always told her. I was glad to get out of there. I did pop into the kitchen to say hey to my wonderful aunt, but she was up to her elbows in flour, so I didn't stay.

As I drove from Mrs. P's mansion on Orange Grove to the Hotel Green on Raymond Avenue and Green Street, I contemplated the dinner-table conversation the night before.

I really wouldn't mind being rich. And if I were, I wouldn't pester phony spiritualist-mediums or wear flashy jewelry, either.

Did God believe that?

Heck, I'm not sure if *I* believed it. But as there was little possibility I'd ever find out, I don't suppose it mattered.

TWENTY-SEVEN

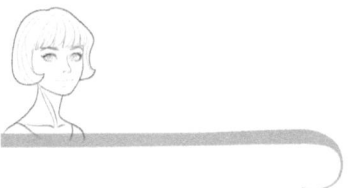

Lucy was delighted when I rang her doorbell and she answered same.

"Daisy! I've been wanting to have you over for the longest time. After all, you've invited us to your house several times, and this is the first chance I've had to reciprocate."

Interesting. I'd never thought of dinner invitations and so forth as events needing reciprocation. Then again, my society manners, while fairly well ingrained due to my profession, hadn't taught me everything about how life is supposed to be lived. I don't think Vi expected us to take her out to dinner every time she fed us one of her delicious meals, which was a darned good thing. We'd be broke in no time flat if she did. Sam sometimes took us all out to dinner, but we didn't think of his invitations as reciprocation exactly. He wanted us to know he appreciated us as a family that had, in a way, adopted him as one of ours.

"Nonsense!" said I heartily. "You needn't reciprocate. We love to have you and Mr. Zollinger over." We hadn't had them to dine but once or twice, so I don't know why I'm going on about this topic.

At any rate, the Zollingers' apartment was lovely, and I could imagine their home on Holliston Avenue would be likewise spiffy.

Mr. Zollinger clearly made a lot of money. I was glad for Lucy. And for him, too, of course.

I raved about Lucy's pretty furnishings and admirable decorating skills until Mr. Zollinger corralled us and led us downstairs via the elevator and guided us to the Castle Green's restaurant, which was mighty fancy.

There we dined on chicken a la king—the Castle Green's pastry wasn't as flaky as Vi's—and then Lucy and her Albert led us to the Valley Hunt Club's parlor. Sure enough, the room was empty save for a grand piano and several chairs scattered here and there.

"What a pretty room," said I as I walked piano-wards. It really was. The walls were decorated with, appropriately, hunting prints and pictures of past Tournament of Roses Parades. The Hunt Club had sponsored the Rose Parade until interest in the parade grew too large for it to handle. Then the Tournament of Roses Association was formed. If anyone cares.

"Yes, I think it is, too," said Lucy. "Why don't we sing the whole song and not just the third verse?" she suggested. "After all, we'll get more practice that way."

"Sounds like a good plan to me," I said.

So I sat at the piano and practiced a few chords. I had to push my sleeves up a trifle due to those puffy bishop sleeves. Too late I realized they actually *did* get in the way. I do believe I'd even picked up a little gravy from my luncheon. Ah, well. Such is life. I could wash the dress.

After I felt comfortable at the piano, Lucy stood beside me, folded her hands in front of her waist like an opera singer getting ready to belt out an aria, I played the introduction to "What Child is This?" and we both began to sing. We started at the beginning and went through all four verses. That is to say we sang the four verses we Methodists had in our hymnals.

For all I know, there are dozens more stanzas to the song, the music for which has been around for a really long time. In fact, I read somewhere that folks in British public houses—we here in the USA call those things saloons or bars, or did until Prohibition when they turned into speakeasies—used to sing the melody as a drinking song in the 1600s, although I'm not sure about that. History contains a whole lot of iffy information. If you want to get to the absolute truth of any matter, you have to do more digging than I usually care to do. Our Methodist version was first published in 1871.

Anyway, by the time we'd finished the fourth verse, I was surprised to learn we'd attracted an audience. Applause came from the door. I spun on the piano seat to see a whole bunch of men standing with Mr. Zollinger, clapping to beat the band. I know I blushed, because my face went all hot. Darn my red-headed coloring.

To my astonishment, Gaylord Wagner shoved his way through the crowd and swaggered over to Lucy and me. I gazed at him and tried to hide my discomfort. What the heck was *he* doing there?

"That was lovely, ladies!" he cried, all ebullience and heartiness. "A gorgeous rendition of a gorgeous hymn by two gorgeous ladies."

Albert Zollinger trotted at Gaylord's heels and put what looked like a restraining hand on his shoulder. Gaylord frowned at him.

"Please, Mr. Wagner, allow me to introduce you to my wife, Mrs. Zollinger, and her very good friend, Mrs. Majesty. They were just practicing the duet they're going to sing at church on Christmas Eve."

"Ah," said Gaylord, disappointment flitting across his face. Unless that was my imagination giving him emotions he didn't feel. "So you're both married ladies."

"Yes," said I, before Lucy could tell him I was a widow.

"I'm sorry to hear it."

His buddies in the background chuckled. I wanted to sneer, but didn't.

"Who was that singing?" came another voice from the door.

When I glanced over to see who had spoken, darned if I didn't espy Vincent Wagner. I didn't know the pernicious Wagner brothers hung out at the Castle Green. Then again, they were rich—or had been, anyway—and rich people frequented fine restaurants, one of which the restaurant in the Castle Green was.

"These two ladies were providing the entertainment this afternoon, Vince," said Gaylord, giving a sweeping gesture meant to encompass Lucy and me. He winked at his brother. "They were practicing for church."

"Church, eh?" Vincent more or less snickered. "Ah, well. Isn't that nice?"

"Not only that," said Gaylord, "but I do believe Mrs. Majesty will be honoring us with her presence at tonight's Christmas party at the club. Isn't that right, Mrs. Majesty?" He smiled down at me. I have no idea why he made me think of a slithering cobra. He was actually rather stocky.

So was his brother, who said, "Really? Will you be singing Christmas carols for us?" Vincent asked.

"Um...No," I said, thinking Christmas carols would be much more appropriate than pretending to be a fortuneteller at a Christmas party.

"I do believe she's going to bring along the tools of her trade," said Gaylord, who seemed to know more about my business than I wanted him to. "Isn't that so, Mrs. Majesty?"

"Yes," I said with something of a snap.

"And what tools are those?" asked Vincent as if he really wanted to know.

"Her crystal ball and so forth," said Gaylord, still smiling down at me. "Claude Dermott told me she'd be attending tonight's shindig."

"Her crystal ball? My goodness!" said Vincent. He looked surprised. Didn't really blame him for that. But I was sick of this conversation. It made me feel ill at ease, perhaps because I just didn't care for the two Wagner brothers.

"Among other things," I said.

"So you're an adept at the mystical arts?" said Vincent, his smile growing wide.

"So people tell me," I said, trying not to sound as nervous as I felt.

"I've never connected spiritualism and Christmas before," said Gaylord. "This evening should be interesting."

"I haven't, either, Gay. But I'll be sure to stop by and have my palm read or whatever."

"I'm only bringing my crystal ball," I said. My throat had gone tight. "I won't be reading palms."

"Ah," said Vincent. I'm not sure what he meant by that *ah*, if anything. He turned to a fellow standing next to him. "Stanley, will you look at this."

"Yes?" said the man whom I assumed was Stanley. "Look at what?"

"Why, Mrs. Majesty here," said Vincent. "She's going to be at the Christmas party tonight. Only she won't be singing Christmas carols. She'll be plying her crystal ball."

"Is that right?" said Stanley, who was also kind of stocky. I wanted to get out of there. Actually, I wanted to *be* out of there. Ten minutes prior to all those men showing up.

"I understand Mrs. Majesty is the finest spiritualist-medium in the entire city of Pasadena," Gaylord told his brother. "Isn't that so, Mrs. Majesty?"

As I said, I wanted to be gone. So I contented myself with a short, "Yes," plucked my hymnal from the piano stand, and stuffed it under my arm. "Let's be off, Lucy. We've practiced enough."

"Yes, indeed," said Lucy's Albert, taking his wife's arm. Then he took mine, too. Fortunately it wasn't the arm under which I'd tucked the hymnal, or the book would have fallen, plop, to the carpeted floor. I don't like bending pages of other people's books, and that one belonged to my church.

"There's no need to rush off," said Gaylord as the three of us marched to the door, where the clot of men parted rather like the Red Sea for Moses.

No one responded to Gaylord's plaintive statement.

Vincent said, "See you this evening, Mrs. Majesty. I'm looking forward to it."

That made one of us.

Then the man called Stanley said, "So am I," which made two of them. I'd begun to dread the mere thought of seeing any of those men again. Ever.

Once we were out in the hallway again, Lucy said, "Who on earth were those men?"

"Two of them, Gaylord and Vincent, are Doctor Wagner's sons," I told her.

"Oh. I didn't care for them. Didn't they seem…I don't know. Insolent? I thought they were."

"So did I," I agreed.

"They are," said Albert Zollinger firmly, letting go of my arm, but keeping his wife's in his grasp. "The both of them. They're useless so-and-sos."

"Goodness. How do you know them, Daisy?"

"I don't know them. I mean, I've met them at parties at rich people's houses. But I don't know them. I don't want to, either."

"I don't blame you." Lucy hugged her Albert's arm, and I wished Sam were there so I could hug his arm.

I didn't spend any more time with Lucy or her husband, but drove home after we'd escaped from the Valley Hunt Club's parlor, the Wagner brothers, and their coterie of friends. A feeling of uneasiness accompanied me from that stupid parlor all the way home. I don't know why.

TWENTY-EIGHT

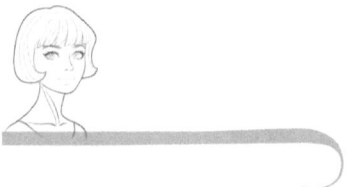

When Sam appeared at our door at about five-thirty in the evening, that danged feeling of uneasiness still pestered me, although I had managed to nap for an hour or so with Spike. I told Sam about it. The feeling, not the nap.

"The Wagners were there?" said Sam, frowning as he hung his hat and coat on the rack next to the door.

"Yes, and they were...I don't know. They weren't mean or anything, but they made me edgy. Nervous. Uncomfortable. Lucy said they were insolent, and I think that's a good word for it. They came over and spoke to us superciliously."

"Superciliously?"

"Yes," I said, feeling a trifle
defensive.

"That's probably because you don't like them."

"I don't *know* them." I gazed upon my intended. "But you might be right. Aren't you going to wear your fancy suit to the party tonight? Harold said you looked like an Italian count when we went to that dinner party at his mother's house."

Sam stared down upon me, clearly appalled. "An Italian count? Precisely how many Italian counts has Mr. Kincaid met in his life?"

Shrugging, I said, "I don't know. I expect at least a couple. He's got all the money in the world and can travel anywhere he wants to, you know."

"Yeah, I guess I do know. My fancy shirt and evening jacket are in the Hudson."

"Oh. Want to bring them in? You can change into them here if you want."

"That's what I'd planned to do," said Sam. "What time are we supposed to be at this Christmas party?"

"I think it starts at eight. We should probably get there a little early so Mr. Dermott can show us where he wants me to sit."

"I'll fetch my shirt and jacket after we eat, then."

"Very well." I reached up and gave him a peck on the cheek. Couldn't do much more than that without shocking my parents.

After Sam had returned my peck with one of his own, he said, "Try not to be nervous. I'll be there, and nothing bad can happen to you." He smiled down at me, and I appreciated him a whole lot.

"Thanks, Sam. I know you won't let anything bad happen to me."

"You betcha." As Sam knelt to pet Spike, who had gone with me to the front door, I fidgeted, in spite of Sam's words of assurance. Sam glanced up at me. "What's the matter?"

"I don't know," I said. Then I added honestly, "I know you'll be at the party and will be vigilant, Sam. You're wonderful to me. But ever since those two Wagners and their group of friends showed up when Lucy and I were practicing our Christmas-Eve duet, I've been nervous as a cat."

Standing up with a grimace—I noticed he hadn't brought his cane into the house—Sam said, "I didn't know cats were particularly nervous creatures." He grinned, but I didn't enjoy his sense of humor that evening.

"Stop being so literal, Sam Rotondo. I've never had a cat, but Samson, Pudge Wilson's cat, always runs away from Spike." The Wilsons lived in the house just north of ours. Pudge was a cute kid.

"That's probably because every time they see each other, Spike chases Samson."

"Probably," I conceded. "But I suspect things become time-honored clichés because they hold a modicum of truth, don't you?"

It was Sam's turn to shrug. "Beats me, but I'm willing to take your word on it."

"It's not my word," I mumbled, irritated. "It's wisdom of the ages."

"And who am I to doubt the wisdom of ages?" asked my darling fiancé, still grinning at me.

"Evening, Sam," said Pa, walking into the living room from the hall. "You all ready to escort Daisy to this fancy party tonight? I can't imagine what crystal balls and Christmas have to do with each other, but Daisy said hers is going to be used in aid of discovering Doctor Wagner's murderer."

"Evening, Joe," said Sam, shaking my father's hand. "I doubt we'll learn anything, but it's worth a try, I guess." His eyebrows dipped as he peered at me. "Daisy's edgy about it, though."

Turning to me, my father said in surprise, "Edgy! When have you ever been nervous about practicing your spiritualist routine?"

"Not often," I admitted. "But I'm not looking forward to this evening's party."

"There's a first," said Sam, still grinning. "You're usually champing at the bit to stick yourself into my homicide cases."

"Am not," I said ungraciously—and, I regret to say, untruthfully. Then I left Pa and Sam to chat while I went to the kitchen to see if Aunt Vi needed any help. I'd already set the table.

"You can take the shepherd's pie to the table. Put it on a trivet." She gestured to some wrought-iron trivets hanging on hooks on the wall.

"Want me to set it at your place?"

"Yes, please."

So I did as she'd asked, and then returned to the kitchen, kind of like an obedient sheepdog. Only all I herded were food and silverware. Sheepdogs have it much harder than I.

After I'd set a basket of dinner rolls on the table, Vi stood back, her hands on her hips, thinking. I could tell, because her brow furrowed. A second or so later, she said, "I guess that's it. I made enough shepherd's pie to feed an army." She grinned at me. "So it should satisfy your father and Sam."

I grinned back, feeling a little better about life in general.

By the way, my aunt has told me more than once that if you make a shepherd's pie with beef instead of lamb or mutton, it's not a true shepherd's pie. If you make it with beef, it's cowboy's pie. I guess that makes sense. I have no idea what one would call if it one made it with chicken. A poulterer's pie? Whatever it's called, I like it a lot.

Ma walked into the kitchen yawning. She got off work at noon on Saturdays, and she liked to take a little nap on Saturday afternoons. I'd done the same thing, being a firm believer in naps if you're facing a long day and a longer night. "Something smells good," she said, sniffing the aromatic air appreciatively.

"Shepherd's pie," I informed her.

"Made with the lamb left over from last night's dinner," Vi added.

"Oh, good. I like shepherd's pie," said Ma.

Vi and I exchanged a glance and a smile, glad we had my mother's approval for something edible. She'd managed to eat and almost enjoy chicken curry the few times Vi had fixed it for the family, but she was basically a meat-and-potatoes kind of gal. If one can call one's mother a gal.

"It smells wonderful," I said. "I think everything's on the table. Anything left for me to set out, Vi?"

"I don't think so. Thanks, Daisy."

"Thank *you*."

"Call the men in for dinner, will you, sweetheart?"

"Sure, Ma."

So I called the men in for dinner, we all took our places, and Pa said grace. Then Vi dished out a heaping mound of shepherd's pie and passed it my way. I passed it on to Pa, who passed it to Ma, who passed it to Sam, who smiled as he stared down at it.

"That sure looks good," he said.

"It is," I told him as I passed Ma's plate on to Pa.

Eventually, Vi got us all served, we passed the rolls and butter, and dug in. What a great meal. When we were finished with the main course, I collected the dishes, and Vi told me to set out bowls. So I did, and darned if she didn't appear at the kitchen door holding a great, big baking dish in which she'd prepared an apple crisp for our dessert! I adore apple crisp. Vi says it's not the same thing as an apple brown Betty, whatever that is, but I don't care. It's delicious, especially served, as Vi served ours, with vanilla ice cream on top.

"I almost feel ready to face that stupid Christmas party," I told Vi after I'd scraped up the last morsel of apple-crisp topping—Vi said it's made with butter, oatmeal, brown sugar, and cinnamon, but you couldn't prove it by me—and sighed happily.

"Glad you liked it," she said, smiling benevolently at us all. As mentioned previously, it amazed me how much she loved to cook and loved having people love her cooking.

"Wonderful meal, Vi," said Sam.

"Delicious," said Ma.

"Superb," said Pa.

Unanimous vote. Happens a lot when Vi cooks.

We all rose from the table, and Ma and I began to clear it.

"I'll wash the dishes tonight," said Ma. "You have to work, and I had a nap this afternoon."

"I had a nap this afternoon, too, but I appreciate the offer. I have to change into my Gypsy fortune-teller costume."

"And I have to go out to the car and get my fancy duds," said Sam, helping Ma and me carry dishes to the kitchen sink.

"I'll meet you in the living room," I told him. "Then I guess we should get going."

"I guess," said he, limping toward the front door.

"Where's your cane?" I called after him.

"In the Hudson."

"Better take it tonight. If you don't need it to walk with, maybe you can bop someone on the head with it."

Sam grimaced at me over his shoulder.

Ma said, "Daisy!"

Aw, heck. "We're trying to find a murderer, Ma," I said in my own defense.

"Still and all, I don't believe you should say things like that."

"Very well, Ma," I said upon a sigh. Then Spike and I went into our bedroom.

I'd already set out my fortune-teller costume, so I just took off my day dress and slipped into the costume. I'd made this particular outfit a couple of years prior. It consisted of a white peasant-style blouse and a multi-colored skirt. I'd sewed together different colored strips of cloth that had ended up in my bits-and-pieces drawer, drew the skirt together at my waist with elastic stripping I'd found at Nelson's Five and Dime, and wore it and the blouse with a bright red sash that dangled. For my head covering, I chose a blue, red, and yellow striped material. Because I didn't know what the night would bring, and also because I always did so, I put on the Voodoo juju Mrs. Jackson had given me. After slipping the juju over my head, I put on lots of colorful, cheap necklaces I'd found in various junk shops around town. I jangled like a ring of keys when I walked.

Right after Sam had been shot, Mrs. Jackson made a juju for him, too. A couple of months earlier, his juju had heated up every time he was in the company of the guy who turned out to be the murderer. Since Sam didn't believe in spiritualist mumbo-jumbo, it kind of irked me that it was *his* juju that had pointed to the murderer and not mine.

Of course, I didn't believe in spiritualism, either, in spite of recent evidence that might point to it efficacy, but never mind. I surveyed myself in the cheval-glass mirror after I'd finished plopping the last bead necklace over my head and around my neck.

"What do you think, Spike? Do I look like a Gypsy?"

Spike, never having seen a Gypsy, didn't answer, although he did wag his tail. I'd never seen a Gypsy, either, but I'd seen photographs in the *National Geographic*. They didn't look like I looked at the moment, but I would probably be hired to play a Gypsy in a minute if I were to audition for a part in a Hollywood movie. The last time I'd worn the same costume, Harold had complimented me on it, so it couldn't be *all* bad.

Anyway, I'd venture to guess nobody else attending that night's party had ever seen a real Gypsy, either.

Spike and I left the bedroom, re-entered the kitchen, and there was Sam, looking as dapper and handsome as I'd ever seen him. Darned if Harold hadn't been right about him.

"You look great, Sam!" I told him, inspecting him from tip to toe. "Wonderful. You *do* look like an Italian count!"

"Yeah?" said Sam, sounding skeptical. "And how many Italian counts have *you* met?"

"None. I've never met a Gypsy, either, but I'm supposed to look like one. What do you think?" I gave a twirl, clanking riotously as I did so.

Sam shook his head. "I suppose you look as much like a Gypsy as I do an Italian count."

"You both look great," said Pa, beaming at us from the door to the dining room. "You make a nice couple."

"Thanks, Pa." I went over and gave my father a peck on the cheek.

"The two of you look wonderful," said my mother, smiling at Sam and me.

"Thanks, Ma."

"But you don't have dark hair," said Sam. When I glanced at him, he'd commenced frowning at me. "Gypsies have dark hair, don't they?"

"I'm going to wear a colorful striped scarf," I told him. "Nobody will know my hair's really red. Sort of red. Dark red."

"Auburn," said Sam.

"How poetic of you."

Sam rolled his eyes. Then he said, "You have gorgeous hair."

In other words, everything was completely normal in the Sam-Daisy romance department.

Harold showed up just about then. We'd agreed he'd escort us to the party, since he actually knew a member of the club in the person of Dr. Fred Greenlaw. No one needed to know Sam and I were there at Claude Dermott's invitation. Claude was still worried he might get killed if Dr. Wagner's murderer actually did reside at the club. Even if he didn't live there, he might attend that night's party.

It occurred to me that we were all assuming a lot of things that weren't facts. Ah, well.

However, after my encounter with the two Wagner brothers earlier in the day, I understood Claude's trepidation. Those two and their friends had given me the willies.

Because Sam's Hudson was so much larger than Harold's Stutz Bearcat, Sam drove us to the club. On the way, he told us two uniformed policemen were going to be at the club with us, in a back room and out of sight, unless and until they were needed.

"I'm so glad," I told him.

He gave me a surreptitious squeeze, leaned over a bit and whispered, "I love you and don't want anything to happen to you."

I darned near cried.

I think Harold snickered, but I'm not sure.

TWENTY-NINE

The Pasadena Golf and Tennis Club was ablaze with lights when Sam pulled up across the street from it and parked his car. I was a trifle startled and wondered if the party had begun without us.

But when we walked to the club, a nervous Claude Dermott greeted us at the door and explained the lights. "We're just getting ready. The party doesn't actually begin until nine o'clock, but the staff is decorating the place for Christmas." He eyed me. "You look really…colorful, Mrs. Majesty."

"Yes. I'm supposed to be a Gypsy fortune-teller."

"You look like one," he told me. I guess he'd believed the folks in the flickers, too. "But come on in here. I'll show you where I set up a table for you to use." He looked at my empty hands. "But weren't you going to bring a crystal ball or something?"

"Here it is," said Sam, holding out the embroidered sack containing my crystal ball and its stand.

By the way, if anyone's interested, I'd found that "crystal" ball in downtown Los Angeles's Chinatown about ten years earlier. It was just a big glass ball and had nothing to do with crystal, but what the heck. It had surprised me a couple of times in the past by showing me things I didn't really want to see. I hope it wouldn't do so that night.

Or maybe I did. Nerts. I didn't know what I wanted, except for the night to be over and to be in bed with my dog. And, of course, to see the murderer of Dr. E.A. Wagner caught. As long as the murderer wasn't one of my friends.

At any rate, I approved of the table Claude had set up for me, although Harold decided it needed to be decorated more festively. So I sat in a folding chair behind the table, which positioned me with my back to a wall. That was fine with me. I didn't want anyone to sneak up on me.

After Harold had decorated my table with a couple boughs of holly—stolen, no doubt from another table in the club—he stepped back and critically surveyed his work.

He shook his head. "I don't know. The table looks festive enough, I guess, but you seem a trifle out of place. A Gypsy at a Christmas party? I just don't know."

"This wasn't my idea," I reminded him, feeling cross and tetchy.

"Now, now. A fortune-teller might not always belong at a Christmas party, but this was a good idea, whoever had it."

"If you say so. Anyway, you're the one who came up with this particular bright idea."

"Oh, come on, Daisy. You know you want to find out who murdered that miserable piece of... er, garbage. If you don't, poor George Grenville is likely to spend the rest of his life in prison with the likes of my father. Nobody deserves that fate. Except maybe my sister."

"You're right," I said upon a weary sigh, although why I was weary I had no idea. I'd had a nap, after all.

"He's right about what?" asked Sam, walking over to us and gazing judiciously at my table.

"He's right about wanting to find out who really murdered Doctor Wagner. We all three know it wasn't George Grenville, no matter who found what in his gardening shed."

"Huh," said Sam.

"Huh," said Harold.

I swear, if one didn't know better, one would think they two men were related. Sam would be horrified if I told him that.

"Is everything all set up here?" asked a harried Claude Dermott. He was actually wringing his hands. You seldom find people doing that except in novels and the flickers.

Because I felt sorry for him, I smiled and said, "Everything is fine here, Mr. Dermott."

"I'm so glad." He pulled a handkerchief from his pants pocket and wiped his perspiring brow. "I'm so nervous about this party, I can hardly stand it."

"I'm sorry," I said, understanding his feelings, but wishing he hadn't admitted to them. I was already nervous enough for the both of us, and maybe a couple of other people too.

Patting Claude on the back, Harold said, "I'm sure everything will go swell. The place looks wonderful. Whoever put up the decorations did a great job."

"Thank you," said Claude. "We keep decorations for various seasons stored in the basement. We only put away the Thanksgiving cornucopias and Indian corn a week or so ago. All these holidays come in a row, and they keep us hopping."

"I'm sure that's so." Harold's voice oozed compassion.

Which it should. I'd never thought about how people who ran businesses like the Pasadena Golf and Tennis Club had to make their places of work look appropriate for various seasons, but it made sense. Especially here in Southern California, where pretty much the only way you could tell one season from another was by the decorations folks put up.

That's not entirely true. For instance, the weather in recent days had been quite nippy. But at least we didn't have to slog through feet of snow.

Sam pulled up another folding chair and we sat beside each other, watching the staff of the club scurry here and there setting out Christmas-related items. A couple of women who were maids, according to their black dresses and white aprons, decorated a gigantic fir tree across the room from my table.

"That's a gorgeous tree," I murmured.

"Yeah," said Sam. "Hope nobody sets it on fire with a cigarette."

"Golly, Sam, I was only worried about being murdered before you said that. Now I can worry about the Christmas tree burning the club down, too. Thanks heaps."

With a grin, Sam said, "Always happy to oblige."

Waiters had begun arriving with trays of food by that time. Two long tables on each side of the room, each with a red table cloth and adorned with fir boughs and holly berries, began filling with what looked like tons of canapés and snacks of all varieties. A small orchestra consisting of mainly brass, along with a with a couple of violins and a cello, tuned up. Their conductor wore a red bow tie in honor of the season.

When the director gave the signal, the orchestra commenced playing "Joy to the World." They sounded quite nice. "The Pasadena Golf and Tennis Club really knows how to throw a party," I muttered.

"Sure does," Sam agreed.

"You all set?" asked Harold, munching on something as he walked to my table. Glancing around, he said, "The place looks great, doesn't it?"

"It does," I agreed. "And I love the Christmas music."

"Aha! Take a gander at who just joined the party," said Harold, hurrying to the door, where I saw Dr. Fred Greenlaw, his sister Hazel on his arm. I liked the both of them really well.

"Good evening, Daisy!" said Hazel, coming to my table. "Harold said you'd be here, offering spiritualist advice to the members."

"It's good to see you, Hazel," said I, meaning it. She was a nurse and a lovely person, two attributes of which I approved. Not that she needed my approval. We shook hands, and then Hazel called her brother over to my table.

Naturally, Sam had stood upon Hazel's arrival. He leaned slightly on his cane, but he smiled at her as they shook hands. His smile didn't waver when he traded her hand for her brother's. I took that as a good sign, given what Sam thought of Dr. Greenlaw, Harold, and their ilk.

Hazel, Fred, Sam and I chatted together for some time, and I was surprised when I glanced up and saw that the room had filled with people. "My goodness. I guess I'd better set up my crystal ball and start looking clairvoyant."

Hazel laughed.

Sam handed me his cane and said, "Will you look after this for me? I don't want to carry it around with me."

"Don't you need it?"

"Naw. I took a couple of aspirin tablets just before we drove over here. I should be all right for an hour or so."

"Very well, if you're sure, but I have more aspirin tablets in my handbag if you need more."

"Thanks, sweetheart."

"You're more than welcome. I hate it that you hurt all the time."

"It's not all the time," said Sam, although I think he was down-playing his pain, poor fellow.

Anyway, I tucked the cane beneath the table, then glanced up at him. "Does it stick out on the other side?"

"A little," said Sam.

"I'll turn it sideways," I said, and commenced to move it with my black Gypsy shoes. " Is that any better?"

"Yeah. Nobody can see it now, since the cloth hangs down to the floor."

"Good. Come back from time to time so we can compare notes." I divided my gaze between Sam and Harold.

Harold saluted.

Sam didn't.

To my surprise, if not total amazement, I realized as soon as my men walked off that most of the people standing close by were waiting for *me*. By gum—so to speak—it didn't look as if anyone else in the world, or at least in the higher echelons of Pasadena society, cared if crystal balls and Christmas didn't go together. The Christmas music helped disguise the anomaly. Or maybe it didn't.

A couple of giggling girls, one with dark hair and one with light hair, whom I'd seen at other people's mansions although I couldn't recall their names, were first in line. As I could only use the crystal ball on one person at a time, I smiled Gypsy-ishly at the both of them. "Who wants to be first?" I asked in my best mystical voice.

The girls each poked the other on a shoulder while I waited, suppressing an urge to gesture for someone else to take the chair across from me. I gave myself a stern reminder that I was there to provide entertainment, not annoy the guests.

Finally the dark-haired girl sat in the chair. Her hair was bobbed in the latest style, and she wore a perfectly smashing gown of bright Christmas red adorned with fabulous beading. I tried not to stare at the beading, but it sure caught the eye. What's more, after squinting at it for several seconds, I decided I could do my own beading in a like style. Therefore, because she'd assisted me even though she didn't know it, I smiled sweetly at the girl. She giggled nervously.

"Merry Christmas," I said.

Evidently she hadn't expected a Christmas greeting from a Gypsy, and she gulped. "Um…merry Christmas."

"Would you like me to consult the crystal ball about anything in particular?"

It occurred to me that people were standing too close to my table. Nobody'd want to ask the crystal ball anything if the whole rest of the room could hear her. Or him, but it was usually ladies who availed themselves of my services.

I held up a hand, attempting to do so in an occult manner. "One moment, please."

The girl blinked as I stood, craned my neck and scanned the room. As soon as I caught Harold's eye, I gestured for him to come to me. He did so, thereby making him the second male of my acquaintance who did as I asked of him. The other one was Spike.

In a low voice, I asked Harold to set a boundary around my table so each person for whom I read the crystal ball could have a modicum of privacy.

"Sure!" he said. "Don't know why we didn't think of that earlier."

"Nor do I, but I'd appreciate it if you'd make my table a little more—isolated or something."

"Absolutely."

And darned if he didn't. He snabbled Sam and Fred Grenville, who set up a barrier of chairs around my table, the backs of the chairs facing me. Therefore, although folks could sit on the chairs, they wouldn't be staring at me or at anyone for whom I was consulting the ball. I know that sounds idiotic. It *is* idiotic. But it's how I made my living, so I respected it.

Again I smiled at the young, dark-haired lady. "There," I said softly, attempting to sound enigmatic. "Now, would you like to consult the crystal ball about anything in particular?"

"Oh!" She covered her mouth with a well-manicured hand and giggled some more. She looked as if she'd visited a beauty parlor that very day, and I recalled her being one of the Wright girls. The Wrights were fabulously wealthy, the head of the family having made a fortune from chewing gum, of all odd things.

By golly, it was the Wrights' missing butler who'd made my crystal ball show me a bunch of fir and pine trees a year or so before! As soon as I recalled that other evening, I wished I hadn't. Anyhow, back to the Christmas party...

"Yes, please," the girl—Veronica Wright, I do believe —whispered.

"Let me see," I said, playing my part for all I was worth and recalling snippets of gossip I'd heard here and there. "You want to know if a certain gentleman of your acquaintance is interested in deepening your relationship?"

"Oh! However did you *know?*" she whispered in awe.

I didn't tell her. Rather, I waved my own personal well-manicured hands over the crystal ball in what I knew to be a mystical manner because I'd practiced in front of the mirror in my bedroom, and said, "Love will be yours soon."

"How soon?" she wanted to know. She would.

"The crystal ball can't give you dates and times," I told her. "However, it can tell you that your gentleman friend will be courting you in good earnest in the coming year. In fact, 1925 will probably be the year of your engagement, if not marriage."

"Oh, my!" Veronica said, thrilled unless I missed my guess. She turned in her chair. "Sally! Do come here! This is wonderful. She can tell you all sorts of things."

So the blonde, whom I assumed to be Sally, tripped up to my table, and Veronica rose and allowed her to sit. Sally waited until Veronica had gone out of hearing range before consulting me. Her question wasn't quite as banal as that of her friend.

Leaning over the table, she whispered, her gaze sliding around the room as if to be sure no one was spying on her, "Can you please tell me if my father's business will get better? He's so afraid we'll lose everything."

I glanced at her and saw tears standing in her eyes. All right. I know she was one of the upper crust of Pasadena society. Still and all, if you're accustomed to having everything you ever wanted and feared having it snatched away from you...well, I felt sorry for the girl.

Therefore, I took my time before I answered her, wishing the stupid ball really *could* predict the future. As I passed my hands over it for about the fifth or sixth time, darned if it didn't suddenly turn a murky gray color. Startled, I lifted my head almost fast enough to break my neck and looked around. No one hovered over us. However, when I glanced to my right, I saw Gaylord Wagner grinning at me.

Mercy sakes.

What did this mean? Casting a glance at the ceiling, I didn't see any light bulbs that might have burned out. Could the crystal ball...?

No. That was absurd.

Nevertheless, I was a trifle rattled as I returned to the subject of this sitting. Fortunately, the ball cleared again. When I took a surreptitious glance to my right, Gaylord Wagner was gone. Very odd.

However, words began spilling from my mouth. I'm not sure how they got in there, but what they said was, "Your father's business, in spite of recent reversals, will recover. Your family will experience happiness beginning at the end of February or in early March."

And where *that* tidbit of information had sprung from, I had—and still have—no earthly idea. Sally was pleased, and I was pleased for her. I also hoped I hadn't lied to the sweet thing.

Anyway, the party went on, and I continued to ply my trade. Occasionally the crystal ball turned an ugly gray, and every single time it did that, when I looked around, darned if there wasn't a Wagner brother, either Gaylord or Vincent, nearby.

At the very first opportunity—in other words, the first time Sam walked over to my table to see how things were going, I took a little break from my duties, grabbed him by the arm, and yanked him outside. It was cold out there, darn it. But I wanted privacy in which to convey my message. So I did.

I'm sure it comes as no surprise to anyone that he looked at me as if I'd lost what was left of my mind.

THIRTY

The front door to the club opened, and I whirled around, afraid one or both of the Wagner brothers had followed Sam and me outside for some fell purpose. I nearly fainted with relief when Harold, shivering, walked over to us.

"I saw the two of you leave. What's going on?" he asked, rubbing his coat-clad sleeves with his hands. "It's too damned cold out here for a tête-a-tête, Daisy."

"I know it is," I said, still shivering. "But Sam doesn't believe me!"

"I believe you," said a clearly cranky Sam.

"What doesn't he believe?" asked Harold, his gaze flipping from me to Sam.

"I *do* believe her!" said Sam, still cranky.

"He doesn't either!" I cried, frustrated and frozen.

"I *do* believe her crystal ball went from clear to gray every time one of the Wagners was near it," said Sam, his own voice sounding frustrated and frozen.

"It's the truth!" I cried, feeling helpless. "It *is*, Harold!"

"I *believe* you," said Sam, still more loudly and frustrated.

"Interesting," said Harold in a judicious voice. Then he

shrugged. "I believe you, too, Daisy, but your mud-colored crystal ball doesn't help us any."

"But…but…but…"

"Harold's right," said Sam, interrupting my stuttered attempt to defend my crystal ball. Boy, I never thought I'd ever even compose a sentence like that one, but there you go. "Even if you're right"—He held up a hand to preclude any more outbursts from me—"we need hard evidence, not a muddy crystal ball."

"I have an idea," said Harold before I could bellow at Sam.

Actually, I had no intention of hollering at Sam because I knew he was right. I could imagine me in a courtroom telling a judge and jury that the Wagner brothers were guilty of their father's murder because my crystal ball had said so. Even *I'd* laugh me out of court.

"What's your idea?" asked Sam of Harold, giving up on me as a lost cause, I guess.

Harold elucidated. "The Wagner brothers have been tippling quite heavily this evening, and—"

"*Tippling?*" I cried, horrified. "You mean they're *drinking? Alcohol?*"

Harold and Sam both rolled their eyes. I swear, if they only knew how alike they were…

"Get a grip on your sanity, Daisy. Of course, they're drinking alcohol," said Harold. "What else would you expect two idiots like them to drink? Christmas punch?"

"But where do they get *alcohol?* In the Pasadena Golf and Tennis Club?"

"They probably have their own bootlegger and stocked up before they even arrived at the party."

"But—"

"Never mind, Daisy," said Sam, annoying me, although I'm not sure why. "It's too damned cold out here to talk about how the Wagners get their booze. What's your idea, Kincaid?"

So Harold explained. "They've both drunk enough that they're being unwise in their communications. They and their pals have been chuckling and guffawing over something, thinking they're being coy. Fred Greenlaw is with them, and he and I just decided he should lure the Wagners into a back parlor, where Fred might be able to find out what they think is so damned funny. I think you and I, Detective Rotondo, should pay a surreptitious visit to the same back parlor. If Fred is a good-enough actor—and I think he is—and if they confess to murdering their old man, maybe Fred will get them to tell all. After all, Fred's a doctor. He also loathed Doctor Wagner because, not only was Doctor Wagner a bad egg, but he also…uh…interfered with Hazel when she was younger."

I gasped and cried "No!" although I don't know why. At that point, I was willing to believe anything atrocious of the late and exceedingly evil and unlamented Dr. Wagner.

Ignoring my outcry, Sam said, "Good idea. You think Greenlaw will be believable? If the Wagner boys are guilty of murder, they probably won't take kindly to people butting in on their revelations."

Harold waived Sam's worry away with an airy hand. "Don't worry about Fred. He's been buttering up the two dim-witted Wagners all evening long. So has Hazel, but Fred has a better chance of prying the truth out of them. They don't want women interfering in their business. They think of women as being stupid and undeserving and good for only one thing."

"The cads!"

All right, all right, I know the old-fashioned epithet was ridiculous under the circumstances, but I couldn't help myself.

"Sounds like they take after their old man," said Sam.

"They do," said Harold.

"I'm freezing to death," said I.

Sam put an arm around me. "Let's get you back inside. You can continue to read your crystal ball, and Kincaid and I will see if we can hear the Wagner boys confess to something for which we can arrest them." He eyed Harold with some misgiving. "You're *sure* your friend will be able to convince the brothers he's on the up-and-up?"

"Fred is an acting genius," said Harold.

"If you say so," said Sam.

So I went back into the club before Harold and Sam so no one would think the three of us had been out there together. Boy, I hadn't realized how many rich people in Pasadena smoked cigarettes and cigars. Coming into the fuggy atmosphere from the clean out-of-doors, made me stop in the doorway and wave my hand in front of my face, trying to clear away some of the smoke. Didn't work.

Nevertheless, eyes watering from the smudgy air, I returned to my table in my little private part of the front parlor and sat once more in front of my crystal ball. Which was, at that very moment, a sickly mud-gray color. I lifted my head and glanced around the room. Sure enough, Gaylord and Vincent stood in front of the wall of chairs, chatting with a few of their friends. I noticed Fred Greenlaw among their cohorts. It looked to me as though Harold had been correct about Fred. He was laughing it up and slapping people on the back, and being as much of a hail-fellow-well-met as any of the other rich young men he huddled with. I also noticed no women graced their group.

As Sam would say, "Huh." Well, Harold would say it, too, come to think of it.

Then Gaylord hollered, "Stanley, old man!" and I jumped a little in my chair.

"Gay and Vince," Stanley hollered back, making my ears ring. Those fellows were loud.

I knew the reason. Since Harold had let me in on their secret, I now understood those pretty flowered teacups each man held *didn't* contain tea, but some kind of illicit alcohol. Well, except for the cup held by Fred Greenlaw. He was no scofflaw, unlike the other men in that group.

But I had to get back to work. I wanted to sneak to the back parlor, where it looked as if the gang of Wagners and their cronies were headed, but I had to leave that up to Sam and Harold. Curse all men! I wanted to *be* there! I wanted to *hear* what those horrible men said to each other. I wanted to *see* Fred Greenlaw practice his acting skills on a bunch of fellows who weren't nearly as smart as he.

Mind you, I was only assuming the last item on that list. But the man was a doctor, for Pete's sake. You couldn't become a doctor unless you were pretty darned smart.

Instantly my mind leapt back to that wet green cemetery where Spike had discovered the muddy body of the late Dr. Everhard Wagner, and I revised my doctor theory. But only slightly. I'm sure medical colleges were much tougher on their students in these modern times than they'd been when Dr. Wagner went to school.

Or maybe they weren't.

It didn't matter. That's because my crystal ball had become the hit of the Christmas party, young maidens were once again lined up, so I had to get back to work. Piffle.

But the young ladies were nice and sweet, all a good deal younger than I—and I was only twenty-five, for crumb's sake—and they appreciated my talents, such as they were. Then again, maybe I felt so much older than they because I'd actually *lived* for a few years. I'd been married; seen the love of my life come back from an unspeakable war the shell of his former self; I'd nursed him through terrible times; and I'd mourned his loss when he finally put himself out of his misery. These young things had been pampered and petted and given everything they'd ever wanted ever since they were born. Our lives were...

Marianne Grenville's face appeared in my crystal ball.

I swear to heaven, it *did*. What's more, Marianne's face was then replaced by the face of Miss Emmaline Castleton, who had lost her fiancé in the late Great War and who also suffered from tuberculosis. I looked around, flabbergasted, but saw no one peering oddly at my ball or at me.

Good. However, I did revise my scenario regarding the lives of the young women who were asking a piece of glass for advice about their various lives. I didn't know what any of them were going through or had gone through, and I had no right to judge a single one of them. I almost wish Johnny Buckingham were there so I could relay to him my profound revelation.

I swear to heaven, I didn't think that line of young women would ever get smaller. It seemed to me every lady in the club that evening wanted to ask something of my crystal ball. Most of them had questions about their love lives, but some actually had problems they wanted advice about. From a piece of glass...

Never mind. It made them happy when I told them the ball had told me something.

I was sitting across from a young woman named Natalie Levine when loud crashing noises came from the back of the club, along with several loud bellows of what sounded like rage. A shot rang out, nearly scaring the socks off of me. Both Miss Levine and I jumped a foot or so and turned to see what had caused the ruckus.

Darned if we didn't see Detective Sam Rotondo, Officer Doan, and another uniformed policeman hauling the handcuffed Wagner brothers from the premises. Fred Greenlaw and Harold Kincaid followed at a distance that made me think they didn't want to be known as having had anything to do with how and why the Wagner boys had been arrested.

Miss Levine, her hand to her mouth, said, "Oh, my!"

I couldn't have said it better myself.

Claude Dermott, looking frazzled, entered the room from another door, casting wild glances around the room. "What happened?" he hollered. "What's going on?" Poor fellow. He was supposed to be in charge of the place.

Harold hooked him by the elbow and led him over to my table. He—Harold, I mean—bowed politely to Miss Levine and said, "I beg your pardon, Natalie, but I need to talk to Mrs. Majesty for a moment or two. I'm sorry for the interruption."

"That's all right," said Miss Levine. "Whatever is going on?"

It sounded to me as if she were more interested in why the Wagner brothers had been hauled away than in my crystal ball. I was glad of it, because I wanted to hear Harold's tale, too.

Therefore, Harold drew up another chair in front of my table, shoved Claude Dermott into it, gestured for Fred Greenlaw to stand guard over us, and both he and Fred leaned over the table.

"It worked," said Harold gleefully, grinning from ear to ear. I know that's not possible, but it's a time-honored expression, so it's fair to use it. Harold's grin was certainly wide.

Astonished, I said, "You mean they confessed to murdering their father?"

Natalie Levine gasped.

"What?" barked Mr. Dermott? "They did *what?*"

"They confessed!" I said.

"Not precisely," said Harold.

"What the heck does that mean?" I asked, irked.

"They said enough for us to know they buried their old man in the cemetery. Sam sneaked away to call in his two outriders, and we listened another couple of minutes. They were *laughing* about it!"

"Who was laughing about what?" I asked.

"The Wagners were laughing about hauling their father to the cemetery and dumping him into a hole."

"Good heavens," I said, my nose wrinkling in disgust.

"I don't think heaven had anything to do with it," said Harold.

"So they were the ones I heard in the locker room?" asked Mr. Dermott.

"I guess so," said Harold. "You didn't recognize their voices?"

"Well, no, but lots of men are members here. I don't know them all, and I certainly don't know what each of them sounds like."

"I guess it doesn't matter. Sam said he thinks he can break them."

"What does that mean?" Claude Dermott asked, appearing horrified, probably because he thought it meant Sam would batter them about the head and shoulders with a blunt instrument until something actually *did* break.

"It's only a figure of speech. He already has them confessing to burying their father, and they wouldn't have done that if the guy wasn't dead. I figure they must have killed him if they knew he was dead and they buried him, right?"

"Oh. Yes. That makes sense," said Mr. Dermott, who wasn't quite as quick-witted as Harold.

"What about the baseball bat in George Greenville's garden shed?" I asked.

"They were chortling about that all night," said Harold, sounding disgusted. For good reason. "They thought that was the cream of the jest. Pin the murder on poor old George, who's never even held a baseball, much less hit one with a bat."

"I guess," said I, thinking Harold was probably right.

"Oh, dear. Oh, dear," said Mr. Dermott. "It looks as if the crowd is getting upset. I think I'd better call the festivities to an end."

"Good idea," said Harold.

I glanced around the room and, sure enough, people seemed to be fidgeting, staring at the front door to the club and looking worried and upset, as if they weren't sure what had just happened or what they should do now. Fred Greenlaw turned to Mr. Dermott.

"Want me to make an announcement, Claude?" he asked.

"Oh, would you? Thanks, Fred. Your voice is much louder than mine."

All it took was a loud voice? Well, who was I to argue?

But darned if Mr. Dermott wasn't correct.

Fred stood on a chair, lifted his arms in the air and hollered, "Friends! Sorry for the disruption of our Christmas party! But it's now..." He shook his arm, thereby allowing his coat sleeve to fall and reveal a gold wristwatch, and said, "...nearly midnight, and it's time to call a halt to the festivities. The recent disruption isn't any fault of the club or the club's fine manager. So if everyone will fetch your coats, hats, et cetera, we'll all go home and have a jolly and happy Christmas!"

The orchestra began playing again. This time it was "Jingle Bells," which got everyone out of their surprised stupors and put grins on all their faces.

"I guess I'd better go, too," said Natalie Levine, whom I'd forgotten all about. "Thank you for your help, Mrs. Majesty."

Had I helped her? I couldn't even remember. Nevertheless, I smiled enigmatically and said, "You're most welcome. Have a lovely Christmas."

"Thanks. You, too." And Natalie Levine hurried off.

I had no idea where Sam was, or how Harold and I were going to get home.

THIRTY-ONE

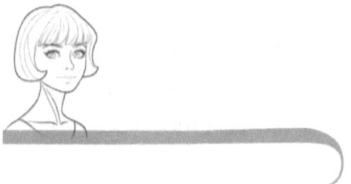

I needn't have worried. As ever, Harold took care of me.

"Just wait here, sweetie. I'll make sure everyone's able to drive home. I'll call a cab for the ones who aren't *compos mentis*."

"Why wouldn't they...Oh." Only then did I recall the imbibing that had been going on in the club that evening.

"Yes," said Harold. "Oh. But put everything away and wait for me. Fred will drive us to the police station. I want to know what's transpiring on the Wagner front."

"So do I." Darn Sam anyhow. He could have scooped me up on his way out the door, couldn't he?

Oh, very well, that would have been unprofessional of him.

Harold and Fred scurried off to see that everyone at the party was able to get home, and I began packing up my spiritualist paraphernalia. I was about to pick up my crystal ball from its stand when I noticed it had turned dead black.

I jumped slightly, my hands flying away from the ball, and sat back in my chair. Black? I glanced to my left and to my right, and then looked at the ceiling, thinking someone had turned off the lights. No one had. Tentatively I peeked again at the ball. Still black.

Lordy, Lordy, what did this mean?

I jumped about three yards in the air when I heard, very softly, from behind me, "Don't say a word, Mrs. Majesty. You're going to help me get my brothers out of jail now."

Whirling in my chair, I saw the fellow I'd heard people call Stanley. Stanley? Brothers? What was the man talking about?

"Wh-who are you?"

"Stanley, Mrs. Majesty." He pointed a teensy little gun at me. I think those things are called derringers, but I'm no gun expert.

"But...Who are your brothers? What are you talking about?"

"Tut, tut, Mrs. Majesty. And here I'd been told you were a clever woman."

"No. I'm not. And I don't know who you are or why you're pointing that gun at me. It's a rude thing to do and I wish you'd stop it."

"Can't."

"Nonsense! You could if you wanted to." All right, it probably wasn't wise to argue with a man holding a gun on me. I was upset.

"Gaylord and Vincent Wagner are my brothers, Mrs. Majesty."

"Your *brothers*?"

Squinting at him, I discerned a vague family resemblance. Gaylord and Vincent were both stockier than Stanley, but they all three had the same squinty weasel eyes and pointy weasel chins. Marianne didn't inherit ugly eyes from her father. Still and all...*brothers*?

"Yes. Their old man knocked up my mother, and I was the result."

"I-I-I—"

"Don't bother trying to figure it out. The dead doctor was a son of a bitch. Everyone knows that. My mother knew it, too, but she kept me anyway after I was born. I got to know my brothers quite a few years ago. They hated Dear Old Dad almost as much as I did."

"Did...Did you kill him?"

"Now why would you think that?"

"Because you're pointing a gun at me."

"You're not as dumb as you look, I guess."

"That's not nice!"

"Shut up," said Stanley, sounding more serious than he had before. He looked it, too. In fact, he looked downright mean and nasty. "Gather your things together, Mrs. Majesty. Then we're going for a ride down to the police station. There I aim to get my brothers and hightail it out of Pasadena forever. I'm sure your tame detective will trade my brothers for you."

"But—"

"I said *shut up*! Damn you, get your things and come with me. *Now*."

He'd walked up to me and now stood directly behind my chair, inducing an anxiety I couldn't recall feeling before in my life, although I'd been in some mighty tight corners, so maybe I'd merely neglected to recall the feeling. If so, I don't blame myself. It was a most unpleasant one. "Um...Um...I'll get my handbag. May I do that?"

"I just told you to do that," he reminded me, snarling. Now he looked kind of like a rabid weasel, although I don't know that for sure, never having seen a rabid weasel.

"Oh, yes. I'm sorry. You're making me nervous."

He shook his head in mock sympathy. "What a shame. Now hurry up."

So I leaned down to fetch my handbag and darned if I didn't first feel Sam's cane. I'd completely forgotten about it. I could use it as a weapon! Maybe. What could I do with Sam's cane? Against a gun?

I had no earthly idea.

"Ready, Daisy?" came Harold's voice from across the room. "Fred's—Hey, what's—?"

The sound of a very loud gunshot ended Harold's sentence for him.

Horrified, I forgot all about being afraid, grabbed Sam's cane from under my table, held it by its curving top, swung it like a baseball bat, and bashed Stanley Whatever His Last Name Was on the side of his head with it. Stanley stumbled, fell over my chair, and crashed onto the table, taking my still-black crystal ball with him.

The gun flew somewhere. I didn't keep track of it. I just kept thumping Stanley's head with Sam's cane.

He screamed. "Stop it! Bitch!"

"What the devil!" came from Fred Greenlaw.

He, too, rushed into the room, and he and Harold raced over to where I continued battering Stanly Whomever on the head. He'd lifted his hands to cover same, so I flailed at his fingers, too.

"Daisy!" Harold cried.

"Daisy!" Fred cried.

"*Make her stop!*" Stanley cried.

"*You shot Harold!*" I bellowed at him. "I'm not going to stop until you're *dead!*"

"Daisy!" Harold yelled, trying and failing to grab the cane from my grasp. "He didn't shoot me. The bullet missed."

"I don't *care!* He *tried* to shoot you! He was going to shoot *me!*"

"Daisy! Stop it!"

Fred and Harold finally managed to grasp an arm each and hauled me away from Stanley. I managed to get one last vicious *whack* in, which effectively did in the cane as a weapon, unless Fred and Harold let go of me. Then I aimed to stab Stanley with the broken, pointy end of what used to be a pretty sturdy cane.

Stanley whimpered on the floor, his hands still over his head and beginning to show bruises, a relatively gory puddle of blood growing around him. Panting, I stood over him, held in four strong hands, longing to finish killing the fiendish whimperer.

"What on earth is going on in here?"

Claude Dermott screeched to a halt in front of what was left of my fortune-telling table. I had no idea where my crystal ball had rolled.

"He pointed a gun at me! He shot Harold!"

"Did not!" Stanley screamed.

So I kicked him. Hard.

He screamed again.

Fred and Harold dragged me a couple of inches farther back. I continued, panting like a winded racehorse, "He's Gaylord and Vincent's brother! He made my crystal ball turn black! He said he was going to take me to the police station to get his brothers out of jail! He said Sam would trade them for me!"

"Huh?" said Mr. Dermott.

"I don't think she's coherent yet," said Harold.

"Can we let you go, Daisy?" asked Fred. "Don't hit Stanley again, all right? Or kick him. He's subdued now."

"He's a *devil!*" I screeched.

"All right, enough is enough, Daisy. Drink this."

And darned if Harold didn't hold a flask to my lips, tilt my head back, and make me swallow something vile that burned its way down my gullet.

My fit of rage ended in a fit of convulsive coughing.

However, thanks to Stanley's having shot a gun in the sacred confines of the Pasadena Golf and Tennis Club, Claude Dermott, when he called the police, learned a car was already on its way because someone else had telephoned to report the gunshot. He and Fred managed to tie Stanley up with some ribbon that had lately decorated a table. By the time the police arrived, he was trussed as neatly as a Christmas package, but he looked nowhere near as inviting. He also bled a lot from various bashed placed on and around his head.

In actual fact, I'd damaged him a good deal. I'd have been ashamed of myself if he hadn't threatened me with a gun and shot at my best friend. Later Sam told me I'd given him a concussion, and he'd probably lose at least some of the hearing in one of his ears. I'd wanted to kill him, so I thought those results were paltry.

When I told Sam that, he only looked at me and shook his head.

Anyway, here's what ultimately happened to Dr. Everhard A. Wagner and the aftermath of the 1924 Christmas party at the Pasadena Golf and Tennis Club.

Of his three sons—Diane and Marianne had no idea Stanley even existed until after that fateful party at the club—Stanley was probably the one who hated him most. That, he claimed at the police station, was because he was a bastard—Stanley, not Dr. Wagner—and he resented Gaylord and Vincent for being born to Dr. Wagner's wife, when Stanley's mother was only one of the doctors many mistresses.

Stanley got to know Gaylord and Vincent, who thought it was a hoot that they had a brother who'd been born out of wedlock. Stanley buttered up the Wagner boys, although he still resented them like fire. He badgered his father to acknowledge him as a full-fledged son, mainly so he could partake of the doctor's wealth, of which he—Dr. Wagner, I mean—seemed to be losing a lot in recent years.

Because of that, and because all three of Dr. Wagner's sons were awful people, they plotted the old man's demise, Gaylord and Vincent promising Stanley a portion of the doctor's fortune after they inherited same. Stanley—whose last name, I eventually learned, was Clarke (with an E, as Stanley was quick to point out, probably because he thought it looked classier than plain old Clark)—did the actual deed by battering Dr. Wagner over the head with a baseball bat. Not, in fact, unlike what I'd done to him with Sam's cane, so Stanley got what he deserved in my opinion. Sam only sighed when I told him so, but that's neither here nor there. After Stanley had done the actual deed, Gaylord and Vincent helped wrap the dead doctor in a rug, carry the corpse up to Mountain View Cemetery in Gaylord's motorcar, and bury it in a shallow grave.

And there he would have stayed had Sam and I not taken Spike to the cemetery that soggy Monday two weeks before Christmas in 1924.

Oh, and my crystal ball had rolled across the room and stopped underneath a lovely wing chair in a corner of the Pasadena Golf and Tennis Club's decorated-for-Christmas parlor. It was clear as a bell when I hauled it out from under the chair, dusted it off, and put it in its embroidered bag. It hasn't turned gray or black since, and I sincerely hope it never will again.

Diane and Marianne were stunned to learn of Stanley's existence, although they weren't surprised. They'd even postulated other children in the doctor's life to me once or twice before. George and Marianne Grenville decided to sell their home on Catalina Avenue and move into the beautiful house on El Molino Avenue. Diane objected at first, wanting nothing to do with the place where she and Marianne had been tortured, but Marianne and George promised her they'd redecorate the home and make a happy, friendly, welcoming place for the three of them—and any children George and Marianne might decide to adopt. Thanks to her loathsome father, she'd never be able to bear children of her own; but she, George, and Diane, all three, possessed loving hearts and wanted to help children in need.

I thought that was sweet of them.

Harold, Fred, Sam and I didn't get home until the wee hours of Sunday morning after that wretched Christmas party. Fred dropped Sam and me off at my family's Marengo bungalow, Sam spent the night on our sofa. Ma, Pa, Aunt Vi and Spike were all delighted to see him Sunday morning. Both Sam and I were still groggy from the night before, but we revived a bit over breakfast as we told my family the story of the party.

"Good Lord," Ma gasped. "He had another son out of wedlock? Oh, poor Mrs. Wagner!"

"Yes, and poor Marianne," I agreed. "Neither she nor her mother deserve what that terrible man did to them. And all the Wagner sons seem to be chips off the old block." I suddenly thought of something and stared at Sam, appalled. "Oh, Lord, Sam, you don't think there are any other Wagner bastards running around loose in Pasadena, do you?"

"Daisy!" my mother cried, horrified by my language.

"I'm sorry, Ma, but that's what Stanley is. I didn't mean it as a bad word." My nose wrinkled, acknowledging my last sentence as a lie. Oh, well.

"I hope not," said Sam, shoveling in a bite of Vi's delicious scrambled eggs.

"What an awful thing to happen, though," said Vi. "Are you sure you're all right, Daisy? He didn't hurt you, did he?"

Sam and I exchanged a long glance across the table. I finally said, "Um, no. He didn't hurt me."

"Daisy, however, nearly killed him," said Sam. He would.

"You *did?*" Pa looked at me with approval.

Ma and Vi didn't.

"Well, he shot at Harold," I said in a lame attempt to justify my out-of-control behavior the night before. "When I first hit him with the cane, I thought he'd just killed my best friend."

"He got what he deserved," said Sam, sticking up for me. And this, after I'd ruined his cane. What a great guy he was. "He murdered his own father, don't forget. And Daisy's right. He would have shot Harold if his aim had been true. I'm sure he'd have shot Daisy, too."

"Oh, my word," said Ma in a horrified whisper.

"Good Lord," said Vi, likewise afflicted.

"Good for you," said Pa.

Have I mentioned I love my father?

Anyway, although it was a struggle, I managed to get dressed and ready for church on time. Sam, wearing the non-evening clothes he'd left at our house what seemed like years before, but had only been the last evening, drove us in his Hudson.

I staggered into the choir room, donned my robe, and got in line behind Lucy Zollinger. I have to admit my eyes teared up during "Savior of the Nations, Come," our anthem for that day, but I think they were only the result of emotions left over from the previous night. We didn't stay for cookies and tea after church, but hightailed it back home, where Sam dropped us off and then took off for his own home. Spike and I went to bed and napped for hours.

Lucy Zollinger and I sang a wonderful duet during the third verse of "What Child Is This" the next Wednesday, Christmas Eve. The rest of the Christmas Eve service was beautiful, the ladies of the church having outdone themselves decorating the church for the occasion.

I bought Sam another cane and gave it to him on Christmas Day when he came over to our place for dinner.

"It's not your real Christmas present," I said, feeling a little silly about handing him a beautifully polished Malacca cane, complete with a horse's-head handle and with a green Christmas ribbon adorning it. "But I thought since I broke your other one, I owed you a new one."

Sam stared down at me for a long few moments, during which I twitched and fidgeted. Then he smiled, said, "Thank you," and kissed me.

I breathed easier after that.

My brother and sister, Daphne and Walter; their respective spouses, Daniel and Jeanette; and Daphne and Daniel's two children, Polly and Peggy, all oohed and aahed when told the tale of the terrible doctor and how Spike had managed to find his foot in a shoe in the cemetery.

They also oohed and aahed over the lovely Christmas gifts I'd made for them, thanked Ma and Pa for the practical gifts they'd given them, devoured Aunt Vi's delicious Christmas dinner, and generally had a great time. I played the piano and we all sang Christmas carols. By golly, Sam sang with us. He, as I may have mentioned, has a glorious bass voice. I love Christmas.

And then came 1925. Oh, my.

The End

SHAKEN SPIRITS

A DAISY GUMM MAJESTY MYSTERY, BOOK 14

When I woke up at home, aching to beat the band, I couldn't remember what had happened. The last thing I remembered was sighing when the last band and the last float in the 1925 Tournament of Roses Parade passed us by, and we got ready to walk home, chatting happily amongst ourselves.

My fiancé, Detective Sam Rotondo, who worked for the Pasadena Police Department, had joined us for the special event. Even though we weren't married yet, Sam was part of the family.

The weather was brisk, it being the first day of January and mid-winter and all, although you can hardly tell one season from another in Southern California. However, winter is colder than summer, even in Pasadena.

Therefore, I worried a bit about Sam's left leg, which had sustained a bullet wound a few months prior to that day. It seemed to hurt him more when the weather turned chilly. "Are you sure you can walk all that way?" I asked him before we left home, being the solicitous fiancée I was.

"Of course, I'm sure," said Sam grumpily. He didn't like to have his weaknesses pointed out, even if they weren't his fault.

"Just asking," said I, a trifle miffed, although I'm not sure why. I knew Sam well enough by then to know he'd be a touchy old grouch if anyone mentioned his leg. "Have you taken any aspirin this morning?"

He heaved an exasperated sigh. "You know I have. You're the one who gave them to me along with the glass of water."

"Yes, yes, I know. I just worry about you, is all."

Sam rolled his eyes ceiling-wards. He was always doing that.

"Well, I *do*! It's because I love you."

"Are you going to be a nagging wife?"

"Yes."

"Good. Just checking."

He grinned, and I felt like smacking him. He enjoyed getting me all riled up, the fiend.

"Anyhow," Sam continued, "I have this lovely new cane to use if my leg bothers me." He brandished same, and I felt my face flush. I'd given him that new cane, a Malacca number with a swell horse's head handle, as one of his Christmas presents. He'd needed it because I'd broken his old cane over the head of a vicious murderer. But I didn't like to think about that.

After we'd settled the cane-and-leg issue, Ma, Pa, Aunt Vi, Sam, and I all began the walk up to Colorado Boulevard, where we aimed to find a place from which to watch the big parade. We were joined in this endeavor by the Wilsons, our next-door neighbors to the north. Pudge Wilson, the young scion of the family, had celebrated his thirteenth birthday not long back and had graduated to full Boy Scout status. He wore his uniform proudly, and always attempted to do at least one good deed every day, preferably early so he didn't have to think about it again.

It became apparent shortly after the Wilsons joined our party that Pudge's good deed on that New Year's Day was to assist Sam Rotondo, who didn't appreciate Pudge's efforts on his behalf. I kind of wanted to take Pudge aside and tell him to lay off that particular good deed, but didn't get the opportunity. We walked in a clump and got to Colorado Street together. Pudge then made himself useful by clearing a spot on the curb for us to stand. I worried about Sam having to stand for so long, but I didn't press the issue. Anyhow,

Pudge had thought to bring his camp stool, which folded up when not in use.

"If anyone gets tired of standing, just sit here," said he, giving Sam a meaningful glance.

"Thank you, Pudge," I said, since Sam didn't seem inclined to thank the boy.

Pudge, who had been sweet on me for quite a while by then, blushed up a storm. He was so cute. I have no idea why his nickname was Pudge, because he was approximately as big around as a broom straw. I'd asked Mrs. Wilson once, and she'd merely shrugged and said she wasn't sure how he'd come by the moniker either.

The Rose Parade was beautiful, as usual. The Tournament of Roses Queen that year was Miss Margaret Scoville, a pretty young woman whom I didn't know personally. Criminy, that made me feel old—and I'd only just turned twenty-five in November! But there you go. All my school friends were married or working or having babies or whatever, and a whole new crop of lovelies had sprung up while I wasn't looking.

After the parade ended, we started the short walk home.

And that was all I remembered.

When I woke up, Dr. Benjamin, our wonderful family doctor, stood at the head of my bed. Spike, my late husband's beloved black-and-tan dachshund—everyone else in the family loved him, too—lay on the foot of the bed, staring at me and looking worried. Sam, Ma, Pa, Aunt Vi, Mrs. Wilson and Pudge had clumped together around my bed. Ma and Aunt Vi were crying into their hankies. Mrs. Wilson had Pudge's hand in hers, and it looked to me as though they were squeezing each other hard.

I'm pretty sure I blinked at the assembly. "Wh-what happened?" I asked. Not original, but I really wanted to know.

"You were hit by a car," said Pa, his voice shaking slightly.

"I was?"

"Yes," said Ma. She sniffled and added, "Sam insisted on carrying you home."

"With your *leg*?" I said with a gasp, my left arm having just given a particularly sharp twinge just then.

"No," said Sam, his voice hard. "In my arms."

I'd lifted my head slightly to ask my stupid question, but let it fall again, exhausted and exasperated. Besides, lifting my heat hurt. "You know what I meant."

"Yeah. I know." Sam brought a chair from the kitchen into my bedroom—which was right off the kitchen and, therefore, easy to fetch—and fell onto it with something of a *plunk*.

"Oh, Daisy, we were so frightened," whispered Ma. Pa put his arm around her shoulder and gave her a hug. "You were bleeding *everywhere*!" She turned and wept onto Pa's shoulder.

"There was blood all over the place," Pudge contributed. He sounded a little more excited than worried. What the heck. He was a boy, so I didn't fault him.

"I-I still don't understand precisely what happened," I said. Looking to Dr. Benjamin, who was probably the most coherent member of the group gathered in my bedroom, I asked, "Do you know, Doc?"

"Just what your father told me. A car hit you and slammed you into a nearby tree. Sam carried you home, and Vi telephoned my house. I rushed over."

"I'm sorry," said I, grieved to have been the one to spoil his holiday.

"I'm not. I'm glad I was at home," said he in his brisk way. "Norma and I were getting ready to listen to the football game. Well, I was, anyway." He grinned, and I got the impression Mrs. Benjamin—Norma—wasn't as fond of football as was the doctor.

"I hurt all over," I said then, taking a mental scan of my body's aches and pains. "Is anything broken?"

"Your left arm," said Dr. Benjamin. "I set it for you and brought a sling. I'll have to make a cast for it, but I can do that tomorrow. You're lucky it was a simple break."

Lucky, was I? Somehow, I couldn't find it within myself to be grateful. "But I need both of my arms!" I cried, appalled.

"Daisy, you need to heal," said Sam. "It'll take time. That's what you're always telling me about my leg." As I've already mentioned, Sam had been shot in his left thigh by an evil woman some months prior to this current event. He wasn't a patient... patient, so I was irked he was giving me the same advice I was always giving him.

"But... but what about my job? Have you ever tried to manipulate the Ouija board while your arm is in a sling? Or shuffle a deck of tarot cards? Or lift a crystal ball?"

"No. I think you're the only who has to worry about that," said Sam tartly. Then he grinned. "But, hey, we're a matched set now. I have a bum left leg, and you have a bum left arm."

"Somehow, that doesn't make me feel better."

"You were all cut up, too," said Pudge, still excited unless I missed my guess. "Like Mrs. Gumm said, after it hit you, that car flung you really hard against that tree and you got scraped all over."

"Oh." No wonder everything hurt.

"But I disinfected all your wounds and got you bandaged. You'll be fine in a couple of weeks. Except for your arm. That will take more time."

"Oh, no," I began to cry and then felt like a fool.

"It will be all right, sweetheart," said Pa, leaning over to give the top of my head a peck.

"And you'll regain full use of your arm," said Doc Benjamin, probably trying to cheer me up.

"Who was driving the car that hit me?" I thought to ask.

"We don't know," said Sam.

"What do you mean, you don't know? You mean whoever it was got away? You didn't even copy the number plate?"

"Didn't have one," said Sam.

Silence filled the room as I contemplated Sam's comment. "Isn't there some kind of law that you have to get a number plate on your motor?" I asked. "And a driving license?"

"Yes. But the car that hit you didn't have a number plate. Don't know if the driver had a license, but if I ever find him, he'll never get another one." Sam sounded grim.

"Good," I said. Then I dripped a few more tears, feeling sore, pathetic, and silly.

"Oh, Daisy, We're all so sorry," said Vi. "But you just rest in bed for a while. Don't do anything. Just rest."

"Yes," said Doc Benjamin. "You need to rest more than you need to worry.

If he said so. But I did worry. I worried about my livelihood and that of my family. You see, I was the primary bread-winner therein, and I won the bread we bought by being a spiritualist-medium to people in Pasadena who had lots of money to waste. I appreciated them for wasting so much of their money on me.

But how could I practice my skills if my arm was in a sling?

And who had hit me with his or her car? Stacy Kincaid, my best client's daughter and the only person I know who'd like to run me over and kill me, was in jail. The reason she hated me was because I'd been, in part, responsible for getting her arrested. But, for Pete's sake, she'd assisted her lover-boy in committing murder! Not to mention that she'd participated in a child-trafficking scheme that kidnapped children and sold them to perverted men. She was evil, and she wanted me dead, but I figured that was only fair. I loathed her and wouldn't be at all upset if someone were to do her in.

That sounds terrible, doesn't it?

I don't care. It's the truth.

"I'm going to sit with you for a while," said Sam, dragging my mind from the swamp of its distressing thoughts. "And then I'm going to do my best to find out who hit you."

I gazed at my darling fiancé with eyes swimming in tears.

"Th-thank you, Sam."

He took my right hand and gave it a little squeeze. I shrieked in pain, and he dropped my hand like a hot rock.

Good Lord, I really did hurt *everywhere*.

Available in Paperback and eBook from Your Favorite Bookstore or Online Retailer

AUNT VI'S "SWEDISH SMOTHERED CHICKEN"

Ingredients:

2 Small Broiler Chickens
Salt & Pepper to Taste
Flour
1 1/2c Heavy Cream
1 1/2c Chicken Stock
Parsley

Preparation:

Dress, clean and split two young, small broilers. Sprinkle
inside and outside with salt and pepper, dredge outside spar-
ingly with flour and fold over. Heat a Scotch kettle*, pour in
one cup heavy cream and chickens. Cook until chickens are
well browned, turning frequently, and adding more cream as
necessary. Cover and cook until chickens are tender and
remove to hot platter. To the three tablespoons fat remaining
in kettle add three tablespoons flour and stir until well

blended. Then pour on gradually, while stirring constantly, one and one-half cups chicken stock and one-half cup cream. Bring to the boiling point, season with salt and pepper and strain. Pour around broilers and garnish with parsley.

* You might call this a Dutch oven

ABOUT THE AUTHOR

Award-winning author Alice Duncan lives with a herd of wild dachshunds (enriched from time to time with fosterees from New Mexico Dachshund Rescue) in Roswell, New Mexico. She's not a UFO enthusiast; she's in Roswell because her mother's family settled there fifty years before the aliens crashed (and living in Roswell, NM, is cheaper than living in Pasadena, CA, unfortunately). Alice would love to hear from you at alice@aliceduncan.net

www.aliceduncan.net

facebook.com/alice.duncan.925